Dear Friends,

It's been more than a decade since I first brought you these three special books in the Forever Faithful Series. In the time since then, I've heard from hundreds of thousands of you about how God has used these stories to touch and change your lives. I'm always amazed by how God puts a story on my heart, but He has your heart in mind. Only He could do that.

When I see the titles in the series, my mind remembers specific readers touched by these books. One young college girl wrote to me after reading *Waiting for Morning*. Her parents had been killed by a drunk driver, and she felt tempted to give up, to let go of her faith in Christ. She wrote: "Your story convinced me that God is still in my life, He is still in control. He has a plan for my life and so I will live out my days in a way that honors my parents. Also, I will forgive the man who killed them. I can't live with the burden of hate another day. Thank you."

I'm also reminded of the woman who read *A Moment of Weakness* and wrote to say: "I wanted to stay pure as a teenage girl, but I gave in to a moment of weakness similar to the one in your book. I've lived in shame, feeling that I'm second best ever since. I figured God couldn't do much with someone like me. I don't feel that way anymore. I am not that same girl, and Jesus died to pay for all sins—even mine. I'm ready to start living again!"

Halfway to Forever has given countless cancer patients the strength to keep fighting—again something only God could do. I'm so grateful for the opportunity to write Life-Changing Fiction™ stories that God uses for His purpose. Looking back on the years since these books first came out, I am in awe over the faithfulness of the Lord.

I always say when Jesus wanted to tell His listeners something straight, He simply spoke it. But when He wanted to touch the heart, He told a story. It is an amazing privilege to be a part of the powerful legacy of story in our culture today.

May God bless you and yours as you read. If this story or another one from the Forever Faithful Series touches your heart in a special way, please send us an e-mail at Karen@KarenKingsbury.com. Your shared personal stories encourage me and my staff so very much.

In His light and love,
Karen Kingsbury

PRAISE FOR
KAREN KINGSBURY'S BOOKS

Halfway to Forever

"*Halfway to Forever* has believable characters you care about. You'll feel their tension, heartbreak, and joy. Karen Kingsbury sweeps readers right in. She really knows how to tell a story!"

RANDY ALCORN, BESTSELLING AUTHOR OF
DEADLINE AND *THE ISHBANE CONSPIRACY*

"Karen Kingsbury's *Halfway to Forever* is an emotionally charged novel of heartache and hope. Keep the tissues handy!"

ROBIN LEE HATCHER, AUTHOR OF *RIBBON OF YEARS* AND *THE STORY JAR*

"Karen's signature style will inspire you and keep you turning pages until the last luscious page."

PATRICIA HICKMAN, AWARD-WINNING AUTHOR OF
KATRINA'S WINGS AND *SANDPEBBLES*

A Moment of Weakness

"Kingsbury spins a tale of love and loss, lies and betrayal, that sent me breathlessly turning pages."

LIZ CURTIS HIGGS, best-selling author of *Bookends*
and *Mixed Signals*

"A gripping love story. *A Moment of Weakness* demonstrates the devastating consequences of wrong choices, and the long shadows deception casts over the lives of God's children. It also shows the even longer reach of God's providence, grace, and forgiveness."

RANDY ALCORN, best-selling author

"One message shines clear and strong through Karen Kingsbury's *A Moment of Weakness*: Our loving God is a God of second chances."

Waiting for Morning

"What a talent! I love her work."

"Kingsbury not only entertains but goes a step further and confronts readers with situations that are all too common, even for Christians. At the same time, it will remind believers of God's mercy and challenge them to pray for America. The book… reveals God's awesome love and His amazing ability to turn moments of weakness into times of strengthening."

BOOK THREE

FOREVER FAITHFUL

Halfway
to Forever

KAREN
KINGSBURY

MULTNOMAH
BOOKS

HALFWAY TO FOREVER
PUBLISHED BY MULTNOMAH BOOKS
12265 Oracle Boulevard, Suite 200
Colorado Springs, CO 80921

Published in association with the literary agency of Alive Communications Inc., 7680 Goddard St., Suite 200, Colorado Springs, CO 80920.

Trade Paperback ISBN: 978-1-60142-540-9

Cover design by Mark D. Ford
Author photo by Dan Davis Photography

Published in the United States by WaterBrook Multnomah, an imprint of the Crown Publishing Group, a division of Random House Inc., New York.

MULTNOMAH and its mountain colophon are registered trademarks of Random House Inc.

Library of Congress Cataloging-in-Publication Data
Kingsbury, Karen.
    Halfway to forever/by Karen Kingsbury.
        p. cm.
  1. Adoption—Fiction. 2. Pregnant women—Fiction. 3. Brain—Cancer—Patients—Fiction.
I. Title.
    PS3561.I4873 H35 2002
    813'.54–dc21

                                              2001007865

Printed in the United States of America
2013

10 9 8 7 6 5 4 3 2 1

Dedicated to...

DONALD, MY KNIGHT in shining armor, my one true love. Can this really be our fourteenth anniversary? Years slip by like hours in a day, but I cherish every one. With you by my side the best keeps getting better, and I thank God that you are such an example to me, to our children, to your students and athletes. Thank you for being my best friend and for believing in forever. Aren't we having a blast? Year after year after year after year... I love you so.

Kelsey, my sweet little "Norm" who has long since shed her little-girl image and traded it in for the look of a young teen on the brink of everything new and wonderful and exciting. You're busy these days, sweetheart, but it does my mother-heart good to know you still remember who you are: a child of God, a daughter, a sister, a student, a friend. I cherish the times we have together even more now that you are in middle school, because in the distant corridors of time I see you, not too very far from here, in a cap and gown. I can't slow the ride, but I can be grateful for every minute, knowing full well that God's plans for you will be nothing less than amazing. I am so proud of you, honey. Always remember that I love you, Kelsey.

Tyler, my handsome, budding young writer. I love when you tell me you're going to act and sing when you grow up—but in your spare time you might write for fun. I guess that's all writing is, after all: fun. The way God intended His gifts to be. I will long remember your "one voice" ringing out across the school's Veteran's Day assembly. May God lead you to always be that one voice ringing out for Him, and may His plans for your life become more evident with each passing year. I love you, Ty.

Austin (or Michael Jordan, depending on the moment). This

past year I have watched you take giant steps away from babyhood and into the strong, strapping young boy you are becoming. I will never forget sitting on the edge of your bed that September evening before your fourth birthday, singing with you, kissing you goodnight, and saying good-bye to my three-year-old. You're not my baby anymore, but you are still my miracle boy. The heart that beats within you is fully devoted—whether slamming a basketball through a net or singing songs for Jesus. Keep that, honey, as God's spectacular plans for your life unfold. Keep it always. I love you, Austin.

EJ, our youngest Haitian son. Adopting you has blessed us beyond words. We have watched you grow from a shy, insecure little boy to a confident, goal-kicking, letter-sounding, smiling child with no limits to your potential. God definitely brought you into our lives for a reason, and I am grateful every day. I can't wait to see what He has planned for you. I love you, EJ.

Sean, our half-angel boy. When we brought you home from Haiti you made an instant place in our hearts for one reason—you were constantly praying to Jesus. Even now, when we give you a present, you drop to your knees and thank God for the giver. When we give you a meal, you won't take a bite—no matter how hungry you are—until proper thanks has been given. And when you finish eating you look to the heavens and say, "Thank you, Jesus." You told me recently that you would grow up and get a good job one day so you could give me and Daddy some money because we'd helped you so much. With teary eyes I told you that wasn't necessary, just love Jesus all your life, Sean. And as God reveals His plan for you, I am convinced that will always be the best advice I could give you. I love you, Sean.

Joshua, chosen by God for our family. When I went to Haiti to adopt your two best friends, I didn't know about you. But you worked your way into my heart in minutes with your sweet songs for Jesus and your sad little smile. How wonderful God is to bring you into our family this past September. You are brilliant at everything you do, from reading, to those soccer foot skills that would make any teenager envious. At six years old you clearly have a great desire to do things right, a determined spirit that will take you far, and a compassion for others that makes you a natural leader. Always remember where your gifts come from…and that God has very special plans for you. I love you, Joshua.

And to God Almighty, my Lord and Savior, the Author of Life, who has—for now—blessed me with these.

Acknowledgments

SO MUCH GOES into the writing of any single book. I couldn't possibly move on to my next project without stopping to thank the people who have made this one possible. First, and foremost, it is my great pleasure to thank God who has given me the gift of writing. I am amazed at the letters pouring in from my readers, letters that prove God is changing lives with the gift of story—just as He did when Jesus walked this Earth. I pray I always use His gift in a way that touches hearts and glorifies God.

Also, thanks to my wonderful husband and children, who understand when life goes on hold because Mommy has a deadline. Donald, you have the most uncanny ability to pick up where I leave off when I need a little extra help. "Thanks" doesn't come close. In addition, thanks to my extended family, many of whom tirelessly continue to spread the word about my novels. I am grateful for each of you.

Beyond family, there are those friends who have prayed for me, supported me, and listened to me discuss story ideas. In that light, a special thanks to Sylvia Wallgren and Ann Hudson, my personal prayer warriors, without whom none of this would ever happen. And to those special friends and sisters in Christ who have made such a faithful impact on my life. You know who you are.

A sincere thanks to Amber Santiago, my dear friend and personal assistant. You have a golden voice, the best I've ever heard. You could be performing for all the world, yet instead you spend each day taking care of my sweet Austin and overseeing dozens of other tasks that make my writing possible. May God bless you for your servant-heart. And to Jenna Hiller who stepped in and helped with our six children during crunch time.

When researching a novel, I often call on experts. For this book and several others I want to thank Bryce Cleary, M.D., and Attorney Stan Kaputska for their valuable insight. Also my father, Ted Kingsbury, who often takes an hour from his morning to brainstorm ideas with me.

Once a novel is written, there are still many people who take it to the next level—the place where you, the reader, receive it. For that reason, a special thanks goes to my agent Greg Johnson and the folks at Alive Communications. I am continually awestruck by your talent, Greg, and humbly blessed that I have the chance to partner with you in bringing these books into being.

Also, thanks to my editor, Karen Ball. Each time you edit a book it's like taking a class from the very best in fiction writing. You are so good at what you do, Karen. Thanks for rubbing a little of your incredible talent on my books. And thanks to Julee Schwarzburg, Chad Hicks, Steve Curley, and Lisa Bowden, who champion my work with the great people at Multnomah Publishers. All of you at Multnomah are like family to me, and always will be. Thanks for taking a chance on me four years ago. In addition, thanks to Joan Westfall, who always does an amazing job on my final edit. I'm blessed to have your help.

A huge thanks to Kirk DouPonce, the brilliantly gifted man who designs my covers. I can only pray that people *do* judge my books by my covers, and that in the end the story measures up. Thank you for offering your best work on behalf of mine.

Finally, thanks to the Skyview Basketball team, you hustling, runnin', gunnin' guys—for giving me a reason to cheer, even on deadline.

Hannah Bronzan rarely visited the cemetery.

The grassy knolls and quiet, sad whispers were not necessary for her to remember Tom and Alicia, because they did not live in the confines of a garden of stone, but in Hannah's heart.

Where they would always live.

But on this day, Hannah climbed out of the car, slipped on her sunglasses, and gazed across a sea of cold, gray tombstones. Her heart ached as she drew a slow, shaky breath.

Much as she didn't want to be here, it was time. Despite the emotions warring within her, Hannah knew she had no choice. She needed to come now, just as she'd needed to come two years ago when Matt Bronzan asked her to be his wife.

By then she had grieved the loss of her first husband, and with a strength that was not her own, she'd survived. Enough to tell Matt yes, to believe there was indeed a new life for her and young Jenny on the other side of a darkness and pain that had nearly destroyed them both.

Coming here had been difficult back then too, but it had given her a chance to say good-bye to Tom, to thank him for all they'd shared, and to release him. To let die a flame she thought would burn forever. Hannah set her gaze in the direction of their tombstones and pulled her sweater tighter.

Her eyes welled up. Now it was time to let go of Alicia.

This was a private moment—one she needed to share with

Tom and Alicia alone. Regardless of shaded grounds, the glasses would stay. She walked amidst the markers, her fingers brushing against an occasional cold stone as she made her way across the cemetery to the place where their markers lay, side by side.

Her eyes drifted from one to the other. *Dr. Thomas J. Ryan...Alicia Marie Ryan.* The birth dates were different, but the date of death was the same: *August 28, 1998.*

A lump formed in Hannah's throat, and she swallowed hard as she knelt down, sitting back on her heels. She wiped an errant tear from her cheek... Alicia would have been nineteen, finished with high school and making her way through college. In love, perhaps, or dreaming of a career.

Alicia. I miss you, baby...

It was harder to picture them now, harder to see the crisp definition in her mind's scrapbook...how Tom's eyes sparkled when she was in his arms, or the way Alicia's smile lit up a room...

They'd lost so much in one terrible moment. A drunk driver, an awful collision...and the life she and Tom had spent years building was shattered.

Hannah exhaled, and the sound mingled with the breeze. *You can do this.* She squeezed her eyes shut, searching for the strength to move ahead. She and Matt had worked out the plans for more than a year. It was the right thing, she was sure of that much. Even now, with sadness covering her heart like a blanket, she could feel the excitement welling within her, convincing her that somehow, sometime soon, it would happen.

She would be a mother again.

"Hi..." She set her fingertips on Alicia's tombstone and dusted off a layer of dirt. "I have something to tell you."

A crow sounded in the distance. This visit was for peace of mind and nothing more. Hannah's precious oldest daughter would never have questioned her intentions, never have doubted her place in Hannah's heart. Her fingers stopped moving and settled over Alicia's name.

"Matt and I have decided to…to adopt a little girl." Her voice broke, and from behind her sunglasses tears trickled down her face and dripped off her chin.

She waited until she could find her voice. "After…after the accident I couldn't imagine ever loving another man," Hannah wiped the back of her hand across her wet chin. "Or another daughter." A sound that was part laugh, part sob slipped from her lips. "But here I am, happy, married, and…convinced God has another daughter for me somewhere out there."

The traffic hummed from the road behind her. "You understand, right, Alicia? I'm not trying to…to replace you, honey." She sniffed. "The bond you and I shared, the one you and Jenny shared, that's something none of us will ever have again. Not like it was."

Hannah paused and gazed up, willing herself to see beyond the blue to the place where Tom and Alicia now lived and loved and laughed.

Gradually her eyes shifted back to the tombstones. "I saw a documentary last night about kids in America, kids waiting for someone to love them, and…I don't know…something inside me snapped." She shrugged and managed a smile despite the fresh tears on her cheeks. "I can't have more babies. We've known that since Jenny was born. But adoption?" She sniffed. "I wasn't sure I could do it…until last night. Then, all of a sudden, I knew. I *could* open my heart to another little girl."

The background noise faded. Hannah traced the *A* in Alicia's name, pushing away the dirt that had gathered there. "We'll adopt a toddler, someone who needs a second chance at life." She blinked, and two more tears slid off the tip of her nose onto Alicia's stone. "I don't know where she is…or who she is. But I know she's out there somewhere. And I wanted you to know bec–"

There was a catch in Hannah's voice, and she held the sobs at bay. "Because she'll be your sister."

Hannah closed her eyes again and waited. The image of her oldest daughter grew clear in her mind once more. "Alicia…"

There she was. The smile, the honey blonde hair, the warmth in her eyes…it was all as close and real as if she were standing there in person.

There were no words, but a distinct sense of approval pierced the darkness. The feeling swelled, and Hannah had no doubts. God wanted her to know Alicia would have supported this decision with her whole being.

Hannah ached to reach out and pull the image of her daughter close, but the lines began to blur. As they did, peace oozed between the cracks in Hannah's heart. It was okay to let her daughter's memory fade for now. The visit had reminded her once more that she no longer needed to feel the pain of Alicia's and Tom's deaths with every excruciating breath, but only as a sad truth that simply was and could not be changed.

Hope wrapped its arms around her as she opened her eyes. It was time to go home, time to let Matt and Jenny know what she'd decided. Of course, Jade and Tanner Eastman would want to know, too. The couple had become their best friends these past years. They'd been there while Matt and Hannah walked through a year of collecting documents and filling out adoption forms, gathering letters and completing a dossier.

The Eastmans understood. They were desperate to have a baby, but so far hadn't been able.

Despite Hannah's tears, a smile tugged at her lips. Yes, Jade and Tanner would be thrilled that Hannah was finally ready to move forward.

She let her eyes settle on Tom's tombstone. "Pray for us, Tom." Two tears landed near his name, and she wiped her cheeks with her fingertips. "Pray for the little girl…whoever she is."

Once more she looked back at the stone, at Alicia's name carved in it. "One more thing, honey. When we bring her home and…and people ask me how many girls I have…" Hannah wiped at her tears again. "I'll always tell them three. Two who live here with me…and one who lives in heaven."

Two

The day had been nothing but salty sea breeze and endless blue skies. Matt and Hannah were gathered on the back deck of their beach home, their picnic with the Eastmans in full swing. They sat there, eating, overlooking the surf and a blazing sunset, and Matt reached for Hannah's hand. He set his burger down on the paper plate and looked around the picnic table at the others—their own precious eighteen-year-old Jenny, and Jade and Tanner Eastman and their thirteen-year-old son, Ty.

"We have something to tell you." He smiled at Hannah, and his presence soothed her soul the way it had since the first day they met. She leaned against him. They had already told Jenny their plans, and Hannah thought her response had been positive. Guarded maybe, but good all the same.

Matt went on. "We contacted our social worker yesterday…and gave her the green light."

Jade's eyes lit up and she clasped her hands together as she caught Hannah's gaze. "Are you serious? You've decided to—"

"Yes." Hannah smiled, and the accomplishment in that one single word hung like a gold medal around her neck. How far she'd come since that awful August day four years ago, how greatly God had blessed them. And suddenly—surrounded by the people she loved, enjoying a barbecue on the deck of the beachside home she and Matt and Jenny shared—the sum of all they'd been and all they were…all they were about to be…was almost overwhelming. "Yes," she said again. "We're ready to adopt."

Tanner's face broke into a grin and he reached across the table to shake Matt's hand. "Congratulations."

There was a brief flicker of sadness in Tanner's eyes, and Hannah understood. Tanner and Jade wanted more children, but since marrying more than a year ago, Jade had miscarried once and been unable to get pregnant since then. Hannah's heart went out to her friends, and though neither of them mentioned their own situation, she knew what they had to be feeling.

Tanner swung his arm over Jade's shoulders. "So, the world's best business partner is going to have a little one running around, huh?" He leaned back in his chair. "Okay, don't keep us waiting…" He took a bite of his burger, and a blob of ketchup landed squarely on his khaki button-down shirt. "Give us the—"

Hannah and Jade exchanged a look, and they both giggled.

Tanner finished chewing. "What?" He looked around the table.

Matt smothered a grin with his hand, and Jenny and Ty laughed into their napkins.

Jade was the first to rescue her husband. She pointed to his shirt, and Tanner glanced down. He chuckled and shook his head. "That settles it. Someone else will have to teach the Bronzans' new little girl how to eat."

Hannah and Jade locked eyes again and burst out laughing. How often had their good-looking, powerful husbands spilled a drink or stained a shirt or broken a chair at their legendary get-togethers? Matt and Tanner might run the nation's most powerful religious freedom law firm, but at home they were often little more than oversized boys.

Matt loosed his grip on Hannah's hand, and his dimpled grin lit up Hannah's heart. "Well, Tanner, I, for one, am appalled at your manners."

Tanner nodded, his expression playful. "That's what I get for hanging out with you."

Amid the laughter, Jade dabbed a wet napkin at Tanner's shirt, giggling so hard her shoulders shook.

Hannah studied her friends through smiling eyes. It was good to see Jade laugh. She'd been dragging for several weeks lately, tired, achy. Jade blamed it on a lingering cold, but after all she and Tanner had been through, Hannah hated to see her sick.

The conversation shifted back to Matt and Hannah's adoption plans. As the evening wore on, Jenny took Ty to a movie with her friends, and the men congregated on the deck around Matt's old guitar. Hannah and Jade took a walk down the beach.

It was mid-March, and though the temperatures were cool, there had been no fog for days. As the sun set, the Pacific Ocean stretched out like a blanket of liquid blue beneath a canopy of crimson and gold. A hundred yards down the beach, Hannah stopped and stared out to sea, breathing in the damp, salty air. "I never get tired of it."

Jade drew up beside her. "It's breathtaking."

"Like a living masterpiece direct from God."

The picnic that day was one of their monthly get-togethers, their way of staying connected and supporting each other. Jade and Tanner lived in a spacious house in Thousand Oaks, twenty minutes away, on two acres of rolling hillside. They had four bedrooms and a bonus room, a monument to Jade and Tanner's dream of having a houseful of children one day.

The women started walking again and Hannah turned to Jade. "You look better, not so pale."

Jade nodded and something in her eyes grew distant. "I felt good today, being with you and Tanner, laughing a little."

Something caught in Hannah's heart. "Things are okay at home, right?"

"We're fine." A smile tried to climb up Jade's cheeks, but fell short. "Just wondering about God's plan."

"Babies?"

"Babies." Jade sighed and her eyes grew wet. "We love Ty so much, but he's thirteen. At this rate, he'll be busy with his own life by the time we give him a brother or sister."

Hannah walked a few steps and stopped. "How does Tanner feel?"

"He doesn't get it." Jade brushed her dark bangs off her face and shook her head. "He missed so much of Ty's growing up years…all he wants is a baby in every room, a chance to be the type of father he couldn't be to Ty."

The cool, damp sand filled in the places between Hannah's toes. "Ty was eleven before Tanner found out about him, right?"

"Right." Jade stared at the sun as it dropped below the horizon. "You'd never know it; the two of them are inseparable. Tanner is such a good dad. Still…sometimes I think the whole baby thing is taking a toll."

"Meaning…?" The soothing sound of a lone seagull punctuated their conversation.

"He's been burying himself at work, staying later, going in earlier. There's always a pressing case…" Jade hugged her arms close to her body. "Lately it's like he could work day and night and it wouldn't be enough." She was quiet, but after a moment a soft huff crossed her lips. "No one believes in his cause more than I do… I'm the one who talked him into it fifteen years ago. But sometimes it feels like he's pushing me away, closing down his emotions."

Hannah nodded and fell in step alongside Jade. "Matt gets that way sometimes. There were times when we'd talk about adoption for three weeks straight, until I needed a break. A day or two to sort out my feelings. Those would end up being the same days he'd work late."

Jade bent down and picked up a broken piece of a sand dollar.

"Then there's my health." She brushed a sprinkling of sand off the shell, and Hannah had the clear impression Jade was refusing to make eye contact with her.

A knot formed in Hannah's gut—a knot made from strings of fear she could no longer ignore. Bad things didn't happen just to other people anymore. They happened. It was that simple. She stopped, and Jade turned to look at her. "The headaches?"

Hannah saw a heaviness in Jade's eyes. She was thirty-five and usually looked ten years younger. But the past couple months…

"The headaches only come once in a while. Nothing to worry about." Jade slipped the broken sand dollar into the pocket of her windbreaker and shrugged. "I'm tired all the time. After a shift at the hospital and Ty's baseball game, I'm wiped. No wonder Tanner has his mind on work."

Hannah swallowed and considered her words. Jade was a trained nurse, after all. Surely if she were worried, she'd go in for tests. "Have you thought about seeing a doctor?"

Jade smiled. "Now you sound like Tanner." She faced the ocean and seemed to stare at something unseen and far away. "You know what I think it is?"

"What?" Hannah took a few slow steps back toward the house, and Jade kept up beside her.

"Depression." A sigh slipped from Jade's lips and blended with the ocean breeze. "Isn't that crazy?"

"Of course not." The knot relaxed. Depression was better than other possibilities. "Lots of people get depressed."

"But me?" Jade stretched her hands over her head and took a slow breath. "I wasn't depressed when my life was falling apart. But now that I'm living my dream, married to a man I've loved since I was a little girl…*now* I get depressed? It doesn't make sense."

Hannah remembered the miscarriage Jade had eight months

earlier. "It makes perfect sense. It hasn't even been a year since you lost the baby."

Quiet fell between them, and Jade wiped at a stray tear. "I think about that child every day. Sometimes it seems like everyone else has forgotten there ever was a baby."

"Even Tanner?" Their steps were slow and easy, the beach empty but for the two of them.

Jade shook her head. "No. Tanner talks about her."

"Her?"

"Yes." Jade sniffed and ran her fingers through her hair. "All my life I've wanted a daughter and…yes. The baby was a girl. She'd be two months old if she'd lived."

Hannah gazed across the watery horizon. "Losing a child isn't something that ever goes away, Jade. Whether that child was miscarried—" she thought about her visit to the cemetery the week before—"or killed in a car accident."

Jade's teary eyes locked onto Hannah's. "I don't know how to let her go. I want a baby so badly." Jade hung her head and gentle weeping overtook her.

Hannah pulled her close, hugging her the way a mother hugs her lost child. Hannah knew Jade's story well. Her mother had abandoned her when she was a child and left her to be raised by an alcoholic father. Jade had no siblings, so though Hannah was only four years older, she sometimes was the next best thing to a mother—or maybe an older sister.

"It's okay." She ran her hand along Jade's shoulder. "You should have said something sooner."

Jade nodded and after a while she pulled back. Her face was wet with tears. "I keep telling myself I'm supposed to let it go. People miscarry all the time, right?"

"But it still hurts. If you don't talk about that kind of pain it'll eat you alive, Jade."

Jade sucked in a deep breath and started walking again. "Maybe that explains my health."

"Exactly." Hannah kept her steps slow, giving Jade a chance to sort through her feelings.

They walked in silence until Jade turned, her eyes searching Hannah's as though looking for an unfathomable secret. "How did you do it, Hannah? How did you learn to live again?"

Hannah knew the answer as surely as she knew her name. "God carried me." She slowed her pace, and after a few more steps stopped and faced her friend. "He'll carry you, too."

She nodded, fresh tears in her eyes. "I know. I feel like this...this depression is keeping me from getting pregnant. Like I'm too tense to conceive."

Hannah angled her head and smiled. "You'll have more children one day, Jade. I believe that with all my heart." She sat down on the sand, pulling her knees to her chest, then patted the spot beside her. "Wanna pray?"

Jade dropped beside her, every motion slow and weary, as though she lacked all hope. They bowed their heads, and Hannah prayed for Jade's broken heart and empty arms. She asked that God bring healing and joy and health to Jade and a deeper understanding to Tanner.

"And please, Lord, one day soon...bring Jade another baby."

Matt drew his guitar close and kicked his feet up on the deck railing. "What else?"

Tanner grinned from a nearby lounge chair and stretched out his legs. He hadn't wanted to come tonight, but like always, time with the Bronzans was medicine to his soul. "Eagles. 'Desperado.'"

Matt plucked at a few chords and began to play. The music filled Tanner's senses, and he closed his eyes, singing along despite the fact that neither of them was exactly on key. They sang about losing all their highs and lows, about getting down from the fences before it was too late… The surf provided percussion in the distance.

When the song ended, Matt studied the fingers on his left hand and winced. "They're shot." He set the guitar down beside him. "I need to play more."

"*We* need to play more."

Matt cast him a lazy grin. "We?"

Tanner tossed his hands in the air in mock indignation. "I'm vocals, you're guitar. A few more nights like this, and we can forget about law. Take this act on the road."

They both chuckled at the thought, but as their laughter faded Tanner crooked one elbow behind his head and uttered a sigh that felt like it came from his feet. He stared at the canopy of stars above, then looked at Matt. "I'm worried about Jade."

Matt nodded once, his voice slow, thoughtful. "She looks tired."

He gazed at the sky again. "She's always tired."

"Maybe she should see a doctor."

"Yeah, maybe…" Tanner could hear Jade trying to reassure him. She was a nurse. She knew enough about medicine to know when she needed a doctor, and she didn't think she did. He'd tried to change her mind, but for now it was a closed subject unless some other symptom came up. Tanner let the worry fade. Whatever was wrong with his wife, it wasn't the Bronzans' problem. And tonight was supposed to be a celebration. Matt had been talking about adoption almost from the first day he started working at the firm. It was Hannah who couldn't make up her mind. In fact, just four weeks ago at lunch Matt had been more discouraged than Tanner remembered ever seeing before. He said he didn't think Hannah would ever make a decision and he wanted to prepare himself for the fact that they might never raise a child together.

He looked back at Matt. "What made Hannah decide?"

Matt crossed his arms, his eyebrows lowered. "It was the strangest thing. We were watching this documentary on TV about kids in the social services system—thousands of them waiting for a permanent home. All of a sudden she started to cry."

Tanner leveled his gaze at Matt. "Because of the show?"

"Because one of the kids—a little girl—really touched her." Matt shrugged. "I put my arm around her and asked her if she was okay, but she shook her head like she didn't want to talk. Then she told me she loved me."

Tanner gestured his approval. "That's always a good sign."

"Yeah. Except after a minute she was crying so hard she went upstairs to bed. I thought it was a setback on the whole idea of adoption. But the next morning she woke up and told me she'd made her decision." Matt's eyes sparkled with excitement. "Now it's just a matter of finding our little girl."

"And Jenny?"

"She's been great. Helps us find web sites with kids up for adoption, made copies of the dossier for us. Nothing but happy about it. Besides, she'll be in college in the fall. UCLA."

"Premed, right?"

Matt smiled. "Just like her dad."

Tanner studied his friend, amazed. "Doesn't it ever hurt? How much she still misses him?"

There was a softening in Matt's eyes. "Jenny loves me; I'll never doubt that as long as I live. I'm her protector, provider, confidante, and safe place. But I'm not her daddy." Matt cocked his head. "I'm okay with that."

Tanner stared at Matt for a moment and then back at the moonlit water. He couldn't imagine raising someone else's child.

Watching Matt, seeing his face light up when he talked about adopting… He shook his head. "I don't think I could do it."

Matt picked up his guitar. One string at a time, he strummed a chord that soothed the anxious places in Tanner's soul. "Do what?"

"Adopt. Raise someone else's child." He clenched his fists and relaxed them again. "I missed watching Ty grow up. Doesn't God know we want another baby?"

"I'm sure He does." Matt gazed up at the moon. "More than any of us will ever know."

Tanner exhaled hard. "I know. I hate when I doubt." He uttered a single laugh, one that was more frustration than humor. "Look at me. Fighting religious freedom battles in front of the entire nation and doubting whether God can bring us a child."

Again Matt moved his fingers over the guitar strings. "Doubts are normal. But don't stop praying, Tanner. God has a plan; He always does."

As they fell into silence, Tanner realized how much lighter his heart felt. His problems hadn't been solved. Jade would still be tired when they left the Bronzans' that night, and the empty long-ing for a baby would still be as real as the air they breathed. But somehow the time spent relaxing with Matt had given him hope again. His friend's enthusiasm about adopting was contagious. It left Tanner believing that one day—maybe one day soon—they'd be celebrating their own good news.

"So, what's the next step?"

Matt let his hands rest on the edge of the guitar, and Tanner was struck by the calm in his friend's face. A calm that was only possible by walking through the fire and coming out refined on the other side. "We've already talked to our social worker and she's looking for an available child."

"A girl, right?"

Matt nodded. "Hannah and I both want a little girl. Three or four years old, doesn't matter what ethnic background. We would have a better choice of children if we were interested in the foster-adopt program. We're licensed for it, but neither of us wants to risk getting a child and having her taken away."

"So you want one who's already legally available?"

"Right. Our social worker doesn't think it'll take long."

Again Tanner was struck by Matt and Hannah's faith. So much could go wrong with a child abandoned to the social services system. Drug abuse, bonding issues, or worse. Watching Hannah and Matt go through the adoption process was like watching a living illustration of faith. "What about that Haitian agency?"

"Heart of God? Great group of people. We filled out the paperwork and paid the program fee, but they didn't know how long it would take until they had a girl that age. Right now, their older children are almost all boys."

"And now Hannah wants to adopt from the U.S.?"

"At first she was afraid to. That's why we looked at Haiti. The statistics are…" Matt's voice drifted and he clenched his jaw. "More than ninety percent of the U.S. kids legally free for adoption have been abused. Some of them so bad it would take a miracle to make a difference."

Tanner narrowed his eyes, barely making out a sailboat on the darkened horizon. "You're taking a big risk."

"Yep." Matt didn't sound worried, only accepting, confident. "There's always a risk."

An easy silence fell between them again, comfortable, meaningful, and Matt moved his fingers over the strings, blending his music with the sounds of the sea.

Muffled voices broke the reverie—Jade and Hannah were back—and Tanner looked at his watch. He swung his legs over the side of the lounge chair and patted Matt on the shoulder.

"Well, friend, I guess we're both in need of the same thing then."

Matt set his guitar down, stood and stretched. "What's that?"

"A miracle. Nothing short of a miracle."

Three

Grace Landers lay in her sleeping bag and trembled. The voices were always loud, but tonight they were too scary to sleep, too scary not to think about.

Besides, the handcuff was hurting her wrist.

The van was small. Grace's sleeping bag was at the very back on the floor, against the double doors. There was barely enough room to sleep there, and she'd had to fold her sleeping bag in half to make it fit.

Mommy slept on the backseat; the front part of the van was where they kept their ice chest. The living room, Mommy called it.

Grace ran her finger over the place where the cold metal scraped against her hand. She would have been a good girl. She tried to tell her mommy, but Mommy wouldn't listen.

"I'm having a man friend over tonight. I don't want you gettin' in the way, ya hear?"

Her mommy locked one part of the handcuff to a pole near the bottom of the backseat and the other part to her wrist. Then mommy made a really mean face and told her to keep quiet or else.

"Not a peep, Grace. If anyone finds out about us living here, the cops will take you away again. This time forever."

Grace was very afraid about that. If the cops took her away, she'd have to live with someone she didn't know. Or maybe even go to jail. That would be scarier than the man her mommy was with tonight.

It was always the same when Mommy had a man friend over.

They'd talk a little and make slurping sounds, like they were drinking pop. Then her mommy's voice would get funny, all tired and slow.

The noises would change after that, almost like Mommy was getting hurt. Then the van would start shaking...that was when Grace closed her eyes and pretended the handcuff was a good thing, that it kept her from being hurt like her mommy. She would lie there in her little bed on the floor at the back of the van and think about something else.

Flowers or butterflies or clouds. Something that helped her fall asleep.

But tonight... It was different.

Mommy's friend yelled a lot, and no matter what Grace tried to think about she couldn't make her arms and legs stop shaking.

"I paid ya for more than that, woman."

There was a sharp sound, like when Mommy spanked her for being bad. Then her mommy started to cry. "You gave me dope, not money, Hank. I need *money*."

The sharp sound came again. "Dope *is* money, idiot. Now lay down."

The man shouted at her mommy for a long time and used words Grace wasn't allowed to say. Over and over the sharp sound filled the van, and Grace began to cry. *Be quiet*, she told herself, and she held her breath so Mommy and the man wouldn't hear her crying. She couldn't let the cops take her away. Never, never.

If only she could get her hand free. Then she could roll under the backseat and sleep there. Maybe the noises wouldn't be so loud, maybe—

There was a loud smack, and her mommy screamed. The noises grew louder and louder, and Grace was too afraid to breathe.

"Help me," she whispered.

Her mother's screams kept coming, but suddenly they were quieter than before. Grace could feel invisible, warm, Daddy hands soothing out the shakes in her arms and legs and heart, making her feel hugged and happy.

She stared around in the dark, but there was no one there. No one at all.

Then she remembered who it was. It was the invisible Daddy, the one Grandma had told her about before she died. Her mouth formed the word *Hi,* but no sound came out. Still she smiled in the darkness, safe and secure in His presence.

Whoever He was, He'd come to her before.

Whenever she thought she might die from being sad and afraid, He'd come with warm hands and a safe feeling. Almost like a daddy taking care of her, the way she pictured a daddy might if she'd had one. He made her feel safe and sleepy and little. Even littler than four years old. And even though she couldn't see Him, He didn't scare her.

She stopped crying, and her mother and the man grew very quiet. Not far away there were sirens, but even though they got louder and louder, Grace wasn't afraid. *I'm okay… I'm okay…* The handcuff still cut at her wrist, but her hand relaxed and she closed her eyes. In a few minutes she drifted off to sleep.

Thinking about flowers and butterflies and clouds.

And an invisible Daddy who loved her even if no one else did.

Four

The headaches were getting worse.

Jade's hands trembled as she took two painkillers from the bottle in her purse and downed them with a glass of water. As she swallowed she glanced around the hospital cafeteria... The edges of the room were blurred.

She squinted. In fact, the edges of everything were fuzzy. Not enough to trigger panic, but enough to frustrate her. Was this all the faith she could muster? An unshakeable sadness over losing a baby? Discouragement at not being able to get pregnant? Depression strong enough to affect her vision and give her headaches?

She sighed. Not much of an example of faith, especially when she had the miracle of Ty and Tanner at home to remind her daily of God's amazing power.

The medicine started working, and the lines became crisper. Jade took another drink of water, then smoothed out the wrinkles in her nurse's uniform. She walked to the closest table, steadying herself on an occasional chair along the way, and sat down. The nausea was back... Maybe it was from the medication.

Or from the one thing she dared dream.

Either way, in seven hours she'd have the results. Her period hadn't been regular for a while, but the past cycle had been completely absent. Susan at the lab had been more than happy to process the pregnancy test. But Jade needed to work her shift before she might know the answer. No matter how she was feeling.

Help me get through the day, Lord...

Jade stood and glanced at her watch. One o'clock. Time for Brandy Almond's chemotherapy.

Jade's head still pounded with every heartbeat as she made her way down the hallway to the children's cancer ward. There were times when she questioned her sanity... It was one thing to work in the general children's ward as she'd done when she was just out of high school. Kids with kidney problems or bad cases of tonsillitis.

Cancer was something altogether different.

Still, there was nothing more rewarding than giving sick children the gift of hope, and Jade seemed to be able to do that better than anyone at Mount Sinai Children's Hospital. Because every now and then, children survived cancer's attack. They grew stronger and healthier, and their hair grew back.

And once in a while those children would go home to live normal lives.

As far as Jade was concerned, *every* child had a chance to go home. Brandy Almond was no exception.

It was nap time at Mount Sinai, so the hallway was quiet. None of the children were touring the ward in wheelchairs or sitting around the schoolroom table or building castles with wooden blocks in the playroom.

On the nurse's station, there was a tray stenciled with Brandy's name. On it were three pills and a bag of liquid poison that would kill the leukemia cells—along with the cells Brandy needed for eating and breathing and living. Jade took the tray and set her sights on a room four doors down the hall. The girl was a high-school track star and the oldest child in the children's cancer wing, and she regularly complained about the fact.

Without making a sound, Jade let herself into Brandy's room. A rerun of *I Love Lucy* whispered from the television. Brandy looked up, her eyes dark and sunken, then shifted her gaze back to the TV.

"You're supposed to be sleeping." Jade smiled and set the tray down.

"I'm not three."

"No, but you're sick and your body needs rest." The bag hanging over the girl's bed was empty. Jade replaced it with the full one from her tray and crossed her arms. "How are you feeling?"

Brandy's eyes welled up and she looked out the window. "Fine."

Jade's heart went out to her. It was prom week at Thousand Oaks High School where Brandy was a junior. She ran track and had been a state contender with one of the fastest miles of any girl her age.

Then she started bruising.

When she was first diagnosed back in February, dozens of teens from the track team frequented Brandy's hospital room. It was all Jade could do to maneuver her way through the maze of visitors to administer the chemo treatments. But over the weeks, as Brandy's long blonde hair fell out and her muscled legs atrophied beneath the sheets, her friends stopped coming. It was track season after all, and Brandy's teammates were busy.

This week especially.

Before Brandy got sick, there had been a boy—a quiet, dark-haired long jumper on the track team. The two of them had planned since September to attend prom together. He'd come by earlier and hemmed and hawed for fifteen minutes before stating the real reason for his visit.

He was taking someone else. He wanted Brandy to hear it from him first.

Jade prepared a needle with anti-nausea medication and injected it in the least bruised area she could find on the girl's arm.

Then she sat on the edge of Brandy's bed and patted her frail hand. "How are you really?"

Brandy clenched her teeth. "It doesn't matter. The whole year's a waste."

"Okay. So start working toward next year." Jade kept her voice quiet, calm...subdued enough that Brandy took her seriously and upbeat enough to do the one thing she believed in, the thing that kept her working in this department: to infuse hope and life and love right alongside the chemotherapy. Drop for drop.

Tears welled up in Brandy's eyes again and she gazed at Jade. "What if there isn't a next year?"

Jade's heart sank as she layered the girl's hand between her own. "There will be. You need to believe that."

Brandy blinked and tears forged their way down either side of her face. "I don't have faith like you, Jade." Her fragile body heaved twice as a series of sobs broke through. "It's hard...to believe anything good will ever happen again."

The moment called for more than a hand hold, and Jade leaned down and hugged Brandy, letting her sob. "Shhh...it's okay, sweetheart. It's okay."

"I'm...I'm afraid." The girl clung to Jade as though she'd never admitted her fears before. "What if I don't make it?"

"Oh, honey, look at you." Jade smoothed the girl's hair. "You're getting better all the time."

"But...but I'm still here. I'm still sick."

Since the day she was diagnosed, Brandy had acted as though her illness were nothing more than a serious inconvenience, a speed bump in what would otherwise have been a wonderful year. She complained about being in the children's ward, complained about the food, and rolled her eyes when she got word that she needed to stay another week. But never for a moment had she acknowledged any fear about the cancer.

Her parents were no different. They were certain that the cancer would go away and their daughter's hair would grow back in time for her senior portrait. That next year at this time she'd be competing at state.

With all her heart, Jade prayed they were right.

Both Brandy's refusal to talk about her cancer and her parents' eternal optimism were normal, but they'd left Brandy nowhere to voice her questions, no one with whom to share her deepest fears.

Until now.

Jade stayed in Brandy's room for half an hour, simply listening. When she left, she hugged the girl and promised to pray.

Brandy sniffed and wiped the tears from her cheeks. "You really think it'll help?"

"Yes." Jade angled her head and smiled. "In every way that matters."

Brandy nodded, and though she stopped short of agreeing, her expression softened.

Help her, God… She's thinking about You. Maybe for the first time.

Jade remembered something Tanner had told her once, when they first found each other after being separated for so many years: Everything happens in God's timing… It was true. First for her and Tanner.

And now for Brandy.

When Jade left her shift at eight o'clock that night her head still pulsed with an aching that almost never seemed to go away. But because of Brandy's questions, Jade felt the breath of God's presence more tangibly than she had in days.

She walked across the hospital to the lab. No matter what the test results showed, she had more than enough reason to be happy. She was fifteen minutes from home, from seeing Tanner.

And if anything could cure her headache, it was that.

Like every case that ever seemed to matter, this one came in to the Center for the Preservation of Religious Rights (CPRR) by way of an anonymous phone call. Matt and Tanner ran the firm as equal partners, but the caller wanted only to talk to "Mr. Eastman."

Though a dozen situations demanded his attention, Tanner took the call. It was a woman, and Tanner could tell from her broken sentences that she was crying. "They're…They're taking our church from us."

Tanner gazed out his office window. "Who's taking it?" There was a chance she was a nutcase or a prank caller. But something in the woman's voice made him think otherwise.

The woman drew a shaky breath. "The city of Benson, Colorado."

Tanner grabbed a legal pad and sat up straighter. Benson was a suburb of Colorado Springs, the hub for a dozen Christian ministries. Rumor on the religious freedom vine was that Benson was run by a city council hostile to anything remotely Christian.

In the past year Tanner had heard of two situations that very nearly became full-blown national cases, both of which were based in Benson. The first involved a judge who refused to remove from his courtroom wall a plaque bearing the Ten Commandments. The judge took early retirement and the issue was resolved before a case could be filed.

A few months later a public school teacher was told he couldn't sponsor a community betterment club. The reason? His beliefs might bias students toward his faith. Just as the situation was gaining public attention, the Benson City Council ruled that it could no longer be responsible for community betterment groups. The high school club was dropped and the situation became a nonissue.

"Okay." Tanner kept his tone factual and prayed it would have a contagious affect on the woman. "Why don't you tell me what you know?"

Once the woman had control of her emotions, her story was clearer than water. The congregation at First Church of the Valley had a lease arrangement with the city to hold services at City Hall. The woman's husband was Pastor Casey Carson, who headed up the church and had worked out the lease deal himself.

According to the woman, three weeks ago the church leaders were notified by someone on the city council that they were in violation of their lease agreement. They were ordered to stop holding services at the hall. Four days later a Sunday morning class on transcendental meditation began meeting there instead.

The woman released a tired sigh. "Not only did the city council cancel services, they refused to refund the remaining lease money. We paid for a year in advance. That's what they asked for and… We had no options."

Tanner felt his heart engage. "How many months were left?"

"Four."

Four months of rent money? "That would be thousands of dollars."

"Right."

Tanner scribbled as fast as his hand could move. "On what grounds?"

"Violation of contract."

"Violation?" Tanner's enthusiasm fell flat. If the church violated some aspect of the contract there would be no case.

"We read the contract and didn't see it—" The woman was clearly on the edge of tears. "We never imagined that by…"

The woman paused, and Tanner tapped his pencil. "By what?"

"My husband believes there's only one way to heaven, through Jesus. And…and that's why they pulled our lease."

The pencil fell to Tanner's desk. He eased his chair in a half rotation and stared out his window, across Warner Center and over the Los Angeles foothills. *Just when I think I've heard it all...* "They pulled your lease because of the content of your husband's sermons?"

The woman's voice was barely a whisper. "Yes."

Tanner made an appointment with her for the next day and met with Matt in the conference room before leaving that evening. "It could be big."

Matt leaned back and stroked his chin. "Could be a misunderstanding."

There was silence for a moment. "Good point." Tanner slid a copy of his notes from the earlier conversation across the table.

That's why he liked working with Matt Bronzan. Matt's considerable experience as a district attorney tempered his reaction to cases like this one, especially in the early stages.

Tanner considered his partner. Matt liked to say that Tanner was the firm's fiery energy, its passion and heart. Tanner was at his best in closing arguments, spilling his guts without reservation as though the jurors were close friends privy to his deepest, most intimate feelings. Tanner seldom failed to win a jury's empathy—and most often its vote. It was what earned him a reputation as the best religious freedom fighter in the land.

But Tanner knew none of it would have been possible on his own.

Matt was the conduit through which Tanner's energy flowed, a stabilizer with an endless ability to reason and debate prior to trial. He brought to Tanner's fire a wealth of research knowledge and an uncanny talent for finding perfect precedent cases. There was no way Tanner could have run the firm without him, and after three years Matt was more than a brilliant partner.

He was Tanner's best friend.

Aside from Jade, of course. The thought of her sent a shot of anxious adrenaline through his veins. What was wrong with her, anyway? He'd waited all his life to love her, to be her husband and share forever with her. So why the headaches? Could she still be struggling that much over the miscarriage?

In a single motion, Tanner pushed his chair from the table and stood. That had to be it. Because he couldn't begin to imagine the alternatives.

Matt looked up from the notes. "Going home?"

"Yeah." Tanner reached for his leather bag, his shoulders feeling suddenly heavy. "Hey, pray for Jade, will you?"

Concern flooded Matt's expression. "The headaches?"

Tanner nodded and exhaled in a way that filled his cheeks. "She can't get rid of 'em."

The office air conditioning clicked off, and a somber quiet filled the room. Matt studied Tanner, and when he spoke, his voice was soft. "You're really worried, aren't you?"

There was no point hiding the truth from Matt. The two of them had seen enough heartache in their days to know better than to lie to each other. "I am." A strange mix of anger and sorrow seized Tanner's heart, and tears stung his eyes. "She *can't* be sick." He blinked twice and worked the muscles in his jaw. "Not now…after all we've been through."

Matt linked his fingers and stared at the floor. When he looked up, he patted the empty chair beside him. "Why wait." His smile didn't erase the worry from his eyes. "Let's pray."

Tanner's fingers relaxed one by one, and the bag dropped from his hand. With small, slow steps, he made his way around the table and sat across from Matt. Then they did the one thing that set their business relationship apart, the thing that convinced them their friendship would outlast anything they might do in the field of law.

They prayed.

In quiet unison, heads bowed, they lifted Tanner's precious Jade to the very throne room of heaven.

An hour later Tanner was tossing a football with Ty out front when Jade pulled up.

"Hey, Dad…" Ty caught the ball and jogged to Tanner's side. "She looks good."

It was true. The heaviness in her eyes had lifted, and there was a spring in her step as she made her way from the car to the place where the two of them stood.

Jade grinned at Ty and then at Tanner. Tanner felt his pulse pick up when he saw her eyes well with tears, but then a smile broke across her face. She wrapped her arms around both of them, drawing them close.

"Guess what, guys?"

There was joy in her voice, and Tanner held his breath as Jade lay her head on his shoulder. "I'm *pregnant!*"

"You are? Yeah!" Ty let out a whoop and tossed the football high in the air.

Elation and relief coursed through every vein, every inch of Tanner's body. "Thank God!" He cradled Jade's face with his fingertips and kissed her, the same way he'd kissed her that night when they first found each other again. His voice was the happiest whisper. "I love you, Mrs. Eastman."

She giggled and kissed him back. "I love you, too."

"Come on." He took Jade's hand and led her to the house with quick steps. "Let's call the Bronzans."

Jade's quick smile ignited fresh sparkles in her eyes. "Can I call?" She grabbed Ty's hand and they headed inside together. "Hannah has to hear the news first."

Tanner stood back with Ty, watching Jade tap out the

Bronzans' number. His heart soared. How long had it been since he'd felt this good? The corners of his mouth felt like they were permanently fixed halfway up his cheeks.

"Hannah, it's me. I went to the doctor today, and they found out what's wrong. You won't believe it…" She squealed. "I'm *pregnant!*" Pause. "I know. Yes, God is so faithful. Always."

The phone conversation between the women continued and Tanner closed his eyes. He refused to think of the what-ifs. They didn't matter anymore; Jade was pregnant! All their prayers had been answered—his and Jade's, Matt's, and Hannah's. They'd each begged God on Jade's behalf, and now the tiny baby growing inside her was His miraculous reply. Her headaches, the nausea…all of it was for the best reason of all.

Jade was going to have a baby, a brother or sister for Ty. The child they'd dreamed of.

And everything about their lives and the happily-ever-after they were building was going to work out just fine after all.

Five

The phone was ringing as they brought in the groceries. Jenny went back for the rest while Hannah set three bags down on the counter and grabbed the receiver. Her heart still felt light within her. The same way it had felt since hearing Jade's good news the day before.

"Hello?" Hannah leaned against the counter and gazed out at the ocean.

"Mrs. Bronzan?" The caller's voice was familiar, but Hannah couldn't quite place it.

A flock of seagulls filled the sky, standing out against the clear blue. "Yes."

"This is Edna Parsons from Social Services." The woman hesitated and Hannah's heart skipped a beat. "We have a little girl for you."

Hannah's breath caught in her throat and her knees went weak. Was it really possible? Had the social worker found the child they'd been praying for? "You…you do?"

Jenny entered the house with the last of the groceries.

"Your file says you're not interested in the foster-adopt program." A heavy sigh sounded across the phone lines. "But I've worked in this department for twenty-four years. Mrs. Bronzan, there's no way this little girl's going back to her mother."

Anger stirred in Hannah's heart. This wasn't the call they were waiting for. It was some sort of mistake. Why were they calling if the girl wasn't legally free? Hadn't Hannah and Matt made it clear that the last thing they wanted was to fall in love with a child they might wind up losing? *I'll say we're not interested…* Hannah drew a deep breath. "Tell me about her."

Jenny came up beside Hannah and arched an eyebrow. Hannah covered the receiver with her hand and whispered, "Social Services."

Mrs. Parsons continued. "Well…she's a Caucasian child, four years old. Our department took an anonymous call up in the Santa Maria area. The child was living with her mother in the back of a van in an abandoned field. Her mother worked as a prostitute and was part of a drug ring, one that police have been trying to bust for months. The woman's been moved to Los Angeles because of an outstanding warrant here. She's in jail awaiting trial; the little girl is in temporary foster care in the San Fernando Valley." The social worker paused. "This is the third time the woman has been arrested for drug trafficking and prostitution. It was her last chance and she blew it. There's no next of kin. The judge has already started the process of terminating the woman's rights to the child."

Hannah's eyes grew wet. "What… What does that mean?"

"The woman goes to trial in two weeks. At that time if she's sentenced to prison—and she will be—the judge will order the child placed in a foster-adopt home pending termination of the mother's rights. In cases like this, the child should be legally free within six months."

Legally free in six months? The thought danced about the surface of her heart. That wasn't so bad, was it? Hannah pictured the little girl sleeping in the back of a van. If anyone needed a stable family, this child did. Besides, life was full of risks.

And if she said yes…if they were willing to look past the technicalities, she might be a mother again in a matter of days!

Hannah wanted to shout out loud with the possibility, but she bit her lip and locked eyes with Jenny. The mix of emotions in her daughter's face made her reach out and take Jenny's hand. Excitement, fear, sorrow. Feelings they were all bound to have throughout the adoption process.

This was only the beginning.

Hannah closed her eyes and pinched the bridge of her nose. "Why us, Mrs. Parsons? We made it clear we weren't interested in taking a child unless she was legally free for adoption."

"I'm aware of that."

Phones rang in the background in the office of Social Services, and Hannah struggled to concentrate. She was dying to tell the social worker yes...yes, they'd take the little girl and give her a real bed, a real home, and a family who would love her forever.

But what if something happened? What if somehow the mother's rights weren't terminated? How in the world would the child survive then? How would *she* survive?

What am I supposed to do here, God? Give me wisdom...please.

Edna Parsons drew a deep breath. "I've met the girl, Mrs. Bronzan. And, well, she's very special. Other than a very rough first few years, she's in perfect health. She'll be very easy to place. I called you first because I can picture her in your family."

Hannah opened her eyes and felt the familiar sting of tears. A lump in her throat made it impossible to speak. She swallowed hard, already drawn to the lonely little girl sitting in a foster home somewhere.

A little girl whose name God was even now writing on her heart.

Mrs. Parsons interrupted her thoughts. "I can give you a few days to think about it. If you're not interested, I need to look through my other files as soon as possible."

Hannah squeezed Jenny's hand and nodded, finding her voice once more. "That'll be fine. I'll call you tomorrow. Thank you for thinking of us." She almost hung up, but then she stopped. "What's her name?"

She could hear the smile in the social worker's voice. "Grace."

Grace...

The moment the phone was on the hook, Hannah led Jenny to a sofa in the next room. Her heart raced and her hands trembled as she faced her daughter, smiling through eyes clouded with tears. "They have a little girl for us. Mrs. Parsons said she could picture her in our family."

Jenny searched Hannah's face. "But—" her voice was barely audible—"she's a foster child, right? Isn't that what you said?"

Hannah shrugged. She released her hold on Jenny's hands and leaned back. "For now. She'll be free in six months. The mother's in jail, and in a few weeks Grace will be placed in a foster-adopt home."

"Grace?" A flicker of hope danced in Jenny's eyes.

"Yes." Hannah smiled and played the child's name over again in her mind. *Grace.* It was a good name, a good sign. It was God's grace that made the risk worth taking. Somehow the Lord would see them through the adoption process.

Jenny folded her hands, her forehead a mass of wrinkles. "How old is she?"

Hannah reminded herself to breathe. Her mind still spun from the information. The phone call felt like something from a dream, and now that Mrs. Parsons had explained the situation, Hannah could already imagine the girl coming home in a few days. "Four. She's been living in the back of a van."

Jenny's chin quivered. She stared out the window at the gentle surf and breathed out, soft and slow. Hannah's heart ached for her daughter and the emotional roller coaster they'd ridden these past years—as well as the one they'd ride in the coming months if they took this child.

Jenny faced Hannah again. There were tears on her cheeks, and she wiped the wetness with the back of her sleeve as the uncertainty in her eyes fell away. In its place a grin formed, one that convinced Hannah beyond a doubt that they were doing the right thing by adopting. "We're going to take her, right?"

"Well…" Hannah laughed and sobbed at the same time. "When Matt gets home, we'll talk about it."

"What's there to talk about?" Jenny's eyes sparkled and she threw her hands up. "God must want her with us. Otherwise he wouldn't have had the social worker call."

Hannah wrapped her arms around her daughter, taking in the warmth of her, the fresh smell of her shampoo. She silently thanked God for sparing this precious child four years ago. Hannah pulled back and searched Jenny's eyes. "So if we take a vote, yours is yes?"

A smile filled Jenny's face. "Absolutely."

When Matt got home an hour later, the decision was unanimous.

Hannah called Mrs. Parsons the next morning and told her the news. "How soon can we have her?"

The social worker laughed. "Within an hour of her mother's sentencing."

From the moment Hannah hung up the phone she was bathed in reassurance, grateful for the little one God was bringing into their lives. It was a miracle, really. In two weeks she would be a mother again, sharing the joys of parenting a child who desperately needed love and security, a home and a family that would be hers forever. A miracle that never would have happened if they hadn't lost Tom and Alicia.

Further proof that God grew fragrant flowers of hope in the ashes of loss.

The days dragged on. More than once Hannah would be out shopping for a toaster or a purse or groceries, and find herself drawn to little girls' dresses. *No*, she told herself. *Not until the hearing*.

But in further conversations with Mrs. Parsons, the social worker explained that some clothing for Grace was necessary if the child was to be brought to them as soon as the hearing took place.

Hannah and Jenny set out one night intending to buy a single outfit and a pair of pajamas. Instead they came home with leggings and flowered T-shirts, jeans and frilly socks, two dresses with smocking and lace, a floor-length pink nightgown, and a package of multicolored hair bows. Just in case she had long hair.

Matt chuckled at the array of clothing spread across the dining room table that night. "I think Grace is covered for the first few days, anyway." He put his arm around Hannah and kissed her forehead.

"Actually, we held back." Jenny grinned as she ran her fingers over the soft cotton leggings. "My little sister needs nice clothes, you know."

Later, when Jenny was out with friends, Matt and Hannah took a stroll along the beach. The night was warm, signaling the coming summer. Matt wove his fingers between Hannah's, and for a while neither of them spoke. Hannah savored the ocean breeze on her face, the warmth of Matt's strong hand in hers, the way she felt safe and protected in his presence. The way he had always made her feel since the accident.

Never in her wildest dreams could she have imagined a life with anyone but Tom Ryan. But now she was in love with life once more, amazed that God had provided her with not one, but two men capable of capturing her heart.

Matt broke the silence first, his voice as gentle and soothing as the winds from the Pacific. "Are you worried? About the risk?"

It was something they hadn't talked about. Mrs. Parsons didn't expect there to be a problem. If Grace's mother was put in prison, the judge would begin the process of terminating her rights that same day. And only then would Grace be placed in their home. The process seemed safe enough to Hannah.

"Are you?" Hannah had already dismissed the risks associated with adopting Grace. If the child's mother was sent to prison and Grace came to be their daughter, no one could ever take her away. Hannah was sure of it. Imagining risks now made Hannah's future feel no more stable than the sand beneath her feet.

"There's a risk." Matt's steps were slow and thoughtful as he caught her gaze and held it. "No matter how small."

Hannah swallowed. "I can't think that far ahead." She side-stepped a pile of seaweed. "If the judge starts the termination process, then the law's on our side. I have to believe that."

They walked a bit further, and Matt stopped. He reached for a piece of driftwood and flung it out to sea, watching as it disappeared beneath the waves. "The law's a funny thing." He looked at her again. "It won't be final until her mother's rights are legally severed. You need to understand that." He paused. "Just in case."

Hannah shifted her gaze toward the dark ocean and felt the sting of tears. Alicia's face came to mind—beautiful, intelligent, and kind. Alicia's future had been brighter than the sun, but today she lived in heaven. "Nothing's for sure." She faced Matt and placed her hands on his shoulders. Her eyes held his, and she waited for the lump in her throat to subside. "I learned that much four years ago."

"Okay." Matt nodded, love overflowing from his heart to hers. "As long as you understand."

"I don't want to think about it, but I understand."

Matt wove his hands around Hannah's waist and clasped them near the small of her back. The chill from the wet evening air disappeared. "What should she call us? Have you thought of that?"

Hannah smiled. "Mommy and Daddy. Because that's what we'll be."

Matt brushed a lock of her long hair back from her face. "So you're not worried."

She smiled despite the tears that pooled in her eyes. "Worrying doesn't help. I worried all the time before the accident and it didn't make a bit of difference when Tom and Alicia were killed." Her throat was thick with emotion, but a single ripple of laughter made its way up. She rubbed the tip of her nose against Matt's. "If Grace comes to live with us, then she's our little girl." She closed her eyes and she could see Alicia waving good-bye from the backseat of the Bronco that long-ago summer day. "Whether we have her for a day or a lifetime."

The waiting was worse than anything Matt could remember. Especially because there was a chance it was ushering in a season that might end in devastating loss. He tried not to think about the fact, but his legal background told him anything was possible.

One week turned to two, and on May 11, Jade and Tanner came over to see Jenny off for her senior prom.

"Jenny, you're breathtaking. You look just like your mother." Jade hugged her.

"Jade's right, sweetheart." Matt stood nearby, his heart all lit up inside. "You and your mother could be sisters."

"I don't know about that." Hannah giggled from across the room, her eyes shining with pride. "But there's no doubt you'll be the prettiest girl at the dance."

Tanner put an arm around Jenny and squeezed her shoulders.

"Ty's at baseball practice, but he says hi. Oh, and not to worry. He'll miss his game the day of your graduation." He winked at Matt. "Thanks for letting us share your day."

Jenny glowed under the attention and adoration, and Matt couldn't help but feel his heart swell. Some days it seemed like only yesterday when he burst into Jenny's room and found her nearly dead, bottles of pills spilled around the bed from her attempted suicide. Watching her now, tall and lean, with the curves of a young woman, it was hard to believe four years had passed since that awful time.

The distance Jenny had come since then was a race that could only have been run with God, and Matt was most thankful for Jenny's faith. A faith that added an angelic glow to her considerable beauty.

Matt pulled Jenny aside before her date arrived and took her hands. "You'll be the most beautiful girl at the dance." He kissed her cheek. "I want you to know how proud I am of you."

"Thanks." Jenny's eyes were watery and she smiled. There was a gentle silence between them, and Jenny's face grew serious. "A long time ago I asked you whether you loved my mom, remember?"

Matt felt his expression soften. "Yes. Outside the jail. After the verdict against the drunk driver."

"Right." Jenny blinked and two tears left tracks across her made-up cheeks. She dabbed at them and laughed at herself. "I wasn't going to cry."

Matt reached for a tissue and handed it to her. Then he told her the same thing he'd always said when her losses seemed overwhelming, when tears overflowed the walls around her heart: "Tears are okay, Jenny. They mean you're breathing."

She smiled and nodded. "Anyway," her gaze met his, and he could see how much of the little girl had faded from her face these past years. "I'm glad the answer was yes. You've made my mom so happy. And you've made us a family again." She sniffed, her eyes more serious than before. "Maybe...maybe I don't say it enough, but I love you, Matt. You may not be my daddy, but you're my father. I think of you that way more than you know."

Matt hugged her tightly. There would be other times like this...the day he would walk Jenny down the aisle in place of the dad she'd lost, the day she would have her firstborn...

But this day, this moment, would remain in the treasure chest of his memory forever. Her feelings for him were more of a gift than she knew, and it took him a moment to find his voice. "I love you, too, honey. You'll always be my oldest girl."

He wondered about Grace then, about raising a little girl who had suffered so little love in her early years. "I hope Grace grows up to be just like you." He grinned at Jenny and reached for his camera. "Come on. Your mom's waiting. I think she wants about a million pictures."

By the time the hearing for Grace's mother arrived two days later, Hannah had the photographs of Jenny's night developed and in a scrapbook. In fact, she was more organized than she'd been in years. Anything to pass the time.

Matt and Jenny both stayed home with Hannah that morning, each of them silently finding ways to keep busy. Hannah pictured the courtroom somewhere on the other side of the Santa Monica Mountains and imagined what stage the proceedings might be at.

Do any of them know what's at stake?

At eleven o'clock the phone rang. Hannah stared at it while Matt and Jenny hurried in from other parts of the house. Her heart pounded as she reached for the receiver. "Hello?"

"Mrs. Bronzan?"

"Yes?"

"This is Mrs. Parsons from Social Services." She hesitated while Hannah held her breath. "Grace's mother was sentenced to fifteen years. The judge ordered termination of her parental rights to begin as soon as possible."

The tears were instant and Hannah smothered a cry with her hand. She glanced at Matt and Jenny and nodded. "So…so you can bring her here now?"

"Yes." The woman's answer was quick, confident. "Grace is waiting. I'll have her home in time for lunch."

Hannah hung up the phone and hugged Matt and Jenny as tight as she could. "She's ours!" Tears spilled onto her cheeks as she shouted for joy. "Grace is coming home!"

They made lunch together, guessing what type of personality their little girl would have. Would she be shy or silly, withdrawn or affectionate? And what would she look like? Most of all they talked about how right they felt about taking her in.

Fifteen minutes later Mrs. Parsons pulled into the drive. With Matt and Jenny at her side, Hannah saw the little girl for the first time—and her breath caught in her throat.

"Dear God…" She stared at Grace, at the child's creamy complexion and the mass of dark blonde curls that framed her face. "I don't believe it."

"Mom…do you see what I see?" Jenny's eyes were wide.

Matt's face was blank as he looked from Hannah to Jenny and back. "What's wrong?" He stared at the child. "She looks like an angel. So?"

Hannah shook her head, her throat dry. "No…she looks like…" She was too shocked to speak, too caught up in the vision of the child before her. Almost as though she were seeing a ghost.

"She looks—" Jenny took her mother's hand and finished the explanation for Matt—"She looks exactly like Alicia."

Mrs. Parsons and Grace were at the door, and Matt opened it, his eyes dancing. He smiled big. "Hi."

The social worker grinned in return. "We've come to bring Grace home."

Hannah stood two feet behind him, mesmerized by the child. Up close it was clear that though the resemblance to Alicia was uncanny, this little girl was more serious, older than her years. She would be her own person, not a replica of a daughter that was no longer with them.

But that was as it should be.

"Come in." Matt motioned to Mrs. Parsons, stooped down, and placed his hands on his thighs. "Hi there, Grace."

The child leaned into Mrs. Parsons and buried half her face. She barely lifted her hand and wiggled her fingers at Matt, looking at him with one wide eye. Then the part of her mouth that could be seen curved into a shy smile.

Grace and Mrs. Parsons stepped into the house, and Grace raised her eyes up at Hannah. "Hi."

Hannah's heart sang within her and she knelt near Grace. "Hi, honey." She ran her fingers over the child's feather-soft curls. "We're glad you're home."

Grace nodded and looked at something near her feet.

A flock of questions invaded. Did she like them? Would she always be this shy? Hannah struggled to force them from her mind. It was too soon to make judgments about Grace's personality. Of course she was shy! She'd never met them, and now she was being told this was her home, her family.

But even in those early minutes, after being brought to yet another family, Grace's quietness faded when she met Jenny.

Hannah watched her teenage daughter kneel before the little girl.

"Hi, Grace. I'm your sister." There was a mist of tears in Jenny's eyes as she took the child's hand. "My name's Jenny."

Grace blinked and let go of Mrs. Parsons. She came to Jenny and leaned into her arms. Then she said the one thing that convinced Hannah beyond a doubt that Grace was destined to be their daughter. More convincing than Mrs. Parsons' phone call a few weeks ago. Even more convincing than the way Grace looked so much like Alicia.

With eyes hungry for love, Grace smiled at Jenny and said, "I always wanted a big sister."

Edna Parsons spent nearly an hour at the Bronzans, taken by the loving way the family had welcomed the child. As Edna left, she gazed at the ocean and thought of the cozy warmth that made up the Bronzans' home. The family had all the necessary means to give Grace a life she'd only dreamed of.

Edna sighed as she made her way back to the car, seized by a pang of fear. What if Grace's birth mother appealed her case and was set free? What if the termination didn't go through? What if something happened and Grace had to leave this family?

She slid into the driver's seat and shook off the feeling. It wasn't possible. Grace's situation was simply too bad for any solution other than a termination of the mother's rights.

She thought about Grace's file, reports she'd read again just that morning. They'd been no different from hundreds of other files she'd seen in the past year, but something about Grace tugged at Edna's heart. Maybe it was the most recent report, the one detailing the child's removal from her mother's care.

The details were enough to turn Edna's stomach, and though she wasn't a praying woman, she took a moment from her schedule and placed before God two very specific requests. First, that the Bronzans be permitted to adopt Grace.

And second, that they never learn the awful things that nearly transpired the night their new little girl was taken into protective custody.

Six

S omething was wrong.

Jade was utterly nauseous, her headaches more severe than before. And on several occasions her vision had doubled. She did everything she could to rationalize the way she felt. Her age must be a factor, she told herself, or her hormones. Maybe the baby was bigger than Ty had been at this point, or possibly the stress of the miscarriage a year ago had strained her system more than she realized.

Maybe she needed glasses.

Jade tried to calmly analyze her symptoms, but each night she lay down in raw, heart-pounding fear, terrified something was wrong with the baby. Sometimes, after Tanner was asleep, she'd sit straight up in bed and stare out the window, willing her heartbeat to slow down, desperate for a grip on her emotions.

Day after day the fear ate at her, but not once did she tell Tanner. Oh, she told him when she didn't feel well or when she had to lie down because her headaches were so bad. But she didn't tell him her deepest fears, that there might be complications with her pregnancy. She barely acknowledged the possibility to herself.

But now, six weeks after learning she was pregnant, Jade was worried about more than the baby's health.

She was worried about her own.

That was why, when she awoke at four in the morning one Monday in June with a splitting headache, she promised herself she'd make the call. Whatever was causing the pain in her head, it had to be checked. She'd start with Dr. Layton, a neurologist friend who worked with her at the children's hospital. He would know what to do.

No matter how great her fear, there was no better time to go in and be seen. Ty had spent the night at a neighbor boy's house, and today he was going to the beach with the boy's family. Jade had no plans whatsoever for the day.

Her head throbbed as she eased herself to a sitting position, careful not to wake Tanner. He would be up in two hours and he needed his sleep. He'd been coming home from the office earlier since Jade's announcement, but he was so excited about the baby that they had talked until after midnight the past few nights.

Despite her pain, the sight of her sleeping husband filled her with joy. There couldn't be anything seriously wrong with her. Not now, not when she had everything she'd ever dreamed of with Tanner.

She brushed a lock of hair off his forehead and admired the angles of his face. He'd been treating her like a China doll since hearing the news, doting on her, bringing her ice water, and encouraging her to rest whenever possible. Because of the severity of her symptoms, he wanted her home from work, and she agreed. Her last day would be at the end of the month. She would reevaluate after summer, since the baby wasn't due until December.

Whenever Tanner worried about her headaches and nausea, Jade would lean close and kiss him into silence. "I'm supposed to be sick. Morning sickness means I'm carrying a healthy baby."

It was enough that she was concerned; there was no point worrying him also. For the most part Tanner was willing to believe her explanations.

She closed her eyes. *Make it go away, Lord, please. Take the pain from my head so I know there's nothing wrong with me.*

Her skull ached in response, and images from the night before filled her mind.

She and Tanner had gone out onto their bedroom balcony to watch the moonlight glistening on the rolling hills behind their home. In the shadows they had spotted a pair of deer making their way to a thicket of oak trees. Tanner came up behind her and slipped his arms around her still-flat mid-section.

"You're beautiful, Jade. More beautiful than anything." He whispered into her ear and she leaned her head back against his chest.

"Mmmm." She closed her eyes. "It feels so good to be with you."

"I'm sorry you're sick." He left a trail of feather-light kisses along her neck. "But I love that you're pregnant. I want to be a part of everything I missed when you had Ty."

Tears had burned in Jade's eyes. "I wish there was a way to get back the years we lost." She drew a deep breath and savored the weight of his body against hers. "Sometimes I still can't believe we're together."

The memory faded, and Jade stared out the window at the still-dark morning sky. Her first pregnancy had been marked by pain and turmoil, all of it orchestrated by Tanner's mother and her web of lies.

Jade thought for a moment of the girl she'd been when she got pregnant with Ty, the way she'd ached for Tanner, yet wound up marrying someone else instead, someone she never loved and shouldn't have married. In the end, it was Doris Eastman's confession that brought her and Tanner together.

It was amazing, really. After marrying Tanner eighteen months ago, Jade had actually come to like Doris. She was a woman changed by Christ's forgiveness during the final days of her life—so much so that Jade grieved alongside Tanner when she died a year ago.

Jade's head pounded harder, and a wave of panic came over her, the same one that seemed to hit with increasing frequency these past months. Against her will, a thought she'd been fighting came back again...

What if the headaches were some sort of punishment? What if God was punishing her for marrying Tanner after being married to Jim Rudolph all those years?

She swallowed hard, reached out, and laid her fingers on Tanner's bare arm. *Were we wrong, God? Were these not the plans You had for us?*

Jade had voiced her fears to Hannah Bronzan before, and each time her friend's answer ran along the same lines: "You did what you could with Jim. You've told the Lord you're sorry for your part in the marriage, but you were never unfaithful, Jade. Jim was. God doesn't hold you guilty for that. Not you or Tanner."

Then Hannah would reiterate what all of them already knew. Jim had moved in with another woman and divorced Jade in a bitter case that nearly cost her full custody of Ty. By the time the divorce was final, Jim had nothing but anger and bitter words for Jade. Three days later he married the woman he'd left Jade for.

Hannah's reassurances came to Jade again: "You made your mistakes, but you didn't cause the divorce. The fact that Tanner entered your life again at that time wasn't some trick by the devil. It was God's way of blessing both of you after a decade of heartache."

Her friend's words sounded right, even now. But still...

There had been women at church who wrinkled their noses at Jade after her decision to marry Tanner, telling her that according to Scripture she was living in adultery.

The idea that what she and Tanner shared might somehow be against God's will was almost more than Jade could take. Especially when she loved him more than life itself. She'd read the

Scripture in Matthew about divorce over and over again. At first she'd been convinced that she was in the right, that God granted exceptions in cases where one spouse had been unfaithful. There was no question that Jim was guilty of marital unfaithfulness. He'd refused to rectify things with her even when she'd wanted to try.

But the stronger her headaches grew, and the weaker and sicker she felt, the more terrified she became that somehow God was angry with her. Her face grew hot and her heart raced wildly. *Don't punish us now, God, please…*

A veil of sweat broke out on her face, and she pushed her fears aside. Nothing good came from worry. She reached for a glass of water and two pain relievers from a bottle on her bedside table. They were a mild, over-the-counter brand—the strongest thing she would consider taking while pregnant. They hadn't worked well in past days, but as she swallowed them she told herself she'd be fine in an hour.

The perspiration on her face was heavier than before. She took her hand from Tanner's arm and ran it across her forehead. As she did, Tanner stirred and blinked a few times before squinting at the clock.

"Jade…it's 4:30, honey." His eyes closed as he snuggled against her and circled his arms around her waist. His voice was thick with sleep. "What're you doing up?"

Her head pounded in response and her mind raced. "I'm hot. I think I'll take a shower."

Tanner tightened his grip on her. "Mmmm, baby, are you sure? Stay here with me."

"I'd like to." Jade ran her fingers through his hair and down the length of his arm. "But the morning sickness is kinda strong."

Tanner opened his eyes again. Even in the dark she could see his growing alarm. "Hey…shouldn't that be over by now? You're what…twelve, thirteen weeks?"

"Yes." Jade forced a smile. Tanner had dozens of briefs he could be studying, but instead she had often found him these past weeks in their office poring over the daily breakdown of what to expect during pregnancy. "You know what it is? This baby of ours is so healthy, my morning sickness might last four months. Who knows, right?"

Tanner thought about that for a moment and the worry left his face. "I love you, Jade." He leaned up and brought his lips to hers.

Their kiss lingered, and for a brief moment Jade forgot about the pain in her head. "I love you, too."

"Go shower." He smiled. "And I'll pray it won't be four months." He settled back into the pillow and closed his eyes once more.

"Okay. Sweet dreams."

Jade studied the image of her husband as she stood and pulled her robe tight. As she headed for the bathroom, his words rang her heart. *I love you, Jade…*

Despite her aching head, the thought of an angry God punishing her for loving Tanner seemed nothing short of outlandish. She knew God better than that.

But five minutes into her shower, her vision doubled and grew so blurry she couldn't see. As she struggled to focus, a piercing pain sliced through her head, and she screamed in agony. "Tanner!" She groped to keep her balance as everything around her began to spin. "Help me!"

His footsteps sounded fast and hard against the floor outside the bathroom, but it was too late. Darkness overtook her as she collapsed on the floor of the shower, unable to move.

"Jade!" Tanner was at her side. "Dear God, help me…"

She could feel his hands on her shoulders, then under her arms as he lifted her from the wet tile, but the sounds around her were fading fast.

And in that moment her symptoms seemed terrifyingly clear. Nausea, morning headaches, double vision. Now this…

How many children had she cared for with similar symptoms? If it was what she feared, then her thoughts hadn't been irrational after all. God must indeed be punishing her. Punishing both of them.

Jade opened her mouth to speak but she no longer could. *No, God…please. Don't let it be…*

She wanted to tell Tanner she was sorry, that she loved him more than words could say, and that he needed to call an ambulance, but she couldn't make her tongue work to form words.

For a while Tanner was gone, and Jade fought to remain conscious. *He's calling for help…everything's going to be fine.* Then he was back and he swept her into his arms again. The last thing she remembered was his breath on her face, his distant voice begging her to hold on, telling her that help was on the way.

And something else…a damp area on her chest. With a jolt she realized Tanner was crying. *Tanner…honey, don't cry. I'll be okay, I promise.*

Then there was nothing but cold, quiet darkness…and the lingering wetness of Tanner's tears.

Tanner could force himself to do only two things as he followed the ambulance in his car: breathe and pray. Neither was easy. The moment he had seen Jade on the floor of the shower, her lips blue, her arms and legs jerking unnaturally, a grenade of raw fear had exploded in his heart.

Over and over he had pictured himself waking to her screams and finding her on the floor. "No, God!" he'd shouted as he stared at her, panic coursing through his veins. He'd had no idea what to do first. Call for an ambulance? Help her stop shaking?

In a split-second decision, he dropped to the floor, took her by the shoulders, and tried to force her body to stop shaking.

When that didn't work he called 9-1-1.

"What's the emergency?" an operator had asked him.

"I don't know…my wife is dying! Come quick. Please!"

In the minutes after that, Tanner hadn't meant to cry, but tears came anyway. Streams of them. As though his heart knew something his mind wasn't ready to grasp. That there was something terribly wrong with the only woman he'd ever loved.

When the paramedics arrived, Tanner told them Jade was pregnant. They noted the information, hooked her up to several monitors, and gave her a shot of something. While they did, Tanner pounded them with as many questions as he dared ask. Was this something they'd seen before? Was she dying? What was the shot for? Could they help her stop shaking?

Two men worked on her, loading her onto a stretcher, and one of them answered Tanner's questions, his tone calm and confident. "It happens often," the man explained while he helped his partner hook an IV line into Jade's arm. "She isn't dying. She's having a seizure. The shot will calm her down."

Seizure? The word screamed in Tanner's mind even now. A seizure? Other people might have seizures, but not his wife. Not his precious Jade.

The memory evaporated in a desert of fear. Tanner swallowed hard and kept his eyes glued on the swirling lights in front of him. He knew nothing about medicine, but he knew this: Seizures were a sign of something bad.

Something very bad.

It was more than Tanner could process, so he continued to pray. Not the conversational prayer he so often shared with God, but a desperate cry for help, for an answer they could live with. One Jade could live with.

At the hospital Tanner tore from his car and raced into the emergency room. Jade was being moved through the lobby toward the back. Tanner was at her side in seconds, his heart racing as he gently leaned over and hugged her close.

"Jade, honey…" He took hold of her hand and walked alongside the stretcher. "How are you?"

She forced a smile, and Tanner tried to keep the fear from showing on his face. She looked small, almost childlike, lost in a sea of sheets and intravenous lines. Her face was pale, her tone groggy. "I have a headache."

"I know. Dr. Layton's on his way."

Her eyelids lowered partway. "I'm tired."

Tanner kept his stride even with the moving stretcher and glanced at the paramedic pushing her. "Is that normal?"

"Yes. It's the medication." The man angled the stretcher around a corner and into a room. He patted Jade on the hand. "Go ahead and sleep. Dr. Layton will be here in a few minutes; he'll take good care of you."

She was asleep before the man left the room, and Tanner stared at her. A chill had worked its way into the marrow of his bones. *What's happening to her, God? She's everything to me.*

Sweat beaded across his brow, and he reached for her hand. She couldn't be sick, couldn't have anything wrong with her. *Please God, not Jade. She and Ty and the baby…they're all I've ever wanted, all I've ever prayed for since–*

A technician entered the room, cutting his thoughts short. "She needs to go to X ray." He positioned himself at the head of Jade's bed and began wheeling her out of the room. "The doctor wants a CAT scan."

Tanner stayed by Jade's side as much as possible, and at eight o'clock that morning, Jade was admitted for observation pending the results. She was still groggy when Dr. Layton entered the room

and walked over to her bed. Tanner was glad this doctor was handling the situation. The two men had met on several occasions,
and Tanner liked his professionalism. From everything he knew
of the doctor, if anyone was up-to-date on current medical break-
throughs, it was Robert Layton.

The man nodded at Tanner, his expression serious. Then he
smiled at Jade. "Looks like you're feeling better."

Jade uttered a weak laugh. "Talk about morning sickness,
huh?"

Dr. Layton's expression fell and his eyes narrowed. "Jade—"
he glanced at Tanner, then back at Jade—"I'm afraid it's more than
morning sickness."

Tanner held his breath and tightened his grip on Jade's hand.
No, God...please... Nothing felt real. The whole scene felt like a
poorly scripted TV drama.

The doctor drew a breath and moved a step closer to the bed.
"The CAT scan shows a brain tumor, Jade. It's about the size of a
walnut." He pursed his lips. "We need to do a needle biopsy."

Even as the doctor spoke, as he delivered the worst verdict of
Tanner's life, Jade's expression went unchanged. She nodded and
listened the way she might if the doctor were talking about a
simple case of the flu or a patient down the hall.

Or one of the kids she worked with.

Tanner wanted to scream at both of them, to shake the doctor and demand to know the odds, the risks. To know if Jade
would be okay when the nightmare that had just begun was
finally over.

Instead, he struggled to still his spinning thoughts and focus
on what Dr. Layton was saying.

"The seizure means that the tumor is growing." He glanced at a
clipboard in his hands and then back at Jade. "If it's aggressive, there's
no time to waste. Even if it isn't cancerous. You know that, right?"

No time to waste for what? Tanner wanted to scoop Jade into his arms and run from the room, find some way to stop the craziness. Instead he stayed stone-still and felt the slightest trembling in Jade's fingers. He clasped his other hand around hers, and the trembling stilled.

There was a pause, and Tanner cleared his throat. "I don't understand."

Jade turned to him. "If the tumor's growing, they'll want to do brain surgery right away." She hesitated, and for the first time he saw tears in her eyes. "But that puts the baby at risk."

Tanner's heart pounded in his throat. Surgery? Risks to their baby? None of it was possible. He tore his eyes from Jade's and stared at Dr. Layton. "What are the options?" His tone rang with frustration.

The doctor angled his head. "It's too soon to say." He set his hand on Jade's shoulder. "Let's get through the needle biopsy and then we can talk."

The test was set for just after lunch, and neither Jade nor Tanner wanted to talk about the possibilities. Instead, Jade slept, and Tanner held tight to her hand while he called Matt.

"Hey, listen, I'll be out of the office for a few days." He squeezed his eyes shut and pinched the bridge of his nose, holding his tears at bay. His heart thudded hard against his chest. "Jade's—" Fear stopped him from finishing the sentence. He couldn't say it, couldn't admit the truth this soon. His hands trembled and his throat refused to let him speak for several seconds. *Control, Tanner. Come on.* He swallowed hard and cleared his throat. "Something's come up."

Matt paused. "Everything okay?"

"Yeah." Tanner's answer was too fast, but he prayed Matt wouldn't ask any hard questions. He wasn't ready to talk about the doctor's findings. Not yet. Not when he was still desperately trying to catch his breath and believe the news himself. "Jade isn't feeling well."

"Oh. Right." Matt seemed relieved. "Morning sickness?"

"Yep." Tanner closed his eyes briefly as the lie left his lips. *If only it were true…*

"Tomorrow then?"

"Sure."

The phone call ended and tiny sweat drops made their way down Tanner's forehead. He hated lying to Matt, but he couldn't admit the awful truth. Not to Matt or Hannah or the neighbor who was caring for Ty that day.

Not even to himself.

Using his wife's name and the words *brain tumor* in the same sentence was too impossible to imagine. Maybe the tests were wrong. Maybe they'd insert a needle in Jade's skull and find out there wasn't any tumor there at all.

The seizure medication made Jade sleep through the biopsy and into the afternoon. Tanner called about Ty and asked the neighbor if he could spend one more night with them.

"Jade's not feeling well." He glanced at her, at the bandage on the small patch near the front of her head where they'd pulled out a sample of the tumor. Despite his sweatshirt, Tanner began to shiver.

The neighbor agreed and put Ty on the phone. "Hi, Dad, the beach was so cool! Me and Karl bodysurfed three hours straight."

"That's great." Tanner dug deep down and found the courage to continue. "Hey, buddy…uh, your mom's not feeling so well. Karl's mom said you could stay over tonight and she'll bring you home tomorrow before dinner."

"Okay." Ty didn't hesitate, and a small wave of relief splashed against Tanner's taut body. Why tell the boy now, when they didn't know anything about the monster they were about to battle? The bad news could wait until tomorrow. Ty's tone was light. "Give her a kiss for me, all right?"

"All right. Be good."

"Okay, Dad. I love you."

"Love you, too."

When Tanner hung up, he was reminded, as he always was, of how many times he'd missed out on telling his son he loved him. Eleven years. Even now it was impossible to imagine that while he'd spent all those years pining away for Jade, wondering why she'd married someone else, Ty had been growing up without his father. It was a tragedy Tanner could only withstand because of the close bond he and the boy shared now.

In the nearly two years since they'd found each other, Tanner had taught Ty how to throw a spiral using the laces of a football, and how to perform the crossover in basketball. He had pitched him a thousand baseballs in the field across the street from their house, and he jogged with him three times a week.

Despite the constant blur of motion he generally made in their home, Ty had a sweet side as well. That semester at school he befriended Karl, their neighbor. The boy didn't have a father. When Tanner and Ty played catch or hit balls, Ty often asked if Karl could come, too.

"Karl reminds me of me back before I knew you," Ty would say when the two of them were alone. "I wish he had a dad like you. You and Mom are the best parents in the world."

Tanner shuddered again. Telling Ty that his mother was seriously ill was more than he could imagine. And so he focused his gaze on Jade's beautiful face, and sometime around midnight, after the night nurse had made her final rounds, Tanner fell asleep.

At ten o'clock the next morning, Dr. Layton appeared again. He was holding a file, and this time the gravity of the situation was etched in the lines on his forehead.

"It's cancer, Jade. I'm sorry."

Tanner stared at the doctor, his eyes unblinking. What had the man said?

Cancer?

The word screamed at him from every wall in the room. Jade couldn't *possibly* have cancer. It was all a nightmare. He was going to wake up at home in their own bed, Jade beside him, smiling at him, assuring him everything was all right, and promising him that she and their baby were perfectly fine.

No, God, not cancer. Not Jade…

Tanner hung his head for a moment, his hands clenching into fists. Then just as quickly, he realized he hadn't said a word to Jade. Ignoring his pounding heart and uneven breathing, he lifted his chin and reached for her hand. She had been watching him, her eyes filled with too many emotions to sort. Sadness, regret, disbelief. And fear, of course. But…Tanner frowned. He saw guilt, too. As though somehow she felt responsible for the doctor's awful news.

Her eyes welled up. "I'm sorry, Tanner."

"No." He forced a partial smile and uttered a single desperate laugh. "It's not true, Jade. Tests can be wrong." His gaze shifted to Dr. Layton. "Isn't that right? Can't the tests be wrong?"

The doctor's mouth formed a straight line, and he looked from Tanner to Jade and back again. "Not this time."

Tanner stared at the man. He wanted to scream or punch a wall, shout at anyone who would listen, insist the diagnosis wasn't true. His gaze shifted back to Jade and he saw quiet tears streaking down her cheeks. He tightened his grip on her hand. "We'll fight it, Jade. People beat cancer all the time."

She nodded, smiling as her eyes filled again. "We'll beat it." She swallowed a single sob. "God's…not finished with me yet."

Tanner nodded, his mouth dry with the blasting winds of hot, merciless fear. "We'll fight it together." He wove his fingers between Jade's and leaned against her arm as the doctor explained their opponent in detail.

"Jade has a glioblastoma, a fairly common type of brain cancer."

Tanner forced himself to concentrate. He still had hold of Jade's hand. "It's curable, right?"

The doctor leveled his gaze and his voice fell a notch. "Yes. In about half the cases." He hesitated. "It depends on how fast the tumor's growing. Of course, there's no way to tell how long it's been there." Dr. Layton let the file fall to his side. "Jade's pregnancy seems to have compromised her immune system and sparked what looks like aggressive growth."

The words were like something from a nightmare. *Tumor…cancer…aggressive growth.* Tanner massaged his left temple with his free hand. The doctor might as well have been speaking Russian for as much sense as it all made.

"I'm recommending two weeks of intense radiation therapy followed by removal of the tumor. At that point we can implant radioactive pellets and begin chemotherapy until—"

"Stop." Tanner held up his hand, and Jade and the doctor looked at him. "Radiation? Removal of the tumor? That's surgery, right? Brain surgery?" He alternated his gaze from Jade to the doctor.

Dr. Layton sighed. "Yes."

Jade opened her mouth to speak, but Tanner wasn't finished. He let go of Jade's hand, stood, and paced three quick steps toward the door and back. "What's that mean for the baby?"

"I know what it means." Jade's tears spilled onto her cheeks and she turned her attention to Dr. Layton. "I won't terminate."

Terminate? What was she talking about? The baby? *Their*

baby? Tanner tried to breathe but he couldn't. The air around him had turned jagged and sharp, cutting at him as he struggled to drag it into his lungs.

"I'm… I'm lost." Tanner crossed his arms and managed to grab a quick breath. "If someone would clue me in here." He sat back down and leaned over his knees, his eyes locked on Dr. Layton's.

The man uttered a tired sigh. "The treatment I'm recommending would require terminating the pregnancy, Tanner. There's no way a fetus could survive the radiation and chemotherapy. Even the surgery holds considerable risks."

"And if she terminates the baby, you think the treatment will…that she'll be okay?" Tanner's heart skipped a beat. He was wandering toward a cliff he'd never come anywhere near, but what choice was there if it meant Jade's life?

"Yes. I think there's a good chance. But I'd like to begin first thing in the morning. First we would—"

Jade shook her head. "No!"

"Jade…" Dr. Layton hesitated.

"I said *no.*" Jade shot the man a fierce look, ignoring the tears that spilled onto her cheeks.

The doctor gritted his teeth. "I'm recommending you terminate this afternoon. I'm sorry, Jade. I don't see any other option. Right now the tumor—"

"Excuse me." Tanner held up his hand. "Could you give us a half hour, doctor?" His palms were suddenly damp, his heartbeat irregular. "Jade and I need to talk."

Dr. Layton nodded and left the room, closing the door behind him.

The moment they were alone, Jade sat up straighter and cried out in a tone that was both angry and hurt. "What are you *thinking,*

Tanner?" She splayed her fingers across her chest. "We don't need a half hour or five minutes. I wouldn't consider terminating this pregnancy. Not for anything."

Tanner was on his feet again, and as he walked to the window, he felt suddenly twice his age. Frustration became anger and it boiled near the surface of his heart. When he turned back to her, his eyes were damp. "I want this baby more than my next breath." He lowered his voice and took a step closer to her bed. "But if it means losing you…" His words were strangled in emotion. "Maybe it's our only choice."

Jade's eyes grew wider still. "Tanner, I can't believe you mean that."

He blinked, and the fog of confusion cleared just enough for him to see through it. Had he really said that? Really alluded to the possibility that he'd agree to abort their baby? What was he saying?

He fell to his knees and then back on his heels. There he let his head hang forward and allowed the tears to come. Jade was right, of course. He'd made a living defending the religious right, protecting people who protested in front of abortion clinics, people who thwarted the efforts of high school nurses to provide condoms and secret abortions for students.

Wasn't he the one whose closing arguments had once included Dr. Seuss's famous story about Horton the Elephant finding an entire town on a dust speck? *A person's a person, no matter how small.* He could hear the sincerity in his voice even now.

He'd never stood on this side of the great debate over life. But he had to face the truth…without a doubt, if he had to decide this minute whether to save Jade or the baby, there would be no question what he would do. He'd sign the termination papers without hesitating.

And that truth terrified him.

What did it say about everything that defined him? His faith, his passion for the law, his integrity…? Was it all a sham? Just something to use in the courtroom?

The only thing he didn't doubt was his love for Jade. His desperate, lifelong love for a woman with eyes as green as Chesapeake Bay, a woman he'd loved since they were children, back when they skipped rocks and rode bikes and spent endless summers growing up in the same Virginia neighborhood.

A woman who could no more terminate the life of the child she was carrying than she could will herself to stop breathing. Life…the love of life was part of who she was. Part of why he loved her.

"Tanner…"

Her voice pulled him up from the floor. His feet moved like they were stuck in mud as he walked to her bedside.

There was no anger in her eyes now. Only a quiet certainty. She ran her tongue over her bottom lip and shook her head. "I can't…"

A sob slipped from her throat, breaking free a dam of emotion. She reached out her hands, and Tanner laid his upper body across hers, working his hands and arms behind her and clinging to her.

"I know." He brought his mouth close to her ear, his own tears mingling with hers. "I'm sorry…"

Tanner remembered a documentary once about two men and a little boy who got caught in severe rapids while boating on a river. When the vessel overturned, the two men were killed, but by some miracle the child made his way to the distant shore and scrambled up a muddy tree root. He clung to the underneath edge of that cliff until help came, knowing that to let go meant certain death.

For three hours the boy hung there, his fingers bloodied and locked into place by the time rescuers showed up.

Tanner closed his eyes and nestled his face against Jade's. He was that child now, clinging to Jade with all that remained of his hope and courage and belief in forever.

Because to let go, to lose her now, would certainly kill him.

Even if it took a lifetime for his heart to stop beating.

Seven

D r. Layton would never suggest terminating a pregnancy for anything but the most serious causes. Jade could remember the man arguing with other doctors about taking extreme measures to save not only pregnant patients, but their unborn children as well. He was not a man of faith, but he was one of the kindest doctors Jade had ever worked with.

The fact that he disagreed with Jade and Tanner's resolve to keep the baby could only mean one thing: He feared for Jade's life.

That afternoon, she and Tanner huddled against each other in the hospital room as Dr. Layton detailed his alternate treatment plan, one that would hopefully take Jade and the baby safely through the next several months.

"We'll deliver the baby at thirty-two weeks. Not a minute later." Dr. Layton's sigh rattled Jade's nerves. *Thirty-two weeks? That's too early, God…the baby won't be able to breathe on his own…*

The doctor continued. "In the meantime we'll watch the tumor."

Tanner gripped her hand, his face pale. "What…what should we look for?"

"Seizures are the biggest concern." The doctor frowned. "Jade's tumor is in the frontal lobe of her brain. That means even the smallest growth could trigger more seizures like the one she had yesterday." He looked from Jade to Tanner. "The solution is an anti-seizure drug. It would be the least likely to have an ill effect on the baby."

Jade nodded. She was familiar with the medication, and terrified at the same time. She had been so busy worrying about Tanner and his reaction to the news, so concerned with having a good attitude toward her ability to fight the tumor and God's ability to heal her, that she'd taken almost no time to consider the road ahead.

Especially if it included five months of anti-seizure medication.

She glanced at Tanner. *Please, God...give him strength.*

The doctor drew up a chair and sat down across from Tanner. "Seizures could be nothing more than a painful inconvenience...or they could kill Jade and the baby. We have to prevent them. Let's talk about the anti-seizure medication." He leveled his gaze at Tanner, and Jade held her breath. She knew what was coming. "The drug has side effects. Personality changes, excessive grogginess, slow speech, slow motor skills. Depending on the dosage, it could temporarily appear that Jade has brain damage."

The remaining color drained from Tanner's face. Jade wanted to rip out the IV line, grab Tanner's hand, and run for her life. She'd seen patients on anti-seizure medication, kids with inoperable brain tumors who sometimes didn't recognize their parents after three weeks on the drugs. This was why brain cancer was the most dreaded of all childhood types—the medication and the fact that the prognosis was usually so poor. Jade thought of Brandy Almond... How was the girl doing? Maybe her cancer was in remission by now.

The doctor was telling them that the side effects were often reversible once the tumor was removed. "I'll start you on a low dose, but as the tumor grows, we'll almost certainly have to increase the medication. We'll have to monitor it."

It was almost four o'clock when the doctor left them alone.

Tanner crossed the room and anchored himself at the window, his back to her. "Did you hear that?" He looked over his shoulder at her. "The drug could change your personality."

Jade ached to climb out of bed and hug him, to promise him that no matter what medication found its way into her veins she would never see him differently, treat him differently. But she wouldn't lie to him. She'd seen the effects of the drug too often.

"Okay." She summoned every bit of faith within her and spoke in a voice that barely carried across the room. "We'll have to pray it doesn't."

Tanner shrugged and came to her side once more. "I guess."

There was something numb in Tanner's tone, and it frightened her. Was Tanner doubting the power of prayer? Was he questioning whether God could help them? The possibility scared Jade more than any cancer ever could. *God, give him faith...help him.*

In response a Scripture came to mind. It was their verse. Their life verse: *"For I know the plans I have for you...plans to give you a hope and a future and not to harm you..."*

She folded her arms against her chest and tried to believe it was still true. "You guess? Is that all, Tanner? After all God's brought us through?"

He gripped the side rails of her hospital bed and locked his elbows. "God allowed a brain tumor to grow in your head, okay? I'm still trying to deal with that. You and I—" his jaw tensed—"we love the Lord with all our hearts but because of my mother's wretched lies we lose a decade together. Ten years, Jade." His knuckles turned white as he tightened his grip on the bed rails. "Now this?" He groaned. "I'll pray. Of *course*, I'll pray. But right now I don't know if it'll make a difference."

Tears filled her eyes again. She hadn't cried this much since she walked out of Tanner's mother's house thirteen years ago believing he didn't love her. "Tanner...please."

He was rigid, tense with anger and fear and confusion. But at the sound of his name on her lips, his hands and arms relaxed, and he closed his eyes. When he opened them, Jade saw something that gave her hope again.

Resolve.

She exhaled in relief. This was the Tanner she knew and loved, the one who would fight to the death for what he believed. And certainly now, in the darkest moment of their lives, he would trust God to lead them through. What choice did they have?

"I'm sorry, Jade. Forgive me, okay?"

She nodded and reached toward him, slipping her hand in his.

He brought her fingers to his cheek and searched her eyes, his voice hoarse. "I'm just scared. Scared to death."

"Me, too."

He looked at her for a long while. Then he closed his eyes again and broke the silence between them with the most intense, most heartfelt prayer Jade had ever heard him utter.

When he finished, he opened his eyes and said the thing they must both have been thinking since getting the results that morning. "Let's call Ty."

Jade held her breath while Tanner phoned Karl's mother. He explained that Jade was in the hospital for tests. The woman was more than willing to bring Ty there, and an hour later, Tanner left to meet them in the hospital lobby.

The few minutes alone in her room gave Jade time to soak in the reality of what was happening to her, of the dark path that lay ahead. She thought of Ty, the years they'd shared when she was married to Jim Rudolph, back when the boy received little or no attention from anyone but her. For years she had tried so hard to forget about Tanner, but it had been impossible. Ty was a perfect miniature of him. Through the boy's pale, blue eyes, Tanner had shared breakfast with her each morning and hugged her each night.

Never back then had she thought it possible that Ty and Tanner would meet, or that somehow she and Tanner would find their way back together again. And now…

Will you take me home, God? Will you leave Tanner to raise our little boy? Is that the plan you have for me?

The questions formed a lump in her throat, and when the two men she loved most in life—one a shorter replica of the other—entered her room, it was nearly a minute before she could speak.

"Mom, what's wrong? How come you're here?" Ty wore a stained baseball shirt. His eyes were bright with panic. Jade held her arms out as he ran to her and hugged her for a long while. When he pulled back, he ran his finger over the IV line. "Dad says you're sick."

"Yes." She found her voice and set her hand on his shoulder. "I have cancer, Ty. Brain cancer."

They had decided to tell him the truth. After all, he would be affected by every stage of her treatment. Especially the difficult months when she'd be on the anti-seizure medication.

"Cancer?" Ty's face went white, and he took several steps away from her until he was snug against Tanner's side. "Does that mean…you're gonna die?"

"No, honey." Jade forced a smile, despite her breaking heart. "Cancer can be treated." She closed her eyes for a moment. *Help me say the right words, God.* Ty had to feel her hope now, at this early stage. That way he'd be more likely to stay hopeful when things got worse. "I'll be sick, though, so you and Dad need to stick together."

After a half hour of questions, Ty seemed content to sit in the chair beside Jade and watch baseball on the hospital television. Tanner took the time to call the Bronzans.

"I'm at the hospital, Matt." Jade watched her husband massage his temples and struggle to say the words. "We got some bad news today."

There was a pause, and she saw her husband's eyes well up. "Jade has…Jade has brain cancer. The doctors told us a few hours ago."

Jade couldn't hear their conversation, but she could tell from Tanner's reaction that Matt must have been shocked. Tanner nodded a few times and then choked out a single request before hanging up. A request that frightened Jade because it was so out of character for her self-reliant, fun-loving husband.

"Please come," he said, his voice cracking. "We need you guys."

The Bronzans were there in half an hour. Jenny stayed at home with Grace, since small children weren't allowed in the room.

Matt vowed to contact the firm's mailing list and request prayer support for the weeks and months ahead. Hannah offered to do what she could to help with Ty. Still, despite their words of encouragement, Jade caught them both wiping tears throughout the evening.

For the first time Jade could remember, Matt and Tanner shared not a single one-liner or smile between them. She wanted to shake them both.

I'm not dead yet! Don't give up on me…

But she kept her thoughts to herself. She was too new in her role as cancer victim to know how to act.

When visiting hours were over, the Bronzans offered to take Ty home with them. Jade would be released from the hospital in the morning, sent home with specific instructions and a month's supply of anti-seizure medication. Hannah would take Ty to baseball practice and bring him home after that.

"Thanks," Jade reached out and held Hannah's hand. Tanner, Matt, and Ty were near the door, not listening to their conversation. "You're the best friend I have, Hannah."

"You, too." Tears filled Hannah's eyes and this time she didn't try to hide them. "I learned something after Tom and Alicia were killed."

Jade nodded, her own tears blurring her vision.

Hannah struggled to speak. "I learned that even in the darkest nights, morning eventually comes." She smiled, her lips trembling. "It's God's promise. Fight this, Jade. Fight it with everything you have."

"I will." She blinked back the tears. "If I ever look like I'm giving up, tell me again, okay?"

Hannah nodded, and soon Ty and the Bronzans were gone for the night.

Tanner turned off the light in the room and pulled his chair near her bed again. He planned to sleep at her side as he'd done the night before. "Maybe..." His voice was a quiet whisper. "Maybe you won't have any side effects."

His statement confirmed what she already knew. The thing that weighed most heavily on both their minds here and now, at the starting line of their race against death, was the medication. What if she suffered from it the same way some of her young patients suffered? Would there be a time when she might look into Tanner's loving eyes and not know him? Feel the precious touch of his hand on her skin and be startled, even frightened?

He tried again. "Maybe you'll be the exception."

She consciously raised the corners of her mouth. "Maybe."

The nurse brought in a tray bearing a glass of ice, a pitcher of water, and a straw. There was also a small saucer with two orange capsules. Jade didn't have to ask what they were. She'd given them to her patients too many times for that.

Tanner looked from Jade to the tray and back again as the nurse poured her a glass of water. There was a heaviness in Tanner's eyes that broke Jade's heart. "Is it…?"

She nodded. "Yes." There was no sense in dragging out the moment. She placed the pills on her tongue and took a long swig of water.

And with that, Jade's uncertain journey into darkness began.

Eight

Nearly six weeks had passed since Grace came to live with them, and Hannah was so giddy about life she felt guilty.

What right did the four of them have to be happy when Jade and Tanner were living through the most difficult time in their lives? Of course it wasn't a question that could be answered. Hard times came to everyone who lived long enough, and as Matt had been there for her during her darkest days, so the two of them would be there for Jade and Tanner.

Still, Hannah found herself consumed with warring emotions. Half the time she was elated by the leaps and bounds Grace made each day, but there were moments, hours, when she was drawn to the sad, quiet pondering of Jade's future.

It was the morning of July 3, and Jenny was upstairs helping Grace get dressed. The three of them were going shopping for the big party the following day, the one she and Matt had thrown each Fourth of July since they were married two years ago.

Hannah worked in the kitchen, taking care of the morning dishes and savoring the sound of Grace's laughter upstairs. Had it been nearly two months since that day when Mrs. Parsons brought her home to live with them? The victories they'd notched since then were unbelievable, making up the sweetest bouquet of memories.

The four of them had learned to trust each other. They had shared tenderness and tears, sunshine and silly laughter. Many nights when Grace was tucked in bed, Hannah and Matt marveled at how far she had come.

How very far.

A breeze filtered in through the kitchen window, and Hannah paused, staring at the endless blue beyond the sandy beach. There had been times during those first two weeks when Hannah wondered if Grace would survive the transition.

Times when she wondered if *any* of them would survive it.

The child would wake in the middle of the night, grabbing at her wrist, of all things. Then she'd scream in a way that would bring all of them, even Jenny, running to her bedroom.

Hannah shuddered as she remembered Grace's first night. After Mrs. Parsons left, they showed the child her room and her pretty new clothes. Grace ran her fingers over the delicate pink things and looked at Hannah, her eyes wide. "Who will wear them when I'm gone?"

There was a pause while Hannah, Matt, and Jenny exchanged a look. Finally Hannah knelt down before the girl and stroked her hair. "Grace," Hannah's voice had been a mix of fear and compassion. "We want you to stay here. With us."

Grace shook her head. "I never stay for very long. The police come and take me back to Mommy."

Hannah hadn't known what to say, so Matt set his hand on Grace's shoulder and took over. "Honey, the police won't take you away anymore."

Grace wrinkled her nose and tiny tears filled her eyes. "Mommy said..." She was crying, but in a way that was different from any other child Hannah had seen. Tears streamed down her cheeks and her small shoulders shook, but she made no sound at all. She wiped her face and looked at Matt. "Mommy said if I got took away from her, then the police would put me in jail."

Jenny covered her mouth, stifling a cry.

The horrible picture Grace had painted made Hannah's head reel. She and Matt circled the child in a hug. "No, Grace, that'll never happen." Matt's tone was soothing. "We want you to stay with us forever."

Hannah had expected Grace to stop crying. Instead her little body convulsed. With the three of them watching, Grace climbed onto her bed, curled in a ball, and said just one more thing before falling asleep. "I w-w-want my *mommy.*"

She came to the table for dinner that evening, but ate nothing. Regardless of their attempts to get her to talk, Grace remained silent, wary through her bath and while she was being tucked into bed.

When they were downstairs and out of earshot, Jenny collapsed on the sofa. Her eyes were dry but frustration was written into every crease on her forehead. "She hates us."

Hannah sat beside her daughter, and Matt pulled up a chair nearby. He spoke in a voice that was low and full of compassion. "She's afraid."

"That's right." Hannah slipped her arm around Jenny's shoulder. "Mrs. Parsons said that would happen."

"I know, but still…" Jenny let her head fall against the back cushion. "How long will it take before she trusts us?" She leveled her gaze at Matt. "Before she laughs and plays like a regular little girl?"

Matt reached out and patted Jenny's knee. "With God on our side, my guess is not long."

Grace's first scream pierced the peaceful silence of the Bronzan home at two o'clock the next morning. Matt and Hannah grabbed their robes and raced down the hall just as she released her second scream.

Matt sat her tiny body up and shook her gently. "Grace, honey…it's okay. Wake up."

The child opened her eyes, but didn't make eye contact with either of them. Instead she stared straight ahead and screamed again. Eyes wide, she grabbed at her right wrist, shaking that hand

and slapping it over and over and over.

Finally Matt caught her fingers midair and brought them down. "Grace, it's okay. Wake up."

In response she shook her head faster and faster and screamed again, this time looking from Matt to Hannah and back. "No! No…no…no…*no…!*"

Hannah anchored the child on the other side, and together she and Matt wrapped their arms around her, whispering words of hope and peace until she stopped screaming.

"I want my mommy; I want to go home." Then she hung her head so that the curls made a tent around her face. "Go away. Please go away."

The floor of Hannah's heart fell that night as she drew back and took in the picture Grace made. She was a little girl alone in the world, unable to let go of the nightmares of yesterday long enough to believe in the treasure of today.

And there was nothing she or Matt could do about it.

On her way out of Grace's room, hot tears slid down Hannah's cheeks. *Get us through this, God…please. What have we done?*

It was a prayer she prayed often that first week, and by the ninth day—with Grace barely speaking to any of them and still asking hourly to go home—Hannah considered calling Mrs. Parsons and asking for help.

Jenny handled Grace's reluctant beginning by being gone more than usual.

Hannah had cornered Jenny that week and tried to reason with her. "You'll never connect with her if you're not home."

"I don't know what to say." Jenny shifted her weight to one hip. "Besides, she doesn't care if I'm here or not."

Hannah took hold of Jenny's arm. "That's not true. She told you she wanted a sister that first day. She may not talk to you, but she likes you."

Jenny narrowed her eyes and lowered her voice. "That's not the kind of sister I was expecting."

There was more that Jenny wanted to say; the intensity in her eyes told Hannah that much. Of course Grace wasn't the type of sister Jenny had been expecting. The only sister she'd ever known was Alicia, and the two of them had been inseparable, laughing and playing together. Delighting in the same kinds of games and music and with that uncanny ability to finish each other's sentences.

The way only sisters could.

Even if Jenny hadn't intended to, she clearly had expected Grace to be something of a companion. A little sister to her the way she had once been a little sister to Alicia.

The situation had been heartbreaking, and there was nothing Hannah could do about it.

Before the night was over, Jenny apologized for being impatient. But the entire situation had Hannah at a breaking point.

Midway through the second week, Matt linked his arms through hers and pulled her close. "It takes time, Hannah. I'm not willing to give up."

"Me, either. I just wish I knew what God was doing."

Matt grinned. "Building a bond between us, maybe?"

Hannah's mind went blank. "A bond? By giving us a child who won't talk or smile or respond to us?"

"Ahh, but remember this..." Matt put a finger to Hannah's lips. "One day when she *does* talk or smile or respond, we'll know it's real, won't we?"

Hannah remained doubtful. Would they ever be able to truly reach Grace? That night she and Matt prayed on their knees in the sand outside their house.

"Give us wisdom, God." Matt closed his eyes and directed his face toward the starry sky above. "It's been nine days and she's so quiet, so locked up inside. What can we do different, God? Just show us, please. We love her. We'll wait as long as it takes."

The breakthrough happened the next day.

Matt was at work and Hannah was making oatmeal when Grace entered the room. She came up beside Hannah and tugged on her sleeve. Hannah smiled at her, but before she had time to speak, Grace tucked her hand in Hannah's and said, "I have something to tell you."

Hannah set the spoon down beside the pan and turned to face her. "What, honey?"

"I'm sorry." Grace lowered her chin, but kept her eyes on Hannah. "I haven't been very good. I miss my mommy."

Tears stung at Hannah's eyes, and she blinked them back, stooping to the child's level. "That's okay. You're still getting used to us, Grace. It takes time." She hugged her and kissed her cheek.

Grace ran her thumb over Hannah's hand; her touch was velvet. "Do you like me, Hannah?"

Hannah framed the child's face with her fingers, brushing the curls back and looking deep into her eyes. "I like you very much."

Grace doodled an invisible design with her toe. "I'm scared the police will come and take me to jail…but I'm still here."

Hannah nodded. "I know you miss your mommy, honey. But sometimes God gives little children a new mommy and daddy. Ones that can take care of them better and—" she was treading on slippery ground, but she forged ahead—"And sometimes love them better."

This time Grace bobbed her head up and down, and throughout breakfast she chattered away about the beach and her toys and Hannah and Matt and Jenny.

"You and Matt are Jenny's mommy and daddy, right?" Grace had long since finished eating her cereal and now sat opposite Hannah, her hands folded on the table.

"Right." Hannah wanted to say more. *We're your mommy and daddy, too, Grace*. But she held her tongue.

"Hannah?" Grace cocked her head.

"Yes?"

"You have only one girl, just like my mommy, right?"

Hannah wondered whether the sting of that question would ever go away. "Actually…" She allowed herself to pause. "I had two girls. Jenny and Alicia. But Alicia died a few years ago."

"Oh." Grace's nod was matter-of-fact. "She's in heaven with Jesus."

The breath caught in Hannah's throat. Mrs. Parsons hadn't gone into detail about Grace's background, except to say it had been challenging. All they'd been told so far was that Grace was a child with no physical, mental, or emotional disabilities. Whatever that meant.

Still, there'd been no reason to think she adhered to any faith.

"How do you know about Jesus, sweetheart?"

Grace shrugged. "My grandma told me."

Grandma? An alarm sounded in the control center of Hannah's soul. Mrs. Parsons had said there was no extended family, no one who would fight for Grace once her mother's rights were severed. "Grandma?" Hannah tried to smile. "I didn't know you had a grandma."

"I don't anymore. She died at Christmastime." Grace folded her arms and swung her feet. "Grandma loved Jesus very much. She told me Jesus was like an invisible Daddy, and sometimes, when Mommy had a bad night, I knew Grandma was right. I could feel my invisible Daddy hold me and keep me safe."

Hannah fought the urge to let her mouth drop open. The child seated before her—who for more than a week hadn't spoken to them or shown any sign that she was capable of loving or being loved—not only knew about Christ, but had felt his love in her life.

Before Grace went to sleep that night, she smiled at Hannah. "Know what, Hannah?"

Hannah leaned down and kissed the girl on the forehead. The burden of frustration from the past week lifted like fog. She could hardly wait to tell Jenny about the change in the child. Hannah's fingers soothed Grace's brow. "What?"

Grace batted her silky eyelashes. "I like you, too."

Over the next two weeks there were more moments like that.

One afternoon she and Grace took a walk on the beach and found a sandy knoll where they watched seagulls swooping low over the water. "Know what, Mommy?" Grace looked at her, squinting in the sunlight.

"What, honey?"

"We should sing a song."

"We should?" Hannah grinned at Grace and reached for her hand.

"Yes. A happy day needs a happy song."

"Okay." Hannah nodded, biting her lip to keep from giggling. "What should we sing?"

"You teach me a song." Grace shaded her eyes with her hand. "Please, Mommy."

Hannah thought a minute. "Do you know 'Jesus Loves Me'?"

Grace's fair eyebrows came together in deep concentration. "I don't think so."

"Oh, Grace!" Hannah brought her hands together in a series of light claps. "It's the happiest song of all."

There and then, with the seagulls providing backup, Hannah taught Grace the familiar tune. Immediately it became Grace's favorite, and after that they sang it at dinner and every time they walked on the beach.

As Grace opened her heart, every day was more of a blessing

than the day before. Not just to Hannah, but to each of them in different ways.

Two weeks ago Sunday, they'd been coming home from church when Hannah checked the rearview mirror and saw Grace and Jenny holding hands. Three days later she came home from the grocery store and found Grace in Matt's lap. He was reading to her, nuzzling the side of his face against her creamy cheeks and giggling with her at the silly parts.

Hannah froze in the doorway, moving in slow motion as she set the bags at her feet. She remembered thinking that it was finally happening, just as Matt had known all along. Grace was falling in love with them, and they with her. Not because they were just another nice family who took care of her for a few weeks while her mother dealt with the legal system, but because Grace was starting to understand the truth.

This time she wasn't going anywhere. She was home. Forever.

A week after that, Jenny took Grace to a park down the street and then out to lunch. When they came home, they both wore gaudy, blue-beaded bracelets and matching grins. "Grace wanted to go shopping." Jenny laughed and swept the girl up onto her hip. "We bought sister bracelets, right Grace?"

Grace planted a wet kiss on Jenny's cheek. "Right." She slid down and ran to Hannah. "Wanna see?"

Hannah studied the band of beads and saw a silver plate on top that read, "Sisters Always." The words were barely legible through her tears. "That's wonderful." She straightened and grinned at Jenny. "I'm sure Jenny won't take it off for a minute."

In the days since then, Grace had established a nighttime ritual. Hannah and Matt would walk her up to bed and pray with her. Then they'd give her a chance to pray, and almost always her prayer was the same.

"Dear Jesus, thank you for giving me a family. Please don't ever take me away from here because this is my home. And I want to live here forever and ever."

Once in a while, Hannah and Matt exchanged a glance as Grace finished praying. A glance that, in a moment's time, spoke both their greatest fears and their greatest faith that certainly God would grant the child's request. Not once in the past three weeks had they voiced concerns that Grace would be anything other than their forever daughter.

With a sigh, Hannah let the memories fade as she worked the sponge into the countertop. They had heard nothing but good news from Mrs. Parsons. The termination process was on schedule, and within six months Grace would be free for adoption. The path ahead looked smooth and without trouble.

Still…

She paused and stared once more out the window at the sea. It would be good when the process was over. When Grace Bronzan would forevermore and legally be Grace Bronzan, and her little-girl prayers could be about schoolwork and making friends and having a good day. The way other little girls' prayers were.

Then they could get on with life.

The thought sent a piercing reminder through Hannah's heart. Once the adoption was complete, they could indeed move on. But what about Jade and Tanner and Ty? What about their unborn baby?

It was still almost too much to believe. Jade had cancer? How could she? After all she and Tanner had been through? Hannah pictured Jade in the hospital room the other day. If anyone could make it through brain cancer it was Jade. Hannah smiled. Her friend always fought for what was right, whether as a parent volunteer in Ty's classroom or by encouraging Tanner in his legal work.

Certainly she would fight now. After all, there could be nothing more right than seeing Jade well again, seeing her baby safely delivered, seeing the four of them become a family, the way Jade and Tanner had always dreamed they'd be.

She thought of the hundreds of conversations she and Jade had held. Together they had shared their life stories, sometimes in laughter, sometimes in tears. They marveled often at how much they had in common, how God had brought both of them through the flames of loss and heartache.

But this time…the situation was as grim as it had ever been. Hannah's heart skipped a beat as she considered the possibilities. It wasn't right that Jade was sick. Hadn't they had enough grief in their lives already?

Hannah held her breath and then exhaled long and slow. As her anxious thoughts faded, she closed her eyes, and with everything in her, she thanked God for the friend she had in Jade Eastman. A friend she had come to love.

Then she begged God to move mountains and part seas…whatever it took, so that one day very soon Jade would be well again.

Nine

The Fourth of July dawned without a trace of fog and by midmorning Jade had stirred together her famous potato salad. She was ready for taste testers.

It had been a week since her diagnosis, a week since she'd taken her first dose of anti-seizure medication, and so far she was holding her own in the battle. There had been no personality shifts, no changes in her gait or speech. She was tired and less focused, but she was determined not to let Tanner and Ty see even that. It was important that they think she was making progress. Their enthusiasm was bound to make her feel better, which would make the few symptoms she was experiencing all but disappear.

Jade didn't know if it was the holiday or the fact that she was one week closer to a safe delivery for her baby, but she felt particularly upbeat. She expected the picnic at Matt and Hannah's later that day to be a huge success.

Jade took a bite of the potato salad and licked her lips. "Okay guys…" She raised her voice so Tanner and Ty would hear her upstairs. "I need tasters."

A moment later there was a galloping sound above her. "Coming!"

It was Ty. Jade smiled and filled a clean spoon with more of the salad just as he pounded down the stairs and rounded the corner. He took the spoon from her and grinned. "I already know it's good."

Jade lowered her chin and put her hands on her hips. "Humor me, okay." She tousled his hair. "I can never get the spices right till someone else tastes it."

Ty ate the mouthful in one bite. "Tastes great." He hesitated. "Well, maybe a few more spider legs."

He ran from her just as she reached out to paddle him with the spoon. When he was a few feet away, he spun around. "Hey—" his teasing expression faded—"You look great, Mom. I'm praying for you."

Joy filled Jade's heart, and she studied her son as she hadn't in months. He was taller, looking more like his father every day. And he was thirteen. A teenager now, with more maturity and wisdom than most boys his age—maturity and wisdom born of a painful past they'd survived together.

But those days were behind them. They were together now, a family like they always should have been. These were the good days, the times of their lives. Jade clenched her teeth. Nothing would change that, not even her cancer.

"Thanks." She walked the few steps that separated them and set her hands on Ty's shoulders. In a year or so he'd be taller than her. "That means a lot."

Ty winked at her. "I'll be out back."

"Okay." She gave the muscles along his shoulders a couple of quick squeezes and raised her brows. "Impressive. The girls will be lining up at the door."

"Girls can wait." He grinned. "I have hoops to play." He kissed her on the cheek and headed for the backyard and the half-court where he spent much of his time.

"Ty…"

He turned back. "Yeah?"

"Where's your dad?" Jade hadn't seen Tanner since that morning.

"Upstairs. We were playing Nintendo, but I beat him right before you called me."

"Oh." Jade felt her smile fade. Why hadn't he come down with

Ty? Was it her imagination or had he been avoiding her? When they were together, all he wanted to talk about was her health, how she was feeling and what changes she was noticing from the medication.

She hid her frustration. "What's he doing now?"

Ty shrugged. "I think he's working."

Jade nodded and Ty disappeared through the back door. She felt suddenly tired, but made her way up the stairs and found Tanner in his office, writing on a legal pad.

The sound of her footsteps caused him to look up. "Hi."

The tension in Jade's shoulders eased. Tanner's tone was cheery. Maybe she was only imagining the distance she sensed between them. "Hi." She came up behind him and worked her hands along the base of his neck. "I called for testers on my potato salad."

Tanner's muscles stiffened beneath her fingers. "I had to work."

"I know." Jade stooped so their cheeks were touching. She spoke softly, her voice a whisper. "But it's my famous potato salad. It won't be the same without your professional tasting ability."

Tanner stared at his notepad for a moment, then back at her. "How are you feeling?"

"Fine." Jade straightened and walked around his chair. She knelt in front of him and sighed. "But why does it seem like that's the only question you ask me lately?"

For a moment Tanner said nothing, then he set his pencil down and wheeled his chair backward so there was some distance between them. "Is this how it's going to be?"

Jade let her hands hang at her sides. "How what's going to be?"

"You have cancer, Jade. Brain cancer." Tanner crossed one leg over the other and leaned back in his chair. He narrowed his eyes, his voice loud and frustrated. "Last time I checked that was something serious." He gestured toward the door. "But there you are, making potato salad and getting ready for some big Fourth of July picnic like everything's fine."

Jade folded her arms. "What do you want me to do, Tanner? Lie down in bed and wait until I get sicker? Turn out the lights and give up on you and Ty?" She placed one hand over her abdomen. "On our baby?" A huff slipped from her throat. "I'm sorry, honey, but I can't do that. I *won't* do it."

Tanner uncrossed his legs and dug his elbows into his thighs. "That's not what I mean, and you know it."

"What *do* you mean?" Jade threw her hands in the air. "Ever since you heard the c-word you've been different. Like you're afraid to touch me, to love me."

"That's not true." Tanner's tone was softer as he stared at her with helpless eyes. His gaze fell to his feet, and he covered his face with his hands. "Ah, Jade. You have no idea."

Jade's anger cooled and she crawled closer, resting her head on his knee. Of course Tanner wasn't put off by her illness or bent on being negative. He was simply afraid.

Scared to death at the thought of losing her.

She reached up, peeling Tanner's fingers from his face until she could see his eyes. "I'm sorry."

He studied her, his gaze layered in pain and fear. "Don't pretend everything's okay, Jade. Please."

"I'm not pretending." She forced a smile despite the tears that stung her eyes. "I feel good, Tanner. Better than I thought I would."

"But you're sick. You can't act like you're not."

"Yes, I can." She uttered a single laugh. "I can act happy and normal and crazy in love. Don't you see, Tanner? You and Ty and our baby, all of you matter more to me than being sick." She brought her lips to his and kissed him long and slow, working her hands along his sides and dusting his neck with her fingertips. "Ty's outside." Her voice was deep with desire as she rose to her feet.

Taking his hand in hers, she led him out of the office toward their bedroom, where she did everything in her power to make Tanner forget about cancer and surgery and the medication's devastating side effects.

Everything except the way she so desperately loved him.

The picnic was going strong and so far Matt thought it had been a huge success.

Jade and Hannah were inside washing dishes, and Jenny and Ty were on the beach playing Frisbee with Grace. Matt cleaned the barbecue while he watched Tanner run a dishrag over the picnic table. The usual afternoon breeze had kicked up and Matt decided against getting his guitar. They almost always sang after dinner, but he wanted to give Tanner a chance to talk

They finished their jobs, found their sunglasses, and took seats in adjacent beach chairs. For a while they watched the kids as they ran through the surf, chasing the Frisbee and splashing each other.

"Grace looks happy." Tanner kept his gaze on the child.

Matt studied her, amazed at how she'd become part of their family. "She's a special little girl."

"Any word from her birth mother?"

Matt shrugged. "She's in jail. The termination should be finished up in four months."

Tanner shook his head. "Amazing."

They fell silent again, and Matt watched as Jenny swept Grace into her arms and ran from Ty. The boy was a miniature of his father. Strong and agile. Beautiful in motion. He caught the girls in ten strides and the threesome tumbled to the sand, laughing and tickling each other.

There was a full feeling in his heart and Matt realized what it was: He was a father, really and truly. Not just to Jenny, whose heart would always belong in part to another man, but to Grace as well. No longer was the child's presence in their home something of an experiment or a way to help a child in need. She was his daughter, through and through.

She had moved into his heart, where she would always remain, regardless of what the months ahead brought. He no longer had even the slightest emptiness in the father's heart that beat within him. That place was filled with a little girl he loved more with each passing day.

A little girl who—regardless of her biological makeup—was absolutely his own.

The wind stung at Matt's eyes and he shifted his gaze to Jenny. *Good for you, Jenny girl.* She was two months from starting college and could have turned her back on the idea of Matt and Hannah adopting a child. Instead, she'd been determined to be a part of the process from the beginning. And now that Grace was part of their family, Jenny had blossomed in ways Matt had never seen before.

He studied her again. What was it exactly? Something in her carefree expression, or the twinkling in her eyes...

Just then Jenny threw her head back and laughed with abandon as Grace took her by the hand and tried once more to outrun Ty.

That was it. Her laughter. Jenny laughed more easily than before. Suddenly Matt remembered a conversation he and Hannah had shared not long after they were married. They were walking together and Matt had commented that Jenny seemed back to normal, content and happy with life.

But Hannah cast him a sad smile and shook her head.

"She's not the same as before the accident."

They kept walking, and Matt asked Hannah what she meant.

"The way she laughs is different. She doesn't throw her head back and giggle like she used to before Tom and Alicia died." Then Hannah had said something Matt still found utterly sad. "You want the truth?"

"Yes." Matt tightened his grip on Hannah's hand.

"I don't think she'll ever laugh that way again."

The memory faded, and Matt stood to get Hannah. She had to see it, had to watch for herself the fact that Grace had helped Jenny laugh again. But as he turned toward the house, he saw Hannah was already outside, standing a dozen feet behind him, seeing the same thing he'd just seen.

Her hand was over her mouth and tears filled her eyes. "I never thought…"

Matt crossed the deck, slipped his arm around Hannah and held her close. "I was coming to get you."

"It's…" Hannah's voice was raspy with emotion. "It's because of Grace. Jenny has a sister to love again." Hannah focused hard on the smaller girl and shook her head. "The resemblance to Alicia is uncanny, Matt."

Matt nodded and watched the two girls for a long while. "I love her so much it scares me." He looked at Hannah. "Ever feel that way?"

"Yes." Hannah shifted her gaze back to their two daughters. "All the time."

After a minute Hannah went back inside, and Matt returned to his seat beside Tanner.

"Everything okay?"

Matt nodded. "It's Jenny. She's really blossoming as Grace's big sister."

Tanner stroked his chin and studied the children again. "They look alike, have you noticed?"

A smile lifted the corners of Matt's mouth. "Yeah, we noticed." Matt shifted in his chair and searched Tanner's face. "Hey, how are things?"

Tanner filled his cheeks with air. He held his breath, then leaked it out again. "Work's good. I like the Benson, Colorado case. The pastor's wife sent me the contract they had with the city. Came in the mail yesterday." Tanner shrugged. "She's right. Deep into the document there's a clause that says City Hall can't be rented by any group who teaches faith in Jesus Christ as the only way to salvation." He grabbed a quick breath. "It's amazing because even without looking at case precedent, we've got a winner here, and personally, I think it'll be—"

"Tanner." Matt reached out and took hold of his friend's wrist. "I wasn't talking about work." He hesitated. "I was talking about Jade."

"Oh, that." Tanner seemed to shrink an inch as he settled back in his chair. "Jade says she's feeling good."

Matt nodded. "She looks good."

"Right." Tanner waited awhile then leaned forward again. "Anyway, I told the pastor's wife we'd set up a conference call after the holiday. That way we could figure out what to do, whether we file suit now and interview people at the church or fly out for a conversation with…"

Matt let Tanner ramble on about the case, but concern for his friend grew with each passing sentence. Since Jade's diagnosis, Tanner had responded one of two ways whenever the topic came up. Either he was angry and full of questions or he refused to talk about it.

Neither response was a solution in a situation like the one

Jade faced. The one their whole family faced. Because even if she felt good now, there were dark times ahead. The premature delivery of their baby, radiation, chemotherapy, and brain surgery.

So while Tanner droned on about the Colorado case, Matt prayed that his friend would stop avoiding the truth and figure out a way to handle the situation.

Because the hardest days of Jade and Tanner's lives were just around the corner.

By the time the two families lined up their beach chairs on the sand at dusk that evening, Jenny was exhausted. Fireworks shot off the pier in Redondo Beach lit up half the sky. Grace cuddled between Jenny's legs and jumped a time or two when a firework was particularly large or loud.

There was no way to explain the change that had come over Jenny's heart in the past few weeks. At first she had been irritated by Grace's silence, but over the days she'd seen a connection growing. After all, Jenny knew what it was to be withdrawn in the face of loss. Even if Grace's mother had been awful, Grace was bound to feel sad and uncertain over being taken from her.

Jenny figured the connection between her and Grace happened about the time they got their sister bracelets.

But now there was something even deeper, stronger. Something she hadn't felt since before Alicia's death. As the fireworks ended, Grace squirmed around and hugged her. It was then that Jenny understood what she was feeling. It was a sense that she belonged to Grace, and Grace to her—a special feeling that couldn't be replaced, not even with a best friend or a loving parent.

After four long, empty years, Jenny was finally a sister again. And no matter their age difference or the fact that Grace was adopted, Jenny knew something else.

The feeling would last forever.

The group was making their way into the house, folding chairs and commenting on the dazzling display and the fact that another Fourth of July was behind them. Jenny stood and took Grace by the hand. "Come on, sweetie. Let's go inside."

After a cup of milk and two more chocolate chip cookies, Jenny led Grace toward the adults. "Grace and I are tired." She smiled down at her sister. "We're turning in for the night."

There was a round of good nights and Jenny helped Grace up the stairs and into the bathroom where they brushed their teeth. After Grace had her nightgown on, Jenny tucked her under the covers and kissed her forehead. "You wanna pray or want me to?"

Grace grinned. "Let's both pray."

When they were finished, Grace blinked twice. "Can I keep the lights on for a few minutes? I want to look at my Bible."

Jenny smiled and reached for the bright blue children's picture Bible near Grace's bed. "Sure, honey." She pointed to the wall adjacent to the child's bed. "I'll be on the other side of that wall getting ready, okay? I'll check on you in a few minutes."

Grace locked eyes with Jenny and smiled the sweetest smile Jenny had ever seen. "I love you, Jenny."

A rock settled in Jenny's gut, and for a long time she stood there, not sure what to say. She *did* love Grace, didn't she? But those words had never been something Jenny said lightly. In all her years, she'd only said them to four people: her parents, Matt, and Alicia. The people who were permanent in her life, people she could count on. It was her way of maintaining the meaning of the words.

Don't let her notice, Lord. Please. I'm just not ready...

Jenny swallowed quick and smiled as big as she could. "You're my favorite girl, Gracie; you know that, right?"

The corners of Grace's lips fell a bit. "Yep. You're my favorite girl, too."

Jenny clenched her fists as she left Grace's room. *What's wrong with me? I do love her, don't I?*

She wasn't sure and she was too tired to dwell on the issue. Five minutes passed and Jenny was taking out her earrings when it happened. Three soft thuds sounded on the wall between her room and Grace's. Jenny's heart stopped, and her breath caught in her throat. Suddenly she was four years younger, and the girl in the next room was not Grace, but Alicia.

It had been a different house, of course, but a similar wall had separated their rooms, and from an early age they designed a code. One thud meant hello; two meant come quick. And three thuds represented the three words she and Alicia shared every day for as far back as Jenny could remember. The words Jenny reserved for only a select few.

"I love you."

Of course there was no way Grace could have known that, but still, the sound of the thuds had been almost like hearing Alicia's voice again, like having her alive once more and as close as the next room.

Before Jenny could unfreeze her legs, the thuds came again. Once, twice, three times. And in that instant Jenny wanted nothing more than to go to her little sister and hold her, share with her all the love that had been building in her heart for the past few weeks.

Without hesitating, she rounded the corner into Grace's room, sat on the edge of her bed, and took her small hand. "Hi, honey. Did you want something?"

Grace nodded and yawned, setting her Bible back on the nightstand. "I wanted to tell you I love you."

This time a partial cry came from Jenny's mouth before she could silence herself. She leaned over the little girl and held her close, feeling a dam of emotion breaking free within her heart.

"Sweetie, is it okay if I sleep with you tonight?"

Grace grinned. "Like a sleepover?"

"Right." Jenny stroked the child's soft hand.

Grace slid over and made room as Jenny turned off the light, crawled in bed, and cuddled up to Grace. "Can I tell you something?" Jenny whispered.

"Yes." Grace wiggled her nose against Jenny's.

The tears were coming now and Jenny knew she had to say it before she was weeping too hard to speak. "I love you, Grace. You're my sister and I love you."

Grace's smile lit up the dark room. Jenny's words seemed to settle something deep within the little girl's heart. She was asleep in five minutes. The moment she was, Jenny's tears began spilling onto the pillow. *Dear God, I can't believe it. These feelings I have for Grace…it's like what Mom means when she says Your mercies are new every morning…thank You. Thank You.*

Without making a sound, she wept until she could barely breathe, holding tight to Grace and stroking her hair. And for the first time, the tears weren't because she missed Alicia, but because she had a sister again.

A sister she loved with all her heart.

Ten

Only one antidote could dim the fear in Tanner's heart: work.

As far back as he could remember, Tanner had wanted to be a religious freedom fighter, and now that the symptoms of Jade's tumor were being managed by the medication, it was easy to convince himself she would be fine. That this whole episode was merely some wild and crazy speed bump on the road to forever, and that if he buried himself deep enough into his caseload, one day he'd wake up and Jade would be better, the cancer behind them.

With those thoughts holding the reins to his emotions, Tanner flew to Denver, Colorado; rented a car; and drove to Benson to determine exactly what had caused the Benson City Council to pull the permit on the church's contract to meet there.

What he learned proved without a doubt that they had a case.

He visited Pastor Casey Carson at home. The man who headed the First Church of the Valley had eyes that sparkled and a contagious energy. Tanner had a feeling the pastor would be easy to work with.

"Just a minute—" Pastor Carson pulled something from his file cabinet and handed it to Tanner—"Here. It's our lease agreement."

Tanner leaned forward and read it word for word, searching for the place where Carson and his congregation might have violated the lease.

On the eighth page, four paragraphs down, Tanner found what he was looking for. There, listed as a stipulation of the lease was this statement: "City Hall may not be rented by any group who teaches faith in Jesus Christ as the only way to salvation."

Tanner had seen the copy, but now, holding the original, he was speechless. He let the document settle to his lap, and for a moment his mouth hung open. He lifted his eyes toward Pastor Carson and shook his head. "I still don't believe it."

"I didn't notice the clause before we signed the agreement." The pastor's face was relaxed, humble. "I'm no attorney, but even I couldn't believe that was right, that a clause like that was legal in a city-sponsored rental agreement."

"It's not." Tanner was on his feet and he read the clause once more. Suddenly an idea hit him, a simple idea that truly could make the case a national landmark. His insides relaxed. This was going to be fun. He sat down once more, smiled at the pastor, and tapped the contract with his finger. "Here's what we're going to do…"

That meeting led to others with the associate pastor, and then with the elders at the church. All of them said the same thing: one Sunday, several members of the city council visited their church service. That next Monday, the pastor received notice that they could no longer hold Sunday services at City Hall because the church had violated the terms of the rental agreement.

At night Tanner got back to his hotel room and used his laptop to research case precedent. He talked to Matt the second night and shared his idea.

"Brilliant." Matt's tone held awe, and the excitement bubbling in Tanner grew. Maybe this was the case that would sway public opinion away from dismantling the country's religious freedoms. Maybe more people would be willing to fight for the cause if they could see what was happening in local government, the extreme to which elected officials were willing to go to squash Christianity from any place remotely public.

"We'll handle it together." Tanner's mind raced as he imagined the soundness of the argument they'd have to make on behalf of First Church of the Valley. "Clear your caseload and you can start research next week." He rambled through a list of ideas and stopped only to catch his breath. "Sound good?"

On the other end of the line, Matt hesitated. "Okay."

"If you have a minute, I'll go over the interviews with you; that way you'll be—"

"Tanner, stop." Matt's voice was stern. More stern than Tanner ever remembered hearing.

"What?"

"Have you called Jade?"

At the mention of her name, Tanner felt the blood leave his face. "Why? What's wrong?"

Matt huffed. "She has cancer, remember? You leave her alone with Ty to do research in Colorado and you haven't even called her? In two days?"

Tanner's heart resumed a normal beat. "I worked too late last night. Besides, she said she had projects to catch up on before…"

"Before she got sicker?" Matt's voice was quiet but his words brought a sledgehammer down on Tanner's heart. "If she's going to get sicker, then these are the days she needs you most. While she's still well enough to love you."

Tanner let his head fall into his free hand. "How'd you know I hadn't called her?"

"Hannah told me."

"So she's mad at me?"

Matt groaned. "She's not mad; she's hurt." Matt paused and Tanner knew him well enough to know he was searching for the right words. "You're running. It's only going to hurt worse if you don't stop."

Tanner clenched his fists. "I'm not running; I'm working. We own a law firm, remember?"

"Your wife is sick, Tanner. There's no case more important than that."

"Fine." Tanner had heard enough. What did Matt know of having a sick wife? What did he know about Tanner's fear that any day Jade's personality could change or the tumor could grow and before they had time to prepare for any of it both Jade and their unborn baby could be gone? Matt had no right telling Tanner how to handle the situation. If Tanner wanted to devote this time to his work while Jade was still well enough to leave at home, then that's what he'd do.

Regardless of Matt's feelings.

"I'll call her. Then you and Hannah can stop worrying about us."

"Tanner. No one blames you for being afraid. We're all scared." The compassion in Matt's tone made Tanner regret his unkind thoughts. Matt was only being his friend.

"You're right." He leaned back against the hotel wall and massaged the bridge of his nose with his thumb and forefinger. "Sorry for snapping."

"It's okay. Just don't isolate yourself. We're all in this together."

Tanner hesitated. "Right. Thanks."

Matt meant well, but Tanner wanted to disagree, to tell his friend there was no one who could really understand how he felt. Jade was his entire world, the reason he had chosen to follow his dreams, the only woman he'd ever loved. There was no one who could truly understand her place in his heart, no one who could share his pain if he lost her.

He made the call as soon as the conversation with Matt was finished. Although it was after eight o'clock, she sounded upbeat and happy to hear from him. "How's the research going?"

"Great." Had Hannah really heard from Jade? Maybe the Bronzans were only imagining that his silence had hurt Jade. "I can't wait to share it with you."

"Think it'll be big?"

"Truthfully, Jade…" His mind shifted to the legal plan he'd been forming those past two days. "It could be the biggest of all."

"That's great."

There was silence between them then, and Tanner thought her tone was perhaps too upbeat. "Hey, I'm sorry I didn't call yesterday. Time got away from me."

When Jade didn't answer him, he knew Matt had been right. He hunched over his knees and stared at the hotel carpet. Why hadn't he called? Was it like Matt had said? Was he running from her? There was hurt in her voice when she answered him. "Ty wanted to tell you good night. Me, too." She drew a sharp breath and sounded peppy once more. "But that's okay; I know you're busy. At least you called today."

"Yeah, well, I should have called yesterday."

"It's okay, Tanner. Really."

He dug his elbows into his knees and tightened his grip on the receiver. What was wrong with him? Why wasn't he home with her where he belonged? "How are you?"

"Fine. Ty and I went to the zoo. The baby giraffe was on display for the first time."

"That's nice, but it's not what I mean." He swallowed back his frustration. "How are you *feeling* Jade? You."

"I told you, I'm fine. No side effects, no more headaches. Everything's okay."

Her response made him want to hang up the phone and dive back into his research. Maybe this was why he was running. She refused to discuss her illness or any of the symptoms, almost as though she could pretend away something as life-changing as cancer. And as long as she wasn't willing to talk about it, Tanner didn't have anyplace to share his fears. No wonder it was easier to invest his time at work. It was the only way to silence the terrifying questions that Jade didn't want to talk about and no one else could answer.

Jade put Ty on, and the boy shared his latest escapades on the baseball field. "You'll be home for my game Thursday, right Dad?"

"Right. Absolutely." Tanner smiled and realized it was the first time he'd done so that evening. "Listen, Ty, could you do me a favor?"

"Sure." Tanner closed his eyes and he could picture his son as clearly as if he were standing in the same room.

"Make your mom some tea, okay?"

"Okay." Worry crept into Ty's voice. "She's doing good, right?"

"Right. That's what she tells me."

"Sure, I'll make her tea."

"Thatta boy. And give her a kiss for me."

Tanner talked to Jade once more, but when he got off the phone, he couldn't get back into his research. No matter how hard he tried, his mind kept drifting back until all he could think of was the way he felt the first time he lost Jade.

The summer of his twelfth year, the summer Jade and her father moved away.

That year Jade and he were best friends growing up in the same neighborhood, spending endless days racing bikes and playing together. Scandal and hatred and gossip swirled around them like a typhoon, but they were blissfully unaware.

"Jade's family isn't good people, like us," he could hear his mother saying. "Her father's a drunk, and her mother's run off with another man. She's always been a harlot. I have my proof."

Back then he hadn't understood what she meant, not that it mattered. With or without her mother, Jade was moving. She had a day to pack her things and tell Tanner good-bye. He could see her still, those green eyes flashing as they sprawled across his front yard picking single blades of grass and staring at a canopy of blue sky above them.

Tanner hated the idea of Jade leaving. More than once on their last day together, he asked her about when she'd be home again. "You sure you're coming back?"

"Yes, I promise." Her tone had been frustrated. "We'll meet Mama in Kelso and then when Daddy's job is done, we'll come back here."

They'd only been kids back then, but she was the most beautiful girl Tanner had ever seen. When they said good-bye an hour later, it took all Tanner's strength not to cry. It wasn't until two days after that Tanner heard his mother say she was glad Jade's family was gone for good.

"What do you mean?" Tanner remembered being angry at her. He couldn't begin to understand why she didn't like Jade. "They're coming back. Jade told me so."

"They'll never be back." His mother patted his head. "Forget about her, Tanner."

"Yes, they will! She promised me."

But summer turned to fall, and one year led to another without any sign of Jade and her parents. Tanner had no way to look for her, no ability to check her whereabouts. Often in the years that followed, he'd ask his mother about her.

"I have no idea where the girl is!" His mother would huff and busy herself in the kitchen. "Why must you insist on asking about her?"

Tanner's youthful answer was as clear today as it had been all those years ago: "Because I'm going to marry Jade one day, that's why."

Eleven years would pass before he and Jade would find each other again.

Tanner leaned back in his office chair and doodled Jade's name on a notepad, taking special care with each letter. It was a miracle they'd found each other at all that summer. He had long since forgotten where she had moved, and his mother pretended the same. Who would have thought his internship with the Kelso Board of Supervisors would place him in the very town where Jade lived?

A quiet chuckle came from someplace deep inside him. He remembered the first time they saw each other again. Tanner had been asked to suggest at a public meeting that the children's ward be eliminated from the Kelso hospital as a way of saving money.

Jade attended the meeting. Her argument that day caused the board of supervisors to change their mind and opt for different budget cuts.

But not before Jade had a chance to verbally slay Tanner and his ideas.

Tanner laughed again at the memory. Neither of them had recognized the other at first, but when the meeting was over, Tanner realized who she was. He caught her before she left and when the afternoon was over, they were old friends again.

Friends who spent the summer falling in love.

"Ahh, Jade…if only things had been different." Tanner whispered the words as his eyes found their framed wedding picture on his hotel dresser. He never traveled without it, and now as he studied Jade's green eyes a piercing sadness poked pins at his heart. "We lost so much time…"

Tanner remembered hurting when he learned the truth about Jade's teenage years in Kelso. Life had not been easy for Jade since she'd moved from Virginia. By the time Tanner found her again that summer, the walls around her heart were so high and thick, there were times he thought their relationship didn't stand a chance.

But gradually Jade opened up and the walls fell. Not only that, but midway through July, Jade became a believer, a Christian with a deep love for God. With everything in common, Jade and Tanner's time together was magic.

Until then, Tanner had kept himself from intimate situations, determined to wait until marriage before sharing himself with a woman. Jade, too, was a virgin, and early in their dating Tanner couldn't imagine their relationship ever becoming physical.

Tanner bit his lip, his eyes still locked on his wife's framed image. The truth was, they both let walls tumble that summer. By the end of August, the day before he was scheduled to go back to college on the east coast, there was nothing either of them could do to resist the temptation of being together.

And that single night—the decision to give in to a moment of weakness greater than either of them—changed everything about the next decade.

No matter how much time passed, the truth about what happened that fall was still depressing. It made Tanner long for a way to go back and change things so he and Jade could somehow share every one of the days they missed.

After their fateful night together, Tanner left for Europe on a lengthy mission trip. He was there, completely out of communication, when Jade learned she was pregnant. With nowhere else to turn, Jade called Tanner's mother, who told her that Tanner was a liar who randomly slept with women and made them pregnant.

Tanner opened his eyes and exhaled in a way that filled the hotel room with sadness. The fact that Jade had believed his mother was always the hardest part for Tanner. That and what happened next.

Alone and pregnant with nowhere to turn, no one who seemed to care about her, Jade panicked. It was as simple as that.

She married Jim Rudolph, a man who shared nothing of Jade's newfound faith. It was a marriage intended to do one thing: give Jade's baby a chance at a normal life.

Instead, it caused all of them a decade of heartache.

Tanner stood and stared out the window at the distant Colorado mountains. There were no words to describe the pain that had suffocated him when he returned from his mission trip that fall and found out Jade was married. Tanner tried desperately to reach her, but to no avail.

Tanner turned back to the hotel room and glanced at the clock. Matt was right. What good was he doing Jade here in Colorado researching his next case? He could finish his research at home.

He wandered about his room, gathering clothes and tossing them into his suitcase. A heaviness settled over Tanner's heart, and he knew it was from the flood of memories that had carried him through the past hour. The pain of losing Jade all those years ago never dimmed, not even a little.

Maybe that's why he was running so fast these days.

He'd been heartsick watching her move away when he was a boy. Then after they'd found each other again in Kelso, after they'd fallen in love and made promises to marry, Tanner had been devastated by losing her a second time. It had taken years before her face didn't haunt him at night, before her name wasn't fresh on his mind in everything he did.

Now the stakes were higher than ever, and Tanner was sure of this much: If he lost Jade again, it would destroy him.

Eleven

Fear coursed through Patsy Landers' veins as she sat on a stone bench amidst the wild daisies, pink roses, and brash violets that took up most of the courtyard outside her small house in Bartlesville, Oklahoma.

This was her prayer garden, the place she came when she wanted quiet time alone with God. It was a place she'd visited often these past four months while she prayed about the situation with her wayward daughter. And now, as her heart raced within her, she was sure of His answer.

It was time to take action.

Not for Leslie's sake. Unless Leslie gave her life over to Jesus, there was no way the girl was going to change. She was twenty-one, hooked on crack, and determined not to take help from her mother or anyone else. At this point she could be living on the streets or with a band of drug runners. There was no way to tell.

Patsy lifted her chin and let the breeze dry her tears. If Leslie were not a mother, it would be time to let her go. Let her come to the end she seemed desperate to reach.

But Leslie was not alone.

She had little Grace with her, even though Patsy had offered—as she always did—to care for the child herself. Patsy folded her gnarled hands and a small sigh slipped from between her teeth. The loan had been Patsy's last-ditch attempt, the only way she knew to be sure Leslie would stay in Oklahoma. She borrowed against the equity in her Bartlesville home and gave the money to Leslie on one condition: Use it to purchase a house around the corner, a small place where she and Grace could start a normal life, one that didn't involve drugs and strange men and living out of various broken-down vehicles.

It was the money Patsy was going to use to have her hips replaced, an operation doctors assured her would ease her arthritis pain. But the surgery could wait.

If the money would mean getting Leslie and Grace out of California and off the streets, it was worth every penny.

Patsy was certain Leslie was going to cooperate. Together they toured the small house she'd chosen and contacted a realtor. Escrow papers were drawn up, and Leslie seemed excited about her new chance at life.

The day the deal was set to close, mere hours before Leslie was to show up with the cashier's check and take ownership of the house, she fled. She left with Grace and the money, and Patsy hadn't heard a word from them since.

At first Patsy considered calling the police and reporting the money stolen, but that wouldn't have helped. Besides, she'd given the money to Leslie. Yes, they'd had an arrangement as to where the money was supposed to go, but either way, Leslie hadn't stolen it. Not by legal definition.

Next, Patsy thought about getting in her car and heading down the highway toward California, because if she knew one thing about Leslie, it was this: If she was running, she'd eventually wind up in California. Santa Maria, to be specific. That was where her drug base was, the place where she could crash at any of a dozen houses and have people smoke and drink and shoot up with her. People who would watch Grace for days on end if Leslie wound up in a stupor that couldn't be slept off.

Patsy was as sure as winter that Leslie was there.

But she was also sure that this time there was no point chasing her. Leslie would do what she wanted, regardless of Patsy's attempts to stop her. That being the case, Patsy chose to take an hour every day and do the one thing she knew with absolute certainty would make a difference: Pray.

She prayed that somehow Leslie would arrive in California and feel compelled to find a new start, that she wouldn't return to her drugged-out friends, and that she'd realize there would never be another time when she'd have so much cash on hand.

"Help her think clearly," Patsy would pray quietly while she sat in her garden. "Let her use the money for a house or an apartment. Something stable for Grace."

Because really, what it all came down to was the child.

Patsy could release her hold on Leslie. She could shelve her concerns that her only daughter would wind up in a gutter someday, facedown, dead from a drug overdose. If that happened, so be it. There was nothing Patsy could do to stop it.

But Grace deserved better.

Sweet, precious little Grace. Patsy loved the child like she was her own and would gladly have raised her, would have fought Leslie in court for the chance to do so if only it seemed like the right thing. The problem was that Grace loved her mother. Every time Patsy considered using legal means to take the child from Leslie, she was stopped by that single fact. It was a terrible inner conflict. What was best for Grace? Life with Leslie, or life with her grandmother?

Now, in light of Leslie's disappearing with the money and remaining silent these past four months, the answer seemed perfectly clear. Grace was four years old, after all, and there was no telling what horrific things awaited her if she accompanied her mother back to the culture of drug users and criminal types.

Patsy thought back to the time that had passed since Leslie's disappearance. The months had been filled with pain, not just emotionally but physically. Patsy's arthritis was worse than before and even simple activities were almost more than she could bear. The weeks had become months, and still Patsy prayed. But not until this morning, with the rich smell of blossoms hanging in the humid air, was Patsy sure it was time to act. She took slow, painful steps toward the house. Once inside, she began making phone calls.

Two days later she had enough information to string together what had happened to Leslie and Grace since they left Oklahoma. The facts acted like so many spears, impaling Patsy's heart further with each devastating blow.

As Patsy had suspected, Leslie headed for Santa Maria, but instead of using the money to find a safe place for her and Grace, she blew the entire amount on drugs. Neighbors who lived near a house that Leslie frequented were able to tell Patsy how wild things had gotten. So bad, in fact, that they'd taken to watching little Grace so she wouldn't be run down in the driveway by the constant flow of traffic and party-goers.

Something the neighbor said knocked the wind from Patsy.

"Leslie told us you were dead," the neighbor woman said. "She said you were sick and died. That's why they left Oklahoma."

It was a full minute before Patsy could speak. "She had…a lot of money. Did she say anything about that?"

The neighbor was quick to answer. "Yes. She said you left it to her in your will."

When she hung up, Patsy felt numb from her toes to the basement of her heart. So that's how it was. The guilt of what Leslie had done was so great that she'd simply written Patsy off.

The rest of the truth was no less easy to accept.

When the money was gone, Leslie did what she always did when reality crashed in around her. She took Grace and disappeared, this time in an old van. Police records told the story of what happened next. Broke and unable to buy food or water for her and Grace, Leslie took to prostitution, something she'd done before. She operated out of the van, which she parked in an abandoned field outside town.

That's where she was when police found her. Details of those final days were hazy, but one thing was terrifyingly clear. Leslie was in jail and Grace had been taken into foster care. The court intended to terminate Leslie's rights as a mother. And that meant one thing.

Grace was about to be a ward of the court, adopted out to strangers, all because Leslie had been too proud to place a call to Oklahoma and give Patsy the chance to raise the child.

The policeman she'd spoken to had been kind enough to trace Leslie's file and relay the information Patsy needed if she was ever going to find Grace again. Patsy thanked the man and scribbled down the name of a social worker, the woman who had placed Grace in the home of someone named Bronzan.

Patsy's heart sank. What if Grace had already been adopted? What if it was too late?

She closed her eyes and held her breath. *Help me get her back, God. She needs me. Besides, Grace is my little girl, my angel baby. She doesn't belong with strangers.*

Finally Patsy opened her eyes and allowed herself to breathe again. Then, without hesitating, she picked up the phone and dialed the number the policeman had given her. Someone answered on the first ring and Patsy cleared her throat and asked for Edna Parsons, Grace's social worker.

There was a pause and then a woman came on the line. "Yes?"

"Mrs. Parsons?" Patsy winced as her body tensed.

"Yes, how can I help you?"

Patsy drew a deep breath. "I'm Grace Landers's grandmother. I'd like to see about getting permanent custody of her."

Edna Parsons' heart skipped a beat the moment the caller identified herself. She hoped it was a hoax, one of Leslie Landers's friends seeking to disrupt the termination of Leslie's parental rights.

But there was something very real and logical about the woman's story. She knew Grace's full name and birth date and had examples of what the child liked to eat and wear and watch on television. The grandmother lived in Oklahoma and promised to fax in documentation proving she was Leslie Landers's mother and showing that she had the means to permanently care for little Grace.

The woman suffered from arthritis and lived on a disability pension and the retirement funds from her deceased husband. She was slow, but not crippled, she explained. "I can care for Grace, no problem. She's a sweet child; she knows I don't get around very well."

By all preliminary standards, Patsy Landers seemed well enough to be named the child's legal guardian, but that didn't make the situation any easier. After all, Grace was adapting beautifully with the Bronzans. Edna had been by their house a few days earlier and had been moved to tears watching Grace run on the beach with her new sister. Hannah and Matt said the change in their family had been miraculous.

"It's like she's always been our little girl," Hannah told Edna when she gathered her things and left that day.

Edna's throat swelled with sorrow. She'd done everything she could to see that something like this wouldn't happen, but still it had. These sorts of disruptions in foster-adopt homes weren't supposed to happen! Leslie Landers had said her mother was dead, after all. Of course, Edna had realized the woman could be lying, so she had done a national name search on Patsy Landers—just to verify that the woman was indeed dead. When nothing turned up, Edna assumed Leslie was telling the truth—but Patsy was listed under the name of her second husband, a man who had passed away a decade ago.

It didn't matter now. None of that would help the Bronzans once Edna notified them of Grace's grandmother's intentions.

Losing Grace would be overwhelming to people like the Bronzans, people who had suffered so much loss already.

Edna wanted to go home, shut herself in her bedroom, and cry for a week. But she knew there was something she had to do first. Not now, not until she had the proper documentation from the woman in Oklahoma, but as soon as she did there'd be no way around it.

She would have to call the Bronzans and tell them the truth.

Twelve

A month into the medication, Jade was still herself—no personality changes, no shuffling gait, no slurred speech or memory loss.

She felt tired, but nothing worse.

It was the end of July and Tanner had been home from Colorado for nearly a week. He seemed less distant, more willing to share with her, talk to her. Whatever had happened while he was gone, the change had been a good thing. In fact, everything about life seemed better than ever lately, and Jade couldn't help but thank God with every breath she drew.

Not only that, but the tumor seemed to be staying about the same size—something Dr. Layton said was nothing short of miraculous, considering pregnancy was often the worst time for cancer to hit. Meanwhile, her nausea had let up and she was beginning to feel the first fluttering of movement deep within her, movement that meant their baby was alive and well.

The whole of it was enough to make Jade sing her way through the days, sure that somehow when she reached the end of her battle with cancer, she would emerge victorious. She and Tanner and Ty and the baby. All of them together, without fear of anything else happening to them.

Of course, every now and then there were still times when she wondered if the tumor was God's way of punishing her for what happened with her and Jim Rudolph. But most often, she refused to allow those thoughts a chance to develop. Yes, she'd made mistakes in her marriage to Jim, but she'd done everything in her power to rectify them. There was no point wallowing in guilt now.

"You have to stay positive," Hannah told her every time they were together. "Keep believing God will get you through this. That's where your thoughts should be."

And that's exactly where Jade intended to keep them.

She finished her salad, drank a glass of water, and sat herself down at the computer. A friend from the hospital had told her about herbal vitamin tablets she could purchase online. The blend was designed to bolster the immune system of pregnant women who were battling cancer.

Jade found the web site, read up on the tablets, and ordered a three-month supply. Then she checked the mirror and headed for the hospital. It was just after noon, and she had an ultrasound scheduled for two o'clock. An ultrasound that would most likely tell her the information she and Tanner were dying to know— whether the child she was carrying was a girl or a boy.

As she made her way into the hospital parking lot, Jade remembered a conversation she and Tanner had shared the night before.

"It doesn't matter to me; you know that, right?" They were lying on their sides, their faces inches apart, wrapped in each other's arms.

"I know." Jade brushed her lips against his. "But what if I can't have more kids?"

"Well…" Tanner smoothed her hair back from her forehead. "Then I'd say a little boy would have Ty as the best big brother in the world." He hesitated and touched his lips to her brow. "And a little girl would be a priceless gift…priceless beyond anything I could imagine."

His words ran through Jade's mind as she entered the hospital and headed upstairs to the children's ward, where she had worked before taking leave. It had been that long since she'd seen her patients, and there was one in particular she wanted to check on.

Jade made her way off the elevator and greeted her friends at the nurse's station, all of whom were full of compliments and thrilled to see her up and around. After several minutes, Jade motioned down the hall.

"How's Brandy Almond?"

The eyes of several of the nurses lit up. "She's doing better," one of them said. "There's something different about her. Go see for yourself."

Jade grinned and hurried toward the girl's room, knocking on her door before opening it and stepping inside.

"You came!" Brandy was sitting up in bed, her cheeks full and more colorful than they'd been. "They told me you were going to have a baby!"

Jade hesitated for a moment. Was that all they'd told the young girl? That she was having a baby? Nothing about the brain cancer? Jade swallowed and considered her choice of words. "Yes. That's right." She placed her hand over her abdomen. "An active baby, by the way my insides feel."

Brandy's eyes danced. "You'll name her after me if it's a girl, right?"

"Absolutely." Jade laughed and sat on the edge of Brandy's bed. "Enough about me. Look at you, Brandy. You're glowing. Like you're ready to run a race or something."

The girl beamed. "I'm getting better. Just like you prayed."

"What?" Jade raised her eyebrows. "Brandy Almond? Talking about prayer?"

Was she…? Did the girl believe now? Was that the difference?

Tears filled Brandy's eyes. "After our talk I decided to give it a try. I told God I'd believe He was real if He'd send me a sign of some kind. Some way so I'd know it was right to trust Him."

"And…" Jade marveled at the light in Brandy's eyes. It was a light that couldn't be manufactured. Jade could hardly wait to hear what had happened to convince Brandy of the truth.

"The next day one of my teammates came in with a Bible." Brandy smiled. "Can you believe that? Just out of the blue for no reason."

Brandy's energy never waned as she shared the story of what happened. The girl approached Brandy and told her she'd been praying for her every day since she'd gotten sick. But that afternoon, the teammate felt sure God wanted her to bring Brandy a Bible and share the truth of Jesus with her.

"'It doesn't matter so much whether you run again or even if you get better,' she told me. 'But if you miss out on knowing Jesus…that'll be a real tragedy.'"

Brandy took the girl's visit as the sign she'd prayed for. "She told me about Jesus and placing my faith in Him. She said if I trusted Him, I'd go to heaven one day."

"And you agreed?" Jade squirmed in her seat, her heart bursting with joy. She took Brandy's hands in her own and squeezed them.

"Yes! I'd be crazy not to. All of a sudden it was like I got it. This Jesus you always talked about, the one my teammate loved, He was not only real, but He loved me. I didn't want to wait another minute to accept that love and start loving Him back."

"Oh, Brandy, that's wonderful." Jade leaned over and hugged the girl close. "You'll never be sorry. And your health…" Jade stood and checked the chart near Brandy's door. "You look so much better."

A laugh bubbled up from Brandy's throat, and she clasped her hands. "Doctor says if my counts stay good for another week I can go home. I'm in remission, Jade. They thought I was done for, and now I'm in remission. Isn't that, like…so *God*?"

Jade fired a grin at Brandy. "Yes, it's definitely, like, so God!"

The file told the story. Jade read it and shook her head. The girl was right; her blood counts had been excellent for the past three weeks. She returned to Brandy's side, hoping she would never find out about the brain cancer.

The expression on Brandy's face changed. "Now tell me why you took off work so early. Don't most people wait until the baby's about to come?"

Jade's pulse quickened. *Give me the words, God…please.* "Yes." She searched her mind for something to say. "But, uh, my morning sickness was worse than most." She lifted one shoulder. "I was too tired to work."

The answer pacified Brandy, and the two of them talked for another thirty minutes before Jade told the girl good-bye. "I have an ultrasound downstairs." She grinned at Brandy. "In an hour I should know if we're having a girl or a boy."

Brandy waved a finger at Jade, her face masked in mock seriousness. "Don't forget, now. If it's a girl, you name her after me." Her eyes sparkled. "Hey, and you can bring her to one of my track meets next year!"

"We wouldn't miss it." Jade laughed. "Get some rest, Brandy. And if they spring you next week, don't forget to stop by and visit."

Brandy grew quiet and she reached her hand toward Jade once more. "No matter what happens, Jade, I'll never forget you."

Sudden tears burned at Jade's eyes and she took the girl's fingers in her own. "I won't forget you, either."

"You saved my life; you know that, right? I was ready to give up, and you told me to pray. Otherwise…"

"Otherwise someone else would have told you." Jade brushed away a tear, leaned over, and kissed the girl on the cheek.

But Brandy shook her head. "No, otherwise I might already be gone."

There was a lump in Jade's throat, and she couldn't speak. Instead she shrugged and pointed heavenward.

"Have that little baby and hurry back, okay, Jade?" Brandy's voice broke and her eyes grew wet. "The kids here need you."

The conversation with Brandy played again and again in Jade's head as she made her way downstairs toward the ultrasound room. *Thank You, God…thank You for healing her. Thank You for sending her teammate that day…thank You.*

Only one part of what the girl had said didn't sit well with Jade.

The part about hurrying back. It wasn't that Jade didn't want to return to her hospital work. Rather, she had stopped making plans that far in the future. As though to do so might be presuming on God's blessing.

She checked in and was ushered to a changing room where she slipped into the blue and white medical gown. *Let me get through the pregnancy, God. Please. My return to work can come later.*

While Jade waited, she wondered again if the baby within her was a boy or a girl. All her life she had wanted a daughter, a girl of her own to mother the way she herself had never been mothered. Deep in her heart, Jade was sure a daughter would be God's way of smiling through the fog of uncertainty caused by Jade's cancer. It would be His way of telling her everything was going to be okay, that He had heard the desires of her heart and now was granting her those desires, even amidst the fear of the unknown.

Of course, a boy would be wonderful as well, a smaller version of Ty, another son to follow in Tanner's footsteps.

The minutes crawled by, and finally half an hour later the technician was ready for her. The young woman wasn't someone Jade knew, but she was kind and gentle and not overly effusive. Though the technician didn't say anything about the cancer, Jade had a feeling she knew.

While the woman positioned the ultrasound wand over her stomach, Jade remembered how terrifying it had been the first time she was pregnant. She hadn't sought medical care until she was several months along so Jim wouldn't be suspicious.

I never should have married him, Lord. I'm so sorry. If I had it to do over again, I'd wait and talk to Tanner first. I wouldn't have trusted Doris Eastman's story until I had a chance to–

"There's a pretty clear picture." The technician smiled and froze the image.

Jade stared at it, but being a nurse didn't help her much. She wasn't sure what she was seeing. Reading ultrasounds required special training. She grinned at the woman and shrugged her shoulders. "What are we looking at?"

"Well, I'd say she's about as perfect as a baby can be. She looks completely healthy."

"*She?*" Tears nipped at the corners of Jade's eyes. Was it possible? Had God allowed her another chance to mother a little girl?

"I'm sorry." The technician looked surprised. "I thought you knew." She looked back at the screen and pointed to the baby. "There's no doubt about it. You're having a girl, Mrs. Eastman."

Jade blinked back the tears and closed her eyes, allowing herself a moment's privacy. God was going to let her survive after all. Otherwise He wouldn't have blessed her with a little girl; He wouldn't have let the baby live this long, past the point when Jade had miscarried the last time. Happiness shot through her veins, infusing hope to every part of her being. Yes, she was going to survive.

She could hardly wait to tell Tanner.

An hour later she was home, fixing pasta on the stove, when an unspeakable pain shot through her head, dimming her senses and shading her eyes in a cloak of sudden black. She sank to the floor and fought for the strength to shout for help.

"Tanner!" Her voice was weak and fading. "H-elp..."

He should be home any minute, but that wouldn't help her now. Her heartbeats came in short bursts without any sense of pattern, and the pain intensified as she collapsed. The cold tile floor smacked against her arms and face, and she lay there, unable to move.

Terror gripped her heart, her mind. If Tanner didn't get there soon, these might be her last moments alive. Their daughter's last moments. *God, I'm not ready to die! I haven't said good-bye to Tanner or Ty or...*

The pain doubled its intensity and Jade moaned. "Tanner!"

The thought that she might not live through the seizure was sadder than anything Jade could imagine. Not because she had fears about where she'd spend eternity, but because she'd miss out on telling Tanner what was supposed to be the happiest news they'd had in a month.

That the precious child inside her was a little girl.

Even if Tanner arrived in time, the seizure meant everything had changed. She tried to call out again, but it was no use. Her breathing was infrequent and shallow and there was nothing she could do to help herself. Her body was rebelling against an invasion deep in her brain. An invasion that could only mean one thing.

The tumor was growing.

Tanner heard Jade's soft cries the moment he opened the door.

"Jade?" He sprinted for the kitchen. Steam filtered up from the stove where a pot of boiling water spilled onto a flame-red burner. "Jade, where are—"

Something on the floor caught his attention and he stared at her. "Dear God, no...not again."

He raced to her, turning off the stove and reaching for the phone as he fell to his knees beside her. Fear made breathing next to impossible. "Jade, baby, wake up!"

Her eyes were wide open, unblinking, and her arms and fingers were frozen stiff. She was still shaking, her limbs jumping off the floor, and he could do nothing to help her stop. It took less than fifteen seconds to call the ambulance; then he remembered Dr. Layton's advice from last time she had a seizure.

Lay her flat…check her pulse, her inhalations. Don't administer CPR unless she's stopped breathing on her own…

Tanner forced himself to concentrate and follow the doctor's orders. Her heart was still beating, but it was weak and irregular. He lowered his face to hers. "Come on, Jade; fight, baby. Don't leave me." His eyes fell on her upper chest. She was breathing, but only the faintest bit of air passed over her lips. Tanner gripped her shoulders and clung to her. "Stay with me, Jade. Don't leave…"

The seconds slowed to a crawl, and Tanner begged God to help them. His eyes remained locked on Jade, looking for the moment when he might need to start CPR. "Keep breathing, Jade…please keep breathing."

Tanner wasn't sure how much time passed, but he felt a hand on his shoulder and turned to see the paramedics. He scrambled out of the way, his body weak from terror. What if it was too late? What if they couldn't help her? Why was any of it happening to them?

As usual, there were no answers.

The paramedics moved fast and spoke quietly. Before Tanner could glean anything from their conversation, they whisked Jade into an ambulance and off to the hospital.

Again Tanner followed behind, his mind numbed by the nightmare unfolding before them. *What's happening, God? Why this? Why her?*

A Scripture from a sermon they'd heard the week before flashed in Tanner's mind. *"In this world you will have trouble. But take heart! I have overcome the world."*

Tanner steadied his hands and kept his attention on the ambulance in front of him. *Is this the trouble you have for us, Lord? That Jade suffer like this?*

It was more than Tanner could bear. He forced himself to believe it was all a mistake, that the seizure was merely an adverse reaction to Jade's medication or maybe somehow related to her pregnancy and not the cancer at all. He was at her side the moment he saw her inside the emergency room. Though she was conscious, she was too exhausted to speak.

"Hang in there, honey. I'm here."

Dr. Layton met them at the hospital and pumped a megadose of anti-seizure medication into Jade's veins. More tests were performed, and Tanner could do nothing but stay by her side, hold her hand, and pray it was all a bad dream. That somehow they'd wake up and Jade would be the same cheerful person she had been that morning. Back when brain cancer seemed little more than a diversion in what was otherwise a perfectly normal pregnancy.

Two hours later, the prognosis was painfully clear. The tumor had grown, and Dr. Layton ordered an immediate increase in Jade's anti-seizure medication.

"At this point, Jade's in a race against her biological clock." The doctor stood close to Tanner, his hand resting on Jade's bed. "And there's something else. The tumor isn't growing neatly like we'd hoped. It's starting to grow tentacles. The more that happens, the less likely we'll be able to operate when the baby's born. I thought you should know."

The information settled like a dense cloud of poisonous smoke over Tanner's consciousness as he struggled to make sense of the doctor's words. The tumor had tentacles? Seizure medication—though replete with side effects—could prevent further attacks. But if the tumor continued to grow, it could cause a stroke or sudden death. The baby was still eleven weeks away from the set delivery date.

"If things get bad enough, we'll have to take the baby and hope for the best." Dr. Layton bit his lip. Jade's eyes were closed, and Tanner doubted that she either heard or understood any of the information the doctor had just shared.

Tanner nodded. "What's the soonest the baby could live?"

"We've saved them as early as twenty-five, twenty-six weeks. Jade's just about twenty-one weeks along now." The man hesitated. "Jade's wishes are clear about keeping the baby. We'll only deliver that early if we have no other choice."

There was no way Tanner could think that far in the future. He smoothed the hair off Jade's forehead and thanked the doctor. "I think we need to be alone, if that's all right with you."

Dr. Layton's shoulders slumped and he nodded. "I'm sorry." He raised the file he had in his hand. "The nurses will explain the increase in medication. I'm afraid…" Tanner understood the pause. The doctor knew all too well that there was only so much bad news a person could handle. Finally he went on. "I'm afraid the extra medication is bound to cause the more serious side effects we discussed earlier."

Tanner clenched his teeth and waited for the doctor to leave. He wanted to scream at him that none of the news they'd received that day was right or fair or even remotely possible. Jade's tumor was growing tentacles? Sudden death was a possibility? None of it seemed real, and suddenly Tanner couldn't sit by his sick wife another moment.

He stood in a burst of motion and strode to the window, staring outside as a rush of tears blurred his vision. Memories from days gone by danced on the screen of his mind. He and Jade finding each other again that summer in Kelso, walking along the Cowlitz River and holding hands in the park while they caught up on the first decade lost.

Jade…I need you. Don't leave me again.

He squeezed his eyes shut and another image appeared.

It was Jade two years ago, the afternoon they found each other again. She was crying and telling him that yes, Ty was his son. Her words echoed in his heart. *"I love you, Tanner…I never stopped loving you…"*

He could hear her voice, feel the touch of her fingers against his face as they realized the devastation caused by his mother's web of lies.

Dozens of memories flashed before Tanner's eyes, a tapestry of happy moments they'd shared in the two years since they'd been back together. He gripped the windowsill as despair worked its way through his veins. He didn't have one single happy memory without Jade. He stared out the window at the sunset over Thousand Oaks, silent tears sliding down the sides of his face.

God, what am I going to do if she dies? Please…don't take her. Please, God…

"Tanner?"

Her weak voice made him spin around. He wiped his hands across his cheeks, determined she wouldn't see him cry. "I'm here, baby." He was at her side again in three quick steps. "How're you feeling?"

The corners of her mouth struggled into a smile. "Did…did the doctor tell you the news?"

Tanner's heart pounded within him. *How do I tell her the truth, God…give me the words.* "Yes. He told me."

Jade's eyes sparkled despite her exhaustion. "You don't look excited."

What? Was the medication messing with her already? He tried to keep his voice even. "Excited?"

"Tanner, it's the best news we've had in a month." She held out her hand and he took it, weaving his fingers between hers.

"Jade…I don't understand…" He bit his lip and shook his head. "What news?"

Her half-closed eyelids opened wider than before. "Then you don't know." A slow chuckle came from her throat. "Fine. Let me be the first to tell you." She brought their hands to her lips and kissed his fingers. "Congratulations, Mr. Eastman. You're going to have a daughter."

Thirteen

The girls were at the grocery store and Hannah was folding laundry in Grace's room when the phone rang. She straightened a rag doll on Grace's pink ruffled pillow and answered the phone in the office down the hall. "Hello?"

There was a pause on the other end and Hannah rolled her eyes. Salesmen. They never came right out and gave you their pitch anymore. Instead there was an annoying three-second computerized delay. Hannah was about to hang up when she heard Edna Parsons' voice.

"I need to speak to you. Can I come by, or would you rather talk now, on the phone?"

Inch by inch, Hannah sank into the chair near the phone. Her heart was in her throat. "Now's fine."

The social worker sighed. "I hate to tell you this…"

Hannah's pulse quickened, and she struggled to breathe. What was this? It couldn't be about Grace. Her mother was in jail, after all. They were just a few months from finalizing the adoption. "Just tell me. Please."

Again Mrs. Parsons hesitated. "I've been in conversation this week with Grace's maternal grandmother."

Hannah's stomach dropped. This wasn't happening; it was impossible. Grace didn't have a grandm—

"It seems…well, she isn't dead after all."

Hannah was falling into a dark and endless pit. She knew what was coming and there was nothing she could do to stop it.

Her grip on the phone tightened. "How…how do you know she's telling the truth?"

"The woman provided us with documentation proving she's Leslie Landers's mother. Apparently she gave Leslie a great deal of money and tried to help her purchase a house in Oklahoma."

Oklahoma? The woman lived in Oklahoma? Did that mean… Hannah squeezed her eyes shut and tried to focus on the social worker's explanation.

"Instead Leslie took the money and ran to California. She blew it on drugs and told everyone, including Grace, that Grandma Landers was dead."

Hannah swallowed. "What does the woman want?"

Another sigh filled the phone, this one heavier than before. "She wants Grace. She says she's been like a mother to the child since she was born. The only stability Grace has ever known."

Until now, Hannah wanted to say. *Until she came to live with us!* The technicality of their situation didn't matter; Grace was *their* daughter. Even if the adoption wasn't finalized. "Don't…don't we have some say in this? Grace belongs to us now."

"Grace belongs to the state. She's a foster child, a ward of the court." Mrs. Parsons paused. "I had no idea this would happen. I feel terrible, Mrs. Bronzan."

Hannah's mind raced for a solution. There had to be a way out. Maybe she and Matt and Jenny and Grace could pile in the car and head for Mexico. Maybe she could hang up and the entire phone call would be nothing but an unthinkable nightmare. Hannah rubbed her forehead and stared at the floor. Her heartbeat was so loud she was sure the social worker could hear it. "Does…does the woman know how happy Grace is? Does she understand?"

"She wants her granddaughter, and according to California

law she has the right to take custody of her as long as she's fit. We checked her out and she's a fine woman, Mrs. Bronzan. She's flying here today from Oklahoma to take Grace home."

To take Grace home? There was a searing pain in Hannah's heart. So that was it? Grace's grandmother figured out where she was and now Grace would have to leave? As though she and Matt and Jenny had never been a part of her life at all? Tears spilled from Hannah's eyes and she struggled to find her voice. "You're taking her today?"

"No." There was a shuffling sound of papers in the background. "We'll come for her tomorrow morning. Say ten o'clock. Her grandmother wants to come, too. She…she wants to thank you for helping Grace these past three months."

"Yes…I see…" Hannah mumbled a good-bye and hung up the phone. As she did, her eyes fell on a framed photograph of Grace and Jenny, their arms slung across each other's shoulders; grins spread across their faces. Her face contorted as the sobs came. "No!" She shouted the word so it sounded throughout the empty house. "No, God! Don't take her away!"

Hannah reached for the picture and clutched it to her chest, weeping over the thought of telling Grace good-bye in the morning. There would be no time to prepare, no time to let her know how much they loved her. Not only that, but after tomorrow she'd be living in Oklahoma.

How would they survive? Any of them? The child had worked her way into the very fiber of their family, into the deepest crevices of their hearts. It would be like losing…

Hannah couldn't finish the thought. Her weeping grew louder, more desperate, and she collapsed over her knees, still holding the photograph. *No, God…not again.*

The pain that wracked her body was as gut-wrenching as it was familiar. Hannah knew all too well what it was to lose a daughter, to receive the kind of news that destroyed a family in an instant.

Her tears were not only for Grace and what tomorrow's loss would mean. They were for Alicia and Tom and everything about that awful day when Hannah first understood how life could change forever in the course of a few minutes.

The last day of summer. Four years ago, almost exactly.

The events of that day were etched in a part of her brain where they would remain for moments like this, moments when drifting back was simply inevitable. And so, still clutching the picture of Grace and Jenny, Hannah was sucked back in time, back to a golden afternoon, the last day of summer vacation, 1998.

She had busied herself that day readying for her family's return from what had become an annual summer's end camping trip. She remembered sneaking a look out the window every ten minutes or so as evening drew closer, impatient for their return.

But time slipped away until they were thirty minutes late, and then an hour. Hannah was still staring out the kitchen window when the police car pulled up that evening.

His exact message was jumbled in her mind, but key words stood out still. There'd been an accident, serious injuries, Tom and the girls were at the hospital.

It was the beginning of a time when Hannah felt like she was walking underwater, as though everything she heard or saw was somehow muffled by a dense layer of pain unlike anything she'd ever experienced.

At the hospital Hannah was ushered into a small room where a doctor used kind, careful words to tell her the news. Jenny had injuries, but she'd be okay. The others weren't so fortunate. Rescue workers had made a gallant effort, but both Tom and Alicia had died at the scene.

Before the night was through she followed the doctor to a room where Tom's and Alicia's bodies lay, and at a time when they should have been laughing and sharing stories over dinner, Hannah bid each of them a final good-bye.

Next she learned that the driver of the other car had been drunk. In fact, he'd been convicted of drunk driving several times before hitting her family.

The news—all of it—turned Hannah overnight into someone even she didn't recognize, someone angry at God and bitter with life, determined to make the drunk driver pay. Someone oblivious to the cost her revenge was exacting on Jenny.

The memory faded and Hannah sat straighter in her chair. She looked once more at the photograph of Jenny and Grace, and though fresh tears swam in her eyes, she knew somehow she'd survive. The Lord would see her through. After all, He'd given her Matt, and with Matt by her side Hannah could survive just about anything.

She thought about her tall dark husband and the way he'd made her life beautiful these past years. Matt, who had walked her through the year-long court battle against Brian Wesley, the drunk driver. Matt, who had represented the spirit of Christ at every turn, seeking not revenge but justice. Matt, who had been Hannah's constant friend and supporter.

It was no surprise, really, that she'd fallen in love with him.

Not that the process had been quick.

It started more than a year after the accident, when Hannah acted on Tom's dying wish. That day she walked into a prison meeting room, sat across from Brian Wesley, and forgave him.

Afterward, when Hannah joined Matt and Jenny outside, something had changed. Hannah couldn't place it at first, but in time she realized that forgiving Brian Wesley had removed ice from around her heart. With the cold gone, she was able to see

Matt in a way she hadn't before. In fact, for the first time since the collision she was able to imagine her future, to admit she still had one.

For a long while she and Matt hid their feelings, each not sure the other was ready for romance. Hannah remembered the turning point.

It was a few months later in late February and Matt had spent the day with her and Jenny. Though the sun was out, a cool breeze filled the air, and the three of them flew kites at a local park. When the sun set, they returned to Hannah's house and Matt barbecued steaks.

As soon as dinner was over, Jenny announced she had plans with a friend. Half an hour later she was gone for the evening, and Matt and Hannah had the house to themselves. They spent the first hour walking to the local high school and circling the track. For the first time none of their conversation centered around Tom's and Alicia's absence. Rather they talked about his dream of joining a law firm that fought for religious freedom and spending the next part of his career upholding rights that too many people took for granted.

"I'm finished with drunk drivers," he told her. Their steps were unhurried and every now and then their arms brushed against each other.

"You met your goal. A drunk driver was convicted of murder one." Hannah gazed at the treetops beyond the school. "I don't blame you for wanting something new."

Matt shook his head. "It isn't that. Murder one was the right conviction for Brian Wesley. But even that won't keep it from happening again. Tonight, tomorrow…every night after that…someone will drink too much and climb behind the wheel. They'll break laws and drive without licenses and kill people like Tom and Alicia and my friends."

Hannah angled her head, curious in a sad sort of way. "So, we should give up?"

"No." Matt slipped his hands in his pockets as they kept walking. "You should keep working for victim rights as long as you feel God wants you to. I think that kind of thing helps, especially with teenagers. There you are talking about your losses, showing pictures of Tom and Alicia. That kind of message is bound to stop some of them from drinking."

He paused for a moment and Hannah savored the peace that resonated in her soul when she was with him. He continued, his tone thoughtful. "But *prosecuting* drunk drivers doesn't keep anyone from drinking and driving."

"It made Brian stop." Hannah wasn't being argumentative. She only wanted Matt to know how important his role was in seeing Brian sent to prison for what he did. Yes, she forgave him. But after numerous drunk driving accidents and convictions, after killing two people, Brian belonged in prison.

It was the only way he wouldn't kill again.

"For now." Matt shrugged. "But Brian won't serve his whole term. And then we'd better pray he finds healing from his alcoholism. Otherwise, it could happen again. You and I both know that."

Hannah didn't respond. The thought of Brian Wesley back on the street, possibly drinking and driving again, was too depressing to imagine. She waited for Matt to continue.

"I'd like to invest my time where I could shape American law, set precedent for generations to come. Cases that would preserve freedoms for millions of Americans."

Hannah remembered her heart swelling with pride as Matt shared his hopes with her that evening. Their conversation shifted to his basketball days in college and she found herself wishing she'd known him then.

"If you played with as much passion as you practice law, you must have been very good." She smiled up at him. The sky was growing darker and without saying a word they shifted direction and headed back to Hannah's house.

Once inside, Hannah made coffee, and they continued their conversation over a board game Matt had given her. He was winning handily when he tapped her foot under the table and flashed her his cards, alerting her to the fact that he'd been cheating.

"Matt Bronzan!" Hannah's laughter rang like wind chimes in springtime. "Here I thought you were a man of honor."

"Well, let's see…" He looked at the ceiling, pretending to be deep in thought while he calculated something. "You've beaten me the last five games. I'd say even men of honor have to resort to drastic measures now and then."

But as he finished his sentence, his elbow bumped the playing board, messing up the meticulously placed chips and putting an immediate end to the contest. "Aha!" Hannah snatched his cards from his hand. "Justice, again!"

In his attempt to grab the cards back, Matt missed and took hold of her hand instead. The air between them changed, and their eyes locked. Both their smiles faded. Time ceased to exist as they stayed that way, his hand clutching hers, while they searched each other's eyes and tried to think of something to say.

He made the first move. Clearing his throat, Matt removed his hand, took hold of his coffee mug, and finished what was left of his drink. "I should be going."

Hannah was confused as much by his reaction as her own. Why was he upset with himself for holding her hand? Didn't he have feelings for her? And what was this sudden ache in her heart? It was only eighteen months since losing Tom… Had she been so quick to fall in love with another man?

She had no answers as she followed Matt to the front door.

Though she planned to merely thank him for a fun day and bid him good-bye, she couldn't stop herself from asking the question. The one that burned stronger in her with each passing day.

"Why, Matt?" They were standing face-to-face near the open door, him filling the doorframe and her leaning against the wall as she studied his eyes for answers.

He cocked his head, his tone soft. "Why, what?"

"Why are you here with me? You could be dating a dozen different women, getting on with your life." She hesitated and she could hear her heart beating hard within her.

For a moment she thought Matt might laugh or launch into an explanation, the kind he was expert at giving. Instead, he moved closer and cradled her chin in his fingertips. Then he brought his lips to hers and kissed her.

When he drew back, his eyes were glistening. "Because..." He kissed her again, his touch gentle and sweet, but burning with a thinly veiled desire. "Because I love you, Hannah."

The explosion of emotions within her that night was more than she could bear. Tears spilled from her eyes and she was speechless. She was in love with Matt Bronzan, and that meant she was healing. Though she had never expected to love any man other than Tom Ryan, here she was, kissing Matt and savoring the sensation of falling once more.

Matt's expression filled with subtle alarm when he saw her tears. He brushed them from her cheeks as his eyes clouded over. "I'm sorry, Hannah. It's too soon. I just...I had to tell you." He glanced at his feet and back at her. "I'm sorry."

A sound that was more laugh than sob came from Hannah and she wrapped her arms around his neck. When the hug ended, she found his lips again and kissed him the way she'd wanted to for months.

The days after that were a blissful bouquet of moments that

were almost impossible to believe. By the end of the week, Jenny caught on to what was happening between them. One night she was on her way out with friends when she winked at Hannah. "Tell your boyfriend hi for me."

Alarm sliced through Hannah's happy heart and she held her breath. "Boyfriend?"

"Yes, *boyfriend.*" Jenny laughed and Hannah's body went limp with relief. "I kept wondering what was taking you guys so long. I figured this would happen months ago."

After that Matt and Hannah were inseparable, and on Easter Sunday he took her and Jenny to brunch and asked Jenny's permission to marry Hannah. Jenny was so thrilled she clapped her hands like a little girl. "Yes! We're going to be a family."

As the summer wedding date drew near, there were many conversations between Hannah and Jenny and Matt, acknowledgments that Matt could never replace Tom, but that what they shared would be every bit as rich. Maybe richer, since great love was often born of great loss.

Though she would never forget Tom and the love they shared and the family they raised, Matt was her closest friend now. The bond they forged in Hannah's time of grief was stronger than anything she'd ever experienced. She loved Matt with a strength that surprised her and made her grateful for every new morning in his arms.

The memories grew distant, and Hannah wiped her tears. She stared at the photo in her hand. Matt had helped her survive the loss of a daughter once before. He would help her again, wouldn't he?

Hannah considered the strength of Matt's love for Grace, the way the child ran to him each evening when he came home from work. Hannah gritted her teeth. How could she call him now and tell him it was all over? That their time with little Grace had ended before it even had time to really begin?

Matt had helped Hannah cope with Alicia's loss, but Alicia hadn't been his daughter. He'd never even met her.

It occurred to Hannah that this loss would be a different matter altogether. Grace wasn't merely a sweet girl whose absence was bound to break Hannah's heart. She was their daughter. Matt's daughter.

Help me be strong for him, Lord, the way he was strong for me. Help us survive…

She prayed until there was nothing left to do but call Matt and tell him. As she dialed his office, her heartache grew. The news about Grace was bound to break off a piece of Matt's heart, a piece that would be gone forever. And so Hannah prayed once more that somehow she'd have the strength to help him survive.

The same way he'd helped her survive four years earlier.

Fourteen

Matt knocked on Tanner's office door and let himself in before his partner could respond. "Got a minute?"

Tanner looked up and nodded to a chair on the other side of his desk. "Sure." He let his eyes fall back to the file in front of him. "What's up?"

Matt wasn't sure how to begin. Tanner hadn't said more than a few words about Jade's condition since her last seizure. He spent hours at the office, working well past his usual six o'clock, and seemed entirely focused on the Colorado case.

Normally that might be fine. That kind of devotion happened once in a while at the offices of CPRR. But not now, not with Jade so sick her life was at stake. Matt sank into the high-backed leather chair across from Tanner and stroked his chin.

It was best to start on safe ground. "How's the case?"

Tanner looked up, a brief smile lifting the corners of his mouth. "Good. We'll file suit against the city tomorrow. I'll need to be there a few days each week for the next month."

"Still going for the sneak attack?" Matt studied Tanner. The man was brilliant when it came to strategy, and the solution he'd mapped out for this case was no exception. In fact, if it went the way Tanner expected it to, the case could serve as a major precedent for a decade to come. Still, with Jade sick, there had to be a better answer than Tanner flying to Colorado.

Tanner laughed. "It'll surprise 'em, that's for sure." He tapped the file on his desk. "It'll be heard in Colorado Springs. You knew that, right?"

"No." Matt raised an eyebrow. "You got the change of venue."

"Last week. I thought I told you." Tanner's gaze fell for a moment. "The judge thought we needed a jury outside of Benson for a fair trial."

"Pretty big news to keep to yourself."

"Yeah." Tanner looked up again, his eyes narrowed as though his heart was a million miles away. "I've had a lot on my mind."

There was a moment of silence between them and in the distant background they heard the ringing of the office phone. Matt softened his tone. "How's it going, really?"

"Good." Tanner shrugged. "I'm praying we get the right verdict the first time around. Maybe we can skip the appeals process if I can make a strong enough argument."

"Tanner." Matt blinked. "I'm not talking about the case." He hesitated. "How are things with Jade? You never talk about her. Hannah and I are desperate to help, but we don't know how."

Tanner pushed back from his desk and leaned deep into his chair. "She's fine. The doctor increased her medication, and she has a full-time nurse in case she has another seizure."

Matt's mind raced, trying to make sense of everything his friend was saying. "The tumor's grown, is that what happened? That's why they had to increase her medication?"

"Yes." The look on Tanner's face was almost angry. "It's growing, okay. But we're handling it just fine. Jade's nurse is taking care of everything."

"Okay…" Frustration built in Matt and he leaned forward, resting his forearms on Tanner's desk. He'd never seen his friend so cold and shallow. It was like someone else had taken over Tanner Eastman's body. "So bite my head off, why don't you?"

For a moment Tanner looked like he might snap back, but instead he exhaled long and slow, his shoulders slumping in the process. "I'm sorry." He rotated his chair so he faced the window, his back to Matt. His voice was hard to hear over the traffic nine stories down. "You don't deserve that."

Matt sat straight again and studied his friend's back. "No. And you don't deserve a sick wife, but that's where you're at. All I'm saying is, Hannah and I want to help."

Tanner was motionless for a while. Then without turning around he began to speak, his voice quiet and broken. "It's hard for her to have visitors. She's...she's slower than before. Her speech, the way she walks...."

Matt's heart broke as Tanner turned around once more and their eyes connected. Tanner's were dry, but only because the fear in his face was stronger than the pain. Matt clenched his jaw and shook his head. "I'm sorry."

Tanner nodded. "The doctor says she should be back to normal once the baby's born and they can remove the tumor. But for now..."

Their eyes held for a moment, and Matt didn't know what to say. No wonder he didn't talk about it much. He was too terrified to voice his concerns. "I can't imagine."

"It's like..." Tanner lifted his hands and let them drop. "It's like I lose her a little more each day." He planted his elbows on his desk and hung his head, his shoulders trembling. There was an ocean of sadness in his voice. "I'm so scared."

There was nothing left for Matt to say. He stood and circled the desk, stopping behind Tanner and placing a hand on his shoulder. "Let Hannah and me come over tonight and pray with you. Please."

Tanner wiped the back of his hand beneath his eyes. "I'm not sure Jade would be up to it."

Matt's heart sank. "Then let us bring you dinner. If she's feeling good enough, we'll stay for a while."

Tanner lifted his head and looked about to protest when

Matt's secretary poked her head in. "Matt, line two. It's Hannah."

Normally Matt would have taken the call there, in Tanner's office, but something told him Tanner needed to be alone. He followed the woman, glancing back at his friend. "Be right back."

Matt's office was next door. He dropped to the chair behind his desk, picked up the receiver and punched the flashing button. "Hannah?"

Her breathing was rough, and Matt heard the muffled sound of sniffling. "Hi. Sorry to call you at work."

There was no question about it. She was crying. A surge of adrenaline coursed through Matt's veins. "Honey, what's wrong? You sound terrible."

"Mrs. Parsons called." Hannah struggled with each word. "Grace's grandmother is alive. The judge is ordering that Grace live with her."

The words hit him like so many bricks. "What?" Matt's reply came out as more of a gasp, as he hunched over his knees and dug his elbows into his thighs. "That's impossible."

Hannah sniffed again. "It's true." She hesitated. "Grace leaves tomorrow."

Not Grace! Matt screamed the thought silently, the pain so deep, so great, it was impossible to voice. There didn't seem to be enough oxygen in the room, no way to take a deep breath. Every thought in Matt's head spun wildly out of control. "They can't do that."

"Well, they are." A small sob made its way across the phone lines. "Come home, Matt. Please."

"Okay." He didn't recognize his own voice. "I'm on my way."

He hung up the phone and stared at his hands, willing himself to deny the fact that Hannah had called, or that the social worker had delivered the news. Wanting to disbelieve all of it. How could their social worker have missed the fact that Grace had a grandmother? And why weren't they told of the judge's decision sooner?

Matt clenched his fists. If only he'd had an hour before the judge. Surely he could have convinced the man that Grace was better off in a family, with a mother and father and sister who loved her. Matt would have argued that the grandmother could have visitation rights, but full custody? To a woman Grace didn't even know was alive?

The effort of standing took everything that remained of Matt's strength. Like a man moving through water, he made his way back to Tanner's office, walked inside, and closed the door.

The moment Tanner saw Matt, his expression filled with alarm. "What is it? What's wrong?"

Matt realized Tanner thought the call had been about Jade, that perhaps the news—whatever it was—was so bad it couldn't come directly to Tanner.

Matt shook his head. "Nothing about Jade."

There was a subtle easing in the lines on Tanner's face. "Hannah, then?"

For a moment Matt did nothing but hold his breath, his eyes locked on those of his friend. Then he shrugged his shoulders, feeling the sting of tears. "They're taking Grace from us tomorrow."

Tanner stared while the news sank in. Then he let his head drop as though the news was more than he could bear. When he looked up he had just one word. "Why?"

Matt worked the muscles in his jaw. "Her grandmother came looking for her. The judge decided—"

"No!" Tanner slammed his fist onto his desk, his voice filling the room. "Why is this happening to us?" He stood and stared outside, gripping the windowsill. His knuckles were white; his back trembled. "It isn't supposed to be like this. We're on God's team, you and me. We fight heaven's battles, and in return we're supposed to get a break, isn't that right?"

Matt let his gaze fall to the floor for a moment. The pain in his heart was crippling; there was no way he could respond.

Tanner exhaled and the noise filled the room. He spun around. "You know what's eating at me?" His voice was saturated in bitterness. "When was the last time He helped either one of us?"

Matt was conditioned to have the list on hand: his health, his marriage, his job, his home, the familiar accounting of God's numerous blessings. But all he could think about was Grace, her apple-cheeked smile, her twinkling eyes and curly hair. And the way it would decimate his family when she said good-bye. "I don't know what to say."

"Me neither." Tanner laced his hands behind his head, clenched his teeth and moaned. "I don't know how much we're supposed to take."

There was nothing Matt could do but agree. He closed his eyes. *Give me strength, God; get me through this.* As he prayed, an anchor appeared before his eyes. It came in the form of a Bible verse he'd memorized as a college senior. Without thinking, the words were on his lips. "'In this world you will have trouble…'" His tone was calm, belying the condition of his heart. "'But take heart! I have overcome the world.'"

"I know." Tanner's shoulders slumped and he leaned against his desk. "It's just…"

The heartache ripping through Matt was getting worse. He had to get home to Hannah, had to see if there was anything they could do to stop the madness that had come upon them. "I need to go."

Tanner drew a deep breath and crossed the room, hugging Matt with the crook of his arm the way he might hug a close brother. "Call me."

"I will."

Moving in a fog of fear and uncertainty, Matt grabbed his things and headed for the car. There was roadwork on Malibu Canyon and the ride home would likely take twice as long as normal. That was fine. Matt needed the time to think.

He stared at the brake lights in front of him and then gazed up.

A blue sky stretched from one mountain range to the other, and the sun overhead sent rays of light along the narrow canyon road. Warmth filled the car, numbing his fear, and Matt shifted his attention to the wheat-colored rolling hills in the distance.

As he did, he was drawn toward the tunnels of time.

It was the pain, of course. The pain reminded him of meeting Hannah for the first time, of looking into the eyes of a woman who had just lost her husband and child.

He remembered the first time he and Hannah met in court, before one of the hearings. He'd never seen so haunting a face before. Hannah was equal parts devastated, determined, and defiant. And more beautiful than any woman he'd ever seen.

With the Pacific Ocean just ahead, Matt gripped the steering wheel with both hands and remembered the depth of despair she had carried that first year of their friendship, the year he spent prosecuting Brian Wesley.

Everywhere she went back then, Hannah wore a pin with the photos of Tom and Alicia. As he worked the case, Matt often relived his own grief from years before, when his best friend in college was killed by a drunk driver. But over the months of working with Hannah, he came to realize no matter how strong his pain had been at losing his friend, it paled in comparison to losing a spouse.

Or a child.

"It's a kind of pain you can't know until you feel it yourself," Hannah had told him.

Memories of her voice faded as Matt reached Pacific Coast Highway. He was five minutes from home. Was it really happening? Would he walk inside and find Hannah crying? And what about Jenny? She'd already lost one sister, and that had just about done her in.

How would she handle losing Grace?

He remembered the night before when he sat on the edge of Grace's bed, holding her hand and reading her a nighttime story.

"Daddy?" She looked at him from a nest of soft blankets and lacy pillows and batted her eyelashes. "Will you always read me stories?"

Matt grinned at this little one who'd so captured his heart. "Forever and ever, Gracie."

"Even when I'm big?"

A lump formed in Matt's throat, a combination of gratefulness and sadness. Grateful because this precious child was his daughter, and sadness because one day she'd grow up and leave them. "Yes," he said when he found his voice. "Even when you're big."

The image disappeared as Matt pulled into the driveway and climbed out of the car. Now there would be no lifetime of storytelling, no growing up together, no little girl to call his own.

And in that moment, Matt knew Hannah was right. Losing a child created a kind of heartache that could only be understood through experience. Because the hurt that weighed on him now was greater than any Matt had ever felt.

He steadied himself before opening the front door. *Carry me, Lord...*

Be still and know that I am God...

The flash of words in his mind was so strong, Matt knew they'd come straight from heaven. Still, the pain remained. And Matt knew that whatever happened next, Hannah would show him the way through it. She knew what to do, how to act, how to grieve. How to survive this kind of loss.

After all, she had lost a child before.

Now it was his turn.

Fifteen

Grace's grandmother didn't look like a monster.

Quite the opposite, in fact. Sitting across from Hannah and Matt in the Bronzans' living room the next morning, Patsy Landers looked nothing short of genteel. She was petite, with fashionably cropped gray hair, compassionate eyes, and a pleasant smile. A strand of elegant pearls lay over her beige cashmere sweater, and despite her considerable limp, she had the polished mannerisms of a cultured woman.

But Hannah couldn't help think it all a clever disguise. After all, she was here for one reason only: to tear their family apart.

Of course the woman claimed to love Grace and want the best for her. But why take her from the only stable home she'd ever known? What kind of love was that? Hannah kept her feelings about Patsy to herself. There wasn't time for ill will toward the older woman. Not now, when they had less than an hour left with a child they had come to love as their own.

Hannah and Matt sat huddled on one sofa, Grace squeezed between them, Jenny close against Hannah's other side. Mrs. Parsons had given them their explanations and made it clear their legal options were reduced to none.

It was time to say good-bye.

Hannah wiped the tears from her cheeks and looked at the two older women sitting across from them. "Would you mind if we had a few minutes alone with Grace?"

The social worker gave a quick nod. "Take your time." She stood and motioned for Patsy Landers to follow. "We'll walk on the beach. Thirty minutes sound okay?"

Hannah nodded and hung her head.

Her life since Mrs. Parsons's phone call the day before seemed like something from a nightmare. Matt had gotten home just after one o'clock and spent the next two hours talking with various officials at Social Services.

He had started with Mrs. Parsons. The questions sounded like something from one of Matt's famous cross-examinations, and Hannah sat cross-legged nearby, staring at the floor, listening to Matt's end of the conversation.

"What if the woman isn't mentally sound?" Pause. "Have you checked her financial records?" Another pause. "Does she have the space to raise a child? The energy?"

When he had exhausted all avenues with Mrs. Parsons, Matt asked to speak to her superior. Again Hannah listened.

"I understand that, but the judge has already given her permanent placement in our house." Silence. "I realize that, but any psychologist would tell you that once a child has bonded to parental figures, it's more traumatic to separate that bond than it is to work within it." More silence. "Maybe you're not hearing me. I said we'd be happy to work out visitation rights with the child's grandmother…Yes, I know she lives in Oklahoma, but right now we're Grace's parents and that's how it should stay even if…"

Matt's efforts went on that way until Jenny and Grace spilled through the front door, giggling and grinning from their day together. Jenny saw Hannah sitting on the floor crying and Matt on the phone.

The smile faded from her face and her eyes grew wide.

Matt got off the phone and they all listened as Grace rattled on in a happy singsong voice about the lunch out with Jenny, the shopping, and the fun time they had playing at a local park.

Hannah had wiped her tears and smiled at Grace. "Sweetheart, why don't you go to your room for a little bit and play with your baby doll. Mommy has to talk to Jenny."

Grace was oblivious to the mood in the room and she skipped off, blowing Hannah and Matt a kiss on her way. Before she left, she ran up to Jenny and kissed her on the cheek. "Can I tell you something, Jenny?"

Jenny's voice was pinched, and Hannah had the feeling her daughter somehow knew what was about to happen. "Sure, sweetie. Anything."

"You're the best sister in the world." Grace smiled big at her and threw her arms around Jenny's neck. "I love you for always and always."

When Grace was out of earshot, Hannah stood and held open her arms. Jenny came to her, hugging her close while Matt stood beside them. "Honey, I'm so sorry to tell you this."

Hannah could feel the heavy thud of Jenny's heartbeat and a wave of nausea swept over her. The entire scene reminded her of that awful day in the hospital room when Jenny regained consciousness after the accident. The day Hannah had to tell Jenny that she'd lost both her father and her older sister. This was different, of course…but it was every bit as painful and just as final.

Jenny had pulled back, searching Hannah's face. "What happened?"

Normally Matt would have stepped up, put his hand on Jenny's shoulder—something that would come across as a show of support…but he was drowning in his own pain. He said nothing as Hannah tried to explain.

"Grace's grandmother has turned up. The judge says Grace has to live with her. In Oklahoma."

Jenny stepped back, her face knotted in angry confusion. "*What?* They can't do that! She belongs to *us.*"

Hannah took careful hold of Jenny's arm, bridging the distance between them. "She's here on the foster-adopt program."

Hannah's voice broke. "We all knew that."

Jenny backed out of Hannah's grip. "But Mrs. Parsons said there were no doubts! Nothing that would stop her from being ours. She said the foster-adopt thing was a technicality, remember?"

Neither Hannah nor Matt spoke.

Jenny struggled to keep from yelling. "Can't Matt do something about it? He's a lawyer; they'll listen to him."

"I tried." Matt took a step closer to Jenny. "Grace's grandma is fit enough to care for her. That's all the courts care about. The law is clear. If an existing relative is suitable for guardianship, then that relative gets the child. There are no gray areas, Jenny. I've tried everything."

Jenny leaned forward and spread her fingers across her chest. "How can God let this happen to us twice?" She hesitated and Hannah could see tears on Jenny's cheeks. *Twice?*

Hannah blinked back a lake of tears. "God brought her to us, Jenny. He'll get us through." It was true—Hannah knew it with every fiber of her heart—but in that moment the words sounded trite and pat.

Jenny's mouth hung open and Hannah wasn't sure if she was going to cry or scream. Instead she turned and ran to her bedroom.

Hannah started after her, but stopped near the stairs. "Jenny…"

The girl stopped and looked back at Hannah. "What?"

"Don't stay up there too long; Grace leaves tomorrow."

The evening had been an emotional roller coaster, one like Hannah had never experienced before. When Tom and Alicia died, none of them had seen it coming. There were no final meals or final bedtime talks or final goodnight kisses.

That wasn't the case this time, and as evening came, the finality was almost more than Hannah could bear. Hannah and Matt decided to wait until after dinner to tell Grace about her impending move to Oklahoma. And since Grace liked the beach better than any place at all, the three of them prepared a picnic dinner they could eat near the water. Before dinner Jenny joined them, and they filled the next two hours with as much joy and love and happiness as they possibly could.

They ate Grace's favorite meal—peanut butter sandwiches with raspberry jam, and chocolate chip cookies. Then they built a sandcastle on the shore and watched as the waves came closer and closer. A minute later they jumped back when a big wave came and washed the castle into the sea. Only Grace clapped with delight as it disappeared.

It was all Hannah could do not to break down right there. The castle seemed to represent everything about their time with Grace. All that they'd spent months building. When Grace was gone, there would be nothing more to show for their time together than a hole in their hearts where once stood a beautiful castle.

They held hands—all four of them—as they walked back home, and after Grace's bath they gathered in her room and told her the devastating news.

Hannah had agreed to do the talking. Matt and Jenny would stay close by, helping Grace know that this decision was not one they agreed with. That no matter what happened she would always be their little girl.

"Grace?" Hannah sat on the child's bed, her heart pounding in her throat. "We have something to tell you."

Grace was lying flat on her back and a quick smile came over her face. "You mean like a story?"

Hannah's eyes filled, blurring the image of Grace. "No, honey. Stories aren't real. The thing I have to tell you now is real."

"Okay, what?" Grace's fingers gripped the satin edge of her

blanket on either side of her chin. "Tell me."

A light-headed feeling came over Hannah and she begged God for strength. *And the right words, God…please. Something that will make the transition easier for Grace.* She managed to grab a mouthful of air, and decided to start with the good news.

"Grace, they found your grandma. She isn't dead; she's alive."

Grace scrunched up her face. "Mommy said she was dead."

Hannah cast a desperate glance at Matt and then turned her attention back to Grace. "Your mommy was wrong. Your grandma is alive and she's coming to see you tomorrow."

Grace sat straight up and stared at Hannah. "My grandma's coming tomorrow?"

"Yes." Hannah took hold of Grace's hand. "In the morning."

"From Oklahoma?"

Hannah had nodded, and her throat grew thick again. Grace was very bright for a four-year-old. She seemed to know more, retain more information than most children. Then again, Grace hadn't ever had a childhood.

At least not until she lived with them.

Hannah steadied herself. "There's something else." She paused. "Your grandma wants you to go back to Oklahoma. She wants you to live with her."

Grace's blonde eyebrows settled lower on her face. "You mean for a bacation?"

"No, honey…" Behind her, Hannah could hear the sound of Jenny stifling her tears, and Matt came alongside her, slipping his arm over her shoulder. She focused on Grace once more. "I mean forever. Your grandma wants you to be *her* little girl."

Tears flooded Grace's eyes. "In Oklahoma?"

"Yes, baby. You'll be moving to Oklahoma with her tomorrow."

"But…" The tears spilled onto her velvet-soft cheeks. "But will you come with me?"

The child's words sliced Hannah's heart to ribbons. She had thought nothing could be more painful than Mrs. Parsons's call earlier that day. She was wrong.

Will you come with me…?

Hannah bit her lower lip and found the strength to speak.

"We can't, honey. Our house is here. Your house will be in Oklahoma." Hannah imagined how her answer must have sounded to Grace and she cringed. "Your grandma wants you all to herself." Tears were tumbling down Grace's cheeks, and Hannah cocked her head, desperate to ease the child's sadness. "You love your grandma, right?"

"Yes." Grace's chin quivered, and two soft sobs came from her throat. "But you're my mommy and daddy and Jenny." She looked around. "This is my room. And if my room is here then this is where I live. I wanna stay, Mommy. *Please…*"

They were all crying now, tears coursing down Hannah's, Matt's, and Jenny's faces alike. Hannah pulled Grace close and smoothed her hand over the child's silky hair, hair that was so like Alicia's at that age. Jenny crawled under the covers on the other side of Grace and Matt knelt up against the bed. They formed a group hug, each of them crying in soft whispers, desperately hanging on to the moment.

Hannah could almost feel herself pushing against the hands of time, begging God for more hours, days. Whatever He might give them. As though by staying there at her side they might somehow avoid the good-bye ahead.

But long after Grace had cried herself to sleep, time marched on, and that morning when the doorbell rang, her two large suitcases were packed and ready to go.

Hannah had imagined Patsy Landers to be an older version of Grace's mother, hard and mean, tarnished from years of drug abuse. The real Patsy couldn't have been more different.

Mrs. Parsons made the introductions. Jenny had taken Grace outside until the given signal, allowing the adults to discuss the matter away from her at first.

When they were seated, Patsy turned to Hannah and spoke in a voice that trembled with emotion. "You have no idea how sorry I am about this." She turned to Matt. "I had no idea Grace had been placed in foster care. I'm afraid…" Her gaze fell to her lap for a moment. "I'm afraid my daughter told her I was dead."

The entire story spilled out, and by the time it was finished, Hannah knew that despite her limp, the woman was obviously capable of caring for Grace. Clearly she had wanted custody of the child long before this, but time and again had been refused by her daughter. What's more, it seemed the woman was a believer, just as Grace had told them from the beginning. Hannah and Matt need not worry; this woman would keep Grace grounded in her faith.

But the most obvious truth was this: Patsy Landers loved Grace with all her heart. And so there was no doubt in Hannah's mind that the child's move to Oklahoma was not only final, it was the right thing. Maybe not now, maybe not in the short term, while Grace was bound to miss them. But in the bigger picture. Grace would not know the love of parents the way she would have if she'd been allowed to stay, but she would have a woman who had known her all her life and loved her since birth. A woman who, like all of them, had been a victim of Leslie Landers's drug addiction.

When their discussion was over, Patsy thanked Hannah and Matt and promised to pray that God would bring another child into their lives soon. Jenny led Grace into the room after that, and now here they were. After months of learning to love a little girl they'd never known before, months of breaking through her silence and isolation and hurt, months of caring for her as though they'd have forever together, it was time to say good-bye.

Patsy and Edna left through the back of the house and closed the door behind them. Hannah summoned all her strength to lift her head and kiss Grace on the forehead. "Your grandma is a very nice lady, Grace."

Jenny bit her lip, and Hannah knew she was trying to stop the tears that flowed from the corners of her eyes. Matt was utterly still, his chin resting on Grace's head. Grace realized the finality of the moment and she, too, started to cry. "Come with me, Mommy, please…" Grace looked up and pressed her cheek against Hannah's. "I don't want to live in Oklahoma."

"But you love your grandma, Grace." Hannah squeezed her eyes shut, wanting more than anything to tell the child she could stay. "This is the best plan for you now. Everyone thinks so."

"But I love *you*. You're…you're…" Hannah opened her eyes. Grace's sobs were becoming too great for her to speak. She struggled for a long moment while Hannah and Matt stroked her back. "You're my…*family*."

Jenny moved off the sofa and fell to her knees in front of Grace. "We'll always be your family, honey. Always. Anytime you think of us, we'll be right there."

Mrs. Parsons had advised that in situations where foster-adopt placements were disrupted, it was best not to maintain contact between the child and the foster parents. "Too much pain for everyone involved," the social worker explained. "Complete severance will give Grace the best chance for a healthy adjustment."

Now Hannah wanted nothing more than to add to what Jenny was saying, to promise letters and pictures and phone calls. But she held her tongue, knowing that somehow Mrs. Parsons was right.

Matt cleared his throat and tightened his grip on Grace's slim shoulders. "In my heart, Grace, you'll always be my little girl." Hannah glanced at him through her tears and saw that he was silently weeping, crying as she'd never seen him cry before. He swallowed hard. "Will you remember that?"

Grace clung to Matt and nodded her head against his chest. "Yes, Daddy. I'll remember for always."

Matt pulled a delicate golden locket from his pocket and Hannah blinked so she could see. She had wondered when Matt was going to give Grace the present they picked out for her. "Here." Matt opened the clasp and fitted it gently around Grace's neck. He opened the locket and exposed a small picture of the four of them—Matt, Hannah, Jenny, and Grace. Matt cleared his throat. "This is for you. So you don't forget."

Grace's eyes grew wide and she stared at the picture. "Oh, thank you Daddy. I never had a necklace of my very own." She looked at Hannah and Jenny. "I'll wear it every day forever and ever."

Their thirty minutes passed in a blur, and the women returned. Mrs. Parsons cast a sad, questioning look at Hannah. "Ready?"

Ready? Hannah almost laughed out loud. How would they ever be ready to tell Grace good-bye? To watch her walk out of their home and their hearts forever? Hannah shook her head and shrugged. "I guess."

Mrs. Parsons explained that she would carry Grace's bags to the car and then they'd need to leave. Grace and her grandmother had a flight to catch. Once she was gone with the suitcases, the rest of them followed and stood near the car. Matt swept Grace onto his hip and wiggled his nose against hers. "Don't forget us, okay?"

Grace tilted her face so her eyebrows met up with Matt's. "Okay."

Matt handed her to Hannah then, and though she tried to be

strong, a sob sounded from her throat. "Oh, Gracie, I love you, honey. I love you."

While she was in Hannah's arms, Jenny snuggled her face against Grace's and kissed her cheek. The words she whispered were for Grace's ears alone, but Hannah heard them. "I never had a little sister before. And you'll always be mine."

Huge tears swam in Grace's eyes again and she whispered in a choked voice, "Me, too."

Finally, Patsy came forward. "Thank you." She put her arms around the group of them. "I'll always be grateful for everything you've done for Grace. And like I said, I'll pray that God fills your home quickly."

Hannah and Matt and Jenny clung to each other as Patsy took Grace and walked her to the car where Mrs. Parsons was waiting. They said one last good-bye while Grace sobbed, begging them to come. The three of them stood there, linked together long after the car had driven out of sight.

The pain was crippling, and Hannah could tell from the steady flow of tears that it was the same for Matt and Jenny. For a long while none of them spoke; then in a voice quiet and strong, despite his wet face and the depth of sadness in his eyes, Matt began to sing.

"Jesus loves me! This I know, for the Bible tells me so...."

Hannah closed her eyes and let the words wash over her. Grace's favorite song...the one Hannah had taught her on their walks along the beach. The one Matt had hummed along with her when they cuddled at night.

Despite the vast desert of hurt in her heart, Hannah couldn't help but feel comforted by the very real presence of God; she felt it hovering over them as they stood together there in the driveway. And before Hannah could find the strength to sing, the Lord gave her one more reason to believe they'd survive.

Jenny was singing, too.

Her voice joined Matt's as the quiet song built among them. When they reached the part about God being strong even when children were small and weak, Hannah's throat grew thick. It was true, and Hannah pulled in tighter to the two people she loved most in life. If it was true when times were good, when life was easy and unfettered, it was true now when the darkness seemed blacker than night. Hannah opened her mouth and somehow, despite the emotions lodged in her throat, the words began to flow, the sound of her voice mixing with the others.

Yes, Jesus loved them. He loved them and He loved Grace. If the Bible told them anything, it told them that. Hannah could feel herself growing stronger as the song continued. "Yes, Jesus loves me… Yes, Jesus loves me… Yes, Jesus loves me…the Bible tells me so."

When they were finished singing, Matt prayed. "Lord, only You could fathom the ache in our hearts this morning, the greatness of loss over saying good-bye…" His voice cracked and again they pulled closer to each other. "Saying good-bye to Grace. But Lord, give us open hearts and open minds. Though we cannot imagine a different little girl in our lives, if there be one out there who needs us, bring her our way. Please, Lord." He hesitated then, and Hannah knew he was trying to compose himself. "And please take good care of our little Gracie."

It wasn't until they were back in the house that Jenny turned to them, her eyes intent, serious. "I know what Grace's grandmother meant, and I understand your prayer, Matt." She looked at Hannah. "But I want you to know something. You can bring another little girl into this house and raise her. But that's the last time I let myself fall in love with a sister." Fresh tears fell from her eyes. "Losing one sister was hard enough. Now…" She shook her head. "I'm sorry, I…I won't do it again. Not unless God answers my questions."

Hannah and Matt watched her go; then they came together, embracing each other like two children who'd long since lost their way and had no idea where to turn next.

Though the song they'd sung minutes earlier still rang in Hannah's heart, though she knew God's promises were true and that somehow they'd survive, she couldn't help but ask herself the same question that had to be troubling Jenny.

Why, after all they'd been through, had God let such loss happen again?

Sixteen

Tanner was gone. Again.

He would have a good excuse. He always did. Over the past few weeks he'd given her dozens of excuses, but the bottom line Jade knew was this: If she was dying of cancer, he didn't want to be around to see it happen. The whole thing was too much for him; the wasting away of her energy and health and even her life was too difficult to watch. And so he had tuned out in every way that mattered.

Emotionally, spiritually, and most of all physically.

He hadn't meant to hurt her; Jade believed that with all her heart. But it hurt all the same, there was no denying the fact. His absence had pockmarked Jade's heart with a loneliness and sorrow she hadn't imagined possible.

After taking the trip to Colorado, Tanner had made a brief effort to spend more time with her. But now Jade hardly ever saw him. She was lonely and afraid and she ached for him whenever she was awake. She missed him more than at any other time in her life, even the years when they'd been apart.

His absence was putting a distance between them that scared her and left her with no one to talk to, no place to vent her fears. During their few minutes together, Jade refused to share her true feelings with him. If fear was what kept him away, she was determined not to give him more reason to be gone.

Especially now, when she needed him so badly.

Because the truth, regardless of what she wanted to tell Tanner, was obvious: The medication was changing her.

She began to notice the changes two days after the second seizure, when Dr. Layton increased her dosage and assigned her Helen, a full-time home nurse.

Jade was more tired than she imagined possible, and no amount of sleep made her feel better. Though her brain might intend to spew out three quick sentences, her mouth would only respond with one. One very slow, very deliberate string of words that sounded monotone and robotic, even to Jade. About the same time walking became difficult. Every step required thought and planning, and so her pace was half her usual quick-footed gait.

Then there was her lack of balance. The medication—or the tumor itself—was affecting her equilibrium. There were times, even when she otherwise felt good, when the room seemed to slant so drastically she would fall to her knees if not for the help of someone at her side—usually Helen or Ty, since Tanner never seemed to be home until after she was in bed.

At first it was easy to pass the symptoms off as coincidence, signs that she needed more rest. But after two days of sleeping practically around the clock, Jade could no longer lie to herself.

These thoughts simmered in Jade's mind while she lay stretched out on the sofa in their den. The den was just off the kitchen and for the past two weeks, since Helen had come to live with them, it was the place where Jade spent most of her time.

She reached for the water bottle on the end table and took a long, slow sip. Her Bible was on the floor beside her, but Jade couldn't remember why. Had she read it? Was she intending to read it? The water slid down her throat, soothing the parched feeling that was almost constant these days.

The sun was making its way toward the western ridge of mountains behind their house, so it had to be afternoon. But was it Tuesday? Wednesday? And where was Ty? She lifted her wrist, struggling to steady her hand in front of her. The numbers on her watch came into focus. Three-thirty. Ty would be home in ten minutes unless he had practice or a game. Jade had no idea what his schedule was. For that matter she had no idea about Tanner's schedule, either.

Helen took care of everything now. The woman was kind and orderly, a believer in her late fifties with no family. She was conscientious about her work and took little time for small talk.

Jade wondered how the woman was with Ty. When she took him to his baseball games, did she cheer for him? Ask him how he made a tough catch?

Tears poked pins at Jade's eyes. Before getting sick, she had never missed her son's games. *Help him understand, God…help me get better so I can be there for him.*

The baby shifted position, and Jade's eyes fell to her swollen abdomen. *Hold on, baby girl. You can make it. Just a few more weeks.*

The number became a giant in her mind, stomping out every other thought she'd been thinking. Three weeks? She had to exist this way, like a rotting vegetable, for three more weeks? The idea seemed as impossible as scaling Mount Everest.

Jade's eyelids grew heavier. If there was a silver lining in the fog of medication within which she existed, it was this: She had no trouble sleeping. When she couldn't remember what day it was or where Ty was supposed to be or whether he had a game or what time Tanner was supposed to be home, she could close her eyes and let all of life slip away.

She drew a slow, steady breath and smoothed her hand over her abdomen. The road ahead was long and dark, wrought with terrible possibilities. What if the tumor grew again before the baby was born? What if it killed her? Would the doctors find a way to save their tiny daughter or would she die, too? And what if they both survived until October 7, the date doctors had set for her C-section?

Instead of relishing the birth of her daughter, she would be faced with two weeks of intense chemotherapy and radiation. And after that there would be surgery—an operation that carried with it dire risks in the best of circumstances.

A sad, shaky sigh leaked from Jade's throat and two tears trickled down her cheeks. *How will I survive, God? I need Tanner...*

Do not be afraid...

The words echoed in her heart, and Jade wondered if she was imagining them. It was terrifying to live with a brain that no longer responded the way she expected. *God? Can you hear me? I'm scared.*

Do not be afraid, daughter...I am with you.

A subtle reassurance settled over Jade, and she knew the still small voice in her soul was nothing less than God's own comfort. She closed her eyes, grateful that He still had His hand on her, still loved her and stayed by her even though she was sick.

Especially because she was sick.

Am I dying, Lord? Are You taking me away from Tanner? Away from Ty and our baby girl?

In response, Jade remembered the verse that had been on her heart constantly the summer she and Tanner found each other again. The words soothed her soul and she played them over in her mind again and again.

"I know the plans I have for you...plans to give you a hope and a future and not to harm you..."

A door slammed in the distance and Jade's eyes opened. "Ty?"

"Hey, Mom."

She heard him trudge inside, toss his backpack in the corner, and fling his baseball cap on the nearby chair. His footsteps grew closer, then his warm face was up against hers, kissing her cheek and stroking her hair.

"Hi." He sat back on his heels. "You look tired."

Jade managed a grin. "Thanks, buddy." .

"Sorry." Ty must have caught her hint of sarcasm. "I didn't mean it like that. You look great, really."

She messed her fingers through his wheat-colored hair. Tanner's hair. "That's okay; I know what you mean. I *am* tired. Too tired lately."

"You're not worse, are you?" Concern flashed in Ty's expression.

"No." Jade reached for his hand. "I'm fine."

"Do you need anything? A cookie or juice or something?"

"No, champ, that's okay." Jade struggled to sit up and swing her legs over the side of the sofa. "Let's get a snack together. We can eat out on the patio."

Helen walked past and stopped at the sight of Jade working herself up onto her feet. "I can get the chair…"

The chair. Jade appreciated the way Helen didn't call it a wheelchair, but that's what it was. A wheelchair in case she wanted to get out or be pushed around the block. Dr. Layton had said she would only need it until the baby was born. Between now and then, too much walking could stimulate tumor growth and more seizures.

"No, thanks." Jade smiled at the older woman. "I'm not going far." She held her elbow out toward Ty, and he took it in a way he'd long since perfected.

When he wasn't at school or busy with sports, Ty was constantly at Jade's side, checking on her needs and offering to help her walk from one spot to another when she felt unsteady. This was one of those times.

Arm in arm, she and Ty moved into the kitchen. Jade sat on a stool while Ty put together a tray of apples, crackers, and cheese. He carried the tray outside, placed it on the patio table, and poured two glasses of orange juice. When the snack was set up, he led Jade across the kitchen and through the back door.

"Sort of a preview, huh, Ty?" Jade's head was spinning and the room tilted. She clung to her son's arm, determined to make the walk without falling. She managed a chuckle. "What life'll be like when your mom's an old lady, right?"

"Nah." Ty led her to a patio chair and helped her sit. "You'll never be old."

Once they were situated, Ty filled a small plate for each of them. Jade reached for an apple slice and took a bite.

"Mom…" Ty wrinkled his brow. "Aren't we going to pray?"

"Oh, sorry." Jade set the apple down. "Go ahead."

Ty bowed and paused a moment before starting. "Dear Lord, thank You for this snack, thank You that Mom feels good enough to eat it with me, thank You that she's not getting worse. And please God, make her better soon." He opened his eyes and grinned. "Now we can eat. I'm starved."

Jade's heart swelled. Ty had always been that way. Even when he was a small boy, he would catch Jade starting a meal before praying. It didn't matter if it was Sunday dinner or a midday snack, her son's dependence on God was as natural as breathing.

"You won't believe it." Ty grabbed three crackers from his plate and shoved them into his mouth. "Guess who quit the baseball team?"

Jade pulled one foot up onto the chair and rested her chin on her knee, pretending to think hard on the question. "Carl the Mugster?"

"No…" Ty made a face and chomped on an apple slice. "The Mugster wouldn't quit. He might be having a bad year, but still." Ty's eyes grew wide. "Really, Mom, guess who quit? You won't believe it!"

The apple tasted like metal and Jade ran the napkin over her mouth, spitting the pulp into the paper and wadding it up in her hands so Ty wouldn't know. "I give up; tell me."

"Okay. It's a long story, but it started last week after we lost to the Reds, remember?"

Jade nodded, doing her best to keep a serious face.

"Well…after the game the other team's pitcher came over to our dugout and…"

The rays of sunshine warmed Jade's shoulders, and listening to Ty and his stories made her dizziness less severe. She couldn't bring herself to eat, but that was okay. Helen was bringing her protein drinks three times a day, so even if food didn't look good, at least she and the baby were getting the nutrients they needed.

The smell of jasmine, rich and sweet, filtered up from the landscaped grounds, and a light breeze stirred up a handful of puffy clouds against the deep blue sky.

Jade breathed it in. She loved this time of the year, the way the heat eased up and the Santa Ana winds cleared away the smog. Would she be alive next year at this time? Or was this her last Southern California fall?

"Mom, are you listening?"

At the frustration in Ty's voice, Jade was pierced with guilt. "You were telling me who quit the team, right?"

Ty huffed and fell back against his chair. "I finished that story. Now I'm telling you why Miss McMacken doesn't like my math work."

Jade shook off thoughts of everything but her son. "I'm sorry. Tell me again."

"Okay." He smiled his forgiveness. "But listen this time."

He was just about to move on to another topic when Helen poked her head out the doorway and held up the cordless phone. "Mr. Eastman, for you."

A current of electricity ran through her heart, the same as it always did whenever she heard Tanner's name. Even now there were times when her life felt like a dream, when she feared she might wake and find Tanner was nothing more than the stranger he'd been for ten years after Ty was conceived.

She reached for the phone. "Thank you, Helen."

"Tell him I got an *A* on my history quiz." Ty helped himself to another handful of crackers. "But don't talk long. My game's in an hour."

Jade nodded and held the receiver to her ear. "Hello?"

"Hey…" Tanner sounded close enough to be next to her. "How're you feeling?"

"Fine." Disappointment blew through the hallways of her heart. If only he'd start the conversation some other way. *Jade, I love you*…or *Jade, I miss you*. The dizziness was back, and she closed her eyes. "How 'bout you?"

He sighed. "Busy."

Jade could almost see him, elbow planted on his desk while he sorted through a file. "Looks like it'll be another late one."

Her eyes welled up, and for a moment her throat was too thick to speak.

"Are you there?"

"Yes." She coughed. "Ty wants me to tell you he aced his history quiz. And he has a game in an hour."

"Good." Tanner's answer was quick. "Tell him I'm proud of him and I wish I could be there. Maybe next time."

Jade wanted to scream. What was so important that he couldn't come home at a decent hour? And why weren't Ty's games a priority any more? Tanner ran the office; he could take the time if he wanted to. But she had neither the energy nor the desire to fight with Tanner now.

Instead she brushed the sleeve of her sweatshirt beneath both eyes so Ty wouldn't see her tears. "Fine."

"Fine?" Tanner sounded irritated. "What's *that* supposed to mean?"

"Never mind."

"That isn't fair. Don't tell me you're mad again. Look, Jade, the cases I'm working are demanding, okay? Maybe it isn't good timing, but what can I do? The office needs me."

She shifted her gaze to the passing clouds, her voice quiet, sad. "We need you, too."

"This isn't the time." Tanner exhaled hard. "We'll talk later. I love you, Jade."

"Okay." Jade pulled the phone from the side of her face and ended the call. *Okay?* Jade had always been quick to confirm Tanner's declarations of love with one of her own. But this time the words simply wouldn't come.

Ty finished his story and brushed the crumbs from his hands. If he noticed the fact that the phone call had upset Jade, he didn't say. Instead, he kissed the top of her head and darted toward the door. "Gotta get dressed. Helen's taking me to the game." He paused before going inside. "I'll hit a home run for you, Mom. That'll make you feel better."

She gave him a thumbs-up, touched by his tender heart. "Can't wait to hear about it."

Jade stayed outside, staring at the hills behind their house. If she focused hard on one thing—a tree trunk or a cloud—her sense of balance seemed almost normal. She stayed that way for a long while, refusing to think of anything but the beauty around her. Eventually she heard the front door open and minutes later the sound of the car pulling away.

Certain that she was alone, Jade let her mind drift back to the conversation with Tanner. It was wrong for him to spend so much time at work. Couldn't he see how badly she wanted him home? Did he think a nurse could replace having him at her side?

Betrayal and anger rocked her soul. There were no answers, at least none she cared to think about. Jade pushed her plate back and stared at her wedding ring. An ocean of tears spilled from her heart and down her face.

She missed Tanner so much she could barely stand it.

What if she died? Tonight even? Was this how she and Tanner would spend their last days, distant and frustrated and rarely together?

"God…" Sobs tore at her, and the sound carried on the breeze. "I'm so scared and alone. I need him. Why doesn't he want to be home? What have I done to push him away?"

Since her diagnosis, life had become a nightmare of second-guessing and doubts.

Sweet Hannah, her dependable friend, had begged Jade not to blame herself for what was happening, but it was impossible not to. If only she hadn't called Tanner three years ago when she needed legal help. If only she'd been a quiet wife for Jim, maybe he never would have left her.

Maybe then she wouldn't be sick.

Jade leaned her head back and lowered her eyebrows. What was she thinking? God wasn't using her cancer to punish her for what happened with Jim. Besides, Jim had tried to take Ty away from her! She'd had no choice but to call Tanner. Ty was his son, after all. And Jim would still have divorced her whether she'd called Tanner or not.

And if she hadn't called, Jim would have taken Ty with him.

Still…

The pendulum of her emotions swung back the other way. Enough people had pointed a finger at Jade since her divorce that sometimes she wondered. Was God angry at her for marrying Tanner? Certainly there were reasons for the hard times they were facing, but was her cancer His way of punishing her? At least in part?

The idea flew in the face of everything she knew about the Lord.

Jade had studied Scripture on the matter and realized there were two schools of thought. The first read that anyone who divorced, except for reasons of marital unfaithfulness, and then married another was guilty of adultery. The second group tended to look past the exception and see only the last part of the verse. Marriage after divorce was adultery, pure and simple.

Most of the time Jade sided with the first group. The idea that God would be merciful to a person whose spouse had chosen to take up with another seemed more like God than the second viewpoint.

But sometimes… Jade wondered. What other reason was there for the trial they were suffering if God wasn't angry with her? With both of them? Her sobs returned with a vengeance.

She didn't know how long she stayed there, silently begging God to forgive her, but after a while, the back door opened and Helen appeared. "Ty's going home with his friend. He'll be spending the night there if that's okay."

"It's fine." Jade hung her head. "Thanks."

Jade couldn't take another evening inside waiting for Tanner's return, trying to stay awake long enough to exchange a few shallow sentences. Her head hurt worse than it had in weeks and she couldn't keep her fingers from trembling. Maybe death was right around the corner; maybe the Lord would come for her tonight.

Her tears came harder. "Helen, I need…to get out of here." She turned so she could see the older woman, and the effort was exhausting.

"Well, I don't know…" Helen was at her side, concern etched between the wrinkles on her forehead. "Maybe you should sleep first."

"No!" The tears made it almost impossible to talk. Jade held her breath and shook her head. *Calm down*, she ordered herself, but her heart raced in response. If this was her last night alive, there was no way she would spend it sleeping. When she could speak, she looked at Helen. "I have someplace to go. I'll need my chair."

Helen helped her into the house and, with a shaky hand, she scribbled a note for Tanner.

I can't take it anymore, Tanner…I'll be out late. Don't wait up. I love you more than you know.

Jade

She studied it through a fresh layer of tears. So what if Tanner didn't know where she was? He hadn't been home enough to notice how bad she'd gotten; hadn't spent time with her and Ty the way he might have. Jade hesitated.

It was fear; it had to be.

Tanner cared, of course—he loved her more than his own life—but whatever had come over him since her last seizure, his absence was more than Jade could stand. Especially now, with death breathing down her neck. All of life had become a race for survival. A race in which she was losing Tanner.

Whether she lived or died, she was losing him.

There were a dozen things Jade was desperate to bring before the Lord—her health, her baby's chances of survival. Her life. But before she left that night, Jade uttered the only plea that really mattered.

God, bring Tanner back to me. Please. Before it's too late.

Seventeen

There was no point trying to concentrate.

Tanner planted his elbows in the open file on his desk and pressed his fingers against his tired, aching eyes. How could he work, when all he could think about was Jade, the hurt in her voice as they'd talked…?

He gave a hoarse laugh. Talked? Who was he kidding? They hadn't talked in days, not really.

His late hours were frustrating her; that much was clear. But what was he supposed to do? The case needed him. Desperately. Every hour at work meant a greater chance for success at the trial. Victory wouldn't come unless he stayed devoted.

Right?

Tanner tapped his pencil on his desk as a dagger of guilt sliced through his heart. The arguments he had created to justify his time away from Jade suddenly collapsed like a house of cards. He covered his face with his hands and tried to settle his nerves. *What is it, God? What's wrong with me? My wife's home dying, and I'm here at work.*

He peered through the spaces in his fingers, and his gaze settled on a plaque near the edge of his desk. Jade had given it to him on the one-year anniversary of his helping her win back custody of Ty. A Scripture that was one of their favorites was carved in the middle…

Be still and know that I am God.

The words played again and again in Tanner's mind, but they seemed to have no relevance to any of the troubles burying him at the moment. He let his hands fall to the desk and stared at the outline for what could be his biggest case yet.

Tanner's research had been exhaustive. He had reams of information he could hardly wait to share with a jury. He imagined their reaction when he revealed his favorite little-known facts. He glanced at his notes. For instance, separation of church and state, the idea most people attributed to the Constitution, was actually not in the Constitution at all.

The First Amendment said only this: "Congress shall make no law respecting an establishment of religion, or prohibiting the free exercise thereof."

His eyes moved down the page.

The idea of separation of church and state came from a letter Thomas Jefferson wrote to a group of Baptists, assuring them that no act of government would infringe on their right to believe. Why? According to Jefferson's letter, because that clause in the Constitution provided a wall separating church and state.

A wall that separated the *church* from the *state,* not the state from the church. The state was the power that threatened the church, not the other way around as was so often interpreted today.

Every case Tanner and Matt had ever fought had somehow been birthed out of that single letter from Jefferson, but never had Tanner turned the tables and used the same argument in favor of a client.

Until now.

His approach would surprise not only the attorneys representing the city of Benson, but in time it would surprise the entire nation. The case could be that big. The reason it was taking so much time, though, was that while Tanner's premise was simple, proving it would be something entirely different.

But if Tanner thought building a precedent-setting case

against a hostile city council was difficult, it was nothing compared to the effort of concentrating on work while Jade was wasting away at home.

He clenched his teeth and turned his chair toward the window. The sun was setting, leaving a trail of pinks and oranges that was characteristic of the Southern California evening sky. Who was he trying to fool? He should be home with Jade, caring for her, waiting on her, loving her.

But watching her waste away was more than he could bear. Even if he couldn't think straight, he was better off at the office, doing his best to push the hands of time to a place where the nightmare they were living might be over.

Besides, Jade didn't miss him. She slept most of the time and when she was awake…

Tanner's eyes burned with the onset of tears. When she was awake, she could hardly carry on a conversation. The medication had affected her that much. Snapshots from the past few weeks flashed in the photo album of his mind. Jade trying to climb out of bed and falling to her knees; Jade picking at a plateful of food, unable to eat.

But worst of all were their conversations. Moments like the one that had taken place the night before. He'd come home late again and found Ty and Helen watching *I Love Lucy* reruns. He kissed Ty and asked about his baseball practice. After a few minutes he looked around. "Is Jade in bed?"

"She wanted to stay awake until you got home." Helen cast him a disapproving look. "But she was too tired."

Tanner ignored the unspoken accusations. "Oh." He looked at Ty. "I'll be back in a minute."

Upstairs he found Jade asleep, propped against a stack of pillows. He took quiet steps toward her and sat on the edge of their bed. "Jade…"

She moaned and moved her head an inch in either direction.

Tanner angled his head, his heart breaking at the sight of her, weak and frighteningly thin despite her pregnant belly. "Jade, I love you."

"Hmmm." She blinked several times, squinting at the light and then recognizing Tanner. "Oh…hi. You're home."

Her words were slow, measured. Tanner steadied himself. "How're you feeling?"

She raised one shoulder, and her eyes struggled to stay open. "Okay. The same."

They looked at each other for a moment, and Tanner searched for the words that might help. There was only one thing that really mattered—whether Jade was feeling worse, experiencing new symptoms. But clearly she didn't want to discuss herself.

He spread his palm out on the bedspread and leaned back. "I'm using the separation of church and state ruling in the case against Benson."

For a moment, Jade's eyes were blank. Then gradually they narrowed as though she were concentrating on something intensely serious. "Sepa…sepra…seprish…" She clenched her fists and uttered a frustrated groan. "Help me say it, Tanner!"

"Hey—" he sat straight up, his stomach churning—"Take it easy. You're tired, that's all." What was wrong with her? Was the medication taking her ability to talk, or was the tumor growing into the part of her brain that controlled speech? Her words were not only slow they were slurred, so either option was equally possible.

And equally terrifying.

He swallowed. "I said I'm using the separation of church and state ruling in the case against Benson."

Jade bit her lip and tried again. "Separsh…sepa…"

That was all. She hung her head, and tears fell on the bedspread. "I can't…say it. The letters get all mixed up."

There was nothing he could do, nothing at all. So he turned off the light, stroked her forehead, and waited until she fell asleep before joining Ty and Helen downstairs.

The memory cleared and he looked once more at the plaque on his desk.

Be still, and know that I am God.

He had no doubt about the last part. God existed as surely as the sun and moon. Tanner might not understand what God was doing in their lives, why after so many years apart Jade had to get sick, but his faith remained.

No it wasn't the belief-in-God part of the plaque that troubled Tanner. It was the being still part. How could he be still? The pain of watching Jade fade away was never more intense than when he stopped moving, stopped thinking about work or Ty or the problems other people faced. People like Matt and Hannah.

He read the verse again…and was struck by a thought. He *had* to keep working. Only by staying busy would the days pass and lead him to the place where their baby girl was home and Jade was healthy. But staying busy was also keeping him from Jade…from the woman he loved with all his heart, the woman who needed him.

Tanner stared at the Benson file and slowly closed it. His head ached and his heart hurt. Even if Jade was sleeping, even if the medication was sapping the life from her, he needed to be home. Maybe that's why the plaque on his desk had shouted at him for the past hour. Maybe God wanted him home with Jade, even if seeing her slow and sick and tired was the hardest thing in his life.

He drew a steadying breath and exhaled through clenched teeth. "Okay, God, I'll go."

Thirty-five minutes later, Tanner walked through the front door and stopped short. The lights were off. It looked like even Helen wasn't home. "Hello?" His voice echoed through the foyer, but otherwise the silence remained.

Typically Helen would have cooked something for dinner, but there was only the faint smell of vanilla, Jade's favorite fragrance, mostly likely left over from a candle she'd burned that morning. "Jade? Ty?"

When there was no response, Tanner's heart skipped a beat and he rushed into the kitchen, flipping on a light switch. There on the island countertop was a note. Tanner pictured Jade seizing again, falling to the floor…Helen calling an ambulance. What if this time it was worse than before? What if…?

He reached for the slip of paper, his voice quiet and unsteady. "No, Jade…not again…"

His eyes raced over the page.

I can't take it anymore, Tanner…I'll be out late. Don't wait up. I love you more than you know.

Jade

At the bottom, in Helen's handwriting, were a few sentences that must have been written to keep Tanner from worrying: *Ty's spending the night at a friend's house. Jade and I are at church.*

Tanner read the note three more times, grabbed his car keys, and headed back outside. As he drove to church, he realized that everything he'd gone through in his life before this—the hurt of losing Jade as a boy and again as a young man, the ache of knowing that he had missed out on raising Ty all those years, even the devastation of Jade's illness—all of it paled in comparison to this pain, this terrible ache that never went away.

Because always before the hurt was someone else's fault. Never had either of them acted willfully against the other. But now, as the words of her note took root in his soul, he knew that only one person was responsible for making Jade feel lonely and let-down in her greatest hour of need.

That person was him.

〜◦〜

Pastor Steve was still in his office when Jade and Helen entered the sanctuary. The man—a kind preacher in his forties—heard them enter, and when he saw Jade in her wheelchair he came to her. Both the Bronzans and the Eastmans attended Los Robles Community Church and took turns doing the puppets for children at second service. All of them considered Pastor Steve and his wife friends.

Jade raised her hand in the pastor's direction. She hated the fact that she was crying, and that being pushed down the center aisle in a wheelchair was obvious proof she was not doing well. She wiped at her tears and nodded to the man. "Hi, Pastor."

"Jade…" He put his hand on her shoulder. "What's wrong, dear?"

There were so many things to say, so many questions to ask, that Jade didn't know where to begin. But the relief of knowing someone was willing to listen brought on another wave of tears. "I…I'm sorry." Her voice cracked. "I need to talk."

Pastor Steve glanced at Helen. "I have time. Would you like me to take her home?"

"Yes." Jade nodded before Helen could answer. "Why don't I do that, Helen? That way Tanner won't worry. Besides—" she looked back at Pastor Steve—"I might be here awhile."

"That's fine. This is my late night. Normally I have counseling appointments but no one showed up." He gave her a smile. "I'll be happy to drive you home."

Helen left, and once they were alone, he took a seat on the edge of one of the pews and faced Jade. "I see a dozen emotions on your face, as clearly as if they were written there."

Jade's gaze fell, and she tightened her grip on the arms of the wheelchair. "At least a dozen."

"Like I said, I have time." The man's voice was patient and

filled with kindness. "Why don't you start by telling me why you're here?"

The memories that had troubled her for so long came to mind again, and Jade leaned back in her chair. She looked at Pastor Steve's face and saw nothing but understanding. Then, with only a few tears here and there, she told him everything. She talked about finding Tanner that summer in Kelso and getting pregnant the day before he left for a six-week mission trip. And she explained the mistake she made in marrying Jim Rudolph, and every sad milestone from that point until their divorce. She told him how, after marrying Tanner, some people condemned her for committing adultery.

"And now I have to wonder..." Jade's heart beat stronger than before. Though she was still weak, telling the story to Pastor Steve infused her with a strength she'd been missing for days.

The pastor leaned forward a bit. "About what?"

Jade crossed her arms in front of her and gripped her elbows. "About whether God is using cancer to punish me. You know, for committing adultery."

"Oh, Jade, no..." Pastor Steve shook his head. "You can't think that."

"But...why else would God allow this?"

The pastor leaned back and crossed one leg over the other. "First, let's talk about illness." His eyes softened. "Bad things happen to God's people, Jade. That's always been true. This is a fallen world, and life here is not the ultimate goal. Heaven is."

Jade had heard the explanation before, but it always fell flat. God was a miraculous God. Certainly he could have healed Jade by now, or better yet, prevented the cancer from growing in the first place. The idea that she was being punished seemed far more likely. "But it feels like God's mad at me."

For the next half hour the pastor reminded her of Bible verses, sharing example after example of something bad happening to someone who loved God. When he was finished, he shared a final verse from the Book of John, "'In this world you will have trouble. But take heart! I have overcome the world.'"

The words soothed the raw places in Jade's soul. She had read the verse dozens of times over the years, but now it was as though she were hearing it for the first time…understanding a truth she'd always missed. The Lord hadn't only overcome the world's trouble, He had overcome *hers*. Personally.

Tears swam in her eyes and she studied Pastor Steve's face. "I never thought of it that way." She reached for a tissue in the pocket of her wheelchair. "Like God had already—" she looked down at her chair and back at the pastor—"overcome this."

Pastor Steve hesitated. "There's more. Let's talk about marriage and divorce. I've been asked about this so often that one day I wrote a brief explanation. It's something I printed up for people like you, people with these questions and concerns." He stood and headed for his office, which adjoined the front of the sanctuary. "I'll be right back."

Seconds later he returned with a preprinted card. The front read, "In case you wonder…"

Jade opened it and began to read:

Dear friend, I appreciate your questions about God's view on marriage and divorce. While I do not have the definitive answer in this matter, I have searched the Scriptures on the issue. In that light, I would like to give you my understanding of Christ's position, as I see it in the Bible.

Each of the Gospels talks about divorce to some degree. However, the text in Matthew 19:9 says, "I tell you that anyone who divorces his wife, except for marital unfaithfulness, and marries another woman commits adultery."

I've thought and thought on this verse, and in trying to understand it I've used the word replacement method. In the following examples I've replaced the key words from that verse, but kept the sentence structure the same. Here goes:

Anyone who eats pizza, except for cheese pizza, will get heartburn.

Who doesn't get heartburn? The person who eats cheese pizza. Let's try another:

Anyone who lies in the sun, except for the one who wears sunscreen, will get burned.

Who doesn't get burned? The one who wears sunscreen. Or this one:

Anyone who misses school, except for illness, will receive a fail.

Who doesn't receive the fail? The one who misses school because he's sick.

Many people will argue that once a married person is divorced, they must never remarry because to do so would result in adultery. Yes, there are verses that say this, but there is also Matthew 19:9.

Now if God said it, I believe it. In this case, the words are God's, not mine. We are left to stand back and look at the larger picture, the picture of Christ as our merciful God and Savior. Why would He say, "Except for marital unfaithfulness?" I have to believe it's for this reason: When a person's spouse is unfaithful—physically or otherwise—and has a hard heart toward reconciliation, God does not seem to condemn the faithful spouse to a life of isolation.

Therefore, though the Lord hates divorce, the faithful spouse who remarries is not guilty of adultery. That's how I read it, anyway. If you have any questions, contact me at the church office.

Sincerely, Pastor Steve

With each clear-cut sentence, a river of peace flowed more freely in Jade's heart. She blinked twice so she could see through her tears. "But I was at fault, too. I lied to Jim about Ty from the beginning."

The pastor bit his lower lip. "Well, Jade, you shouldn't have lied, but the test God gives us isn't one of perfection, it's one of intent." He studied her. "Did you intend to see your marriage end in divorce? Even at the end?"

Jade shook her head. "No, even after I found Tanner again I wanted to make things work with Jim. *He* was my husband. But by then Jim had made up his mind."

There was silence between them for a moment, and Jade remembered her feelings from earlier that afternoon. "I guess there's only one other thing." Her eyes settled on her hands and she noticed they were trembling. "I feel like I'm dying. Maybe even tonight."

At that moment, a door opened in the back of the church, and Jade turned just as Tanner rushed in. When he saw her, he stopped, his eyes locked on hers. Even from a hundred feet away, Jade could feel his apology, read it in his face and hear it in his unspoken words.

Her heart filled with a joy so strong it nearly eclipsed her fears. She soundlessly mouthed the only thing that came to mind, a truth that started her crying in earnest and made her ache for his touch: "You came."

Pastor Steve nodded toward Tanner, cleared his throat, and patted Jade on the knee. "I'll be in my office if either of you need me."

When he was gone, Tanner came to her, lifted her from the chair, and cradled her close to his body as though she were a small child. His tears mingled with hers as he brushed his cheek against her face. "Jade. I'm so sorry, baby."

With every ounce of her remaining strength, she held on to him, breathing in the smell of him, savoring his heartbeat against her chest. Careful not to bump her arms or legs, he sat down in the wheelchair, still holding her close.

She wrapped her arms around his neck and buried her face in his shoulder. "Don't let go of me, Tanner, please." Two quick sobs slipped from her throat. "I'm so afraid."

"Of what, sweetie?" He drew back enough to see her face. His voice was like a caress. "Tell me."

"Of dying." She sniffed. "I think I might die tonight."

"Tonight?" Tanner's eyes grew wide and his expression softened even more. "Honey, don't say that."

"But I'm so scared…"

"You?" He looked genuinely puzzled. "I thought you were…you always say everything is fine." He nuzzled his face against hers. "Baby, how long have you felt this way?"

Jade swallowed back several small sobs. "Since…since the day we found out."

His body responded to her words, tensing and flexing beneath her. When he spoke, his voice was choked with sorrow. "All this time I thought I was the only one who was afraid." He tightened his hold on her. "I didn't know, Jade. I'm so sorry, baby. So sorry. You said you were okay."

"I *wanted* to be." Her forehead fell against his shoulder. "I thought if I got scared everything would spin out of control."

"No, honey, that wouldn't happen. It's okay to be scared."

Suddenly Jade's fear of dying that night faded like a winter sunset. Tanner stroked her hair and continued. "It kills me to see you like this…hurting, unable to walk." He paused and touched his lips to hers. "And when you pretended it didn't matter…"

She lifted her shoulders. "I knew you were scared, Tanner. I thought if I told you the truth you'd…you'd be gone more." She clutched his shirt and drank in his sweet breath near her face. "I love you, Tanner. I need you more than ever."

He placed his hands on either side of her face and positioned her so he could see straight into her soul. "What do you need from me, Jade? Whatever it is, I'll do it."

She didn't take even a moment's consideration. Blinking back an onset of fresh tears, she kissed him as she hadn't in weeks. When she pulled away, she studied his face, praying that this would be a turning point, because the battle she was fighting could not be won without him. She knew that now. "Are you serious?"

Tanner's eyes glistened and he nodded. "As serious as I've ever been. What do you need from me?"

"Okay." She drew a steadying breath. "I'll tell you."

And for the next hour, with Tanner hanging on her every word, Jade did exactly that.

Eighteen

Each time the dream was the same, and that September night was no different.

Jenny stood in front of her house, her mom and Matt on either side, and together they waved to Grace. The car Grace and her grandmother left in was maroon, and Jenny watched it back out of the driveway, stop and shift gears, then take off down the street.

The whole time, Grace's face was up against the window, tears running down her cheeks, her hand pressed against the glass as she said her final good-byes.

Two seconds passed, three, four…

Then the car glided into an intersection, and suddenly from out of nowhere a giant white pickup came from the side and there was a horrendous crash. Jenny's senses filled with the assault of grinding metal, shattering glass, screeching tires, and flying debris.

"*No!* Not Grace. Not her, too."

She raced as fast as she could toward the accident scene. But when she came upon the spot where the collision occurred, there was nothing but pieces of the car. Small, maroon pieces. Tires and car doors and engine parts. The giant white truck had continued on its way and was long gone.

There were no seats, no floorboards, and no sign of Grace or her grandmother. Only Mrs. Parsons stood there in the midst of the mess, her body intact and free from injury.

Jenny ran to her and grabbed her by the shoulders. "Where is she? Where's Grace?"

"I don't know." Mrs. Parsons' expression was unsympathetic. "I guess I lost her."

"No! You can't lose her. She's my sister! We have to find her!" Then Mrs. Parsons disappeared.

"Grace!" Jenny darted from one piece of the broken car to another, lifting it and looking for Grace's small body. "Honey, I'm here." She yelled the words, still frantically searching the intersection. "I love you, Grace. Where are you? I need to find you and—"

There was the sound of screeching tires and the roar of a powerful engine. Jenny looked up and gasped. Something terrifying was hurtling toward her. There was no way out, no way to avoid being run down, and in that instant she screamed in terror.

Because the thing coming at her was the giant white truck…

Her eyes flew open and she jumped out of bed, the scream still coming from deep within her. Her heart pounded in her throat, her face damp with sweat and tears.

"Jenny!" Her mother tore into her room, eyes wide with fear. "What is it?"

It didn't matter how often she woke up this way. Each time the sound of her frightened scream terrified both of them. They stared at each other for a beat and then Jenny shuffled across the room and into her mother's arms.

"I'm sorry." She let her head fall against her mother's shoulder and tried to stop sobbing. "I dreamed it again."

The two of them were quiet, but Jenny knew what her mother was thinking. At first, after the accident four years ago, Jenny only dreamed about the happy times, the days when Alicia was still alive. But two years later, Jenny began having horrifying dreams about a giant white truck.

Brian Wesley, the drunk driver, had been driving a white pickup when he hit them.

After a month of nightmares, Hannah and Jenny both agreed

she needed counseling, needed to talk through the feelings she bottled up back when the accident happened. Twelve weeks of regular sessions with a Christian therapist seemed to be just what Jenny needed. The nightmares stopped and never came back.

Until now.

"Honey." Her mother was calmer now. "We can take you back to the counselor if you think it would help."

Jenny eased out of her mother's arms. The terror of the dream took minutes to pass and even now her entire body shook. She ran her fingers through her hair and dried her face with the sleeve of her nightgown. "No. I'm okay. I just…" A lump in her throat kept her from speaking.

Her mother pulled her close once more and stroked her back. "I know honey, I miss her, too."

Jenny swallowed and found her voice, new tears spilling onto her face. "I want her back with us, Mom. She's my sister; nothing can change that."

They were silent for a while; then her mom drew back and kissed her cheek. "Let's talk about it in the morning."

Jenny nodded. "I'm sorry."

"Don't be sorry. We all want her back."

"It's not just Grace." Jenny's voice was the softest whisper. "I miss Alicia, too. Losing Grace makes everything worse."

"I know. It's the same for me."

Jenny studied her mother in the moonlit room as the sobs came once more. There had been a time when Jenny doubted her mother would ever understand. But in the past three years they'd become incredibly close. Jenny was grateful. "I love you, Mom."

"Love you, too." Her mother took hold of Jenny's hands. "Let's pray."

They whispered in the darkness, begging God to bring them both peace in light of Grace's absence. And Alicia's. And to help

Jenny's nightmares go away. When they were done, her mom blew her a kiss and headed for the bedroom door. "See you in the morning."

They returned to their separate beds, and Jenny glanced at the clock. It was just after three in the morning. Though she was tired, Jenny lay awake, staring at the ceiling and thinking about the dream. The counselor had told her that the giant white pickup seemed symbolic, because Jenny had never wanted to hate Brian Wesley over what happened.

Even that first year after the accident, when her mother was determined to see the man locked up for life for what he'd done, Jenny couldn't hate him. She'd never hated anyone in her life and feelings that strong scared her. The pain in her heart was great enough simply dealing with the loss of her dad and Alicia without adding hatred to the mix.

But since she refused to hate the drunk driver, her fear and anger about what happened somehow focused on the white pickup Brian Wesley was driving. After all, that was the only thing Jenny remembered about the accident. One minute she was talking to Alicia about school starting the next day and what teachers they hoped to have and which boys might have changed over the summer.

The next minute she saw a white pickup barreling down on them.

Then there was nothing but darkness.

Jenny rolled over in bed and curled up as small as she could. It was a good thing she had no memory of what happened next. She'd heard the entire story, and that was all the information she needed. If she'd been conscious she didn't think she would have survived.

The idea of seeing Alicia dead at the scene from head injuries and her dad trapped in the car while firemen used torches to cut through their car and get him out was more than she could take in. To hear him gasp for breath, knowing that the paramedics were frantically trying to save his life…

She thanked God she'd seen none of it.

Her injuries had been minor—a concussion and a broken arm. And the next day when she woke in a hospital bed, her mother was at her side. It was then that she found out what had happened. Since the last thing she remembered was the white pickup truck headed straight for them, it was no wonder that was the source of her nightmares.

"Daddy, I miss you…" Fresh tears rolled across the bridge of her nose and onto her pillow. "Give Alicia a hug for me."

Her whispered words faded into the night and Jenny drifted back to their last camping trip. Everything about that weekend was still as clear and vivid as if it had happened days and not years ago.

She and Alicia had been inseparable, despite the fact that they were so different. Alicia was pretty and popular, a cheerleader with more friends than any girl at West Hills High School. Jenny was nearly two years younger and had none of her older sister's charisma and confidence. She was shy and awkward, with a secret desire that one day she might grow up to be like Alicia.

But despite her busy social schedule and the attention she received from her peers, Alicia preferred spending her free time with Jenny. After school—even up until the day she was killed— she and Alicia would listen to music, or take a walk, or ride bikes together.

They were more than sisters; they were best friends.

And the campout with their dad had long been the highlight of every summer vacation. That year they camped at Cachuma Lake, a place known for its fishing spots. The Ryan father-daughter campouts were always marked by lots of time fishing. Fishing and talking.

Jenny saw that now. Back then she and Alicia would roll their eyes and slip into their old jeans and sweatshirts before the sun came up, complaining about the cold or the early morning hour. "Do we have to fish today?" they'd whine.

He always acted shocked by their question. He'd silently mouth the question back at them as though nothing could be more outrageous than to wonder about such a thing. "Of course we're going fishing! Ryans fish; it's what we do."

Jenny blinked away the tears and her sniffle broke the dark silence that surrounded her.

That last day, the day of the accident, had been just like that. They'd gotten up early and fished by flashlight until the sun came up. When it was time to go, she had the most fish. They were making their way up the shore, Alicia in the lead, teasing Jenny about her catch and how maybe fishing was her talent, when Jenny spotted a coiled rattlesnake and screamed.

They all froze, which prevented Alicia from stepping squarely on the snake. Their dad, a doctor when he wasn't fishing, spoke in a voice Jenny remembered still. In his most serious tone, calm and even, he directed Alicia to back away from the rattler one step at a time. Seconds later she was out of danger and the snake slid away.

For months after the accident Jenny remembered the close encounter with the snake. She couldn't help think that if she hadn't screamed, Alicia would have stepped on the snake and been bitten. Though that would have been bad, it would have meant leaving the campsite immediately, before packing up. That way they wouldn't have passed through the intersection of Fallbrook and Ventura Boulevard at the same exact instant as Brian Wesley.

And they would have been alive today.

If only Jenny hadn't screamed.

She knew thoughts like that were crazy, but they came anyway. Now that Grace was gone, it made her wonder what she could have done to prevent *that* from happening. Maybe if she hadn't given her heart over so quickly, so completely…maybe if she'd allowed the precious girl to be nothing more than a welcomed guest…maybe then Grace's grandmother never would have come looking for her and today she'd still be living with them.

Jenny dried her face with the edge of the sheet and turned onto her other side. This time she kept her words silent, allowing them to echo only in the most private places of her heart.

Lord, I know You can hear me. I have a favor to ask. Please, God, when You see my dad and Alicia today, could You tell them to pray? Have them pray for Grace. Because I don't believe she's better off in Oklahoma; I believe she needs to be here with us. And right now I need my dad and my best friend to pray for me. But You see, God, I can't ask them, because they live in heaven with You. So please, God…ask them for me, okay? And when You do, tell them I miss them. Tell them I always will.

The idea that she could ask God to give her dad and Alicia messages was one that always brought peace to Jenny's soul. Despite nightmares about giant white pickup trucks or a little sister she might never see again living a thousand miles away, Jenny drifted off to sleep, resting in the arms of the only One who could keep her dad and Alicia—and now little Grace—alive in her heart.

The only One who could make them feel close enough to touch.

Nineteen

The next morning, nothing felt right to Hannah. She waited until Matt and Jenny were gone for the day, poured herself a cup of coffee, and curled up in a deck chair outside. The fog had settled in overnight, and the damp gray of the sea and sky fit Hannah's mood.

When Grace was taken from them, she made a decision to handle it well, to show the world and her family how much she'd changed since losing Tom and Alicia four years ago. Losing Grace would not set her back a year, wouldn't make her turn against God or renounce her faith. It would be painful, but she would survive.

At least that was the plan.

Instead she'd been short with Matt, distant from the Lord, and several times she'd canceled her volunteer work at the hospital so she could stay home and clean the house or take walks along the beach. Of course, she always wound up in Grace's room, straightening her pillow and dusting her shelves. Jenny was the only one who understood. Poor precious Jenny was suffering at least as badly as Hannah.

The hot steam from her coffee warded off the chill in the morning air, and Hannah held the mug closer to her face. She took a careful sip, wishing the hot liquid could somehow burn away the anger and doubt and bitterness that had crept back into her heart.

She gazed across the water and bit hard on her lip.

Why?

Why did God bring Grace into their lives in the first place? And why had they agreed to take her? She was a foster-adopt child, after all. A child with risks she and Matt had agreed up front not to take. The reason was easy enough. Mrs. Parsons had convinced them. She had told them the chances were basically non-existent that anything would disrupt Grace's adoption. And so they'd agreed.

Many times in the past three weeks, she'd mentioned to Matt that someone ought to do something about the social worker, file a complaint against her or notify her superiors that she'd reneged on a promise. How dare the woman bring Grace into their home and give them time to fall in love with her unless she was absolutely certain that nothing would stop the adoption.

And what about Patsy Landers? How could the woman call herself a Christian, then without the slightest hesitation take Grace from the most stable home she'd ever had? How could she deny the girl a lifetime of love from two parents who cherished her?

Hannah's eyes welled up. She wasn't sorry they'd taken Grace in. The little girl had been worth every minute. The memory of watching her blossom into a talkative, confident little girl in the months they had her was something all of them would cherish forever.

But still it didn't seem right. Mrs. Parsons should have checked Grace's background better, researched to see if Grace's mother was telling the truth about the grandmother in Oklahoma.

Hannah took another sip of coffee just as the door opened. Matt stepped outside and sauntered over, taking the seat beside her. "Hey."

Immediately a ray of sunshine pierced the darkness around Hannah's heart. "Hi." Matt rarely came home in the middle of the day, and almost never in the morning. She situated herself so she could see him. "Did you get fired?"

"Nope." His eyes twinkled. He leaned back in the chair and lifted his chin, letting the ocean breeze wash over his face. "I'm home for two reasons."

"One…"

He reached for her hand and wove his fingers between hers. "One, I had something profound to tell you."

She raised her brows, hearing the teasing tone in his voice. "Two?"

The corners of his mouth rose a notch. "Two…I forgot a file I need for a meeting this afternoon."

"I knew there had to be a catch." She dusted her thumb over the palm of his hand. "Okay, what's so profound?"

Matt's expression grew serious. He shifted his weight forward and met her gaze. "We need to talk."

Hannah's stomach tightened. "You sound serious."

"I am." With the fingers of his free hand, Matt traced her cheek. In his eyes she saw love, but something else. Concern, maybe. Or disappointment. "You're doing it again, Hannah."

His words hung together and formed something she didn't recognize. "Doing what?"

"I know you don't mean it—" he rested his forearms on his knees and studied her— "but ever since Grace left…" He met her eyes. "You're angry again. Like you were after Tom and Alicia died."

The hairs on the back of Hannah's neck rose as quickly as her temper. How *dare* he accuse her of being angry! Who did he think he was, telling her how to feel? "I have a right to be mad."

"Okay." Matt leaned back in his chair. "At who?"

"At Mrs. Parsons…at Patsy Landers." Hannah balled her hands into tight fists. "At myself for agreeing to take Grace in the first place. At you for not stopping me. I don't know." She released a loud huff. "I'm just mad! It wasn't right what happened with

Grace. She was our *daughter,* Matt."

Something about the calm in his eyes made Hannah even angrier. She raised her voice, her tone harder than she intended. "That was the profound thing you wanted to tell me?"

"Yes." Matt shrugged. "And that I found something in the Bible today that might help you."

His suggestion felt like a slap in the face. "My faith is fine, thank you."

He studied her as though weighing what he was about to say. "You wasted a year hating Brian Wesley, Hannah. Where did it get you?"

She narrowed her eyes. "Don't throw that at me, Matt. I had a right, and you know it."

"Hey…" He reached for her hand, but she jerked it back. He hesitated, and she knew he was trying to maintain his cool. "You gave up your rights when you agreed to be a Christian, remember? The only real right you have now is to ask God for help in forgiving your enemies. Whoever they are." He softened his tone. "Isn't that what Tom's last words were all about?"

The reminder tightened like a noose around her neck. Frustration multiplied within her, and she hissed her response. "That isn't fair." She stood and glared at him. "I don't need Scripture or a lecture or a reminder about Tom's dying words, okay?"

Matt cocked his head, his expression harder than before. "What do you need, Hannah?"

"I need Grace, okay? And I need you to leave me alone." Before he could say another word, she stormed inside, through the kitchen and upstairs to their bedroom. There she slammed the door and flopped on the bed.

Fifteen minutes passed, and she heard Matt leave. She sat up and watched through the bedroom window as his car pulled away, and regret welled up within her. She balled her hands into fists. Why was she taking it out on Matt? He'd coddled her fragile emotions since Grace left; it wasn't his fault. Hannah exhaled through clenched teeth.

Still she was angry. Even at him.

Matt's words came back to her.

You're doing it again…being angry only hurts you more…

Was it true? Was this the same way she responded four years ago after losing Tom and Alicia? Memories moved across the screen of Hannah's mind. The times when she shut everything from her mind except her desire to see Brian Wesley pay for what he'd done. Times when she asked Matt to stop praying for her, stop mentioning God, stop making references to Scripture.

She had been too angry to hear any of it.

Hannah crossed her legs and dropped her head in her hand. Since Grace left, she'd told herself that she was handling it better than before, especially when it came to her faith.

I still believe in You, God, don't I? I haven't turned my back on You.

There was no response, no whispers of holy assurance…and Hannah realized it had been days since she'd prayed. She stared at the pattern on their bedspread. Maybe she wasn't openly against God like before, but she certainly hadn't gone to Him for help.

Tears spilled onto her ankles, and a mountain of discouragement settled on her shoulders. She hadn't learned a thing about forgiveness. She was right back where she'd started all those years ago, back when she and Tom were kids growing up in the same neighborhood.

Hannah pictured the basketball game when Tom first noticed her problem. A boy from two streets over had beaten her at a game in Tom's driveway. Afterward he turned to her and told her, "You play basketball like a girl."

The comment infuriated her. Years later the same boy was in a class with Tom and Hannah, and she constantly fired rude comments at him.

"What's your problem," the boy shot back at her one afternoon.

Even now Hannah could feel the way her eyes narrowed at the boy. "I play basketball like a girl, remember?"

Tom had witnessed the exchange, and later that day he shoved her playfully in the shoulder. "When you're mad you never let up, do you?"

Hannah remembered feeling somewhat embarrassed, but her ability to hold a grudge came up a handful of times in the years that followed.

Especially the year Tom began dating a girl at Oregon State University while he was playing baseball there. Some of the biting comments Hannah made about the girl were legendary even a decade later. Comments they laughed about, but comments that were wrong all the same.

At least for someone who professed faith in Christ.

Hannah had studied the Scriptures over the years and read verses about mercy being better than judgment and how anyone who judged another would also be judged. She read about forgiving a brother not once or seven times, but seventy times that. And still she struggled.

Of course the ultimate battle was really more of a war, one that had been waged against Brian Wesley, the drunk driver who killed Tom and Alicia. For an entire year Hannah could barely think about anything but her determination to see Brian Wesley punished. In the end it hadn't been a conviction or a Bible verse or anything Matt said that helped her live again.

Rather, it had been Tom's dying words.

She leaned over her legs and dried her cheeks on her jeans. It had been three years since Hannah had looked through Tom's Bible, the place where she kept the letter containing his last message to her. There had been no reason to dig it out during that time. And now…now that there was reason, she wasn't sure she wanted to.

She stared out the opposite window at the still foggy coastline, trying to convince herself she didn't need the painful reminder of Tom's last bit of wisdom to help her let go of Grace. But the more time that passed, the more she knew she was wrong. Hadn't she kept the letter for this very purpose?

She moved from the bed into the hall closet and there, on the top shelf, pushed toward the back wall, was the leather-bound, cracked blue Bible that once had been Tom's daily morning companion. Hannah took it down and stared at it a moment. *Thomas Ryan* was engraved in the lower right corner on the cover. She ran her fingertips over the name and hurt with a sadness that hadn't crossed her heart in months.

Regardless of how happy and in love she was with Matt, a part of her would always miss Tom, the man she'd fallen in love with as a girl, the one she'd fully expected to share her life with. She pushed those thoughts away and carried the Bible back to her bedroom, holding it the way she might hold a bouquet of dried flowers. This time she found a chair and once she was settled, she took a slow breath and opened it to the page, halfway through the book of Proverbs, where the letter lay tucked inside.

Her name was scrawled on the envelope, but it was neither Tom's paper nor his handwriting. He'd spoken those final words to a police officer at the scene of the accident, a man who failed to pass them on for more than a year because he didn't think them logical.

Hannah took it from the envelope and remembered how the flood of emotion had been unleashed in her soul the first time she read it. She opened it, and with eyes blurred by tears, she read it once more.

Dear Mrs. Ryan,

My name is Sgt. John Miller. I worked the accident scene the day your husband and daughter were killed. I came to your house with the news that day, and later I talked with you at the hospital. You may not remember me, but I remember you. For the past several months I've been thinking about the accident, almost as if God wanted me to remember something.

This morning I remembered what it was. I was with your husband in the minutes before he died, and he wanted me to give you a message. He wanted you to know he loved you and the girls, but there was something else. And that's what I finally remembered this morning. At the time it didn't make sense, and I figured he must have been hallucinating or suffering the effects of blood loss. But now I am convinced that I need to deliver his message to you in its entirety.

Tom told me to tell you to forgive, Mrs. Ryan. He wanted you to forgive.

Even now it was amazing to imagine Tom, trapped in the twisted remains of their car, yet having the wherewithal to know exactly what Hannah needed to hear. *Tell Hannah I love her…and tell her to forgive. Tell her to please forgive.*

But here, now? Did Tom's words apply to this situation also? To the hurt she'd harbored since losing Grace?

Hannah read the letter once more, and one by one the walls around her heart began to collapse. *Tell Hannah to forgive…*

Yes, the words applied as much today as they had three years ago.

She pictured Edna Parsons and Grace's grandmother and even Matt. She'd been angry with all of them and for what reason? Mrs. Parsons hadn't meant to cause them pain; she truly believed Grace's adoption would go through. Otherwise she never would have called in the first place.

Patsy Landers was only doing what *any* grandmother would do in her situation. Certainly if Jenny were jailed and left a baby to the care of the social services system, Hannah would search the country looking to care for that child.

She couldn't be angry at them or unforgiving, not when neither of them was guilty.

And Matt...

Hannah's stomach churned as she folded the letter, placed it back in the envelope, and returned it to its place in Tom's Bible. Then she spent the rest of the day waiting for Matt to come home, praying he'd forgive her.

She went to him the minute he walked through the door. When he saw her, he set his briefcase down in the entryway, and his eyes told her she had nothing to worry about. He forgave her even before she asked. That was the kind of man he was.

"I'm sorry." Hannah took his hands in hers and stood so their toes were touching. Her voice was thick with pain over what she'd done. "I've...I've been awful."

His arms intertwined with hers and he hugged her for a long while. "It's no one's fault, Hannah." His words were a sad whisper, and he pulled back so he could see her face. "Anger is contagious." He lowered his chin, their eyes locked. "When I left here earlier, I felt just like you. Mad at the state, mad at Grace's grandmother." He gave her a sad smile. "Mad at you for being mad at me."

Hannah's insides melted. How could she have been angry at

Matt? When all he'd ever done was try to help her? She bit the inside of her lower lip, then let her mouth hang open for a moment, searching for the words. "I took your advice."

He raised an eyebrow, and she giggled, breaking the tension of the moment. "You…Hannah Bronzan…took *my* advice? Should I call the press?"

She spread her hand on his chest and pushed him with her fingertips. "Stop. I'm serious."

"Okay." His smile faded, but the light in his eyes remained. "What advice?"

"I found Tom's Bible and read the letter, the one from Sgt. Miller."

"With Tom's message, right?" Matt's voice lacked any element of smugness. "About forgiveness?"

"Right." She hung her head for a minute and then looked at him again. "You were right about all of it. There's no one to be mad at, just a—" tears burned at the corners of her eyes—"Just a great big hole where that little girl still lives." She nuzzled her face against his neck. "I miss her so much, Matt."

"I know." He worked his fingers into her back and stroked his hand over her hair. "We all miss her."

Hannah sniffed and a single chuckle came from her throat. "I'm tired of crying all the time."

Matt shifted his head and brought his lips to hers. "I'm tired of it, too."

She kissed him then, savoring the feel of his body against hers. She hadn't felt this alive since the day Grace left. When the kiss ended, Hannah whispered against Matt's cheek. "What are we supposed to do? Where do we go from here?"

Their noses brushed against each other and Matt caught her gaze once more, his face masked in peace. "We take Tom's advice. We forgive and we move on."

"So, you forgive me?"

"Forgiven." Matt kissed her once more and afterward his expression changed. "I had an interesting day."

"Interesting?" Hannah lowered her brow.

Matt grabbed his briefcase, slipped it into the closet, and led the way into the living room. When they were seated side by side on the sofa, he laced his fingers behind his head and exhaled long and slow. "We had a good-bye lunch for one of the guys at the firm."

Confusion roused Hannah's curiosity. "Who's leaving, one of the interns?"

"Not an intern."

Hannah folded her arms. "Okay, I give up. Who?"

Matt settled back into the cushion and angled his head, his eyes locked on hers. "Tanner Eastman. Today was his last day."

Twenty

Grace's smile was missing.

Patsy Landers looked out the back window of her Bartlesville home and realized that was what was different.

Outside, Grace sat in the swing, still and alone, staring at the sky. Her expression was wistful, far away. It wasn't that she was sad, exactly. The past three weeks had gone better than Patsy expected. Sure, Grace had cried some and asked about the Bronzans, but that was to be expected. But by all standards—her sleep patterns, her personality, her behavior—she was adjusting.

She just wasn't smiling.

Patsy had enrolled her in preschool, and three days a week a van with cartoon characters painted on the side picked her up at eight and dropped her back at home at three. Grace brought home artwork, sheets of carefully printed letters, and tales of playground antics.

Patsy studied the child through the window once more. It wasn't what she brought home that troubled Patsy.

It was what she didn't bring—the ear-to-ear smile that had always been a part of Grace even when life was at its worst.

"What's wrong, honey?" Patsy would ask. "Is someone making you sad at school?"

Grace would shrug her thin shoulders, barely lifting the corners of her mouth. "No, Grandma. School's fine."

Patsy watched her now as the child shuffled her feet in the dirt beneath the swing. Maybe that was it. Everything was fine, but nothing was good.

A sigh filtered through Patsy's lips as she limped across the floor to the dining room table. They'd gone to the library earlier in the day, and Grace had picked out two Dr. Seuss books. Patsy chose something more practical. She stared at the book on the table and ran her hand over the cover. *101 Things to Do with Your Kids*.

The book was full of activities for parents and their children. If even ten of them brought a spark of life to Grace's disposition, it would be worth the time spent reading. Besides, there was no time like the present to invest in Grace. Patsy hadn't done enough of that with Leslie. And look how she had turned out.

If there was one thing Patsy was determined to do, it was prevent Grace from going the way of her mother. The idea that she had a second chance to raise a little girl, another opportunity to rectify the mistakes she had made, to make up for the things she had missed out on the first time around…it made Patsy's heart swell. And it made losing Leslie almost bearable.

Patsy opened the cover of the book and gazed at the table of contents. *Take an Adventure Walk…Build a Birdhouse…Knit a Scarf…Jump Rope Games…Learn a Song…*

The suggestions seemed endless, and just reading them lightened the load on Patsy's heart. She might be slow with her cane, but she could take an adventure walk if she saved up her energy. And knitting scarves was something she'd done back when Leslie was a small girl. Certainly Grace would have fun doing those things.

If they spent that kind of quality time together, Grace was bound to be happy. And maybe then she'd find something more than good times together.

Maybe she'd find her precious granddaughter's smile, as well.

Twenty-One

Tanner clicked the remote control and a sports program filled the television screen.

"ESPN?" Jade moaned.

"Sports are good medicine."

She giggled. "Okay, but my movie's on in fifteen, deal?"

"Deal."

Tanner wrapped his arms around Jade, savoring the way she snuggled in close to him on the sofa. Her hair smelled like fresh soap. He closed his eyes and rested his cheek against the top of her head. He could have stayed that way forever. Jade cradled against him, Ty asleep upstairs, happy and content and unaware of the impending danger his mother faced.

It was one week until Jade's early due date, the day that would give both her and the baby the best chance at surviving. Since the day he'd walked out of the office for the last time—hours after his talk with Jade in the church that night—Tanner had spent nearly every waking moment at her side.

Briefs and case precedents and troubled files meant nothing to him. Not anymore. Instead his days were filled with everything about her—the way her eyelashes looked when she slept, the sound of her voice over morning coffee, the brush of her skin against his. He'd fallen in love with her all over again, and no matter how much time they spent together, it wasn't enough. Tanner cherished every moment, even the difficult ones.

In the process, something amazing had happened. Jade's speech was still slow, but no longer slurred. And though she shuffled her feet, she got around most of the time without the wheelchair.

"I don't get it," Tanner had told Dr. Layton at Jade's last visit. "What's the difference?"

Jade had smiled at him. "I already told you."

Tanner gave her a skeptical look and then leveled his gaze at the doctor. "Jade thinks it's because I'm around more, but that wouldn't change someone's physical condition. Maybe the tumor's shrinking."

Dr. Layton glanced at Jade's file on his desk and stroked his chin. "It isn't growing, but it isn't shrinking, either." He looked at them. "I think Jade may have a point."

Tanner remembered thinking he hadn't heard the doctor right. "Meaning what?"

"There's a growing body of research showing that love—the physical touch and closeness of someone we care for—has a positive influence on the body's immune system. Some studies say it's more powerful than diet, weight, fitness, and heredity combined."

Jade had smiled at him. "See?" She squeezed his hand. *"You're why I feel better."*

After hearing Dr. Layton's information, Tanner wanted to cry for a week. If his nearness to Jade had helped her improve in so short a time, imagine what it could have done if he'd been there since the beginning, since she was first diagnosed.

The memory faded and Tanner was glad. There was no point beating himself up over what he hadn't done. He was here now and there was no place he'd rather be. Matt called every few days and gave him updates on what was happening at the office. But only updates.

Tanner had made his departure clear to all of them. He was taking an indefinite leave of absence. Whether that would be three months or a year or even two, he had no idea. Until he returned,

Matt was in charge. All questions would go to Matt and occasionally, a few times a week, Matt would call Tanner and keep him posted on the current caseload.

"I want to know what we're taking on," he told Matt after the good-bye lunch. "But stop me if I get specific. Strategies, case precedents, meetings with opposing attorneys. None of it. I need to be completely focused on Jade and Ty."

"You're sure about this?"

Tanner had looked straight at Matt and given him a sad smile. "Right now I'm not sure if Jade will live to see tomorrow. I'm not sure I'll ever see our baby girl, and if I do, I'm not sure she'll survive her first month. I have no idea how Ty and I will go on if we lose Jade, but leaving work?" He patted Matt on the shoulder. "I'm absolutely sure about that."

"Good." Matt's eyes were thoughtful. "It's just what you need. Time together."

Tanner gazed at the ceiling for a moment and shook his head as his eyes found Matt's again. "Why'd it take me so long to see it?"

"Life's like that sometimes." Matt hesitated. "Was this time off...did Jade ask you to do it?"

"Not in so many words." Tanner's eyes grew wet. "She told me she needed me. That she'd take as many minutes as I could give." He blinked back the tears. "In that moment, everything here paled in comparison to spending even one more minute with Jade."

"If I was in your shoes, I'd do the same thing." Matt slipped his hands in his pockets. "Exactly."

"Probably sooner."

Matt grinned. "I wasn't going to mention that, but..."

Tanner reached for a thick file on his desk and handed it to Matt. "I'm giving you the Benson, Colorado, case." He hesitated. "My strategy is outlined in the first document. After that you'll find my interview notes, case precedent research, and copies of the lease contract that started the whole thing."

Matt thumbed through the file and then looked at Tanner again. "This case meant a lot to you."

A lump formed in Tanner's throat as he leveled his gaze at Matt. "Jade means a whole lot more."

Matt held the file up. "I'll give it my best." As he left Tanner's office, Matt pointed heavenward. "I won't be working alone."

Tanner grinned. "I have no doubts."

The memory faded again and ESPN went to a commercial.

"Time for my movie." She batted her eyes, and for a moment Tanner was lost in them. Whether she was sick or not, Jade's eyes were a gorgeous green, green as the water in Chesapeake Bay.

He sighed in mock frustration. "You sure you don't want another half hour of SportsCenter?"

"Positive."

This time he sighed long and hard. "Okay…what's the movie."

She grinned, and for an instant looked like the little girl he'd befriended back in Virginia. "*The Way We Were.* Channel Eight."

He silently mouthed the title. "Chick flick, right? Tearjerker?"

Jade nestled in closer to his side. "Yes, but you'll like it. I promise."

Tanner groaned. "And if you're wrong?" He kissed the top of her head.

"We can watch war movies for a week." She giggled hard at the thought, and the sound was like nourishment for his soul.

How would he survive without the melody of her laugh, the feel of her body against his? He forced the question from his mind. "Okay. Channel Eight it is."

For the next two hours, they watched Barbra Streisand and Robert Redford fall in and out of love until finally, at the end, they went their separate ways. Through the last fifteen minutes, Jade dabbed at an occasional tear and sniffled without being loud. When it was over, Tanner flicked off the television and turned down the light.

"See?" He twirled a lock of her hair between his fingers. "I told you it was sad."

"It reminds me of us. Before we found each other again."

Tanner thought about that, how empty life had been when they'd been tricked into going their separate ways. "Yeah." He danced his fingers down the length of her arm. "But our story..." He stopped himself.

"Our story what?"

He wanted to say their story would have a happy ending, that there would be no final parting for the two of them...but there was no way he could finish that sentence. Not yet, anyway. Not while Jade was fighting for her life. "Nothing. Hey, what should we do tomorrow?"

Jade let the issue pass. Instead, she gazed up at him and traced his lips with a trembling finger. "Have I told you how much I love you, Tanner Eastman?"

Her question made his knees weak, and though he never would have dreamed it possible, the feelings he held for her were stronger than they'd been that summer in Kelso, the summer they first fell in love. Stronger than they'd ever been before. He kissed the tip of her finger. "You don't have to tell me."

"Yes, I do." Her eyes glistened. "I never asked you to walk away from the office, but here you are. The past two weeks I've hardly thought about being sick."

"Good."

"Remember that night at church, when I told you I thought I might die before morning?"

A lump formed in Tanner's stomach. "Too well."

"I never feel like that anymore." She laid her head on his chest and sighed out loud, the same way she did when she eased herself into a hot bath. As though being beside him was the greatest feeling in the world. "It was my fault you kept your distance before. I should have told you how I felt."

"I should have asked."

"It's over; we both learned something." She took his hand and set it on her pregnant belly. "Can you believe she'll be here in a week?"

The lump in Tanner's gut twisted into a knot. "Thirty-two weeks. How early is that?"

She sat up a bit, staring at her swollen abdomen. "It's early, but her lungs should be developed. It could take a month before she can go home, but maybe not. It depends on her weight."

Tanner ran his hand over her stomach and hesitated. As he did, the baby pushed against his palm. "Ohhh. So you're a fighter, little girl." He grinned at Jade and pretended to whisper, "Just like her mother."

A dreamy look filled Jade's expression. "I feel like you're closer to her lately."

"Yeah—" Tanner moved his hand and the baby kicked him again—"Me, too."

They watched the baby moving beneath her maternity shirt and laughed. "She's rowdy tonight."

Tanner's heart was filled with awe. "It's all so amazing. How could anyone question whether God created life?"

"Especially when you know what's happening inside me, how a real person is being knit together. It's the most beautiful miracle of all."

Sorrow streaked the moment. "I wish I'd been there when Ty was born. All the time I missed...it still kills me."

Jade shifted onto her side and wrapped her arms around Tanner's waist. "You've more than made up for it." She hesitated.

"If something happens to me, I know you'd be okay. The three of you."

Tanner's back stiffened. "Don't say that."

"I'm sorry." Jade was quiet. "I just want you to know I trust you, Tanner. You're a wonderful dad. With or without me."

"You aren't going anywhere. God and I already talked about it."

"I know. But just if…if God takes me home, you and the kids will be fine. You're wonderful with Ty and you'll be amazing with our daughter."

"Daughter…" Tanner let the word dangle in the air like a delicate wind chime. "Are we ever going to name her?"

"Last time we talked about it you wanted to wait. At least until we got this far."

"That was before I left work."

"True." She gripped his shirt and clung to him tighter than before. "We weren't talking about a lot of things back then."

"Well…I think it's time." He brushed his thumb along the side of her arm. "What names do you like?"

"The same ones we talked about before, I guess. The names we would have called our last little girl."

Tanner worked the muscles in his jaw. "How old would she be now?"

Jade did not hesitate. "Seven months."

"You always know, don't you?" A pang of guilt struck him and he paused a moment. "I miss her, too. I just…I don't know. What am I supposed to say about her? 'She would have been beautiful? Precious? She still lives in my heart? We'll see her one day in heaven?' Anything I say won't bring her back." He leaned to the side and met Jade's eyes. "You know?"

"I know. But Tanner, do me a favor." Her eyes traveled a path deep into his heart. "When you're feeling those things, say them. It's all right to talk about her."

"Okay." He looked into her soul. "You know what I think?"

"What?"

"I think we should name her, before we name this little girl. So we're not always talking about her like she was only an idea."

Tears filled Jade's eyes as a smile filled her face. "Okay."

"So let's name her."

They thought for a moment and Jade wiped at a single tear. "I have an idea." She tilted her head and her eyes grew cloudy, as though she was remembering something from a long time ago. "Back when I was a girl, after we left Virginia and I thought I'd never see you again, everything about my life was lonely. My mother was gone forever, Dad drank every night, and, well… You know the things he said to me when he was drunk. He forbade me to go out or have friends in, not that I would've brought anyone home." She hesitated. "Know how I survived that time in my life?"

Tanner hadn't heard this part of her story before. "How?"

"I had an imaginary friend." Jade's smile softened. "She would sit with me on the front porch and read with me in my bedroom. I could tell her my secrets and she would laugh at my silly stories. Best of all, she looked just like me."

An understanding dawned in Tanner's mind. "What was her name?"

Jade lowered her chin. "Jenna."

"Jenna…" Tanner let the word play on his tongue for a moment. "I like it. So that's what you want to name her?"

Jade nodded. "Jenna Eastman."

"Our first daughter. The daughter who lives in heaven."

Jade's eyes grew wet again. "Let's not tell anyone about her name. Let's make it our secret, just the two of us." Her words were slower, and Tanner knew she was getting tired.

He looked at her, curious. "Why?"

Jade lifted one shoulder. "I don't know. That way, whenever we're thinking about her or wondering how old she'd be, we can talk about it together. Alone. Besides, when you miscarry, most people don't think of it as losing a child. We're the only ones who miss her."

Tanner's heart swelled. How good God was to give him Jade, this woman who cared so deeply and loved him so much. "Okay. Jenna's our secret."

Jade tapped her fingers on her stomach. "I'm kinda tired. Can we talk about this one tomorrow?"

Tomorrow. A shadow fell over the moment. "You have an appointment at the hospital tomorrow, remember?"

Peace masked Jade's face. Peace and acceptance. "Yes, to check the tumor growth."

Tanner pictured Jade sliding slowly, steadily, through the MRI tube, motionless and pale under the fluorescent hospital lights, her pregnant belly protruding through the hospital sheets, a stark contrast of life in the shadows of death.

"I hate those tests."

"It'll be okay. The tumor hasn't grown; I'd know if it had." Jade's face lit up. "Besides, if we use the waiting time to talk about names, I won't be so nervous."

"Okay." He relaxed some. "Sounds like a plan."

They were quiet a moment; then Jade leaned against him again. "Did you ever love someone so much it hurt?"

Tanner cradled her body against his and closed his eyes. Again he longed to stay that way, holding her, breathing the same air.

"Yes, Jade, I've loved someone that much… Every day; every hour. Every minute."

Twenty-Two

J ade and Tanner arrived at the hospital at nine the next morning and were ushered into a private waiting room. Everything about the place was familiar since the facility was adjacent to the children's hospital where Jade had worked these past years.

The test was not particularly grueling—there were no strange liquids to drink or painful positions to maintain—but Jade felt as uneasy about it as Tanner.

Lying on a flat tray, being moved through the white cylinder one inch at a time and then back through it again set her nerves on edge. Only by praying constantly—for Tanner and Ty and their unborn daughter, for Matt and Hannah and Jenny, and anyone else that came to mind—was she able to keep her thoughts from the place where they were tempted to be.

On the fact that her brain was being examined by microscopic rays that would determine the course of her life. And even whether she would live at all.

Ty was staying at his friend's house, which meant Jade and Tanner could spend most of the day at the hospital. In addition to the MRI, Jade was scheduled for an ultrasound and appointments with both Dr. Layton and her obstetrician. The team of doctors was working together to make sure the baby's birth would come at a time when Jade's brain tumor seemed stable.

The day was bound to wear on her, so Jade had allowed Tanner to bring the wheelchair. Before they left the car, they held hands and prayed about the hours ahead. Now that they were in the waiting room, Tanner eased her from the wheelchair onto a vinyl sofa next to him.

She eyed the chair and tried not to hate it. It represented such failure and desperation, such proof of her illness. *It's temporary*, she told herself. Then she turned to Tanner. "Okay, I guess it's time."

"Time?" Tanner's blank expression made her laugh.

She pointed to her belly. "Time to figure out a name for little Miss Eastman here."

A knowing look filled Tanner's eyes and he slipped his arm around her. "Oh, that. Right."

For the next half hour they talked about a dozen different names, but finally they settled on Madison. Jade remembered that she had jokingly promised to name her daughter after Brandy Almond, her teenage patient at the children's hospital. But Brandy would understand. Besides, Madison was the name of Tanner's grandmother, a woman who had been rock-solid in her faith and drove Tanner to church long after his own parents stopped attending. Years after her death, her favorite Scriptures played in Tanner's mind and often helped shape the strength of his views.

"Besides that, she was beautiful."

"Of course." Jade smiled and traced her finger along Tanner's cheekbone. "She was related to you, wasn't she?"

"So, you like it?"

"I like it a lot. I only wish I'd known your grandmother."

Tanner kissed the tip of her nose. "She would have loved you."

Jade leaned her head back and stared at an aquarium in the corner of the waiting room. She pictured heaven and having the chance to meet the elderly Madison Eastman, and Jenna, and Hannah's Tom and Alicia. Calm reigned in her soul, and her heart felt full to bursting. "Sometimes I can't wait to get to heaven." A smile played on her lips. "All of us and Jenna. Together forever…"

Concern flashed in Tanner's eyes. "Don't say that, Jade, please."

"I'm not ready to go today." She eased his face nearer and kissed his cheek. "Sorry."

She could feel the muscles in Tanner's arms relax. "It'll be great—in another sixty years or so."

Jade smiled. "Madison what? What's her middle name?"

"Well…" Tanner's eyes twinkled. "Let's make her middle name after this woman I know who loves God and would go any distance to take a stand for her beliefs. If I could only remember her name…" He stroked his chin and stared at the ceiling as though he were trying to conjure up the woman's memory. "Hmmm. She's gorgeous beyond words, dark hair and eyes as green as Chesapeake Bay…"

Jade rolled her eyes and giggled. "Gorgeous?"

A mock indignation filled Tanner's expression and he flashed her a sharp look. "Absolutely!" He returned his gaze to the ceiling and then suddenly snapped his fingers and stared at her. "I remember, now. Jade. Her name is Jade Eastman."

She laughed harder. "You're crazy."

Tanner pointed at himself and mouthed the word, "Me?"

"Yes, you." Her laughter faded. "Come on, Tanner. I'm serious. She needs a middle name."

"I *am* serious." He took her hands in his and studied her eyes. When he spoke again, his voice was softer, more serious. "Madison Jade Eastman. I love it."

Lately it seemed Jade was constantly discovering new depths to the love she and Tanner had for each other. This was one of those times. "You really mean it?"

"Yes." He leaned in and kissed her lips, in a way that took her breath. He drew back only an inch or so, his whispered voice racked with sincerity. "Please."

Jade blinked back tears, and a sound that was more laugh than sob came from her throat. Tanner was right. The names sounded beautiful together. And there was something neither of them was saying. Jade's name would live on, even if somehow the cancer...

She squeezed her eyes shut and let her head drop for a moment. She wouldn't think that way, not now. Not when their baby was about to be born. She had to believe there was life ahead for them. For both of them. When she looked up, she found Tanner's eyes again and smiled. "I like it."

He kissed her, and his face lit up. "It's perfect."

They were talking about nicknames for Madison when the technician entered the room and motioned for them to follow. As Tanner was helping her into the wheelchair, Jade had an idea.

"Don't I have an hour between tests?"

Tanner glanced at his watch as he eased her into the chair. "You do."

"Let's go see Brandy."

"Who?" Tanner was behind her now, easing the chair through the doorway and following the technician down a long hallway.

"Brandy Almond, the high school track star with leukemia. Actually she should be home by now, but I want to try, just in case she's here. Besides, I'd like to see the nurses. It's been a while."

Tanner nodded. "It's a plan."

The test was tiring but uneventful. When it was over and Jade was back in the wheelchair, the technician found them in the waiting room. She handed them a folder. "I'm not supposed to give you results," she said, grinning at Jade. "But you're a nurse."

Jade waited, her heart in her throat.

The technician continued. "I compared these results with the last ones, and there hasn't been any growth. If anything, the tumor's smaller than before." She winked at the two of them. "But you didn't hear that from me."

The woman left, and the moment she was gone, Tanner took

hold of Jade's shoulders and lowered his face next to hers. "I *knew* God would get you through this."

Jade reached up and took hold of his hands. She closed her eyes and a single happy sob came from somewhere deep within her. "Thank you, Jesus. Thank you."

Their moods were higher than they'd been in months as they followed a long corridor into the adjoining children's hospital and made their way to the cancer ward. At the front desk, Jade's former coworkers fussed over her and agreed that she was looking wonderful.

They talked about the department and the victories that had taken place in the time since she'd been gone. Finally everyone drifted back to her work except Linda, the head nurse. She looked from Jade to Tanner then back again. "So what do the tests show?"

Jade's heart soared. "I get the results later today." It was wonderful to have hope again. "But it looks good. I'm going to make it, Linda. I really think so."

Linda brought her hands together and lowered her voice. "We're praying for you Jade. All of us."

Jade reached for Linda's hand and squeezed it. "Thanks."

Linda was a new believer, one of the many people Jade knew who became a Christian after terrorists attacked the United States a year earlier. Across the country, in the aftermath of that tragedy, there were barely enough seats in churches for all the people looking for answers, looking for peace and hope and stability in a world gone mad.

And many of them had found the answers they needed in the One who so clearly was watching over Jade and her baby. Without saying a word, Jade raised her hand and, from where he stood behind her wheelchair, Tanner took hold of it.

It was time to find Brandy.

Jade gazed down the familiar blue-carpeted hallway, which

led to a dozen hospital rooms…places where Jade had administered medicine and held the hands of crying children and parents. Places where children had been healed.

Places where they had died.

She looked back at Linda. "I came to see Brandy." She smiled, anxious for the visit. "Tell me she's gone home."

Linda's smile faded. "Oh, Jade…" Tears welled in her eyes and her chin quivered. For a moment the woman couldn't seem to speak. "You didn't hear."

"Hear what?" Alarms sounded in the sanctuary of Jade's soul. What had happened? Was she sicker? Had she slipped out of remission? Whatever it was, there was still hope. Jade and Tanner would spend the hour at her side, cheering her up and praying with her. But even as those thoughts flitted through her mind, the next question stuck in Jade's throat.

"Last time I was here she looked great." Jade's voice sounded hollow. From behind her, Tanner tightened his hold on her hand. "She was…she was in remission. I kind of hoped she might be back at school by now."

Linda shook her head. "I'm sorry, Jade. I know she was special to you." The woman moved closer to the wheelchair and placed her hand on Jade's shoulder, the way nurses do when they're about to deliver bad news.

Jade's head began to spin, and she had the urge to leap from the wheelchair and run out of the building. What had Linda said? Had she used the dreaded past tense? *I'm sorry, Jade…I know she was special to you…*

No! Jade wanted to scream. *Not Brandy. Not when she was doing so well. This was her year, the year she was going to run again and win the track meet. Please, God, no.*

Tanner must have known how she was feeling, that she could hardly breathe, let alone speak. He cleared his throat and voiced the very thing Jade wanted to ask. "Is she sick again?"

Two tears spilled onto Linda's cheeks and she brought her hand to her mouth. "A week after your visit, Brandy got pneumonia." Linda looked from Tanner to Jade. "She was very sick. A week later...the leukemia came back full force." The woman paused. "She never recovered, Jade. We lost her three weeks ago."

Three weeks ago?

How come no one had called her? Jade's heart ached. She would have wanted to be at the funeral. At least then she could have comforted Brandy's parents or known the peace of telling Brandy's friends that she was in heaven with Jesus. That somewhere Brandy Almond was running again, her long beautiful hair blowing in the breeze of heaven's wind. Running faster and freer than at any other time in her life.

Anger mingled with excruciating feelings of loss, and Jade forced herself to speak. "How come...no one told me?"

Linda's gaze fell to the ground for a moment before finding Jade's once more. "We didn't want to upset you." Linda released the hold she had on Jade's shoulder and folded her arms. "We figured you had enough to deal with."

"Well..." Jade's heart pounded in her throat. "I appreciate that. But you figured wrong." She splayed her fingers against her chest. "I loved that girl...very much."

"I'm sorry." Linda shook her head and wiped at another tear. "We didn't know what to do."

Jade hung her head, and Tanner squeezed her hand, silently assuring her that he shared her grief. Every bit of it. Tears flooded Jade's eyes and spilled onto her stretch pants. She wanted to fall to the floor, crawl to Brandy's room, and climb up in her bed. She wanted to weep and wail and demand that God tell her why. Why He would take one so young and precious and new in her faith, one who would have had such an impact on her friends if she'd lived.

Jade lifted her head and noticed that it took most of her strength. *God, get me through this…*

I am your refuge and your strength, an ever-present help in times of trouble…

The Scripture from Psalms worked its way through her being and she drew a steadying breath. When she lifted her head, she looked at Linda and nodded twice. "It's not your fault. You did what you thought was best."

Linda squirmed, clearly anxious to get back to work. "Her friend—the one who told her about God—comes in once in a while and brings toys for the sick kids. I could give her your number if you want."

Jade managed a smile. "I'd like that. Thanks." She tightened her grip on Tanner's hand. "I have an appointment next door in a few minutes. Tell everyone I said good-bye."

They were halfway down the corridor toward the other building when Tanner pushed her into a quiet waiting area where they could be alone. He came around the front of her chair, knelt by her feet, and hugged her knees to his chest. "I'm sorry, Jade."

Tears, hot and steady, streamed down Jade's face. Yes, death was a reality, especially in a children's cancer ward. Illness was always a threat when a person's immune system was unstable. But Brandy had looked so good the last time they were together…

Jade squeezed her eyes shut and took quick breaths through her nose, trying to slow the sobs that sought to overtake her. "I can't…believe…she's gone."

Tanner laid his head in her lap and clung to her. "She's with Jesus; we both know that."

A thread of terror stitched its way across Jade's heart. "Is that what people will say about me a month from now? 'She's with Jesus?'"

Tanner lifted his head and stared at her, his eyes stark with pain and fear. "Don't say that! What happened to Brandy has nothing to do with you."

She sniffed and grabbed two more quick breaths. She didn't want to attract attention so she kept her tone low. "You…you say that, but actually it does." She tossed her hands in the air. "We get a good report so we think, great, maybe I'm going to get through this thing. But the truth is cancer can turn on you like that." She snapped her fingers. "One week you can be heading toward your senior year in high school, hoping to break a state record in track and field, and the next week you're gone."

Tanner studied her, his eyes helpless and desperate. "Just because Brandy lost her battle doesn't mean you'll lose yours. You can't think that way." He leaned in closer to her. "I need you, Jade."

"I know." She released another series of quiet sobs. "I'm sorry. I'll get a grip." She looked at her watch. "We need to go."

The rest of the day was filled with nothing but positive reports. The baby was perfect, healthy and big enough for the scheduled C-section next week. Dr. Layton examined the results from the MRI and confirmed the technician's assessment. The tumor had stopped growing and perhaps had even shrunk some.

They left with plans for Jade to see her obstetrician once more that week. If everything looked fine, he would do a C-section on Jade Monday, October 7.

It was an evening when Jade should have been walking on air, convinced that God was working miracles both in her body and that of her baby. Instead, she and Tanner spent the evening at Ty's football game, huddled together despite the fact that temperatures were still in the high eighties.

There were no words. When it came to feeling optimistic about cancer, Brandy's death had said it all.

Twenty-Three

The sound of screeching tires out in front of Los Robles Medical Center snapped Hannah to attention and brought her to her feet. She searched for the admitting clerk. "Tina! Quick!"

The tall, graying woman hurried around the corner, back to her spot behind the counter. "Patient?"

"Yes." Hannah pointed outside. "Look."

It had been a slow morning, the type that made Hannah wonder if they really needed her volunteer services. Lately she'd been thinking about helping at the children's hospital instead, in the ward where Jade used to work.

Either way, at least she was back in a regular schedule. Reading the note from Tom's Bible and talking to Matt that evening had helped her hear God's voice in her life once more. Despite the pain of losing Grace, Hannah could feel His merciful hand of healing upon her broken heart. They would survive, even if no other children came their way.

Hannah was convinced of that much.

Now she and Tina stared out the double glass doors as a beat-up Lincoln lurched to a stop in front of the emergency room entrance. The driver's door inched open, and a rail-thin woman spilled out, struggling to stay on her feet. She was holding something, a rag or a blanket. Hannah couldn't quite—

Something moved, and Hannah gasped. "Dear God..." There was a baby in the woman's arms, an infant no more than a few months old. "Tina, call someone!"

Tina didn't wait. She shouted over her shoulder, her eyes still on the woman and baby outdoors. "We need a doctor outside. *Stat!*"

Down the hallway, a doctor and two interns dropped the charts they were working on, grabbed a wheelchair, and ran through the waiting room toward the woman outside. One of them took the baby; the other two helped the woman into the chair. Hannah couldn't hear the doctors, but their expressions were dark and troubled. They raced the woman through the double doors and back into one of the rooms. Tina followed, and Hannah knew she needed to make a chart on the woman.

On his way past, the third doctor handed the baby to Hannah. "Can you hold him? I'll check his vitals in a minute, but he looks okay."

Hannah cradled the baby against her chest and looked at the doctor. "What happened?"

The doctor's mouth formed a straight line and his eyes narrowed. "Drugs." He spat the word as though it tasted bad. "The woman can barely breathe."

A gust of anger blew against Hannah's soul. *Barely breathing?* She let her eyes fall to the woman's baby, snuggled in her arms. He was dressed in a tattered blue sleeper and he was wet through his blanket.

Barely breathing? How dare that woman drive in that condition, drugged and half-dead? What if she'd killed this precious child? Or hit someone else—a family, or a father and his daughters coming home from a fishing trip? The baby wasn't crying, but he was waving his hands and working his mouth.

"There, baby." Hannah kissed the infant's forehead. "It's okay, honey; I'll take care of you."

She clenched her teeth and stared down the hallway toward the room where the woman was being worked on. Holding the baby close to her chest, Hannah walked to the nurses station and nodded to a supply of diapers behind the counter. "He needs changing and a fresh blanket."

An older woman sat behind the desk. "Poor little tyke. I sure hope his mama makes it."

Hannah ignored the comment. People who drove drunk or drugged didn't deserve children. They deserved jail. Even when she was feeling compassionate and forgiving, even in light of Tom's dying words, that much was true. "Call up to labor and delivery and see if they'll bring me a few bottles of formula, will you?"

"Sure."

Hannah took the diaper and found a gurney just outside the drugged woman's room. While she changed the baby's diaper, the woman began thrashing about the bed, screaming and flailing at the doctors around her. "Stop it! You're killing me! Where's my baby?"

A nurse came up beside her and gave her a shot of something, and in less than a minute, the woman calmed down. Doctors took her pulse and checked her heart, rattling off numbers as they worked. "Ma'am, what did you take this morning?"

Hannah wrapped the baby in the clean blanket and held him against her heart. Then she positioned herself so she could see the woman. Hannah's stomach turned at the way the woman's bones stuck out, as though they were trying to break free from her skin. Hannah had never seen anyone so thin.

"I…didn't take nothin' until…until after the baby was b-b-born." She was shaking now, her limbs lurching beneath the sheets. "Don't let me d-d-die…I didn't mean to do it. Please! Don't let me die."

A doctor moved, and Hannah got a better look at the woman's face. What she saw made her breath catch in her throat. It wasn't a woman at all, but a girl. A young girl no more than sixteen, seventeen years old. She was so frail and damaged by whatever drugs she'd been taking that her posture, her eyes looked forty years old. But there was no mistaking the youthful skin and hair.

The doctor leaned over her and yelled near her face. "Ma'am, we need to know what you took! Tell us what you took this morning." The girl's eyes were still open, but she didn't respond. Gradually her legs and arms lay still.

"We've lost her pulse!" A doctor on the other side of the bed tore back the sheet and began performing CPR.

Hannah's eyes filled, and the infant in her arms began to squirm and cry. Soundlessly Hannah swayed the baby back and forth and cuddled her face against his.

Meanwhile, another doctor slapped paddles on the girl's chest and gave a signal. Her body convulsed grotesquely up and off the bed and then settled back down in what looked like a heap of brittle bones. "It's not working!" The doctor's voice was grim. "Again!"

Hannah's heart raced and she shook her head, backing away from the room with quick steps. The baby's mother was dying before her eyes. She had to get out of there before she was sick to her stomach. She hurried to the nurses station, and the woman behind the desk handed Hannah a bottle. "Poor little guy," the woman whispered.

There was nothing Hannah could say. She took the bottle, carried the baby down the hall into a private examination room, and closed the door. In the quiet of the small room, for the first time, Hannah studied the baby's face. He was beautiful. Big blue eyes, and lips that formed a perfect rosebud mouth. He sucked his fingers, hungry and threatening to cry again.

"There, baby, it's okay." Hannah put the bottle near his mouth and he found it, latching on with practiced skill. "You're all right, honey. You're safe now."

He stretched his baby hand out and Hannah placed her finger against one of his palms. With a strength that took her by surprise, the baby gripped her finger and held on.

In all her days volunteering at the hospital, she'd never done this, never held a baby while his mother clung to life in the next room. Her pulse quickened, her thoughts anxious and scattered. *How should I pray for him, God? He made it here safe this time, but if his mother lives…*

Hannah knew only too well the risks the baby would face if his mother took drugs and drove with him again.

Be still, and know that I am God.…

The verse filled her heart, and she realized she'd been holding her breath. She breathed out and kissed the baby's velvety cheek.

Be still, and know that I am God.

It was the Scripture Jade had given Tanner for their first anniversary. Hannah had been with her when they picked it out. "When life gets tough," Jade had said, "that verse is a hiding place."

It was always true at the CPRR law firm, and it was true now. Hannah brought the baby's face against hers again and prayed for his mother. She prayed the girl would live and find help in recovering from her drug problems. And she prayed the girl would never again drive intoxicated.

Then she placed her hand on the baby's head, his finger still gripping hers. *Sweet baby, if only I could protect you from everything happening down the hall.* Hannah took a slow breath, her heart breaking for the child in her arms. "Jesus, I bring You this little one, this nameless boy who You created, and I ask You to bless him. Make his home a safe one and let his mother love him all the days of her life. Let him know the touch of a father's hand and the peace of Your salvation. And bless him to be the young man You would have him be. Keep your Spirit on him, Lord…" Hannah hesitated. "Even now, when his future seems so uncertain. In Jesus' name, amen."

It was the same type of blessing she had prayed over Jenny and Alicia when they were born.

The baby's eyes had grown heavy, and his milk was almost gone. When he stopped sucking, Hannah set the bottle on the floor. Then in a way that felt as familiar as it had eighteen years ago with her own children, she held the baby up against her shoulder and patted his back, cooing at him the whole time. "It's okay, sweetie, Jesus loves you. It's okay."

When she was sure he had no air bubbles in his tummy, Hannah cradled him again. The chair she sat in was rigid and hard, but she rocked him gently, singing songs she'd sung to her own babies.

Including Grace's favorite.

"Jesus loves you! This I know, for the Bible tells me so. Little ones to Him belong; they are weak but He is strong." Hannah nuzzled her face against his, her voice soft and low. "Yes, Jesus loves you… Yes, Jesus loves you… Yes, Jesus loves you…. the Bible tells me so."

He fell asleep in her arms, but still she sang, studying him, mesmerized by his beauty. After nearly an hour there was a knock at the door. She answered as quietly as she could so the baby wouldn't wake. "Come in."

It was one of the doctors who'd been working on the baby's mother. He stepped inside and closed the door behind him. Then he studied the baby with heavy eyes. As he did, he breathed out, discouragement written across his face. "There was nothing we could do."

Fresh tears stung Hannah's eyes and her heart filled with a sudden, overwhelming sense of protection for the infant. "She's dead?"

The doctor nodded. "Traced her to a women's shelter. Seventeen-year-old runaway, clean her entire pregnancy. Got hooked up with one wrong guy and overdosed in a single hour." He ran his thumb over the baby's forehead. "It's a miracle they got here alive. The baby rode in on his mother's lap." He lifted his eyes to Hannah's. "If she'd had even a fender bender he could have been killed."

Hannah's throat was thick with sadness. She stared at the baby, ignoring the tears that fell on his blanket. "What happens now?"

"Police will be here any minute. They'll take the baby to a short-term foster home until Social Services can determine the next of kin."

Hannah nodded and swallowed hard so she could speak. "Poor baby."

And poor family who would care for him over the next few weeks. She couldn't imagine having this precious boy for even a day and then letting him go. Even now, after their short hour together, there was no question about it. Hannah had bonded with him. It made sense. In his mother's dying hour, Hannah had been the one to love him, feed him. Pray for him. Of course she was connected to the baby.

The doctor studied him once more. "He looks like an angel."

Hannah nodded and smiled through her tears. "I hope he gets to live like one."

Edna Parsons got the call just after noon that a healthy baby boy needed short-term foster care. Her job was to find next of kin—a task she took far more seriously since the incident with the Bronzans. If there was a grandparent or aunt or uncle or father somewhere in the world capable of raising the child, Edna would find out.

She met the police at the house where the baby would live for the next few days. Once he was safely placed, Edna visited St. Anne's Shelter, where the baby's mother had been living until her drug overdose.

Edna met with a pleasant woman who ran the shelter. There were Scripture verses stuck to various places on her office wall.

"Milly Wheeler was the mother's name." The woman bit her lip and brushed at the corners of her eyes. "She was seventeen, a runaway."

"I see." Edna scribbled the details on her notepad.

"We do drug testing here." The woman lifted one shoulder. "Milly was clean through her pregnancy. She attended Bible studies twice a day." The woman's voice caught. "I...I really thought she was going to make it."

The woman explained that in the course of their Bible studies, Milly had shared much about her life and background.

"I've got it all right here." The woman handed a folder to Edna. "It's Milly's file."

Edna opened it and the story began to unfold. Milly's mother was a drug addict, a street person in San Francisco, who died three years ago from an overdose. At first Milly tried to live on her own, scrounging food from other street people and digging through trash bins behind restaurants when all else failed.

"She was determined not to follow her mother's footsteps, to stay away from drugs." The woman frowned. "She kept that determination until she turned fifteen."

At that point, Milly apparently assessed her options and decided there was only one way she could make enough money to survive: prostitution.

"The trouble was, with every trick she turned, Milly saw another piece of her soul fade away." The woman crossed her arms. "Finally she could only describe herself as dead. Breathing, moving, existing…but dead all the same."

Edna glanced at the notations in the file. "And that's when she took her first hit of speed."

"Right."

Edna shook her head, her heart heavy for the girl whose story was so familiar, so like that of dozens of girls she'd worked with or taken children from over the years. Drugs were a wicked, evil prison, and once a person willingly walked through the doors, there was seldom any easy way out. "And then…?" Edna scanned the file once more.

"She stayed in San Francisco, turning tricks and taking speed until she got pregnant. The minute she knew for sure, she took a bus to Los Angeles and came here. Her withdrawals were so bad we thought she'd lose the baby. But we got her help and she never took another hit." The woman paused. "Until last night, I guess."

"Yes. She had enough crack in her blood to kill a horse."

Edna closed Milly's file. Across from her, the woman's eyes grew wet again. "She wanted her baby to be a preacher or a writer, someone who would help people be strong in God." She lifted her hands off the desk and let them fall again. "I don't know what happened. She didn't come home last night. I guess she went with one of the guys who hang around here. Even with her faith, Milly was very lonely."

"So you think the baby's clean?"

The woman nodded. "Definitely. Milly was clean through her pregnancy right up until two days ago. Clean and determined to give her baby a life different from that of hers and her mother's."

Edna made several notations on her clipboard. "What about the father?"

"Milly was a prostitute, Mrs. Parsons. The baby's father lived in San Francisco and could be any one of a hundred different men."

"What about AIDS?"

"She tested negative for HIV. Almost a miracle really, coming from San Francisco."

Edna had all the information she needed. She'd still run a name check in the San Francisco area, but Milly's story—the way she'd told it to the people at the shelter, anyway—seemed very plausible.

The women stood and shook hands. Before she left, Edna hesitated. "Is there any way we can prove that her mother's really dead?"

The woman reached for Milly's file once more and thumbed through it. Seconds later she handed Edna a photograph. "This is pretty good proof if you ask me."

Edna took it. "You're right." It was a picture of a small gravestone carved with the name Henrietta Mae Wheeler. The dates of birth and death made the buried woman the right age to be Milly's mother.

The photo was worn on the edges and peeling at the corner. Edna gave it back to the woman, her heart heavy for the tragedy young Milly had suffered. "Why would she keep a photo like this?"

"As a reminder to stay away from drugs." The woman reached for a tissue and held it beneath her right eye. "She didn't want to leave her baby orphaned, the way her mother left her."

If nothing showed up on the name check, Milly's baby boy would be a ward of the court, legally free for adoption. Suddenly a flashlight of hope shone on the day's dismal events. "Do you mind if I take Milly's file?"

"Not at all." The woman handed it to Edna. "Is Kody okay?"

"Kody?" Edna's heart beat faster as a plan took shape.

"Kody Matthew. That's what Milly named him."

Kody *Matthew*? Edna nodded. The irony was almost too

243

much. "Kody's fine. He's a beautiful baby."

The woman nodded. "I hope you find him a good home."

"Yes." Edna smiled and realized it was the first time she'd done so since hearing about Milly's death. "I think I know just the place for him."

Twenty-Four

Leslie Landers hated prison.

A door slammed in the cell next to hers, and the sound echoed through the unit. There was no way to escape the stench of body odor and bacon grease that filled the air. Leslie huffed in disgust. Even her senses were behind bars.

In prison, every single sound echoed. Every scream and cry and loud burst of laughter. Every slamming door and slamming fist. Twenty-four-seven, the place was a madhouse of animalistic behavior, loud voices, and violent actions. A place where the outside world all but ceased to exist.

Prison proved that at least one thing her mother said was true. Hell was real. No question about it, because she was now a resident. Wore her residency numbers on the pocket of her shirt.

But at least her residency was temporary.

None of this lifer stuff for Leslie, no sir. Not like the women on either side of her, women who had killed parents or husbands or strangers and didn't mind saying so. Leslie was different from them. She would bide her time, put in her hours and days and weeks, and one day—before a year was up, if her attorney was right—she'd walk out of here and never go back again.

Even if it meant dying instead.

The minute she was out, she knew just what she'd do. She'd take the pittance of money they give to parolees and buy a bus ticket to Bartlesville, Oklahoma. Then she would take Grace, and this time the two of them would disappear for good.

Leslie grabbed hold of two bars and pressed her nose in the

space between. She'd never been claustrophobic before, but now... There were times when the urge to break free of her cell was so strong she thought she could bend the bars in two. Times when she tried, even. But never when the guards were looking.

Good behavior was the only way she'd get out again, the only way she'd save Grace from a lifetime of preaching and Bible verses and suffocating control by Leslie's mother.

Leslie remembered hearing from her attorney that Grace's adoption had fallen through. She spun around and threw herself on her bunk. Good thing. Strangers shouldn't be raising her kid.

Still, Leslie had been confused until the attorney mentioned her mother. "Apparently Social Services thought your mother was dead." Her attorney shrugged. "Once they found out about her existence and her desire to adopt Grace, they pulled her from the foster-adopt home immediately."

There was no information about which foster home or who was going to adopt Grace before her mother intervened. Not that it mattered. Those people were out of the picture. And now that Grace was in Bartlesville, she'd be easy to find. Probably being spoiled rotten, poisoned with lies about the mistakes her terrible mother had made.

The whole situation made Leslie want to puke. Grace was already spoiled enough. Imagine what living with her mother for a year would do to her?

No, Leslie couldn't let Grace stay in Bartlesville. That wasn't the type of life she should have. She wasn't a Bible kid, a Christian kid. Grace was *her* kid. Leslie Landers's kid. And that meant that, yes, sometimes she'd have to hang around while Leslie made a little money in the sack. And sometimes the kid would have to sit loose while Leslie partied with the guys in Santa Maria, guys who would want to see her when she returned.

But that was no reason to take Grace away and put her up for adoption. The street life that Leslie could give Grace was a good thing. It toughened kids, made them wise to the world and ready for whatever the future held.

Whatever Grace's future held, it didn't involve Leslie's mother or some family of strangers taking over as Grace's parents. Leslie was doing just fine, thank you. The problem was, they needed more money. Which meant Grace needed to pull her weight.

The idea hadn't occurred to her until that last night, the night the cops busted her. The guy she'd been with that night roughed her up pretty good, and in the process he knelt on the seat and spotted Grace on the floor.

She could still hear his words, still feel the way they spawned the idea that just might save them. "You didn't tell me you had a little beauty hiding in the back."

Leslie had been angry with the man. Angry and high. At first she didn't understand what he meant. Before they could talk about it, the police showed up. And only in the days since she'd been in prison had she considered exactly what he was saying. Grace *was* pretty. Pretty enough that if their money started running low, Leslie could put her to work. Films or short projects. Whatever. Nothing dangerous, just something to help them survive.

Besides, it was time Grace made herself useful. Leslie had catered to her long enough, busting her own tail to make sure their cooler was full of milk and cookies and sometimes bananas. It was only fair. Grace needed to make money, too.

And if they worked together, maybe...just maybe, they'd find a way to survive. Then they could set up an apartment somewhere and go about the business of living. Of course, Leslie shared none of this with her attorney. But she did tell him one of her intentions.

"I want Grace back. The minute I'm out of here."

The attorney, an older man who worked for the state, looked

concerned by Leslie's request. "It's possible. With good behavior and a series of letters, maybe."

"Letters?"

"To your mother, sent to my office. I'll make copies and send them on. That's the only way you'll be able to prove how much you miss your daughter."

Leslie wasn't excited about the idea of writing letters, but if that's what it took, she would do it. Her mother probably loved the fact that she had Grace now. Probably figured she was being given another chance at raising a child, since she'd blown it so completely with Leslie.

She grabbed a piece of paper from a pile beneath her bunk. Her mother had been a terrible excuse for a parent. Busy all the time and spewing Bible verses as though they might make up for the lack of time they had together.

Leslie gritted her teeth and stared at the blank sheet of paper. No wonder she'd turned to drugs. At least those friends wanted to spend time with her. She grabbed a pencil from beneath her foam mattress and began to write.

Dear Mother,

Things are going good here. My attorney says I will be out in less than a year. At that time I will come to Bartlesville and take over custody of Grace. I know you think she belongs with you, but my attorney says that isn't true. She's my daughter; I can raise her.

Leslie tapped the pencil on the paper and thought about what else to say. She put her pencil to the paper again.

Please let Grace know about my choice. I'll be out very soon.

Leslie hesitated for a minute and smiled, her heart pinched with hate.

Besides, I've thought of a way we can make enough money to survive. I know we'll never go hungry. Kiss her for me. Leslie.

Twenty-Five

T he moment had finally arrived, and Jade was neither anxious nor afraid.

A strong Santa Ana wind rattled through the canyons, and before daybreak, Jade and Tanner gathered in Ty's bedroom and prayed. Jenny Bronzan was meeting them at the hospital, where she would spend the day hanging out with Ty.

Jade settled on the edge of Ty's bed and watched him slip a sweatshirt over his head. "Now remember, the whole time you're having little Maddie—" Ty's voice was muffled until his head poked through the hole—"I'll be praying for you. The whole time."

"Okay." A surreal calm had come over Jade days ago and now, on October 7, it was still in place. "I'll remember."

"And the minute she's born, you'll tell her what I told you, right?"

Jade stared up at the ceiling and rattled off the words she'd long since memorized. "'Welcome to our family, Maddie. You have the best big brother in the world.'"

"Yes!" Ty pumped his fist. "I can't *wait* to be a big brother."

Tanner poked Ty in the ribs and gave him a partial grin. "It won't happen unless we take this show down to the hospital."

The three of them formed a circle, Jade still sitting on the bed. Tanner drew a steadying breath and began to speak. "Lord, this is it, the day we've been waiting for. Father, You know all things, even down to the timing of Madison's birth." He paused, and Jade could hear the concern in his voice. "Please, God, keep Your hand on Jade and Maddie. Help them come through the operation healthy and strong, and please, Lord, bring them both home soon. We trust You...we thank You ahead of time."

The sun was just peeking over the horizon as they gathered Jade's things and loaded the car. They needed to be at the hospital by seven o'clock, and Jade knew Tanner didn't want to be late. In the myriad of emotions they'd experienced in the months since Jade's diagnosis, they'd done a role reversal once again.

There was no question that, at first, the news of Brandy's death set Jade back, set her and Tanner both back. But after a few days of deep prayer, times when only clinging to Scriptures pulled her through, she had somehow emerged clothed in peace.

Tanner was the anxious one now, but this time he shared his feelings with her. Even last night, hours before they would leave for the hospital, he admitted the depth of his fear.

They'd been in bed, and Jade was quiet, praying silently as she fell asleep. Next to her, Tanner was a study in motion. He tossed and turned from his left side to his right and back again. Finally, Jade leaned up on one elbow and whispered in his direction. "What's wrong, Tanner? Talk to me."

He rolled onto his back and an anxious sigh slipped through his lips. "I'm sorry, Jade. I didn't mean to keep you up."

She laid her head down on his bare chest. "Talk to me. What's on your heart?"

For the first time in an hour, Tanner was still. He pounded his fist into the mattress between them and groaned. "I want to grab the alarm clock and smash it against the wall. Every time the hands move, I feel that much closer to tomorrow."

Jade touched his face. "Is that a bad thing?" She was careful not to sound condescending or unnaturally optimistic. "Our baby's going to be born tomorrow."

"But there are risks, Jade. You and I both know it." His body relaxed beside her. "Assuming you get through the delivery okay, there's the baby to worry about. She's still so small."

"I know."

"And then we'll have maybe a day before they assault your body with the worst kind of chemicals known to man. The thought of it kills me, Jade. It kills me."

She leaned over and kissed him, silencing his fears and smoothing her thumb along his eyebrows. "You're beautiful, do you know that?"

"What if…" His whispered voice was choked with concern. "What if something happens?" He hesitated, searching her face. "I couldn't live without you."

She prayed for the right words. "Remember a long time ago in Kelso, when I didn't think God would ever love me, didn't feel I belonged in a church? Remember the Scripture you gave me back then?"

The anxiety in Tanner's expression eased some. "Yes."

"'I know the plans I have for you,' declares the LORD, 'plans to prosper you and not to harm you, plans to give you hope and a future.'"

"Right."

She searched his eyes. "Believe it, Tanner. Believe it now just like you believed it then. God has a plan for us. For me and little Madison and you and Ty. His plans are perfect." She kissed him again. "You don't have to be afraid."

A single tear slid down his face and he nodded, easing her head back down to his chest. "Don't leave me, Jade."

"Never, Tanner. Never ever."

After that they slept…but now that they were driving to the hospital, Jade could see the tension in the flex of her husband's jaw, feel it in his lack of conversation. He believed, of course. God had brought them back together, after all. But they both knew there were no guarantees that this time God's plans would be the ones they hoped for.

They met Jenny at the hospital, and she produced a bag holding milk and a muffin for Ty. "Looks like we get a day together, huh?"

Ty nodded. He wasn't as chipper as he'd been earlier that morning—probably because of the tension he sensed from Tanner—but so far he hadn't cried, and Jade was glad. Glad that he'd been busy in this season of her illness, glad that he didn't fully comprehend the risks or the hard road that lay ahead.

Jade was in her wheelchair, but she hugged Jenny around her waist. "Thanks for being here."

Jenny gave a half smile and squeezed her hand. "Mom and Matt will be here later. Before the baby's born."

"I can't believe it's already time."

"Mrs. Eastman—" Jenny met her gaze, and Jade saw that the girl's eyes were wet—"We're all praying for you. All of us."

"I know." Jade pulled away and reached up for Tanner's hand. "We feel it."

They followed Jade to a private room where she could wait with them until it was time for the delivery. Tanner would stay with Jade in the operating room, but Ty and Jenny would have to wait down the hall.

After a while a nurse came in and announced it was time. Jenny left the rest of them alone, and Ty came to Jade's side. "I love you, Mom."

"Love you, too, buddy."

"Talk to you in a little while, okay?"

"Okay."

She kissed him on the cheek and smiled, determined not to cry, determined that this would be a happy moment for their family. God knew there would be plenty of harder moments ahead.

Ty left, and the nurse wheeled Jade down the hall with Tanner at her side. They situated Jade on an operating table and gave her an epidural, all the while watching her vital signs, looking hard for clues that her body might be shutting down or seizing.

Jade felt only an occasional prod and poke until, at 7:23 that morning, the doctor lifted Madison Jade Eastman for Jade and Tanner to see. "Congratulations!" The doctor beamed. "She's a beauty."

Through teary eyes, Jade stared at their tiny, fighting-mad daughter, and then at Tanner. "She's *here*." A relieved ripple of laughter came from her throat. "Can you *believe* it?"

Tanner was crying without any sound, as though a leak had sprung on either side of his face. He smiled bigger than she'd seen in months; then he turned to Madison, her arms flailing as she spouted soft baby cries of protest. "It's unbelievable, Jade. I can't believe this feeling." He raised both fists and stared toward heaven. "I have a daughter!"

Madison's cries grew more lusty in response, and Tanner laughed. "Her lungs are healthy." He grinned at Jade, and she tried to imagine which was better—seeing Madison for the first time, or seeing Tanner so happy. He lowered his voice and stared at their newborn daughter, his eyes dancing. "She's perfect, Jade. Absolutely perfect."

Tanner hovered near the doctor as Madison was passed to a nurse, cleaned up, weighed, and wrapped in a blanket. "Four pounds, two ounces," the doctor announced. "Bigger than we expected."

Jade closed her eyes for the briefest moment, overwhelmed with gratitude. *Thank You, God. Whatever happens after this, thank You...* She opened her eyes in time to see the nurse hand Madison to Tanner.

"Okay, little girl, go to Daddy."

Tanner took her in his arms, holding her like a priceless piece of china. The minute his arms were around her, Madison stopped crying and squinted at the fluorescent lights. "That's right, sweetheart. No more tears. You're with Daddy now." He cooed at her. "You're the most beautiful baby in the world, little Maddie."

"I knew it!" Jade giggled. "A true daddy's girl; love at first sight." She was tired, and her words slurred, but nothing could have dimmed the happiness bursting within her.

Jade studied her husband and daughter, and for the flash of an instant she wondered if she would live long enough for their baby girl to know her. The thought didn't dredge up sorrow in her as it might have a week ago. Because Jade knew that if all Maddie had was the love of a father like Tanner, she'd never want for anything.

Fresh tears came, but Jade blinked them back. She didn't want anything to blur the image of Tanner and their newborn daughter. Madison looked lost in Tanner's muscled arms as he cradled her against his body and carried her to Jade. He leaned down and nuzzled his face near hers, with Madison snuggled between them.

"Everything's going to be okay, Jade," he whispered. "I can feel it."

She wanted to say something, but her throat was too thick for words to pass. Instead, she nodded and ran her finger lightly over Madison's silky dark hair.

"Time for the incubator." A nurse came up behind Tanner and held out her hands. "We don't want her to get too cold."

Reluctantly, Tanner eased their daughter into the nurse's arms. When she was gone, Tanner spoke in a soft voice near Jade's ear. "You see it, don't you?"

"What?" She brushed her cheek against his.

"She looks just like you."

Jade smiled and settled back against the operating table. She had been thinking the same thing. There were few pictures of her as a child, but the box of belongings she took from her father's house included one baby photo. There was no question that Madison looked like a small version of her. "I think you're right."

"I know so." He kissed her cheek. "She'll be a knockout."

Jade was quiet for a moment. There was something she'd wanted to tell Tanner, but the timing had never been good, especially this past week when Tanner had been so fearful of the looming delivery date. "You brought the video camera, right?"

"Right. I'll take pictures when I visit her down the hall."

"Keep it here, okay? In the room. I have something I want you to do tomorrow."

Tanner didn't seem concerned with her request. He was too taken with the giddy reality of witnessing Madison's birth and the fact that Jade had come through the surgery so well. "Whatever you want, honey. I have everything I've ever wanted. I can't think of anything I wouldn't do for you."

Jade was still strapped to the operating table, the doctor working to stitch her closed. Despite the IV tubing, she managed to drape her arm around his neck. "There's only one thing I really want."

He brought his face up against hers. "The video camera?"

She shook her head.

"Pickles and ice cream?"

Her laughter rang through the room. He'd teased her throughout her pregnancy about the fact that she never had cravings. "No, silly. Not that."

His face grew serious and he framed her cheeks with his fingertips, kissing her in a way that needed no words. "What then? Anything..."

"You, Tanner." She whispered her answer straight to his heart. "Always only you."

It had been four days, but still Hannah thought of the baby boy with every passing hour. Where was he and who would raise him? Would they teach him to love Jesus? God had heard the prayers she'd prayed over him, that much was certain. Even if they were the only prayers ever said for the boy, somehow she knew God would answer.

But still she wondered. Because in their short time together, the baby had left an indelible mark on her heart. She'd told Matt about him over dinner that night, how he'd looked into her eyes and how she'd fed him and sang to him, prayed over him for more than an hour.

"If I could have, I would have brought him home then and there, Matt. I'm sure of it. He felt like my child."

"I wish I could have seen him."

"So you'd be okay with a boy? One day down the road, I mean?"

"I only want a child, Hannah. Whatever child the Lord gives us." Matt cocked his head. "What happens to the baby now?"

"He's in short-term care until his relatives can be notified. I'm sure someone in his family will take him."

In the days since then, Hannah had tried to push thoughts of the boy aside. She even wondered if she was dwelling on him as a way of letting go of Grace. Whatever it was, the feel of him in her arms, cradled against her chest, was not something that was fading with time.

Now it was Monday morning, and she and Matt had planned to be at the hospital by seven. Instead, she'd burned the oatmeal, and by the time the two of them had cleaned the mess, they were running late. Hannah was sitting at the kitchen table putting on lipstick and Matt was washing the breakfast dishes when the phone rang.

He dried his hands on his jeans and grabbed the receiver. "Hello?" He cradled it against his shoulder as Hannah threw him a dish towel from the table. "Okay." Matt winked at her. "Just a minute."

"Salesman…" He mouthed the word and handed her the phone.

"Thanks." Hannah pointed to the clock. She kept her hand over the mouthpiece. "We have a baby to meet."

"Sorry." Matt shrugged and chuckled. "They asked for you."

Hannah brought the phone to her ear and dropped the whisper. "Hello?"

"Mrs. Bronzan, I'm sorry to call so early. This is Edna Parsons at Social Services."

The floor fell away beneath her. Why on earth was the woman calling now? To give them an update on a little girl they'd never see again? To offer more false promises? Hannah clenched her teeth. It did no good to be bitter now. "Yes, Mrs. Parsons." She motioned for Matt to join her. "What can we do for you?"

Hannah heard the woman draw a deep breath. "First, I want you to know that what happened with Grace was…well, it was devastating for me." She hesitated. "It was the first time in my career that anything like that took place, where a birth mother lied about her existing family members. It's changed the way I handle cases."

Matt pulled up a chair and sat across from Hannah, his eyebrows lowered. A streak of regret pierced the walls around Hannah's heart. Maybe her thoughts about the social worker had been too harsh. "It was hard for all of us."

"Anyway, that's not why I called."

"Okay, what's up?" A part of her didn't want to know, didn't want to hear about another child who would almost certainly, positively, practically, for sure be theirs if only they were willing to ride out the process. She held her breath and waited.

"We have a healthy baby boy, an infant. He's been cleared for adoption, Mrs. Bronzan. No foster care involved. You're the first person I've called."

Hannah could feel the blood draining from her face. A healthy baby boy? Could it be…

It wasn't possible.

The woman couldn't be talking about the baby from the hospital the other day, the little boy who had grabbed so tightly hold of her heart and held it every day since?

Hannah closed her eyes and reached for Matt's hand, her grip on the phone tighter than before. There was no way it could be the same child. Thousand Oaks had become a big city, and besides, Mrs. Parsons worked with families from all over Ventura County.

She blinked back tears and ordered herself to be calm. Mrs. Parsons was waiting for an answer. "What…what do you know about him?"

"Well…he's six weeks old and very healthy. His mother's name was Milly Wheeler; she was a teenage runaway from San Francisco…"

Hannah squeezed Matt's hand while Mrs. Parsons continued.

"Apparently the mother was a drug addict. She stayed clean through the pregnancy, but took an overdose of drugs early one morning last week. On Thursday morning she showed up at Los Robles Medical Center, barely alive. Her baby was on her lap and—"

"Dear God, it can't be…" Hannah's hand flew to her mouth and she hung her head, her mind spinning. It was a dream; it had to be. The baby, the one she'd loved through the most defining moment of his life, couldn't possibly be the one Mrs. Parsons was talking about.

Could it?

"I'm…I'm not sure I follow you, Mrs. Bronzan."

"Thursday morning? At Los Robles Medical Center?"

"Yes. His mother died in the emergency room. He's been in foster care ever since. I've checked out his background, and he has no one. Late Friday afternoon, the judge made him a ward of the court and cleared him for adoption."

Matt leaned back, searching Hannah's face for clues. She held up a single finger and closed her eyes. She had to hear it for herself before she could tell Matt. "He…he was wet. He needed a diaper and a blanket and a bottle."

Mrs. Parsons paused. "Who?"

"The baby. I was there that day. I held him while his mother died in the next room. I prayed for him and sang to him and told him everything would be okay. I wanted to take him home and never let him have another day like that again in his life."

There was a long pause, and when the social worker spoke, Hannah could hear the tears in her voice. "Then I guess God really does answer prayers. Yours and Milly Wheeler's."

Hannah moved her chair beside Matt's and rested her forehead on his shoulder as her tears soaked through his shirt. "What did Milly Wheeler pray?"

Mrs. Parsons cleared her throat. "She prayed her son would grow up to love the Lord and one day tell people about His miracles." She paused. "And what did you pray, Mrs. Bronzan?"

"That God would make his home a safe one…that his mother would love him all …all the days of her life." She brushed her face against Matt's. "That he would know the touch of a father's hand and the peace of Christ's salvation."

There was silence for a moment, and Hannah knew they were both soaking in the impossibility of what had happened. The social worker broke the silence first. "Does this mean you're interested?" Her tone was light and happy, and clearly she was sure of Hannah's answer before it was spoken.

Hannah locked eyes with Matt and remembered what he'd told her four days ago over dinner. Whatever child God blessed them with would be fine. She smiled through her tears and spoke her answer clearly. "Yes, Mrs. Parsons. We're interested. How soon can you bring him home?"

They worked out the details, and at the end of the conversation Mrs. Parsons told Hannah the baby's name. When Hannah hung up, she was at a loss for words. Matt searched her face and chuckled, his eyes brimming with tears. "Why do I have the feeling our life just changed?"

"Remember how I said we had to hurry? Because we needed to meet a baby?"

Matt nodded and wove his fingers between hers.

"Well, we do. But not Jade and Tanner's baby." She kissed him, pulling back only enough to study his eyes. "Our baby, Matt. The little boy I prayed for, remember?"

"The one whose mother died…"

"Yes." She struggled to find her voice. "He's ours, Matt. And get this…his name is Kody *Matthew.*" She uttered a single laugh and ran her fingers through her hair. "Can you believe it? I feel like I'm dreaming, but it's true! Mrs. Parsons is bringing him home this afternoon. I prayed that he'd have a safe home, that he'd know his mother's love and his father's touch—and the whole time I was praying for— " Her breath caught on a sob.

Matt wrapped her into a hug and held her close. "You were praying for us."

In the hallways of Hannah's heart, she could still hear Grace's little-girl laughter, the laughter of a child they would never know again, a child they would miss forever. But in that moment, she knew again the truths she learned four years ago. Nighttime might be long and dark, but eventually morning would come, because that was God's way. His mercies were new every morning.

Just when it seemed like the darkness would last forever, morning would come. Hannah and Matt were living proof of that. In the end, even the bleakest night would always pass away.

Just like God said it would.

Twenty-Six

Hannah and Matt had less than eight hours to prepare a nursery.

But before they could do anything, they needed to go to the hospital. Jenny had called immediately after Mrs. Parsons to say that Jade and Madison were both doing well. Hannah kept the phone call short and exchanged a knowing glance with Matt. This was not the time to tell her about her new brother.

They arrived at the hospital half an hour later and found Jenny and Ty in the waiting room watching television. Jenny grinned at them. "Nice of you guys to show up."

Hannah was bursting with the chance to talk to Jenny, but she played along. "You know how I am in the kitchen..."

Jenny laughed and stood to hug them. "Tanner says the baby's beautiful. Looks just like Jade."

"You haven't seen her?"

Jenny tapped Ty's tennis shoe with her own. "Ty has, lucky guy. Got to wear a gown and a mask and scrub up like he hasn't done for a year or more."

Ty chuckled, and Hannah thought he looked tired. He'd probably been more worried about Jade than anyone knew. Hannah smiled at him. "What's she look like?"

"She's so tiny."

Matt patted Ty's back. "She'll grow. How's your mom?"

"Good. I got to see her, too. She told me she feels a lot better now that Madison's out."

They all laughed, and when the room grew quiet, Hannah

motioned to Jenny. "Can we talk to you a minute? Out in the hallway?"

The slightest sense of alarm filled Jenny's eyes. "Everything okay?"

"Yes." Hannah glanced at Matt. "We want to tell you about a phone call that came this morning."

Jenny's expression went blank, but she followed them to a quiet place in the hallway. "What phone call?"

"Mrs. Parsons called…"

The expectancy in Hannah's voice caused a knowing look to cross Jenny's face. "No, Mom. No more sisters. I told you, it's too hard."

"Hold on." Matt placed his hand on Jenny's shoulder. Hannah's insides melted at the compassion in his eyes. "Not a sister…a brother. A baby brother."

"What? You're serious?" Jenny's face went pale. "I'm going to have a brother?"

Hannah reached for Jenny and pulled her close so the three of them were huddled together, much as they'd been that awful morning when they said good-bye to Grace. "Remember the baby I told you about, the little boy at the hospital whose mother died?"

"You prayed for him and held him while the doctors tried to save her."

"Right. Mrs. Parsons ran the check on him, and he's legally free for adoption. Today! She's bringing him home this afternoon."

Jenny looked from Hannah to Matt and back to Hannah again. She let loose the sweetest ripple of laughter. "Wow, I don't know what to say. You guys and the Eastmans having babies on the same day? Isn't that kind of like a miracle?"

Hannah laughed. "I hadn't thought of that." She looked at Matt. "We need to tell Tanner."

At that moment they spotted him trudging down the hallway,

still wearing the scrubs he'd worn for the delivery. He saw them and waved, his face taken up with an enormous smile. Relief washed over Hannah. A smile that size could only mean one thing: Jade and the baby were doing well.

Hannah crooked her arm around Tanner's neck and hugged him. "Jenny told us she's beautiful. Looks just like Jade."

Tanner nodded and shifted to hug Matt as well. "They're both fine." The smile remained, but from this close, Hannah could see the concern in his eyes. "Jade's tired. Ever since the baby was born, all she wants to do is sleep."

"That's normal." Hannah squeezed Tanner's hand. "Having babies is hard work."

Tanner relaxed a bit. "She got through the surgery without any seizures. The doctors were worried about that."

"Fantastic." Matt looked at Hannah and winked. "Looks like October 7 will be a day we'll all remember."

Tanner looked from Hannah to Matt and finally to Jenny. He grinned at her as he elbowed Matt. "What're your parents up to now?"

Jenny ran her fingers through her bangs and shook her head. "You'll have to ask them about this one."

Hannah giggled. She knew how overwhelmed Jenny must feel. The day had been nothing but a series of life-changing announcements. The sum of them was draining, and she and Matt still had to set up a nursery.

"I give up." Tanner scratched his head. "Someone tell me what's going on."

"Okay." Matt tried to hide his smile. "Hannah and I are going to be parents."

Tanner studied Matt's face. "Seriously?"

"Seriously. The social worker called this morning. She has a healthy baby boy for us. Six weeks old. His name is Kody

Matthew, and she's bringing him home tonight." Matt tousled Jenny's hair. "So—" he checked his watch—"in six hours, Jenny's going to have a baby brother."

Tanner raised a fist in the air and hooted out loud. "Is God good or what? That's awesome." He hugged the three of them, and then he took Matt's shoulder and looked him straight in the face. "We can draw up the papers next week."

Now it was Matt's turn to be confused. "Papers?"

Tanner tried to look indignant. "Of course, papers. Madison Jade will need a fine upstanding husband one day, right?"

"And…?" Clearly Matt didn't see the connection, but Hannah did and she laughed out loud.

Tanner anchored his hands on his hips. "If we're going to arrange the marriage now we'd better draw up papers next week. That way there'll be no question about it. No dating until she's twenty-two and out of college, at which point she will be free to marry Mr. Kody Matthew Bronzan. Sounds good to me."

They all laughed, and Hannah was glad to see Tanner so happy. When the laughter died, she asked about Jade. "Should we wait and see her tomorrow?"

"I think she'd like that." The teasing left Tanner's eyes and his face was filled with gratitude. "I'll tell her you were here. It'll mean the world to her."

They said good-bye and made plans for Jenny to meet them at home early that afternoon, before the baby arrived. A neighbor friend of Jade's would take over with Ty at the hospital and watch him overnight. Then they would all meet at the hospital again tomorrow to visit Jade and see her baby.

Before they left, Tanner thanked them again for coming. "And give my future son-in-law a big kiss, will you?"

It was a happy moment, and as Hannah and Matt left the hospital, she prayed that memories of this day would stay with

Tanner for weeks to come. Because there was no question about one thing: The hardest days for Jade and Tanner were right around the corner.

The next twenty-four hours passed in a blur for Tanner.

Hannah and Matt brought their new baby boy to the hospital and gave Tanner a chance to hold him. It was strange, really. Here he was at the hospital having his own child, but the baby he got to spend more time holding was Matt and Hannah's.

The constant twist of events was enough to make him dizzy.

Jade seemed to know what was going on around her, but she was tired most of the time and that worried Tanner. She passed her congratulations on to the Bronzans, and after Matt and Hannah got a chance to see Madison through the window of the neonatal intensive care unit, they did the same. It was a giddy time—a time when doctors assured them Madison was thriving, given the timing of her birth. She had no lung problems, no cerebral palsy, and no serious dangers. They would keep her in the hospital only as a precaution until she reached five pounds. Then she could go home.

Jade's situation was another story.

Though she had survived the surgery without seizure or signs of trouble, her white count was high. Dr. Layton explained that was because she was fighting an infection somewhere. Maybe at the site of her C-section, maybe in her brain. It was hard to tell.

Either way, an MRI done late the previous evening showed that the tumor had grown a fraction of an inch in the past week. Enough to cause Dr. Layton to worry. Treatment couldn't wait any longer, and the doctor detailed the plan they would follow.

"First of all, we're keeping Jade in the hospital." He directed his comments to Tanner, because even now, with so serious a discussion going on, Jade could hardly stay awake. "We'll start massive chemotherapy and radiation tomorrow and administer treatment for two weeks." He paused. "I'd hoped for three. But I think it's more important to get the tumor out. A woman's hormones change radically after a baby's delivered. Sometimes that can cause a stable tumor to double in size overnight, which in this case would have grave consequences for Jade. Other times it can cause the tumor to send tentacles into the brain. In which case the tumor would become inoperable."

He went on to say that they'd do an MRI each day to monitor the tumor's behavior throughout the two-week treatment phase. "By then the most we can hope for is that the tumor will have shrunk and stayed intact."

Tanner stared at the doctor, speechless. Sometime around the point where Dr. Layton started describing treatment, the floor had shifted. Since then, he'd had the constant feeling that he was falling.

Why hadn't the doctor explained these things before? The tumor could double in size? With grave consequences? What was *that* supposed to mean? Tanner grabbed hold of the nearest chair to steady himself. And what would happen if the tumor grew tentacles…? Tanner was too terrified to ask. He forced himself to slip into lawyer mode, so he could ask questions without allowing his emotions to get in the way. "What are her chances?"

"If the tumor does what I want it to, I think they're good. There are risks of course, but we can talk about those later."

It was after three o'clock on Tuesday afternoon, and Tanner was exhausted. He'd stayed in a vinyl reclining chair, which the nurses set up adjacent to Jade's bed. Though he was comfortable enough, Tanner couldn't bring himself to sleep. Instead he watched the monitors flashing Jade's vital signs. And when he grew restless, he would visit the neonatal intensive care. They'd told him he could come any hour of the day or night to see Madison, and even though he could only stroke her tiny arm through the holes in the incubator, he wanted to spend as much time with her as possible.

Now that everyone was gone, Tanner leaned back in the chair and took Jade's hand in his. Maybe he could grab an hour's sleep before dinner was delivered. He studied Jade and thought it strange that her stomach was so flat. Overnight she looked as though she'd never carried Madison.

Something sank in Tanner's gut as the reason dawned on him. Her lack of excess weight was because of the cancer. She'd barely gained ten pounds. No wonder her stomach was flat. In fact, if anything she looked thinner than before she got pregnant. Too thin.

He sighed out loud. One more thing to worry about. His eyes closed and he turned his thoughts toward God. *How do I get through it, Lord? It feels like we're walking through a minefield and everywhere we turn there's danger.*

In response, he pictured the plaque on his desk, and the inscribed words filled his mind: *Be still, and know that I am God…*

The words soothed his heart and shone a ray of light through the dark tunnel they were traveling. That was it, really. The answer to life's most difficult moments. Life was full of craziness, chaos and inexplicable tragedy. Like the tragedy a year ago of the fallen Twin Towers in New York City or the damaged Pentagon in Washington, D.C.

What sense did life make at all if not for that one single verse.

He could almost hear the Lord whispering the words directly to his soul.

Be still, Tanner, My son. Be still, and know that I am God.

The words calmed him and lulled him to sleep. Two hours later he felt something on his arm and he was instantly awake.

"What is it?" He looked around and found Jade studying him from her hospital bed.

She giggled at him. "Sorry. I didn't want to wake you."

He sat straight up and moved to the edge of the chair, searching her face for signs of weakness or trouble or any one of the myriad of troubles Dr. Layton said might come to pass. "How are you?"

"Fine." A smile filled her face. "How's Maddie?"

The tension left Tanner's neck and shoulders. "She's beautiful. No problems, just a bit small. The doctor said she can go home as soon as she hits five pounds."

Jade's face glowed in response. "God's so good to us, Tanner."

Dr. Layton's warnings from earlier that morning ran through Tanner's mind, but he pushed them back. "Yes." He took Jade's hand in his and ran his finger over the bruise marks where the IV had been for her C-section. "God is very good."

They were quiet for a moment. "I know what you're thinking." Jade's eyes were brighter than they'd been since the surgery, and Tanner was flooded with relief. Maybe Hannah was right. Maybe Jade was only tired because of the delivery, like any other woman.

"What?"

"You want to know how I'm feeling, right?"

Tanner grew serious. "Always."

"I feel good, Tanner. I was half-asleep but I heard Dr. Layton. The tumor isn't going to double overnight…it isn't going to grow tentacles into my brain. God wouldn't bring us this far only to let that happen."

"But you said yourself sometimes God's plans aren't ours."

"I know. But right now, right here, I don't feel like a cancer patient. I feel like a new mother, alive and awake and anxious to hold her baby. Thrilled beyond words to be married to the man of my dreams and certain I'll be around…" Jade paused as tears glistened in her eyes. "Long enough to see that man walk our little girl down the aisle someday."

Tanner's throat was so thick he couldn't speak. Instead, he lifted Jade's hand to his mouth and kissed it, soft and tender, as though it might break.

"But just in case…I have a favor to ask."

He looked up and coughed, still struggling to speak. "Favor?"

"Yes. Remember? I told you I needed the video camera for something today?"

Tanner nodded. "Vaguely." He cast her a silly smile. "I was a little distracted yesterday."

"Well, it's time. Now. Before dinner."

He had no idea what she was leading to, but he reached for the camera and took off the lens cover. "Okay, what am I shooting?"

"Me." She pointed to the closet. "I had the nurse set a bag in there. Inside is a pink journal. Could you get it for me?" She cast him a sweet but tired smile. "Please."

Tanner knit his eyebrows together. He had no idea where this was going but he did as she asked. The journal was where she said it would be, and he gave it to her without pausing to see what it contained. Then he returned to his seat, positioned the video camera, and saluted her. "Tanner, the cameraman, at your service."

Jade sat up a bit straighter, wincing. "They don't tell you how sore your stomach'll be." She smiled and straightened first her bathrobe, then her hair. "Okay, I'm ready."

A strange, uneasy feeling made Tanner lower the camera. His teasing tone was gone. "Wait a minute. What's going on?"

Jade leveled her gaze at him, her face every bit as peaceful as before. "I have something to tell Maddie, something I want her to have when she's older."

Tanner's heart raced and he shook his head. "You just got done telling me you feel fine, that you know you're going to make it and everything's going to work out."

"Yes…"

"So, I don't get it—" He stopped, aware his voice was louder than before and bordered on angry. He started again. "Are you saying you want me to tape some…some sort of good-bye message to Madison?" He paused and glanced about the room, searching for the words. Finally his eyes found Jade's again. "I can't do it, Jade. Ask the nurse, ask Hannah. But I can't sit here and watch you say good-bye through the lens of a video camera."

She waited until he was finished. "It doesn't have to be a good-bye video, Tanner. It's simply a message from me to her. And I want you to tape it." Her eyes grew more intense than before. "Please."

A light huff slipped from his lips. His gaze fell to his lap and the camera lying there. He wanted to do this for her, but how? Tanner thought back over the months, how he hadn't been there for Jade after her diagnosis…

If she was brave enough to speak a message to Maddie from the bed of her hospital room, looking into their family video camera, then in God's strength alone he would be strong enough to film her.

He looked up and his eyes met hers. "I'm sorry." He held the camera up and flipped the screen on the side. "Of course I'll film it."

Jade cleared her throat and nodded to Tanner. At her signal, he began filming and she smiled into the camera. "Hi, Maddie. I'm here in the hospital room the day after you were born, and—" she held up the pink journal—"I wanted to share a few things with you."

Tanner did his best to keep the camera still.

"This is a gift for you, Maddie. Something I've worked on for a long time. It's a book of letters from me to you." She smiled and opened the journal, pointing to the pages inside. "Each letter is sort of a talk, really. Something I might tell you when you take your first steps or say your first words. The encouragement I'd give you on the first day of kindergarten or the first day of middle school."

The book was full, front to back, with handwritten letters. Tanner could see the tears in Jade's eyes, but only if he looked hard. His own silent tears blurred the image of Jade, and he blinked, fighting for the strength to continue as Jade kept talking. "One letter tells you how I like to apply mascara and the best way to blend foundation. Another tells you what to look for in a friend and what kind of boy to stay away from."

Jade flipped through the pages. "I wrote you a letter for the day you get your first kiss and the day you leave for college. And I wrote you a letter for the day you get married, sweetheart." She closed the journal and held it close to her heart. "Those and lots more, honey. They're all here."

She hesitated and her smile faded just a bit. Tanner blinked back another wave of tears and tried not to sniff. He didn't want anything to ruin the miracle he was capturing on tape. Jade swallowed hard. Her eyes narrowed as though she could see the face of their daughter in the camera lens. "My prayer, honey, is that you and I are watching this together. That we get the chance to watch it together lots of times and even share it with your children one day." Jade plucked at her terry cloth bathrobe. "We can laugh at how silly I look and talk about how much time has passed and how quickly. But whether I'm there or not, you'll know that at this time in my life, I got sick. Very sick."

Tears slid from Jade's eyes and she wiped them with her fingertips. Tanner wanted to rescue her, help her through the moment, but there was nothing he could do except keep the camera rolling.

Her voice trembled as she continued. "Tomorrow I'll start treatment, medicine and radiation that the doctors hope will make me better. Then in two weeks I'll have an operation. One that we all believe will save my life."

Jade steadied herself. "Your father and I have prayed about it very much, and we believe God's word is true. He has a plan for me, for you. For all of us. A plan to give us hope and a future and not to harm us."

Her composure broke then. She brought her hand to her face and for several seconds she hung her head, staving off the sobs Tanner knew were just beneath the surface. When she looked up, she bit her lip and smiled through her tears. "But sometimes, honey, God's plans are not our own. Even if that means I don't make it through this, I want you to know how great God has been to our family. Your dad will tell you the stories, but…but I wanted you to hear it from me. If I'm not there beside you, Maddie, I'm in heaven with Jesus."

Tanner's tears were coming in streams, and it took everything in him to keep the camera in place. Jade shook her head. "Don't ever blame Jesus for the things that don't go as we plan, sweetheart. He's the only One who always knows what's best. Even if it isn't what we want."

Jade paused, drawing in a deep breath. "Whew." She stuck out her lower lip and blew her bangs off her forehead. "This is harder than I thought." She smiled and ran her fingers beneath her eyes again. "There are a few things I don't ever want you to forget." She tightened her grip on the journal. "They're in here, written in the front of the book, but I wanted you to hear them from me. Just in case I don't get another chance to tell you."

Tanner held his breath, his heart breaking.

"I want you to know I love you more than you could ever imagine. I dreamed about you for two years before you were born, and now I feel like God's granted me the sweetest miracle by giving you to me and your dad and Ty."

Her smile faded. "I also want you to know how much I love your father. He is the greatest man I've ever known, and no matter what happens, I pray you and Ty will follow his example as long as you live. He is my strength, my song, my protector. Ever since I've known him, he's led me to Christ again and again. And Christ is the only One who could give me the peace that's in my heart right now. Your father will lead you there, too, if you let him." Jade's voice broke again. "So let him, baby. Please let him lead you to Jesus."

Jade kept her gaze straight at the camera lens. "Finally, I want you to love your brother. He's older than you, yes, but he loves you so much. And he's very, very special to me. A time may come when he wonders about life and God and why I had to get sick. If that happens, be there for him, Maddie. Be his friend. Be the one he talks to…especially if I can't be there."

Tears streamed down Jade's cheeks again and she shrugged. A smile filled her face and a sound, more laugh than sob, came from her throat. "I guess that's all. I hope you like the book, honey. I'll love you forever and no matter what happens, I'll see you at home."

Jade lifted her eyes to Tanner's and he turned the camera off. Moving like a man who had aged twenty years in fifteen minutes, Tanner set the camera on the floor, stood, and embraced Jade across the bars of the hospital bed.

They stayed that way a long time, weeping without a sound as they lay on each other's shoulders. No words were needed. Regardless of what Jade had said about the video, its message had only one purpose.

When she could speak, Jade whispered against his face. "The hardest thing…is to think of leaving her…the way my mother left me."

Tanner's eyes were swollen, his nose completely stuffed from crying. Still he found his voice and spoke it into her hair, the hair that would be gone in a matter of weeks. "It would never be like that, Jade. Your mother left you on purpose."

"I know." She muffled a sob in his shoulder. "But I still missed her. I wondered what she'd tell me on the first day of middle school, or when I came home in love with you after our first night out in Kelso." She took three quick breaths. "I don't ever want Maddie to wonder. I want her to feel me there with her even if it's only my words."

Despite the depth of his pain and fear, Tanner couldn't have been more proud of her. "When did you have time to write that?" He drew back, his voice still a whisper. "And how come you didn't tell me?"

"I wrote it when you were still working. I kept looking for the right time to tell you, but finally I decided this would be the best way. Besides, I wanted to make sure she was here and…and healthy before I did the video."

"What about Ty?"

Jade smiled. "I wrote him one, too. I'll give it to him before my surgery. But I already videotaped my message for him. It's in my top drawer in the bedroom."

Tanner's mouth hung open. "I had no idea…"

"I used the automatic setting." She angled her face. "It worked fine."

There was a knock at the door and a nurse entered with two trays of food. Tanner returned to his seat, and they ate their meal side by side with few words.

Jade was tired after making the video and needed sleep. The next morning treatment would begin, and she had to be strong if her system was going to handle the strain of both chemotherapy and radiation, especially while she was still recovering from the C-section.

The only bright spot was that Dr. Layton had promised her a visit to the nursery in the morning so she could spend an hour with Madison before starting treatment. Tanner knew the entire next day—the next two weeks, in fact—would be the hardest in his life. But that night he was determined to be upbeat. For Jade.

They laughed about some of the silly things Ty had said in the past, and then Tanner read Psalms 23 and 91 to her. When he was finished, she yawned and held out her arms. He leaned over the hospital bed bars and kissed her. "I love you, Jade."

She smiled, and though her eyes glistened, she didn't cry. "No matter what happens tomorrow, no matter how bad it gets, I'd do it all again to be with you, Tanner. No one will ever love you like I do."

Fifteen minutes later she was asleep, and though he'd ordered himself to be strong, Tanner was helpless to stop the tears. Dr. Layton had said her hair would most likely be the first thing to go once the chemotherapy began. He gulped back a sob and wove his fingers through her hair. It looked thick and shiny dark against her pink robe. She'd never worn it long, but in light of the impending cancer treatment, she'd grown it out.

Jade had made light of it. "I'll be bald soon enough anyway."

But Tanner couldn't imagine Jade without hair, couldn't picture her silky dark head bald and cut open.

The room was so quiet he could hear his heartbeat, and he wrapped a thick strand of her hair around his finger and held it that way. He stared at her, studying her, watching her breathe through most of the night. Terrified that if he fell asleep, Jade—the Jade he knew and loved and cherished—would disappear from his life.

Not just for a day or a week or a season.

But forever.

Twenty-Seven

G race's absence and Jade's illness were the only marks on an otherwise perfect time for the Bronzans.

During the next two weeks, Hannah prayed daily about both situations.

Grace's curly hair and contagious smile still flashed in Hannah's mind every morning, and occasionally—although less often than before—it took several minutes to remember that she was no longer their daughter, no longer living in the frilly bedroom down the hall.

They had talked about converting the room into Kody's nursery, but there was a small room across the hall that Hannah had used for odds and ends that worked just as well. Besides, she and Matt still believed that somehow, sometime, God would bless them with another daughter.

Becoming parents to a son, however, was nothing less than an act of God. A complete surprise that none of them would have sought out and that had made their home a place of hope and miracles. Overnight Jenny had taken to spending long hours rocking Kody and cooing at him. They marveled at his glowing skin and clear bright eyes, at the fact that a runaway teenage girl had managed to care for her baby so well, and herself so poorly.

Long before Kody awoke each morning, Hannah would find herself restless, missing the weight of him in her arms and wanting to hold him, feed him, sing over him as she'd done that first time in the hospital room. More often than not, she would tiptoe into his nursery, sit in the rocking chair next to his crib, and stare at him, awed by God's hand in her life.

Hannah Bronzan? The mother of a son? It was something she had never imagined, something she had even avoided when they first entered the world of adoption. All she'd ever known were girls. But now, holding Kody, she could sense a difference in the strength of his fist around her finger, the lust of his cry. He was a good-natured baby, yes, but he was all boy. A fighter with strong will and determination that overshadowed anything she'd seen in her girls at this age.

Hannah often sat in the dawning shadows of morning and studied his face through the crib bars, imagining what great thing God had planned for him. Maybe he'd be a preacher, like poor Milly had prayed. Or the faithful president of a company, leading his employees by example. Or maybe a teacher, a coach. A freedom fighter like Matt, or a doctor like Tom.

It didn't matter really. Whatever Kody was, he'd always be a miracle first. A boy whom God had handpicked for their home, their arms. Their family.

That was something else. After Grace was taken from them, Hannah doubted the entire idea of adoption. It was too painful. Besides, other families could take in hurting children. She wondered if perhaps she had only agreed to adopt in an attempt to re-create what she'd lost that awful day four years ago. Not that she could ever replace Alicia, but maybe she could re-create the busy family atmosphere that had marked her life before the accident. Hannah had desperately missed that.

Grace's presence had restored a sense of that, but not really. She was so mistrusting at first, so delicate. They had only just begun to feel like a real family, to sense the balance and laughter and safety a family represents, when she was taken away.

But now, since the moment Mrs. Parsons brought Kody Matthew home, everything about their home seemed different, warmer. More focused on love and life and faith.

Hannah spent hours pondering the change Kody had brought to their family, and she figured it was because Jenny was practically grown up and gone. Before adopting, their family hadn't spent great amounts of time together. Rather Hannah and Matt lived like newlyweds, learning what it was to share a bathroom and a bedroom and a kitchen.

Jenny was a part of it all, of course. But she was gone much of the time, busy with friends and football games and study groups at school. Now Jenny made a point of being home. She and Hannah and Matt spent most evenings circled around the living room, cuddling with each other and taking turns holding Kody.

They talked more and laughed more and somehow, in the process, they loved more.

The sum of it made Hannah's heart swell, and on Sunday, at the end of the first whole week with Kody, she stood at the front door and told Matt as much. The next day would be the first in the trial against the Benson City Council, and he had plans to be there most of the week.

It was six-thirty, and upstairs Kody and Jenny were still asleep. Hannah rose up on her tiptoes and circled her arms around Matt's neck. "Be careful." It wasn't something she used to think about, but after losing Tom and Alicia, and after that fateful day last September, it was impossible not to. Yes, there were more security measures in place, but there were also more angry terrorists. Not that fear had kept them from flying, but Hannah made a point of telling Matt how she loved him before he left for an airport.

Just in case she never got another chance.

He smiled at her and brushed back her bangs with his fingertips. "I will." He kissed her. "Take care of Kody. He'll probably cry more with me gone."

Hannah giggled. "He might need therapy when he's older."

"Actually," Matt pretended to look hurt. "I think you're right. He's very bonded with me."

They both laughed, and Hannah straightened the collar on his suit coat. "Knock 'em dead, will ya? Tanner could use something positive right now."

Matt's eyes narrowed. "I care about every case. Pray about it, search the Bible for help." He shook his head. "But this one's more important than anything I've done in a long time."

"Because of Tanner?"

"Yes." Matt's expression was pensive. "Tanner has such passion, Hannah. Such heart for what we do at the firm. This case mattered a lot to him; it's precedent-setting stuff."

Hannah bit her lip, her heart heavy. "And he gave it up for Jade."

"That's just a glimpse of how much Tanner loves that woman." Matt looked at the ceiling as though he was searching for the right words, words that might come close to describing the relationship between Jade and Tanner. "He's loved her since he was a boy."

Hannah nodded and tears welled in her eyes. "I know."

Matt narrowed his eyes, his jaw clenched, and stared at her a long moment. "What'll he do if something happens to her?"

"No." Hannah shook her head. "We can't think that way."

"I know." He hesitated. "I'll be home before Monday. I promised Tanner."

Hannah stared at her slippers. "Next Sunday night, before the surgery, let's pray around her hospital bed."

"Definitely." He studied Hannah's face. "God's in control. Nothing will happen to Jade that isn't somehow part of His plan."

Tears threatened to spill onto her face and Hannah bit her lip to keep from crying. "I feel so helpless." She let her head fall against his chest. "Pray that God gives me a way to help her this week, okay?"

Matt nodded. "I will." He glanced at his watch. "I've gotta run. Keep me posted on how she's doing."

"I will." Hannah opened his suit coat and slipped her arms around him, hugging him long and close, relishing the feel of his strong, warm body against hers. Since the day they met, Matt had made her feel safe and protected. And lately—as they shared the role of parenting Kody—she was falling more in love with him every day. "I love you."

Matt drew back, his hands still locked near the small of her back. "I may not have known you since I was a boy, Hannah, but I've waited a lifetime for you. And now...I can't help but know that God had me wait because He knew. He knew one day a beautiful woman with a broken heart would come into my life."

He brought his lips to hers and kissed her in a way she would remember all week long. His voice was thick with emotion when he continued.

"And He knew that only together would either of us find the strength to love like this."

Twenty-Eight

From the moment he stepped foot in the courtroom, everything that could go wrong for Matt did.

More than half the jurors were single women in their late thirties and forties. Two jurors were high school teachers, one a college professor, and two were entertainers—young men who had, respectively, a pierced eyebrow and tongue, and a full-neck tattoo.

Usually, in the cases he and Tanner handled, it was best to stay away from anyone too liberal or artsy, anyone in entertainment or academia. Those types of people often, though not always, made jurors who already had their minds set against anything remotely involving God. Some of them would have bought completely into the current-day separation of church and state mind-set. There was a chance these people walked through life believing even the mention of God was illegal.

Matt remembered attending a book conference once in which he and Tanner were promoting a title, *Stand up for Freedom*, that had come out of their early work at the CPRR. The book was intended to appeal primarily to Christians, but the publisher had seen its crossover potential for the general market and asked them to attend the conference.

Midway through the morning, a woman approached Matt and Tanner and looked at their book. Then, as though she were a covert operative in an underworld spy game, she leaned close and asked, "Is this book…you know—" she looked both ways— "religious?"

Matt remembered Tanner's grin. He leaned close in turn, looked both ways as she had done, and whispered, "Yes! It's about religious freedom." He dropped the whisper and stood tall. "The good news is in America you don't have to whisper about religion. It's your right to talk about it." He glanced around the room—a place where every topic from mysticism to magic arts to a dozen Middle Eastern practices was highlighted in dozens of books. "In fact, you can even talk about it right here." He handed her the book. "Read it and see for yourself."

Monday morning, Matt assessed the jurors and wondered what Tanner would have done about it. Thanked God, probably. Assumed there was a reason and moved ahead. So even though the jury selection was grim at best, Matt committed the case to the Lord and carried on.

The premise of Tanner's case, which he'd built long before Matt took over, was simple. After interviewing everyone involved, after studying the contract signed by the Benson City Council and Pastor Casey Carson of the First Church of the Valley, Tanner had thought of something new, something he'd never considered before.

If the Benson City Council was requiring First Church of the Valley to refrain from teaching that Jesus Christ is the only way to salvation, then, in a sense, a local public governing body was defining religion.

Maybe not defining it for the entire state of Colorado, or even the town of Benson, but in drawing up a contract that allowed any group to use City Hall except those who preach the Gospel of Christ, they were, without a doubt, defining religion.

Tanner's tactic, therefore, was this: The city of Benson was in violation of the Constitution, wherein no law should be made "respecting an establishment of religion or *prohibiting the free exercise thereof.*"

In other words, for the first time since religious freedom cases had become necessary, Tanner intended to use the very argument his opponents had used for years. Instead of spending an entire case trying to prove his client had not violated the separation of church and state clause, he would turn the tables and accuse the defendant of that very thing.

So Matt's task was twofold.

First, he would have to depict the First Church of the Valley as a law-abiding organization with as much right to rent City Hall as any other group. Then he would present the biased contract and accuse the Benson City Council of making a law that established a Christ-less religion and prohibited Pastor Carson's church from the free exercise of their faith.

Matt had never prided himself in his opening or closing arguments. He preferred the behind-the-scenes research and examination phases of a case. But now, with Tanner holding a bedside vigil at Jade's side, counting down the days until her brain surgery, Matt had more righteous fire stirring within him than at any time in the past few years.

Because their side had filed the suit, Matt presented his arguments first. He stood and made his way toward the jurors, meeting each of their gazes with a warmth usually reserved for church friends and business associates. "Good morning," he said, nodding in their direction. "Thank you for being here today, for believing that in this courtroom over the next few days there might be something more important happening than your routine schedules. Something in which each of you obviously believes."

Matt glanced at the notepad in his hands and his confidence grew. Tanner had to be praying for him; the words coming from his mouth sounded so much like Tanner it was uncanny.

Thank You, God; give me the words...

Be strong and bold, for I am with you.

The answer resonated in his soul and came straight from the Scripture he'd read that morning. A sense of peace and sureness filled his senses as he began explaining his case for the jury in clear and passionate detail.

He told them that the First Amendment to the Constitution involved a safeguard for people like Pastor Casey Carson. "People whom the founders of this great nation wanted to protect." Matt stopped, slid his left hand into his pants pocket and moved his gaze from one juror to the next. "Do you know why? Because they were familiar with religious persecution. It was something that troubled them enough to leave the comforts of England, their homeland, and venture into a new world, a new life."

Matt's tone grew stronger. "No one would tell them whom to worship and how. No, in America a person would be free to worship as they chose, and the government—no matter how many generations would pass—would never, ever establish a law prohibiting the freedom of religion."

Out of the corner of his eye, Matt saw the attorneys for the City of Benson conferring in silent whispers. Tanner was right! They were surprised by this argument. No doubt they had planned to take the very same approach, accusing Pastor Carson and the First Church of the Valley of crossing the line that separated church and state by daring to preach the name of Christ in a public building.

But now, just minutes into the trial's first day, partway through Matt's opening arguments, there was a current of electricity running through the courtroom that Matt was sure everyone could feel. The church hadn't crossed a line, the Benson City Council had.

Matt took three sure steps over to the plaintiff's table and pulled the lease agreement from a file. When he was back in front of the jury, he held it up. "I hold a lease agreement written and agreed upon by the Benson City Council." He paused and paced a few steps. "Now keep in mind, when the founders of the Constitution referred to Congress, they meant *any* public governing body. Therefore, the First Amendment applies to the Benson City Council as strongly as it applies to the president of the United States."

He raised the lease agreement higher and uttered a single, humorless chuckle. "I'm about to read you a clause in this lease agreement that will astonish you. It will make you wonder how it is that the U.S. Constitution has come to be taken so lightly by people like the Benson City Council members."

Matt could almost picture Tanner in the corner of the room giving him a thumbs-up. Encouraged by a strength that could only have been from God, Matt continued. "At first this…lease agreement…looks like the ordinary sort. It includes the names of the lessor—in this case, the City of Benson—and the lessee—in this case, First Church of the Valley. It requires that a specific amount of rent be paid on time each month and that the facility is cared for in a specific manner."

He flipped the page. "It details how the building may be set up for community events and how it must be cleaned after each use." He pointed to a section highlighted in yellow near the bottom of the second page. "The part you won't believe is down here."

There were still a few feet separating him from the jury box, and now Matt took a step closer, leaning on the railing and angling his back slightly toward the jury. That way when he held up the lease agreement, most of them in the middle section could read the words over his shoulder. "Right here, on line forty-three, item seventeen, is a stipulation to the agreement that reads: 'City Hall may not be rented by any group who teaches faith in Jesus Christ as the only way to salvation.'"

Matt turned and faced the jury again. The outrage he'd felt upon first reading the clause was fresh within him, and Matt let it show in his eyes. "Give yourself a minute to let that sink in. City Hall, a place that may be rented by any group willing to pay and follow a lease, may *not* be rented by a group who teaches faith in Jesus Christ…as the only way to salvation."

He paused and leaked the air from his lungs, giving his expression time to relax. "There's a name for people who teach that type of doctrine. In this country, we call them Christians." At this point Matt returned to the table and exchanged the lease for a hardback copy of the Bible, paper-clipped at a verse in the book of John.

Matt opened it and stood squarely before the jurors. "Many of you may not read the Bible; you may not even like the Bible." He leveled his gaze at them. "But you are Americans, and for that reason you must hear what I'm about to read. He'd memorized the verse decades ago, but he read it from the Bible now, so the jury would have no doubts about the teaching and where it came from. Matt cleared his throat. "In the book of John, chapter fourteen, verse six, the Bible quotes Jesus as saying, 'I am the way and the truth and the life. No one comes to the Father except through me.'"

There was utter silence in the courtroom as Matt closed the Bible and met the faces—some curious, some troubled—of each and every juror. Matt's voice was so quiet they had to strain forward to hear him. "Jesus told the people that he was the only road to heaven. And that, friends, is the very belief banned by the Benson City Council."

Matt set the Bible back on the table, selected another document, and tossed his hands in the air, his voice loud once more. "Sure, you can rent the City Hall in Benson if you believe in voodoo or witchcraft. You can preach a doctrine of multiple gods or no God at all." He raised a single finger. "Ah...but preach the Christian doctrine, the one established by Jesus, and here's what will happen."

The jurors were clearly spellbound. Across the room Matt saw the opposing attorneys scribbling furiously on their legal pads. He leaned against the jury box and positioned the document in his hands so the jury could see it. "This is a letter Pastor Carson received from the Benson City Council eight months after he and the First Church of the Valley—a Christian congregation—began renting out the Benson City Hall."

He glanced at the document, holding it in the air just in front of his face so he had no trouble reading it. "'Dear Mr. Carson, this is to inform you that your right to meet at the Benson City Hall has hereby been reneged due to a lease violation by you and your group.'" Matt raised an eyebrow at the jury and then returned his attention to the letter. "'Our records show that because of this violation, the city of Benson owes you and your organization no money in refunded lease payments. This enforcement goes into effect immediately, as your time slot at City Hall will be filled by another organization this coming Sunday. Sincerely, the Benson City Council.'"

Matt went on to explain how the letter took the First Church of the Valley by surprise.

"See—" he gazed at the jurors—"the church leaders had missed the clause at the end of the lease agreement. They had no idea why they were in violation of the lease." Matt paced several steps back and forth, making eye contact with each of the jurors. Any doubts they may have had about him and his argument were dissolving like sugar in water.

The church, Matt told them, had paid one year's rent up front— seven hundred dollars per month for a total of $8,400. "In addition to kicking the church out of their rented facility with virtually no warning because of a lease clause that clearly violates the U.S. Constitution—" he paused for effect—"the Benson City Council made the poor decision to keep thousands of dollars in lease money. Even though the building was no longer available to the church."

For the next twenty minutes Matt gave the jury the gist of the story, the fact that Pastor Carson contacted the City Council and talked to a secretary who told him about the overlooked clause in the lease and then added, "Your church's name convinced us you wouldn't be in violation."

Matt allowed his tone to grow incensed for a moment, and he could read the same emotion in the eyes of several jurors. "The church's *name?*" He shook his head. "In other words, since the name Christ or Jesus wasn't in the name of Pastor Carson's church, the Benson City Council thought they were safe. Safe enough that they didn't need to check what doctrine was being preached each Sunday." He shifted his weight and cocked his head. "But then someone told someone, and they told someone else, and the Sunday before Pastor Carson's church lost their lease, three members of the Benson City Council showed up at the Sunday service."

Matt prayed his closing words would leave an impression. "This was a case, ladies and gentlemen, that *had* to be brought to trial. Because the Benson City Council had the audacity to make a law prohibiting the free exercise of religion—in this case, the Christian religion. An action that flies in the face of our Constitution and everything this country stands for. An action our founding fathers hoped to avert when they wrote the First Amendment."

He paced to the far end of the jury and noticed that each pair of eyes followed him. "We cannot allow that, friends. Not here, not in Benson. Not anywhere in the United States. Because once we let our government decide what's acceptable in church meetings taking place in City Halls, we're only a short jump to letting them decide what's acceptable in churches." Matt's voice rang with sincerity. "And that would mean everything our forefathers stood for, every battle fought in the name of freedom, would be for nothing."

Matt shrugged one shoulder. "And so, honestly, ladies and gentlemen, this is not a case about separation of church and state. It's a case about standing up for freedom. My freedom, your freedom." He pointed to the front row of spectators where Pastor Carson was seated next to his wife among fifty people from First Church of the Valley. "Their freedom. On that note, we are not only asking that this church be allowed to maintain their lease with the Benson City Hall. We're asking for damages. Certainly the money kept by the city these past months, when Pastor Carson's church has had to meet in various less desirable facilities. But also punitive damages."

He glanced at the attorneys for the city of Benson and several City Council members seated behind them. "Because what the Benson City Council did in this matter is inexcusable and deserves some type of punishment. That way word will get out: We're serious about freedom in America. Dead serious." He gripped the jury box and looked at them with a heart full of compassion. "You can't write laws that fly in the face of the Constitution and expect that act of defiance to go unpunished." There was a beat. "Each of you is here today to carry on where Thomas Jefferson and his peers first began. Protecting freedom for this generation and every generation after it." Matt nodded. "Thank you."

The lead attorney for the City of Benson was an older, distinguished man whose tone was irritating and who focused on the appearance of things. Leasing City Hall to a Christian church would give the appearance of state-sponsored religion; allowing

First Church of the Valley to preach Jesus Christ as the only way to salvation would give an appearance of narrow-mindedness, a lack of political tolerance. The entire matter gave the public the appearance that the Benson City Council had crossed the line between church and state. The attorney barely brushed over the fact that Pastor Carson had signed the lease agreement, binding him to whatever stipulations it contained. If a clause in the contract violated the U.S. Constitution—as Matt was suggesting—the fact that the pastor signed it would be of no significance.

Matt took notes and knew exactly how he'd play out the examination phase. His witnesses were simple, trusting people. People like Pastor Carson, who had never intended to rile up a case that was drawing sparks of national attention; and the church secretary, who kept the books and related in chilling detail the fact that the Benson City Council had no intention of refunding the church's lease money or restoring its lease unless, "You people stop talking about Jesus Christ."

Throughout his examination, Matt inserted questions involving the appearance of things. "So did the Benson City Council give you the appearance of not returning your lease money?"

"No. They actually didn't return it. They kept it even though we'd done everything right. Everything except preach the doctrine they wanted us to preach."

And to Pastor Carson, "Once the clause about doctrine was pointed out to you, did you feel it gave the appearance of discriminating against your group because of your religious views?"

Two people in the jury box stifled a giggle, and Matt knew they understood the point he was trying to make. Pastor Casey twisted his forehead into a grid of lines. "The appearance? I'd say it was more like the left foot of fellowship. We were kicked out of that building because of what we believed. Appearances had nothing to do with it."

Halfway through the first day, Matt had no doubts whatsoever that he would win the case. The jurors were bored and often hostile to the cross-examinations of the Benson attorneys. Every question they asked just looked like another attack on what the people at First Church of the Valley believed, and though the jurors may not have believed the same way, they had clearly caught Tanner's vision about standing up for freedom of choice. Whether that choice involved believing in Jesus Christ or not.

Attorneys for the Benson City Council brought very few witnesses, none of whom were effective. Matt tried to keep a straight face while the examination took place, and rarely bothered to add anything on the cross-examination. There was no point. With each passing hour the jurors were looking at their watches, appearing bored.

Each night back at his hotel room, Matt would call Hannah and give her the report. "You can't believe how well it's going." His heart soared with the way the case was progressing. "There were a dozen newspapers there today, and tomorrow we're expecting at least one national news show."

"That's wonderful."

"Usually they'd be coming to watch us lose, to witness another church group take a fall. But this time they're on our side. Can you believe it? We're not defending religion this time around; we're defending America. The word's getting out, and everyone wants a piece of the story."

He could hear Hannah clap her hands in the background. "Oh, Matt, it's just like Tanner dreamed it would be."

"Have you told him?"

"Every day when I go to the hospital." Her tone grew more somber. "I think it's helping him get through the week."

Matt leaned back on his hotel pillow and kicked his feet up. "You must have everyone we know praying."

The trial wrapped up late Thursday and deliberations began Friday morning. One of the jurors wore a T-shirt that bore the American flag and the words, "United We Stand." Matt took it as a good sign.

The judge informed the jury that First Church of the Valley was seeking fifty thousand dollars punitive damages, but that it was up to the jury to decide the actual amount—higher or lower.

Tanner had called Matt the night before after seeing a segment about the case on the evening's national news. "Hey, I heard the highlights of your closing arguments on CBS." Tanner sounded tired, but there was no denying his enthusiasm. "You're brilliant, buddy. I could never have pulled it off so well."

"That's where you're wrong." Matt grinned into the phone. "I'm only imitating everything I've ever seen or heard from you." Matt hesitated, his voice softer. "Hey, how's Jade?"

Tanner paused and Matt figured he was struggling to speak. "She's…she's very sick, Matt. The treatment is tearing her up. Hurry home, will ya?"

"You tell her to hang in there. I'll be there the minute I'm done."

Throughout deliberations, Matt interviewed with thirteen local and national news anchors and a handful of print reporters. He answered questions about expectations and the Constitution and national freedom, but he refrained from predicting a certain victory. His experience had been that no matter how sure the win, the jury should break the news first.

Finally, at just after four o'clock, the jury foreman notified the court clerk that they'd reached a decision. Matt was almost always anxious at this point in a trial. Bird-sized butterflies would attack his gut the same way they'd done before every basketball game he ever played in. This time, though, the butterflies were still.

In their place was the familiar calm that had comforted him all week. Matt knew it was because people were praying: Hannah and Tanner and the staff at the firm. Even Jade, sicker than she'd ever been, had sought God's divine help for this trial. And only God could have pulled off the type of trial and the accompanying media interest that had taken place that week.

Matt took his seat at the plaintiff's table and watched the jury file in. Several of them cast confident glances in Matt's direction. The clerk took the decision from the jury foreman and handed it to the judge. With little fanfare, he revealed the outcome.

"We, the jury, find in favor of the plaintiff. In doing so we agreed that the defendant must award the plaintiff—" The judge paused and appeared to study the number. Matt's eyes were glued to the man, urging him to continue. The judge cleared his throat and looked at Benson's attorneys. "Five hundred thousand dollars…half to be paid up front, and thereafter five years of fifty-thousand-dollar payments until the judgment is paid in full."

The moment the judge spoke the words *five hundred thousand dollars,* Matt let his held breath out and thanked God. Thanked Him because this case would have a ripple effect that would be unprecedented in the fight for religious freedom. And a half-million dollar judgment? It would put every civil rights group and governing body in the country on alert that the time had come to back off. Americans had the right to practice their religious freedom. In a church…in a school…in a public building. Even in a rented City Hall.

Matt could hardly wait to tell Tanner.

Interviews with reporters took place immediately after the verdict, and time and again Matt gave credit to God and Tanner.

"No one understands the severity and importance of our battle to maintain religious freedom in this country like Tanner

Eastman." Matt looked straight at the cameras, believing every word. "This was his strategy, his victory. I'm glad for the chance to carry it out."

The media circus over what had happened took three hours to die down. Of course, it all paled in comparison to the vigil being held at Jade's bedside several states away. Back at his hotel room later that evening, Matt tossed his things in his suitcase and took a shuttle to the airport.

By ten o'clock he was on a flight home.

Twenty-Nine

Hannah's desire to help Jade had been there long before Matt left for Colorado.

Despite the joy of having Kody as their son, Hannah's heart ached almost constantly for Jade. Yet until Matt returned from Colorado, Hannah couldn't think of anything tangible she could do. In fact, if anything, she felt more disconnected than ever. Here it was, the most trying, painful time in Jade's life, and Hannah was busy buying blue bedding and baby bottles.

And with Matt gone, she'd had no time to do anything but care for Kody.

Now that he was home, she had an idea, something she could do that just might make all the difference for Jade. That Sunday morning, the day before Jade's surgery, Hannah called Pastor Steve at church and told him her plan.

"I want to form a prayer chain for Jade Eastman. Different from any prayer chain ever done before."

During announcements that morning, Pastor Steve explained the plan to the congregation. Hannah listened, praying they would catch her vision.

"You've heard of prayer chains before," the pastor told them. "Well, Hannah Bronzan has put together something a little different. It's called the Jade Chain."

Hannah sat between Matt and Jenny, and without hesitating she took their hands. She looked around and saw that people were listening, some of them nodding, eyes teary. Nearly everyone knew the battle Jade was facing and the very real possibility that she wouldn't survive.

The pastor continued. "Most of you know that Jade is battling brain cancer and that even now—days after delivering their baby daughter—she is undergoing severe treatment. Tomorrow morning doctors will perform a delicate brain surgery on Jade, and truthfully, her chances are not good. She could lose her memory, her personality...her life." He gave Hannah a sad smile. "Hannah's idea is this: Anyone wishing to participate will sign up for a half-hour block of prayer time, starting with midnight tonight. During that block, you will pray for Jade. Pray for her newborn daughter, her husband, and her son. Pray that God heals her and that nothing happens during the surgery to rob her of the person she is, of the dynamic personality she's been blessed with."

He searched the faces of the five hundred people in attendance. When he spoke, Hannah could hear the ache in his voice and she wasn't surprised. "I guess what I'm asking is that you'd sign up. Please. And pray for a miracle for Jade Eastman."

After the service Matt and Jenny went to get Kody from the nursery, and Hannah found the pastor. "Thank you." She blinked back tears. "I'll call you tomorrow as soon as we hear anything."

"No need." The pastor took Hannah's hand, his expression more serious than she'd seen before. "I'll be there first thing in the morning. I'm planning to stay all day."

Hannah hugged him, losing the battle with her tears in the process. There was no question that Pastor Steve understood how ill Jade really was. She thanked him again, then hurried off to the foyer to check on the Jade Chain sign-up sheet.

What she saw stopped her in her tracks. What was this? Why were so many people bottlenecked in the church foyer?

Then it hit her, and her hand flew to her mouth. *Father, I don't believe it...You're so good, Lord.*

She stared, open-mouthed. The scene before her was the most amazing, breathtaking picture of a church family she'd ever seen or imagined in her life.

Snaking in a line up and down the length of the foyer were easily two hundred people.

Men, women, children…baseball players from the local high school, elderly men with canes and wobbly knees, a diabetic woman in a wheelchair. People Hannah knew well and others she wouldn't have recognized if she'd met them on the street. All of them waiting in line to put their name on the sign-up sheet.

Each of them as desperate as Hannah to find a way to help Jade Eastman.

Patsy Landers stared at two handwritten letters spread out on her kitchen table and considered her options.

At first, the activities she and Grace had been doing seemed like they might be enough. Taking a walk, building a birdhouse, singing a song. Each had been fun, and once in a while Grace would even seem happy. Patsy knew this because every now and then Grace would smile.

But it was never her old smile, the one that used to light up a room.

Concerned that something might be seriously wrong with Grace, Patsy took her to see a counselor, a Christian woman whose office was across the street from Patsy's church. For two days, the woman spent an hour with Grace, talking to her, asking her questions. Listening. At the end of the second session, the woman pulled Patsy aside.

"I'll be candid with you; Grace shows all the signs of post-traumatic stress disorder."

Patsy blinked. "Post what?"

Grace was sitting ten feet away. The woman glanced at her, and lowered her voice. "Mrs. Landers, the events that have taken place recently in your granddaughter's life are affecting her deeply. In my opinion, she's suffering from depression."

Depression.

The word was like a tourniquet around Patsy's heart even now. Depression? How was it possible? Yes, the child was bound to miss the Bronzans, but certainly she'd get over it. After all, Patsy had loved Grace since she was an infant. There were times in Grace's four short years when she stayed with Patsy for months on end before Leslie would come around and whisk her away somewhere.

Patsy had been a rock for Grace.

So why now, when Grace knew she would never have to leave, was she struggling with depression?

Patsy sighed. As if those troubles weren't enough, ten days ago she received the first letter in the mail. She stared at the letters again. The first was from Leslie; the second, from a woman who claimed to have a cell next to Leslie's in prison.

Leslie's letter was written in pencil. Patsy picked it up, feeling the same queasy feeling she'd felt the first time she saw it. Leslie's attorney's name and address were on the return corner of the envelope, and the moment Patsy received it she knew there had either been a problem or a miracle.

Leslie simply wouldn't have written otherwise.

The letter took up less than a page, and Patsy studied it once more. Leslie had written it for one reason: to inform Patsy that the minute prison officials released her, she'd be back for Grace. Not only that, but apparently she'd dreamed up some way to make a living.

Patsy's eyes ran over the strange last line in the letter: *Besides, I've thought of a way we can make enough money to survive. I know we'll never go hungry. Kiss her for me. Leslie.*

We? Who was we? Leslie and Grace? What possible way could Leslie and Grace make money? Patsy had studied the line for a long time and decided Leslie must have been referring to a boyfriend, someone she planned to live with once she was out.

However Leslie intended to make money, Patsy doubted her methods would be legal. That afternoon, when Patsy finished reading the letter, she was on the phone with Edna Parsons. "She can't take Grace, can she?"

When Edna hesitated, panic raced through Patsy. "Well, that's tricky. If Grace were adopted to another family, the answer would be no. But since you're her mother, the courts see it as a gray area."

The social worker went on to explain that if Patsy welcomed her daughter into her home and allowed her to visit with Grace, it would be very possible that one day Leslie would be given custody again.

"Besides, you haven't actually adopted Grace yet. You're her legal guardian, but even that becomes open to interpretation once the courts deem Leslie has paid her debt to society."

"You mean she could hire an attorney and fight me for custody?"

Mrs. Parsons let loose a small huff. "If you welcome Leslie into your home, she could leave with Grace, and unless she breaks a law, no agency in the country would consider it a kidnapping." She paused. "The alternative is to get a restraining order on her as soon as you know she's out of prison, but even then you'd have to give cause."

The conversation had played in Patsy's mind a dozen times since then. Especially after she received the second letter. Three days after opening the first, Patsy found a letter in her postbox addressed to Mrs. Landers. The handwriting was unfamiliar.

Patsy set down Leslie's letter and picked up the other one. The message was brief and to the point.

Dear Mrs. Landers,

My cell is next to your daughter's. I heard her talking the other day about making money with her little girl. Grace, I think it was. She was talking about some pretty bad stuff and it made me remember my little girl. Bad stuff happened to her, too. But I ain't never tried to make money off her. I hope you understand what I'm telling you. I don't want any more little girls hurt that way. I got your address from Leslie's notebook when she was on duty.

Candi

Patsy tried every way she could to read something other than the obvious into Candi's note. It wasn't possible. Leslie wanted to make money with Grace? In a way that someone sitting in prison thought was "pretty bad stuff"?

Horror filled Patsy as the possibilities slammed against her mind. Leslie had done some awful things in her life, made some terrible choices...but making money off Grace? The idea and all it entailed was more than Patsy could bear.

Again she called Grace's social worker, Edna Parsons, and read her the note over the phone.

"Sounds like Leslie's made some dangerous connections in prison." Mrs. Parsons's tone was troubled. "Save the note. It might help you get a restraining order."

"But...do you think she's talking about..." Patsy couldn't bring herself to finish the sentence.

"Pornography or prostitution." The words were hand grenades in Patsy's heart. "I'd say it was one or the other. There's an entire network of children Grace's age trapped in that underworld. Police are constantly working to arrest the adults behind it, but it happens. I won't lie to you."

"And you really think Leslie could…could do that?"

The social worker sounded tired. "Mrs. Landers, I haven't told you this information before, but maybe now it's time you hear. The scene at that deserted field, when police found Leslie and Grace, was a grim one."

The things Edna Parsons told Patsy then left her weak and in tears. Her stomach hurt, and she covered her eyes, confused about one thing. "But she asked for her mother for weeks after going to live with the Bronzans."

"That's normal. At that point she could transfer all blame for her situation on to the bad guys her mother spent time with. After spending time with the Bronzans she knew differently." Mrs. Parsons drew a quiet breath. "I saw how Grace changed with that family. For the first time she knew what a real mommy was supposed to be like."

The picture was becoming clearer. "That whole time she thought I was dead."

"Right."

Patsy's tears felt hot on her weathered cheeks. "She must have believed she'd been given a new life, a chance to have a family who would never leave her. Never hurt her."

"Exactly."

The despair in Patsy's soul was worse than anything she'd suffered in all the years of disappointments with Leslie. "What am I supposed to do, then? How can I make Grace feel secure?"

"It takes time."

"And what about Leslie's threats. She'll take Grace whether it's legal or not, by the sounds of it." Patsy's voice trembled and she felt utterly weak.

"First, you should get an attorney and see about officially adopting Grace. Second, I'd follow through with the restraining order. And you might want to consider moving, as well."

Attorney? Restraining order? Moving? Patsy's head swam and she could barely find the strength to speak. "In other words, I'd never see Leslie again."

The social worker's answer rang with finality. "Quite possibly. But then, she considered you dead before any of this ever happened."

Memories of the conversation faded.

Patsy reached for a manila envelope on her lap and tucked the letters inside. She craned her neck and saw that Grace was still on the recliner where she'd been an hour earlier, watching television with the same dazed look she'd had since she'd arrived in Oklahoma.

God, what am I supposed to do?

There was no loud answer, no letters from heaven giving her step-by-step directions on how to raise little Grace. Patsy shifted her gaze forward once more and stared at her hands. Her shoulders shook and tears formed a logjam in her throat.

For years she'd prayed daily for Leslie, begging God to change her heart and bring her closer to Him. Now, in some ways, Patsy was being asked to choose. Give Grace the home and safety she deserved, but eliminate Leslie from her life entirely. It was the most gut-wrenching thing Patsy had ever been asked to do.

She closed her eyes, folded her hands, and brought them to her face. *Please, God, give me wisdom. I feel like I'm going to lose no matter what I do.*

Ask and you will receive…seek and you will find…for the LORD gives wisdom.

The Scriptures soaked through her frightened soul as though God Himself were writing them there.

Bit by bit, an idea began to form in Patsy's head. One she would never have considered if not for Leslie's threats and Candi's warnings—and most of all her own conversations with Mrs. Parsons.

Ever since receiving Leslie's letters, she'd seen only one way of carrying on, a way that grew darker and bleaker with every passing day. But now…in light of God's gentle whispers…she saw a way she'd never considered before. It wouldn't be easy or pain-free, but suddenly it loomed as the answer to her prayers.

The idea grew and took root and by that evening, Patsy was sure it was the best answer. A way that, in the end, would not involve losing, but winning. Not just for Patsy and Leslie and Grace.

But for the Bronzans as well.

Thirty

Only Tanner knew exactly how hard the treatment had been on Jade.

In two weeks she had lost fifteen pounds and most of her hair. She vomited several times a day and was often too exhausted to do anything more than make a short trip to the nursery to see Madison.

Ty visited every afternoon, and Jade made sure she had a scarf around her head before he came. He had a hard enough time understanding her cancer without watching her hair fall out. Finally he'd brought her his Los Angeles Lakers baseball cap.

"Here, Mom." He helped position it over her balding head, pulling the sides down carefully over her ears. "This way you'll have a part of me with you even when you sleep."

Jade had worn the hat every day since, even when the convulsions in her stomach left her doubled over a bedpan for nearly an hour.

They had arranged with their neighbor to watch Ty any time that Tanner wasn't home. And since the second day of Jade's treatment, that had been almost constantly. He came home to sleep and spend time with Ty, but only when Jade insisted. At least four times he'd stayed the night, holding her hand and pulling back the thin clumps of hair that remained on her head so they wouldn't fall in the bedpan.

For all the ways Jade loved Tanner, the time they spent together those two weeks raised her feelings to another level. By letting him see her now, when death was pulling at her from every side, she had shown him everything there was to see, allowed him into every closet in her heart.

Tanner had seen her collapsed on the bathroom floor, clinging to the toilet, and he'd wiped vomit from her mouth when she was too exhausted to move. He'd applied ointment to her C-section incision and spoon-fed her when she was too weak to lift her hands. When she needed to soothe the radiation burns on her face and neck, Tanner worked tirelessly to keep her washcloth cool.

He'd done all that, seen her at her worst and weakest, yet Jade could tell by his touch that he had never loved her more.

The days passed in a slow, sickening blur. Rarely did they talk about the impending surgery when it was all they could do to survive each day. The news was both good and bad. While the tumor hadn't grown tentacles—which would have made it very difficult if not impossible to remove surgically—it had not shrunk nearly as much as Dr. Layton hoped.

Because of that, and because the treatment was taking such a toll on Jade, Dr. Layton decided to go ahead with the scheduled surgery date of October 21. Two weeks after she'd given birth to Madison.

"There's no point waiting," the doctor had told them after one week of chemotherapy and radiation. "Not since we're not seeing a dramatic response to the treatment."

Finally, mercifully, it was Sunday evening.

Dr. Layton had spent an hour with her and Tanner that afternoon, explaining once more the benefits and risks of brain surgery.

"First of all, it's the only way to rid Jade of the cancer." He looked from Tanner to Jade and back again. "Otherwise her condition would be terminal."

He detailed that if all went well, they would remove the entire tumor without disturbing the surrounding brain tissue. If the margins around the tumor tested clean, there was a very good chance Jade would be cured, and that five years from now, if she had no recurrence of cancer she could be given a clean bill of health. Her battle with cancer would be over forever.

If not…

Jade had barely been able to tolerate hearing the list of things that could go wrong. First, they might not get the entire tumor. In that case, if the margins around the tumor showed remaining cancer cells, Jade could easily face a second brain tumor down the road or cancer in another part of her body—most likely her lungs.

Even if they managed to remove every cancer cell, there was a possibility that Jade's brain would be permanently altered in the process.

"That's the part I'm a little foggy on." Tanner leaned forward, holding tight to Jade's hand with one hand and resting his chin in the palm of his other.

Dr. Layton studied the floor for a moment and then looked at Tanner once more. "It means she could lose her memory or suffer a change in personality. When we remove a tumor this size, we try to leave the brain undisturbed. But some tissue is bound to be lost in the process."

Jade watched the blood drain from Tanner's face. These details had always been clear to her, but apparently Tanner had not fully understood until now. "How…how will you know?"

Dr. Layton folded his hands, his brow lowered, eyes dark with the severity of the situation. "We won't know until she regains consciousness. After the surgery."

When the doctor finally left, Tanner hung his head and cried.

Jade wanted desperately to crawl out of bed and go to him, to sit on his knee, wrap her arms around his neck, and promise him none of those terrible things would happen. That tomorrow at this time she'd still be with him and that everything was going to be okay.

Instead she ran her fingers through his hair, praying that her touch would be enough to help him through. "He has to tell us that, Tanner. We can't be blind to the risks."

Tanner shook his head and wiped the sleeve of his shirt across his eyes. "I'm sorry." She saw raw fear in his eyes. "I want to wake up at home with you beside me, with Maddie and Ty down the hall, and know that every bit of this was just some awful dream."

A nurse came then and brought Jade her last meal before the surgery. Now it was six o'clock, and before they could talk about what the morning might bring, there was a knock on the door.

Tanner looked up. "Come in."

The door opened and the Bronzans filed through. First Matt, then Hannah.

"Hey, guys!" Jade smiled at them and pushed a button on the remote control, raising the back of her bed several degrees. "Where's Jenny?"

Matt gave her a partial grin that didn't quite reach his eyes. "Downstairs with Kody."

Jade nodded. She had seen their baby once earlier that week and marveled at the grace of God, the perfection of his timing and design in bringing them this child. Especially while the pain of losing Grace was still so real.

Matt and Hannah crossed the room toward her bed. Hannah carried a large envelope and already Jade could see tears in her eyes.

"How are you?" Hannah took hold of Jade's hand, her face intent.

Jade's throat was suddenly thick with emotion and she could only nod.

Tanner stood, and he and Matt hugged. They'd talked at

length the day before so Matt could fill Tanner in about the trial and the judgment and how all of it had been more than they could ask or imagine.

There were no words between them now, though.

Everyone in the room knew why they were there. They'd come to say good-bye.

Hannah moved close to Jade's side and held up the envelope. "We have something we'd like to hang over your bed."

Jade smiled and adjusted her baseball cap. "Not a Lakers poster, right? Ty already tried that. The head nurse is from Portland. A Blazers fan." She glanced at Matt. "It's all she can do to let me wear the hat."

"No…" The tears in Hannah's eyes spilled onto her cheeks. She managed a sad smile as she took Jade's hand. "It's not a Lakers poster."

Hannah pulled out a small stack of notebook paper. "It's a prayer chain, Jade." Hannah's smile faded and she leaned closer. "Pastor Steve agreed to ask the congregation for forty-eight volunteers." Hannah passed the stack to Jade. "But 240 people signed up."

Tanner positioned himself on the other side of the bed and stared at the pieces of paper. "Are you serious?"

Jade stared, speechless, at the names listed before her.

Hannah Bronzan, midnight; Amy Hannan, 12:30; Adam Sonney, 1:00 A.M.; Ben Bailey, 1:30…

The list of names flowed the length of the sheet and continued to the next page and the next. Ten pages of names. People whose children she had taught in Sunday School or women she'd sat next to in church. Girls in the high school youth group and boys barely old enough to drive.

Names jumped at her from the page: *Brandon Daves, 5:00 P.M.; Ann Hudson, 5:30; Sylvia Wallgren, 6:00 P.M.; Landon Heidenreich, 6:30…*

It was overwhelming.

Her hand began to shake and she let the stack fall to her lap. Her hands fluttered to her throat and she worked to find her voice. "I...I don't know what to say."

There were tears on all their faces now as Hannah took the list and pulled a roll of tape from the envelope. With Matt's help, they taped each sheet above Jade's bed, and finally they placed a small banner over the list of names that read simply: "The Jade Chain."

Jade craned around to see the list as two quiet sobs shook her body. All this time she'd wondered if her church family really liked her or not. The comments about her being an adulterer had only come from two older women, but still, Jade had wondered.

Until now.

When she needed them most, they had stepped up and agreed to pray for her every hour of the day until she was no longer in danger. Jade buried her face in her hands. They loved her... They loved her after all.

She steadied herself and let her hands fall to her lap while Matt and Hannah finished with the wall. "I can't believe it..." Jade looked at Hannah. "Thank you so much, Hannah. I've never...never had a friend like you."

Hannah leaned over and hugged Jade, and the two stayed that way for a long while, holding on to the moment, weeping from someplace deep inside them at the thought of what would come next.

When Hannah straightened again, Matt put his arm around her and patted Jade's knee. "We wanted to pray with you and let you know we'll be here all day tomorrow, helping with Ty and checking on Madison so you and Tanner can be alone."

Jade's heart hurt, swollen with equal parts grief and joy. How blessed she was to count the Bronzans as family, to know that if anything happened to her, Tanner and Ty and Madison would always have friends who understood. Friends who had been there since the beginning and would be there to the end.

Whenever that might be.

Jade tightened her grip on Hannah's hand and searched her eyes. Matt cleared his throat, and Jade shifted her gaze to him. "We love you, Jade. We'll always love you." Matt's voice broke. "We're here for you and Tanner and the kids whenever you need us. Whatever you need."

Matt reached out and took hold of Tanner's hand so the circle was complete. "Can we pray for you?"

"Yes." Jade choked back a sob. "Please."

Jade watched the others close their eyes and bow their heads, and she did the same. Matt spoke in a shaky voice. "Lord, the time has come to place our friend, Jade, in Your arms. We trust You, God, that whatever happens tomorrow will be perfectly part of Your will, Your plan. But we beg You…"

When he halted, Jade knew he was crying.

"We beg You to heal her. Guide the surgeons' hands and give them Your eyes, Lord. To take out every bit of the cancer. Please let the time pass quickly and…and bring Jade back to us very soon. In Jesus' name, amen."

If the good-bye with the Bronzans wasn't painful enough, an hour later their neighbor brought Ty up and turned him over to Tanner. The surgical procedures would start too early in the morning for Ty or anyone else to see Jade. Only Tanner was allowed in her room until she was taken into surgery, and that would happen sometime around six the next morning.

Beside her on the bed was the journal Jade had written for Ty. Tanner had wrapped it a week earlier. Jade held her hand out and studied her son. "Come here, buddy."

He still hadn't cried, not once since Jade's diagnosis. But now, as he shuffled across the slick hospital floor toward her bed, she could see his nose was red and his eyes were puffy. When he was next to her, he scrunched his face into a mass of wrinkles and gripped his temples with his thumb and forefinger.

Tanner stood at his side, his hand on Ty's shoulder, too distraught to speak.

Jade swallowed hard and somehow found her voice. "Ahh, buddy, it's okay." Jade released the bed rail and pulled him close, hugging him and stroking his back while he sobbed in grunts and small gasps as only a thirteen-year-old boy can. The sound of it broke what was left of Jade's heart, and she realized how hard he'd worked to mask his fears before this.

"I…I don't want them to hurt you." He clung to her as he hadn't done since he was a small boy, as he hadn't done since sheriff's deputies showed up at their door to take him away that awful morning three years ago. The week after Jim had won full custody of him.

"Ty, it's okay, honey." Jade whispered the words close to his ear. "The doctors aren't going to hurt me; they're going to help me. So I can get out of here and come home with you and Daddy and Maddie."

"I'm…I'm so scared, Mom. I need you." He pulled back, and she saw terror in his eyes. "What if something happens?"

"God's in control, Ty. You believe that, right?" Jade ignored her own tears and wiped her thumb across Ty's wet cheeks.

He nodded and sniffed hard. "It's just that…well, other than Dad…" He glanced at Tanner and back to her. "Other than Dad, you're my best friend. You *have* to be okay."

Jade pulled his head to her chest once more and let him cry. There was no way she could give him the journal now, not with him worrying about whether she'd survive. Without letting Ty see what she was doing, Jade moved the package beneath her sheets. She would give it to him later, when she was on the other side of this nightmare.

And if not…

Jade squeezed her eyes shut and refused to let her thoughts go that way. Tanner moved in closer, sheltering the two of them with his body, lending his strength whatever way he could.

After a while, Ty pulled back, reached for a tissue, and blew his nose. "I'm sorry for crying. I—" he blew his nose again—"I wanted to be strong for you, Mom."

Jade caught his hand in hers once more. "Never be afraid to cry, son. It means you have a heart."

"Yeah…I guess." Ty tried to grin, his eyes nearly swollen shut. "I love you."

"I love you, Ty." She wanted to tell him something positive, something reassuring. A promise he could hang on to no matter what happened in the morning. She settled on something truthful. Whatever the outcome might be. Their eyes locked and she directed her words straight to his soul. "We'll be home together soon, okay?"

He nodded, missing the double meaning, and this time his smile came more easily. "Okay. Be safe."

Be safe…

The words washed over Jade, and she steeled herself against another wave of tears. They were the words she'd told him since he was small, words she said whenever it was time to say good-bye. She answered him with the words that were his typical response. "Always."

Tanner put his arm around Ty, and together they turned for the door. Before they walked out, Ty turned once more and looked at her. The tears were back in his eyes and hers. Jade managed a smile and raised her hand—her two middle fingers tucked in close to her palm: sign language for, "I love you."

He did the same, and then together he and Tanner left, shutting the door behind them.

Only when they were gone did Jade give in to the tears and heartache that had been building inside her since Ty arrived. *God, help me…I want to see him again. I want to see him grow up…*

I am here, daughter…I know the plans I have for you.

The answer was as real as if God had announced it over the hospital PA system. Jade's body relaxed some, though her sobs continued. She was still crying when Tanner returned.

"He's going home with Matt and Hannah."

Jade nodded and grabbed four quick breaths. In every way that mattered, she was exhausted, but she had to get through this. In the past few hours, she'd had to say good-bye to everyone that mattered to her.

Everyone but Tanner.

And now, before she fell asleep, she would have to do that, too.

Without saying a word, Tanner flipped off the overhead light. The glow from the monitors lit his way as he walked toward her bed. Careful not to bump the machines or disturb the tubing that bound her to them, he climbed onto the mattress and lay beside her on the starchy sheets. The smell of sterilized hospital bedding mingled with his subtle cologne and filled her senses.

I'll remember this smell as long as I live…

He held his face against hers, letting their tears mix and fall to the pillow together…inseparable. Just as she and Tanner were inseparable.

He ran his fingers along her arm and the sides of her face, and Jade savored the feel of his body against hers. For a long while, neither of them spoke. Then, Tanner leaned up on one elbow and studied her face.

His voice was a caress. "When I was in college, I hated English Literature."

The corners of Jade's mouth raised a bit. Even now, at the saddest moment in their lives, Tanner could make her smile. "I didn't know that."

"I did." He ran his thumb along her cheekbone. "I couldn't understand why reading William Shakespeare would ever help me in life."

Jade had no idea where he was going with this, but the diversion felt wonderful. Though her voice was scratchy and weak, for the first time that day it held a trace of humor. "I can see that."

"But yesterday I remembered a quote from Shakespeare."

Jade lifted her eyebrows. "'Wherefore art thou Romeo?'"

"No." Tanner smiled, though the sadness in his eyes remained. His voice grew more tender, if that were possible. "'Give sorrow words: the grief that does not speak whispers the o'er-fraught heart and bids it break.'"

The quote played over again in Jade's mind. This was so like Tanner. Whether he was in front of a jury or sitting beside her on their back deck, his thoughts were always profound. Still, there was no way she could give her sorrow words. Not now, with a thousand yesterdays blocking her ability to speak.

Fresh tears spilled onto Tanner's cheeks and rolled off the end of his chin. "And so I have to speak, Jade. Otherwise...otherwise my heart will break."

She nodded and tried to lift her head from the pillow. When her body wouldn't cooperate, Tanner lowered his face to hers and kissed her—not the passionate kiss of two lovers, but a kiss of longing and sorrow and grief. It was Tanner's attempt to express the depth of what he was feeling.

When he pulled back, he shifted to his elbow again. "I love you, Jade. In all my life I've only loved you."

She forced back the lump in her throat. "I love you, too, Tanner."

"I keep asking myself, what if you don't know me when you wake up? What if you don't remember Virginia or Kelso or Ty or Maddie? And if something happens, how long before I'll see you and Jenna in heaven…what if…"

Then, despite his obvious desire to say something eloquent and memorable in these, her last hours before surgery, he hung his head and wept. Taking great care, he positioned his face over hers and wrapped his arms beneath her, much as Ty had done earlier. "Don't go, Jade…" His voice was racked with torment. "Don't leave me. Please… Come back to me, baby."

"I will…" She kissed his neck, clinging to him. "I will, Tanner. I will…"

Jade wasn't sure how long they stayed that way, but at some point they fell asleep, side by side. As though they might be back at home, holding each other through just one more happy night instead of clinging to their final moments before Jade's surgery.

At five the next morning, a nurse woke them. "They're ready for you, Mrs. Eastman."

Jade squinted at the machines surrounding her and tried to remember what was happening. Then it all came flooding back. It was the morning of the surgery. Her surgery. And after today…

Tanner coughed and eased himself from the bed. Jade could see that he wanted to ask the nurse to leave the room, give them another few minutes alone. But it was too late. Preparations for the surgery were already in motion.

Minutes later two technicians and Dr. Layton entered the room. "Good morning, Jade." He smiled and she appreciated his upbeat manner. He would be assisting in the surgery, after all, and she needed him and the other doctors to be positive.

"Good morning."

The doctor looked from Jade to Tanner and back again. "Well, Jade, this is the first day of the rest of your life."

Jade nodded and glanced at Tanner. He was whiter than the sheets, and his expression was a contrast of trust and sheer terror. She leveled her gaze at Dr. Layton. "I'm ready."

Tanner stood back while they lifted her from the bed to the gurney. She winced as they gave her the first in a series of shots that would knock her out for the operation. Before they took her away, Tanner came alongside her and whispered, "I love you, Jade. Come back to me, okay?"

A warm sensation made its way through Jade's veins and her eyelids grew heavy. "I will, you'll see."

"I'll be praying."

"Thanks…" Her words were slurred, and everything faded around her.

The last thing she saw as she was wheeled from the room, as the medication took her under, was Tanner's face. After that she closed her eyes.

Somewhere she'd read that the last image a person saw before brain surgery would be the first they'd remember when they regained consciousness. If that was true, only one image could help her brain survive the coming hours, help preserve her personality and memory and everything else she held dear.

The precious image of Tanner Eastman's face.

She fought the medication's pull, doing everything in her power to hold Tanner's image there, but no matter how hard she held on, the crispness of his face began to blur and fade until finally the image disappeared entirely.

Then there was nothing but darkness…and the strangest sense that she was being carried. Not by human arms, but holy ones. The sensation grew stronger until finally, despite the total darkness, Jade fell into the deepest, most peaceful sleep she'd ever known.

Six hours later, Tanner was sitting in the waiting room with his loved ones when Dr. Layton came up to them. Tanner was immediately on his feet, his heart soaring over this one fact:

Dr. Layton was smiling.

"Well...?" Tanner's heart raced and he struggled to breathe. "How is she?"

"The surgery went beautifully. We're almost positive we got all the cancer."

A chorus of, "Thank You, God" and "Thank You, Jesus" came from Matt and Hannah and Pastor Steve.

Ty ran across the room and hugged Tanner. "I *knew* she'd make it, Dad. I knew it."

Tanner's knees trembled. She was alive! Thank God, she was alive. He closed his eyes and clenched his fists, his voice merely a whisper. "Thank You...thank You..." Almost at the same moment, he shifted his attention back to Dr. Layton. "Can I talk to her?"

"Not exactly." A shadow fell across the doctor's face. "You can sit with her, but she's unconscious, remember? That's what we expected. We'd like to see her come around in the next few hours." He hesitated. "The longer she stays in a coma, the more likely she'll have some memory loss or personality changes."

"Personality changes?" Ty looked up at Tanner, his eyes wide with new concern. "What's that mean, Dad?"

Tanner narrowed his eyes and tried to keep from collapsing. He was riding the wildest roller coaster of his life. After hitting the highest high in the past six months, he was right back where he'd been all that morning. Begging God to heal his wife and bring her back to him, where she belonged.

Where she had always belonged.

"Well..." Tanner tightened his grip on Ty and spoke with as much strength as he could muster. "It means we keep praying, son. We just keep on praying."

Thirty-One

At eight o'clock that night in the hospital waiting room, Matt was talking in quiet whispers with Pastor Steve when his cell phone rang. He cringed, realizing he'd forgotten to turn it off when he arrived at the hospital. He snatched it up and headed for the door, shrugging when Hannah cast him a curious glance. He stepped outside and took the call.

"Hello?"

"Mr. Bronzan?"

The connection wasn't very strong, and Matt plugged his other ear so he could hear the woman. "Yes?"

"I'm sorry to call you so late, but Edna Parsons gave me your number." The woman hesitated. "This is Patsy Landers, Grace's grandmother."

Matt's heart skipped a beat. "Uh…hello, Mrs. Landers." Matt ached at the sound of Grace's name. He still missed her more than he talked about, more than he admitted even to himself. "How is she?"

"Well…" The woman's tone grew higher-pitched, as though she were upset. "She's been having some trouble."

Matt closed his eyes, overcome with sorrow. If only there were a way to hold Grace right here, right now, he would rock her and soothe away the pain. Whatever had caused it. "Is she okay?"

"She's healthy, if that's what you mean. But she's…she's not happy, and I think I finally understand why."

Confusion rang through Matt's mind. Why was she calling him about Grace? The child was no longer a part of their lives. It killed him to think of her troubled or sad, but there was nothing he could do about it.

Nothing at all.

Matt inhaled, waiting until his lungs were full before speaking. "Mrs. Landers, if you'll excuse me, I'm not sure I understand why you're calling."

"Because…" The woman on the other end was quiet for a moment. "Because I have an idea and…well…I'd like to share it with you."

"Yes…" An idea? About Grace's happiness? Her future? Matt's heart began to pound. "I'd like to hear it."

The days blended one into the other, and still Jade remained in a coma.

Whenever he met with Tanner, Dr. Layton's voice was somber and he frowned often. Clearly the man was discouraged, though Tanner thought he tried to hide the fact. Either way there was no dancing around the obvious. Every hour, every day that passed, the chances of Jade making a full recovery grew more and more slim.

Tanner existed in a fog of prayer and encouragement from Matt and Hannah and the others. At least once a day Ty was allowed in the room, and that was usually when Tanner was at his best. He would encourage Ty to talk to Jade, to touch her. And in the process he would find himself believing she could really hear them.

It was strange how his fears had changed time and again since Jade's diagnosis. Before her surgery, Tanner was most afraid that somehow she'd wake up a different person, no longer knowing him or loving him.

Now, though, at dawn of the fourth day since her operation,

Tanner only hoped she'd wake up at all.

He studied her face, serene and still, and glanced at the prayer chart above Jade's bed. It was still happening. Somewhere in the city of Thousand Oaks someone was praying for Jade's recovery. Tanner was grateful. There were hours when he couldn't find the strength to form another prayer, times when the knowledge of the Jade Chain was all that pulled him through.

His eyes fell back to Jade. The medication had made her face look full again, like it had been before she'd lost so much weight. Her head was still swathed in bandages, but otherwise she looked better than she had in months.

He took her limp hand in his and massaged his thumb over her wedding ring. "Jade, baby, good morning." Tanner cooed the words, inches from her ear. "Today's the day you wake up, honey, okay?"

It was the same thing he said to her every morning. And every time, when she failed to respond, he would start telling her stories. Dr. Layton had told him that conversation was one of the greatest ways to rouse a person from a coma. Memories were another.

That being the case, Tanner had decided to talk about the past. Every day, every hour if necessary. As much as was humanly possible.

"Remember that trust game we used to play when we were kids?" He searched her face for signs of a response. When there was none, he continued. "You'd close your eyes, and I'd lead you around the backyard. Remember? And when the weather was good, remember how we'd ride bikes around the neighborhood?" He relaxed back into the chair, his fingers still clutching hers. "Back then my favorite times were when we'd race. Really, Jade, I used to let you win. I mean, I wouldn't tell you back then, of course, but I loved the way your eyes sparkled when you'd win. It was worth losing just for that."

He took a sip of water and continued, sharing stories about her leaving for Kelso and him promising anyone who would listen that one day—no matter how long it took—he would marry her. Even if he had to search the whole country to find her again.

Tanner tried to sound upbeat. "It worked. I'm here, aren't I?"

Story after story spilled from him, even the sad ones, and in Jade and Tanner's years apart there had been plenty of those. He talked about finding her in Kelso that summer and how attracted he'd been to her, how difficult it was to keep his distance. He celebrated again the choice she'd made that summer to become a Christian and the strength she'd roused in him by challenging his intention to be a politician.

"I would have hated that lifestyle. I can never thank you enough, Jade, for helping me follow my dreams."

His voice grew somber. "After I came back from that trip and found you gone, married to someone else, I thought I'd die from grief. It was all I could do to—"

Tanner froze.

Had it been his imagination or had Jade moved her foot? He leaned forward and stayed utterly still, silent. Then he remembered Dr. Layton's advice:

It's especially important that you talk to her as she's waking up. Help her find her place again. But don't overwhelm her. Take it slow.

Tanner gulped hard and searched for the right words. "Jade, baby?" He waited. "Can you hear me?"

There it was again. Only this time, she moved the fingers on her right hand, too. She was coming out of it! *Please, God, let her come back all the way…please…*

Jade's head moved back and forth, and she moaned like a toddler waking from a long nap.

Tanner was on his feet, his eyes burning with unshed tears. "Jade, baby, it's me, Tanner. You're okay, honey. The surgery was a success." His eyes scanned her body and there was no question about it. She was moving the toes on both feet! Suddenly her hand wriggled against his, then gripped it with the faintest movement.

"Jade, wake up, honey. I'm here with you. Me, Tanner. Can you hear me, honey?"

Her eyelids began to flutter, and in seconds she opened them, squinting from the light. At first she looked around the room and Tanner held his breath.

Please, God…let her know me.

A heartbeat later, she turned her eyes on him…and the corners of her mouth lifted a fraction of an inch. Her voice was slow and croaky. "Hey…"

Tanner's heart jumped. She *knew* him! Jade knew who he was! He grabbed a quick breath and tried to keep from shouting out loud. *Calm. Stay calm.* "Hi."

This time there was no question, she was trying to smile. "Is your…o'er-fraught heart still in one piece?"

Tanner tried not to react, but a flash of concern set him back in his chair. "What?"

"Can I…" She sounded like she'd been sleeping with cotton in her mouth. "Can I have water?"

Water! Tanner grabbed the plastic pitcher at her bedside and poured a cup. "Here." She lifted a shaky hand and took the cup. There were a million things he wanted to ask her, tell her, but Dr. Layton wanted her to lead the conversation once she was awake.

Tanner tried to help her out. "What…what were you asking about?"

Jade's face filled with exhaustion as she raised her head several inches and took a sip. Her head fell back against the pillow, but when she looked at him, Tanner saw her eyes sparkling. "I'm guessing that your…o'er-fraught heart…is still in one piece."

"Because?"

"Because…" She grinned this time, and he could see a familiar teasing in her eyes. His heart soared as she continued. "I heard *everything* you said for the past two hours and…you, my dear attorney husband…have definitely given your sorrow words."

"Yes!" He shouted the word again and flew to his feet. She was back!

Only Jade, his Jade, would have used humor in a moment like this. Now there was nothing anyone could do to keep him quiet. "Thank You, God!" He raised his hands to heaven, staring through the ceiling at a God who was not only his Savior and Lord, but his deliverer. Because only a deliverer could have walked them through the valley of the shadow of death and brought them to this point.

He stared at Jade, wonder seeping into his every pore. "You're back. You're okay!" He wanted to swing her out of bed and into his arms, but he settled for leaning his upper body along hers, careful not to disturb the bandages on her head or put pressure on her. He wove his hands beneath her shoulders and hugged her close. "Thank God you're back. I was so afraid I'd lost you."

"How long have I been out?"

"Four days, Jade. Four of the longest days of my life." He drew back and searched her eyes. "We thought…Dr. Layton said we had to prepare for the worst."

"And the surgery…you said it went well."

There were questions in her eyes, and Tanner wanted to allay her fears before any more time passed. "Tests on the margins came back negative. There's no sign of cancer cells anywhere. They got it all, Jade."

"What about Maddie?" Jade's eyes were heavy again. "I missed you all so much, Tanner."

"Maddie's perfect. She's gaining weight. Her doctor said she might be able to go home in three weeks."

"I knew it." A look of peace filled Jade's face and her eyes closed for a moment. "God is so good."

"What do you remember about the surgery? Anything?"

Jade smiled. "Two things." She took another sip of water. "Your face." She moved her free hand up and traced his jawline with her forefinger. "And the strangest sensation."

Tanner studied her face. No matter how long he lived, he would never get enough of her. "What?"

"Right from the moment I went under I felt the Lord pick me up and hold me, like I was lying in Jesus' arms from then…until now. Isn't that something?"

Tears burned in the corners of Tanner's eyes. "Maybe that's what happens when people are praying for you around-the-clock."

"Maybe. I just know I felt it. As real as if you'd picked me up yourself." Her hand was trembling and she let it fall back beside her. "I'm tired, Tanner."

"I know."

"But before I sleep…I want to see Ty. He needs to know that I'm okay."

Tanner nodded. He didn't want to exhaust her on her first day, not with days of tough recovery ahead. His eyes fell to her hands and arms. The coma had atrophied what little muscle remained on her thin frame. Dr. Layton said she'd need another week of radiation, just as a precaution.

But the days would go by quickly…and very soon they would walk out of the hospital, a family again.

He was reaching for the phone to call Ty when it rang. Surprised, he hesitated a moment before answering it. "Hello?"

"How's she doing?"

It was Matt.

Tanner beamed, the joy of what had happened that past half hour still bursting in his heart. "I have her back! She came to thirty minutes ago." His tone was filled with disbelief. "Can you believe it, Matt? I have her *back.*"

"She knows you? Everything's the same?"

Tanner grinned at Jade. "She's as ornery as ever."

"Thank God…" Matt paused and coughed a few times. When he spoke again it was with tears in his voice. "Tell her we love her… We can't wait to see her." He uttered a single laugh, one that sounded like part cry. "Tell her it's going to be a miracle day for *both* of us."

Tanner lowered his brow. "Both of us?"

"Hi, Matt, it's Hannah on the other line."

"Hi." Jade was watching him, and he mouthed the fact that Hannah was on the phone also. "Okay, so our miracle is obvious. What's yours?" At this point Tanner figured anything was possible. After all, miracles had been sprouting like springtime tulips since Maddie was born.

Hannah did the talking. "We've been in conversation with Grace's grandmother these past few days. At first we weren't sure where it was headed, but yesterday afternoon our social worker called us. Grace's grandmother wants to give her back to us, Tanner. She wants to visit once a year, but that's all. She told us God had showed her it was the best thing for Grace." Hannah's voice broke. "She'll be here this afternoon."

"That's not all." Matt sounded happier than Tanner could ever remember, and the combination of his friend's joy with his own was enough to make his heart burst. "We found out that Grace's mother's rights have been permanently severed. Our Grace is free for adoption. We'll start the process Monday."

"That's wonderful. I never stopped thinking of her as your daughter."

"Jenny's beside herself." Hannah sounded like she was ready to burst. "She slept in Grace's bed last night, thanking God."

They talked a few more minutes before Tanner explained he had to go. They hadn't called Ty yet and needed to do that as soon as possible. When they were off the phone, he explained the situation to Jade.

She smiled, and for the first time since she'd come to, her eyes filled with tears. "Hannah loves that little girl so much." She shook her head, searching for the words. "What can I say? God is so good."

Tanner was about to dial the neighbor's house where Ty was staying when a thought occurred to him.

He glanced up at the Jade Chain still taped to the wall above the hospital bed. Then he checked his watch. Just after eight o'clock. He calculated back. That meant Jade had come out of her coma at 7:15.

Narrowing his eyes, he leaned closer to the prayer chart and used his finger to follow the list. "I wonder who was praying for us at—"

Jade rolled onto her side, craning her neck to see what Tanner saw. "What?"

Tanner could only stare at her, his mouth open. "People have been praying for you around the clock, right?"

"Right…" Jade looked confused.

Tanner studied the chart again and huffed. Chills ran down his arms and legs and he turned back to Jade. "Guess who was praying for you from seven to seven-thirty this morning? When you came out of the coma?"

"Who?"

Tanner checked the name once more and then leveled his gaze at Jade. "Ty Eastman."

Jade's eyes widened and she gasped. Before either of them

could say another word, the phone rang.

Tanner answered it on the first ring. "Hello?"

"Hi, Dad, it's Ty." He waited a beat. "Can I talk to Mom?"

"Wait a minute…" There was laughter in Tanner's voice, laughter and an unrestrained joy that hadn't been there for a very long time. "How did you know she was awake?"

"You mean she really is?" He hooted loud enough for Jade to hear. "I *knew* it!"

Tanner's head was spinning. "You knew what?"

"When everyone was signing up to pray for her, I got in line and signed up, too. 'Course I've been praying every day and stuff. But this morning when I was praying I felt like the Lord touched me on the shoulder. That ever happen to you, Dad?"

"Yeah…sure."

"For a minute it was like He was sitting beside me, and you know what He said?"

It took a while for Tanner to find his voice. The entire morning had been nothing less miraculous than the parting of the Red Sea. "What, buddy?"

"He told me Mom was awake and she was going to be fine."

"Is that right?" Tanner reached for Jade's hand and held it against his heart. "What else did He say?"

"He told me Mom was never in any danger."

"No?"

"No." Ty took a quick breath. "Because Jesus was holding her in His arms the whole time."

There was a knock at the door and Hannah's breath caught in her throat. "She's here." Her voice rang through the house. "Come on."

From different corners of the house, Matt and Jenny bounded into the foyer. Matt took a single step forward, grinned back at them and then opened the door.

There stood Edna Parsons and Patsy Landers, her eyes brimming with unshed tears. And beside her, the child whose face had haunted Hannah every day since she was taken from them.

Their precious little Grace.

"Mommy! Daddy! Jenny…I'm *home!*" She squealed, hands clasped, eyes shining. Then she ran into their arms and clung to the three of them. The locket on her neck bounced with every step. "I'm back. I'm back forever and ever!"

There were murmurings of welcome home and declarations of love between the four of them, and after a moment Hannah fell to her knees. There, with the rest of them gathered around, she held her youngest daughter close to her heart. *Tell me I'm not dreaming, God. Please…*

So often after losing Tom and Alicia she had longed for one more day, one more chance to hold them or talk to them or tell them she loved them. Then after losing Grace, she'd felt the same way, longing for the chance to somehow, somewhere see her again.

But she had never dreamed of this.

Jenny and Matt dropped to their knees, and the four of them formed a huddle. Hannah could only imagine the sacrifice it had taken for Patsy Landers to bring Grace back, to admit that this sweet child was better off living with strangers who loved her than in a home where her birth mother might one day harm her again.

From her place on the floor, Hannah locked eyes with Patsy Landers. Then silently, in a moment meant for the two of them alone, she muttered the only words she could think to say. "Thank you, Mrs. Landers. Thank you."

The older woman nodded, her cheeks wet, chin quivering. When she answered, it was loud enough for all of them to hear. "Grace is home now." She bit her lip to keep from crying. "She has a wonderful family and she has something else. Something she hasn't had since I took her from you."

The rest of them stood and faced Mrs. Landers, their arms around each other. Grace snuggled in the center, smiling from ear to ear.

Matt gazed at Grace, then back at her grandmother. "What's that?"

Mrs. Landers took Grace's hands, her wise, old eyes brimming with love and tears. "Her smile." She looked at each of them. "She has her smile back."

With that, Hannah's heart soared, despite her tears. They would never have to wonder about this little lost daughter, where she was living, how she was doing, who she was with.

Or whether she was still singing "Jesus Loves Me."

Grace was theirs for good now.

They were a family, without any missing pieces, whole and complete, back together as only God could have fixed them.

Thirty-Two

The breeze from the Pacific Ocean was warmer than usual for April, and Jade was grateful. The sun warmed her face and filled her heart as she gazed at the blue sky. It was the only appropriate backdrop for the party that afternoon.

It had been six months since she woke from the coma, six months since little Grace had come home to be with the Bronzans forever. There was no place any of them wanted to be but there at the beach, together. The way they always wound up eventually.

Jade drew a cleansing breath and smiled at the scene below her on the beach. Matt and Tanner, tossing a Frisbee down on the shoreline. Not far from them, Jenny, Ty, and Grace worked diligently on a sand castle that already boasted turrets and tunnels and intricate shellwork.

She shifted her gaze to the stroller beside her. Inside, Maddie was sleeping, her face washed in peace. Jade touched her daughter's fingers and marveled at her tiny perfection. Maddie had come home the day before Thanksgiving, and though she was small, she'd thrived every day since.

The door opened behind her, and Jade turned. Hannah came out, Kody on her hip. He was eight months now, six weeks older than Maddie and twice her size. Hannah sat down, cradled Kody in her arms, and put a full bottle in his mouth. "Feeding time."

Jade laughed. "When isn't it?"

The sound of their families playing and laughing mingled with the pounding of the surf, and Hannah eased her head back. "I never get tired of the miracles around us these days."

"It's amazing." Jade turned toward Hannah. "Did I tell you about my doctor appointment?"

Hannah shook her head and grinned. "Good?"

"Better than good. They took pictures of my brain again, and there are no detectable signs a tumor was ever there."

"Oh, Jade…" Hannah's eyes danced. "That's wonderful."

"You know…" Jade shifted her gaze back to their families. "There was a time when I wondered what God was doing to us." She paused, breathing in the sweet, salty ocean air. "I mean, here we were, all of us, halfway to forever, and suddenly everything that could go wrong, did."

Hannah looked at Grace and nodded. "You're right."

"But you know what?"

Hannah adjusted Kody's bottle so she could see Jade better. "What?"

"I realized something that will stay with me forever, something I needed to learn."

There was a peaceful silence while Hannah waited.

"When I first became a Christian, the only truth God wanted me to know was that He loved me and had plans for me, good plans." Jade smiled. "That was enough back then." She paused and a seagull cried out in the distance. A familiar peace came over her. "Now I understand that even when life is going along perfectly, trouble will come. As long as we're breathing, it will come."

Hannah sighed, and her sad smile told Jade she understood. She, better than any woman Jade knew, understood how swiftly trouble could come. Hannah gazed at Jenny and Grace as they carried a bucket of water from the ocean to the castle. "It's so easy to take the good times for granted."

Jade nodded, feeling wiser than her years. "But we can't afford to, can we?"

"Never. Every day is a gift all by itself."

The afternoon slipped away in a blur of play and laughter, and after dinner they all gathered on the deck except the babies, who were asleep inside. Jade cozied up against Tanner, with Ty on her other side. There was a chill in the air, but the warmth of Tanner's body made it disappear.

Across from them, Matt moved his fingers over the strings of his guitar. "Tanner and I have a musical announcement to make."

Jade shifted and raised her eyebrows at her husband.

Next to Matt, Hannah grinned. "Sounds important."

Grace was sitting in Jenny's lap nearby, and both girls giggled at Hannah's tone. Jenny looked at Hannah. "This should be good."

"We—" Matt kept his face serious and nodded in Tanner's direction—"have decided to give up law for one year and hit the road."

"Hit the road?" Ty wrinkled his nose and stifled a laugh. "With what, a hammer?"

Tanner poked Ty in the ribs as he stifled a grin. "Come on now, we're serious. Let the man finish."

Matt tipped his head at Tanner. "Thank you." He winked at Ty and glanced at the group. "As I was saying, we feel the many evenings spent singing here, for all of you, have prepared us for a career as professional musicians." He looked at Tanner for support. "Isn't that right?"

Tanner gave a firm nod. "Absolutely."

Matt gave a formal plucking of his guitar strings. "On that note, we thought we'd share our opening song with you. The one that will—what can we say—" he cocked his head slightly and tossed his hands in the air—"bring down the house."

"Not while we're in it, okay?" Jade whispered the comment to Tanner but made sure it was loud enough for everyone to hear.

Giggles came from everyone but the men, and Jade brought

her hands to her face, trying to keep from laughing out loud. This was what she loved about the Bronzans. Not only were they the type of friends who stood by when troubles came—even terrifying trouble—they were friends who laughed and loved life.

Friends who made life fun.

There was a twinkle in Matt's eyes when he continued. "Fine." He shrugged in Tanner's direction. "Partner, it looks like the only way to silence our critics is to sing."

Tanner cleared his throat and leaned forward, his expression as serious as he could manage. "Hit it."

Matt began strumming the tune to the Eagles' "Desperado," and Hannah bit her lip to keep from laughing as she rolled her eyes at Jade. The music filled the deck, and Jade giggled in Hannah's direction.

Four times the guys forgot the words, and three times Tanner was noticeably off-key. Jade listened, covering her mouth whenever she was tempted to laugh.

When it was over there was silence. Jade looked around and saw Hannah run her tongue along the inside of her lip.

"So…" Hannah used her hands to show she was doing her best to understand. "Your act will be sort of an offbeat, off-tune, missing-word impression of the Eagles? For all the hip concert-goers craving that type of music, is that it?"

Matt grinned and pretended to hit her with the backside of his guitar. "I told you, Tanner…"

"You did." Tanner lifted one shoulder.

"True artists get no respect."

Jenny laughed out loud, and the sound snapped what remained of Jade and Hannah's restraint. Soon even Matt and Tanner joined in, and when the laughter died down, Tanner leaned closer to Jade once more. "Fine. We'll keep our day jobs."

"I was going to say…" Hannah bit her lip. "Good thing."

Matt shook his head in mock disdain. "If we're not ready for the road, at least we can take requests." He tapped Grace's knee. "Okay, sweetheart, what do you want me to sing?"

Grace lowered her chin, and batted her eyelashes at Matt. "'Old McDommer's Farm,' Daddy. Pleeeease!"

Jade's heart swelled as she watched the scene. Grace had come so far since her return to the Bronzans' home. Patsy Landers had been out for a visit already, and there was even talk of her moving to California to be closer to Grace. But never, no matter what, would she ever tell her troubled daughter about Grace's where-abouts.

It was part of the deal they'd made six months earlier.

Matt made a sweeping bow at Grace. "Your wish is my com-mand."

Hannah chuckled and leaned into the circle, pretending to share private information with the rest of them. "That's for sure..."

"'Old McDonald' it is!" The melody sprang from Matt's guitar as he worked his fingers over the strings.

When they were done, they did "Jesus Loves Me" for Grace's second request, and a silly camp song for Ty. When the children were finished making requests, Matt angled his head toward Jade, his eyes more serious than before.

"Okay, Jade, you're the reason we're all celebrating." He gave her a gentle, knowing smile. "How about you?"

Tanner took her hand, and she leaned her head back, staring at the starry sky and trying to imagine what song summed up the wealth of love and hope and joy in her heart.

Then she knew exactly what she wanted to sing "I've got it." She grinned at Matt. "'Great is Thy Faithfulness.'"

"Ahhh." Hannah nestled closer to Matt and gazed at him for a long moment. "Our favorite song."

The air between them filled with a sense of quiet holiness as

Matt began to play. The music mixed with the sound of the distant surf and Jade closed her eyes as they started to sing.

"'Great is Thy faithfulness, O God my Father; there is no shadow of turning with Thee.'" Their voices joined together, and Jade savored the sound, every word a prayer to heaven. To think she'd believed her cancer a punishment from that same faithful God seemed almost ludicrous now.

She'd learned that, too, these past months.

A smile filled Jade's face as the song built. "'Thou changest not, Thy compassions, they fail not; as Thou hast been, Thou forever will be.'"

Jade opened her eyes and looked at the people around her, people who, just six months ago, she thought she might never see again. Hannah, whose passions were so like her own, but who had been more like a sister these past months; Matt, who had helped Tanner be strong when he had no strength of his own; Jenny, whose sweet heart had been broken far too many times, but who now seemed happier than she had in years; and Grace and Kody and Maddie, who would be a part of all of them forever.

The song played on and Jade shifted her gaze to Ty on her left side, strong in character and handsome like his father, but still so much a boy. He grinned at her and she hugged him.

Then she turned to Tanner. Their eyes met and held, the words to the song dancing on both their lips. She studied the shape of his chin, his jaw, and cheekbones. Everything about him was written on her heart, and she realized that she could read his thoughts more easily since the cancer. Although there were no words spoken between them, his voice played in her heart, telling her he had never been happier, that he needed her more than air.

She leaned into him again, and turned her attention once more to Matt.

He was starting the third verse, one that Jade was not familiar with. Only Matt and Hannah knew this part of the song, and Jade listened, hanging on every word.

"'Pardon for sin and a peace that endureth, Thine own dear presence to cheer and to guide; strength for today and bright hope for tomorrow, blessings all mine, with ten thousand beside!'"

Jade could hardly believe it.

Every word was as though Jade had written it herself. It was the story of her life. God had pardoned her sin and brought her peace. He'd cheered her on through the darkest days of her life and given her an inhuman strength to carry on. She thought of her verse from Jeremiah, about the plans God had for her. There was no question that her tomorrows were filled with hope.

Hope brighter than the sun.

Gratitude flooded her heart to overflowing. Ten thousand blessings, indeed! All of them had so much to be thankful for. Suddenly Jade had a vision of their two families gathered together this way, singing this song, ten years from now…twenty. Thirty.

Tears filled her eyes as one final time they joined their voices for the chorus.

"'Great is thy faithfulness! Great is thy faithfulness! Morning by morning new mercies I see. All I have needed Thy hand hath provided; great is Thy faithfulness, Lord, unto me!'"

Dear Reader Friends,

First, I must share with you how hard it was to let go of the characters in this book. Matt and Hannah and Jade and Tanner have become like close friends, and as I neared the end of *Halfway to Forever* the impending good-bye was almost painful. Of course, my husband thinks I'm delusional. Crying over stories I made up, missing people that don't exist. He says I'll make an interesting old woman one day, when I start wondering why it's been so long since Jade and Tanner have visited.

But for now he humors me.

Halfway to Forever has been close to my heart for a long time. I got the idea for the book on a cross-country flight, thirty thousand feet closer to heaven—the source of all my ideas. Thoughts began to come, and before long I was jotting down plotlines as quickly as I could write. Within an hour I was dabbing at tears. It was the first time I've ever cried when outlining a book.

The thing that struck me most about *Halfway to Forever* was the truth that trouble comes…even for us who believe. I've heard it said that we are either leaving a crisis, entering one, or smack in the middle of one.

It's true, isn't it?

The tragedy of September 11 told us as much. We can make our plans and determine our paths but only to a small degree. So much of life is out of our control. Disease comes, jobs go, children move away. Plans dissolve with a single phone call or newsflash. What seemed so strong and certain today can be reduced to nothing but ash tomorrow. We know that; we've seen it happen. Not just on television and in New York City or Washington, D.C., but in our own lives as well. We all have "twin towers" we hold dear, things or people that seem indestructible until one fateful moment.

The good news is no matter what happens, there is One who

ultimately is in control. He has promised us that if we love Him, He will work all things out for good. All things. Think about that for a minute.

Of course, that doesn't mean every burning building or flash of fear on the landscape of your life will turn out the way you'd hoped. That's not how God works. Rather, He sees the bigger picture. We have the comfort, the peace, of knowing that we can rest in His hands because He will take care of everything. Whatever the trouble is.

As many of you know, my husband and I have six children—three by birth, three from Haiti by means of adoption. When we're taking a long road trip, we often hear multiple voices asking,

"Are we almost there?"

"Where are we going?"

"Why don't we stop here?"

"How come we didn't take that road?"

"I'm tired of this trip."

We try to answer the questions patiently, but the bottom line is we *know* where we're going. We wouldn't take the trip if we didn't think it was going to be good for all of us in some way. Still, children often don't understand and so they question.

Aren't we the same way with God?

There is much we want to know about our journey through life, and God tries to meet our needs by way of His Word and others in the body of Christ who comfort us. But sometimes there are no answers except one: He is God.

He is in control; He will lead us safely home in His timing.

The other day we took our four-year-old to his first professional basketball game. This is the same blonde, blue-eyed boy who tells people his name is Michael Jordan; the boy who plays basketball two hours every day—rain or shine—and can't get enough of the round, leather ball. We thought he'd be thrilled about going to a Portland Trail Blazers game. The problem was he had to leave a birthday party early to go. His sad little pout made for a quiet ride to the stadium.

It wasn't until we got to the game and took our seats that everything changed. His eyes grew wide as saucers, and he sat on the edge of his seat throughout the entire contest, cheering and shouting and raising his chubby fist in the air. It was the time of his life.

The analogy was striking for my husband and me.

In the here and now, we are having fun at the birthday party, but ultimately God wants to take us somewhere else, to a heavenly place where we'll have the time of our lives. The wonderful place where young Brandy Almond went in *Halfway to Forever.*

Yes, we will question. But only God holds the answers, and many of them won't be clear until we get to the Big Game.

While writing *Halfway to Forever,* I was reminded of the Israelites wandering in the desert for forty years. God's provision for them was daily. He never gave them more than enough to get through one, single day. That's how it was for the Bronzans and Eastmans. Yes, there was crisis. Yes, troubles came. But God provided enough grace and strength for each sunup, one day at a time. At first their situations felt overwhelming, as though God had abandoned them.

But that is never the case, is it? Not for these characters, and not for us in real life. If there was anything Hannah and Matt learned, it was that through the darkest night, morning would always come. If there was anything Jade and Tanner learned, it was that God's plans were always good, no matter how they seemed at first.

Just like our son's trip to the Blazers game.

I pray that in journeying with me through the pages of *Halfway to Forever,* you've been reminded of these truths as well.

No matter what, God is in control. He loves you and He'll never let you go.

On a personal note, our family is adjusting beautifully to the adoption of our three new little boys. Sean, EJ, and Joshua are in first grade, learning to read, and loving American sports, American customs, and most of all American food. They pray often and know the One from whom our blessings come. All the terrifying possibilities we imagined and sometimes entertained in the days leading up to their adoption never materialized. Not one.

Our children love each other and are living testimonies to the power of prayer. Our prayer and yours. Thank you for being a part of the miracle of their lives. Your continued prayers are so appreciated.

Until we're together again, I pray God will bless you and yours and leave you with a deeper understanding of his Holy provision.

Day by day by day.

As always, I'd love to hear from you. You can reach me through my website at www.karenkingsbury.com or at my e-mail address, Karen@KarenKingsbury.com.

Love and grace in Christ,

Discussion Questions

1. The strength of Jade and Tanner, Matt and Hannah, was their friendship. Why is friendship important to us all? How is it specifically important to you?

2. Explain how friendship is a tool God uses to bring us closer to Him.

3. We meet up with these characters during a season in their lives when they are all undergoing hardship. Explain those hardships and how they are different from each other.

4. Are you more like Jade, Tanner, Matt, or Hannah when it comes to handling the troubles life sometimes brings? How so?

5. Think of a time when you and a friend shared a difficult season. Describe that time and tell how friendship made a difference.

6. Sometimes when we come against hard times, we're tempted to compromise. Discuss the compromise Tanner considered when Jade's brain tumor was threatening her life. What was his final choice, and why?

7. How did Tanner's determination to stay the course contribute to the way this story played out?

8. In *Halfway to Forever,* Matt was torn between two struggles. Have you ever felt caught up in a fight for your faith? If so, discuss that time and what you learned from it.

9. Jenny goes through a transformation in this book. Explain that, and share about a time when God allowed circumstances to transform you.

10. Describe the miracle that occurs with Hannah toward the end of this book. Name a time when God worked a miracle in your life. How are the situations similar?

THE
FOREVER FAITHFUL SERIES

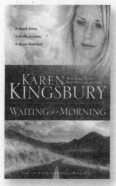

WAITING FOR MORNING—*Book One*

A drunk driver...a deadly accident...a dream destroyed. When Hannah Ryan loses her husband and oldest daughter to a drunk driver, she is consumed with hate and revenge. Ultimately, it is a kind prosecutor, a wise widow, and her husband's dying words that bring her the peace that will set her free and let her live again.

A MOMENT OF WEAKNESS—*Book Two*

When childhood friends Jade and Tanner reunite as adults, they share their hearts, souls, and dreams of forever—until a fateful decision tears them apart. Now, nearly a decade later, Jade's unfaithful husband wants to destroy her in a custody battle that is about to send shock waves across the United States. Only one man can help Jade in her darkest hour. And only one old woman knows the truth that can set them all free.

HALFWAY TO FOREVER—*Book Three*

Matt and Hannah...Jade and Tanner—after already surviving much, these couples now face the greatest struggles of their lives: Parental losses and life-threatening illness threaten to derail their faith and sideline their futures. Can Hannah survive the loss of an adopted daughter? Will Tanner come through decades of loneliness only to face losing Jade one final time?

READ AN EXCERPT FROM THESE BOOKS AND MORE AT
www.WaterBrookMultnomah.com

OTHER NOVELS BY
KAREN KINGSBURY

WHERE YESTERDAY LIVES

In the wake of her father's sudden death, Ellen Barrett must journey back to the small town where she grew up and spend a week with antagonistic siblings. In the process, she must reckon with a man who once meant everything to her.

WHEN JOY CAME TO STAY

Maggie Stovall is trapped inside a person she's spent years carefully crafting. Now the truth about who she is—and what she's done—is revealed, sending Maggie into a spiral of despair. Will Maggie walk away from her marriage and her foster child in her desperation to escape the mantle of depression cloaking her? Or will she allow God to take her to a place of ultimate honesty before it's too late?

ON EVERY SIDE

Jordan Riley, an embittered lawyer, sues his hometown to have a public statue of Jesus removed. The conflict causes him to cross paths with a spirited young newscaster named Faith, who opposes Jordan's suit in surprising ways. Perhaps most amazing of all is how Faith begins to disassemble the walls around Jordan's heart. Will love be enough when the battle rages on every side?

READ AN EXCERPT FROM THESE BOOKS AND MORE AT

www.WaterBrookMultnomah.com

What People Are Saying about

KAREN KINGSBURY Fiction...

"Karen Kingsbury has been such a godsend. Her books have brought me to God and have motivated my husband and me to remarry after a bad divorce. After not being able to have kids, we now have an adopted boy and are trying to adopt another. Your books show faith, love, and tenderness, and I love them."
—KATHY, Rancho Santa Margarita, CA

"Karen Kingsbury's fiction has changed my life by reminding me that there is hope amid seemingly hopeless circumstances and that faith in God's redemptive plan is the anchor I can hold on to when life's compasses fail."—AMY, Lawrenceville, GA

"Karen Kingsbury is our book club's favorite author. We often discuss how each of her books not only entertains us, but inspires us to live out our faith in a real, everyday, every-moment way. Thanks for your stories, which challenge us to be better disciples of our precious Lord Jesus."—LYNDA, Covington, WA

"Karen Kingsbury's books have touched my life in many different ways, but *Where Yesterday Lives* really helped me in the death of my father-in-law... Thank you for the great stories."—CHRIS, Zeeland, MI

"I have read every book Karen Kingsbury has written. Each book has brought me to a place of repentance and helped me to forgive myself for things I've confessed to no one but God. Her books have given me hope for the future, the assurance of forgiveness, and the strength to look forward to what the Lord would have me do and that I can accomplish it in His strength! Thank you."—KAREN, Campbell, CA

"The Lord prompted me to find a Christian author I enjoyed, and I found Karen Kingsbury. I have struggled with depression to a certain degree all my life, but when I read her book, I was at the bottom. This was the beginning of a wonderful journey to recovery for me."—DANNELL, Brawley, CA

"A dear friend handed me *A Time to Dance,* and it was the beginning of some much needed deep healing in my marriage. Just knowing that others could walk through muddy waters and make it through to the other side gave me hope and a sense of relief that maybe, just maybe, I too could be okay again. Thank you, Karen Kingsbury!"—JO ANN, Dickinson, ND

"Karen Kingsbury's work always reminds me of God's grace in my own life, especially the times I really didn't deserve it! After each book, my faith is stronger, and I can't wait for the next book to come out!"—NANCY, Salem, IL

"I just love all of Karen Kingsbury's books. Every one has touched me in a very deep way, relating to one or another 'storm' I have gone through and yet giving me hope that God is always there, carrying us when we don't care anymore whether we live or die. I have been to that place, and God did lift me up from the depths of sorrow and pain! Thank you so much!"—HENRIETTA, British Columbia, Canada

"Karen Kingsbury's books never cease to amaze me. When I finish reading one, I not only feel connected to the characters and the events; I feel that I have walked in the presence of Christ and that He has spoken mightily to me. I always cry when I finish one of her books…tears to say good-bye to the friends I've come to know and love and tears of thankfulness to my heavenly Father. I can't wait to read the next one!"—LINDA, Batavia, IL

"My grandmother has been diagnosed with dementia… Right after her diagnosis, she asked me to bring her some books. I took her everything I own by Karen Kingsbury, which is about ten books. She devoured them! They encouraged her and gave her hope."—DONNA I.

"A friend recommended *A Moment of Weakness*. I gave it to my teenage daughter at the time and she read it as well. It opened up a chance to discuss remaining pure until marriage. She is now twenty-two and married a few months ago as a virgin. We had many other discussions, but your book hit home where my lecturing may not have. God has given you a very special talent, and I am sure He is smiling at your use of it. Thank you!"—KATHY, Livonia, NY

"Karen Kingsbury's novels have not just touched my heart but also my soul. When things go topsy-turvy in my daily life (as with four children they sometimes do), I often think of the Scriptures I've read in your books. Your books have not only kept me up at night anxiously waiting for what is going to happen next, but more important, they have helped me in my walk with the Lord."—STEPHANIE H.

"As a biblical counselor, I have used several of Karen Kingsbury's books to reach the hearts of many of my clients. They have been most helpful in this respect, but I also admire Karen's courage in speaking out on tough issues within our Christian culture."—SANDY K.

"The greatest impact Karen Kingsbury's works have had on my life was to help me with forgiveness. Not just to say the words, for that's what's expected of me, but to actually feel it in my heart… I marvel at how God has used you to work in my life and the lives of countless others."—HARRIETTE, Durham, NC

"I've read several of Karen Kingsbury's books, and after finishing them, I was challenged about the depth of my surrender to whatever the Lord allows in my life. Thank you for taking me to another deep place with my Father."—PAULA M.

"From Karen Kingsbury's very first book to her most recent, she has inspired me to be a better person, have a stronger faith in God, and to question how I am raising my family in a world filled with hate and evil."—PATTIE, Oceanside, CA

"When I went off to college, I fell into a dark depression but convinced myself that Christians not only don't suffer depression, but that it is inherently un-Christian to be depressed… I bought *When Joy Came to Stay* and read it in one sitting… I was able to receive treatment for my illness and work on dealing with events and behaviors that led to this depression. The book made it easier for me to see that God can use even dark times to bless us and help us grow."—DEIDRE E.

"Karen Kingsbury's fiction has helped me with my family problems. Karen's books have taught me how to stick together with my family through thick and thin. They have taught me that even when your family may be having a tough time, never give up."—ASHLEIGH, Fairfield, CA

"I can't tell you how much Karen Kingsbury's books have blessed my life. The novels make me think seriously about what commitment means, sticking it out even when all seems gloomy, and understanding the covenant of marriage."

—NATA, Nigeria

"Karen Kingsbury's fiction is so easy to identify with. These books have been a source of refuge in my emotional struggles after going through marital difficulty and divorce. It helps to know that someone understands what people like me go through!"—MELISSA, Bethel Springs, TN